Rook

The Abled Chronicles: Book Four

R. G. Hurley

Hurley Books

Copyright © 2023 by R.G. Hurley

All rights reserved.

No portion of this book may be reproduced in any form without written permission from the publisher or author, except as permitted by U.S. copyright law.

Contents

Preface   1

Prologue   2

Part One   7

1. Chapter 1   8
2. Chapter 2   17
3. Chapter 3   24
4. Chapter 4   36
5. Chapter 5   41
6. Chapter 6   54
7. Chapter 7   60
8. Chapter 8   68
9. Chapter 9   82
10. Chapter 10   91
11. Chapter 11   109
12. Chapter 12   120
13. Chapter 13   127
14. Chapter 14   142

15.	Chapter 15	153
Part Two		159
16.	Chapter 16	160
17.	Chapter 17	178
18.	Chapter 18	188
19.	Chapter 19	192
20.	Chapter 20	200
21.	Chapter 21	209
22.	Chapter 22	219
23.	Chapter 23	222
24.	Chapter 24	230
25.	Chapter 25	233
26.	Chapter 26	236
27.	Chapter 27	244
28.	Chapter 28	254
Glossary		260
Author's Note		262

Preface

Thank you for your interest in Rook, the fourth book of the Abled Chronicles. As I have written Rook to do double-duty as both a continuation of the series, and as a second entry point for readers who don't want to start at the beginning, I want to take a moment to explain some things.

First and foremost, Rook does come with a content warning for several instances of sexual assault. The scenes are not explicit and would not break a PG-13 rating, but I want to be respectful of my readers and their potential triggers. The scenes in question start on pages 25, 110, and 181.

Secondly, to help my new readers get up to speed without over-summarizing the events of the past three books, I've added a glossary to the back of the book. Hopefully, new readers will appreciate learning more about the world, and old readers will enjoy the refresher.

I sincerely hope you enjoy reading this book as much as I enjoyed writing it. The Author's note at the back of the book contains my contact information, along with my plan for the rest of the series.

Prologue

Nova looked out the window of her family's home, finding something magical about the clean white drifts that graced the backyard. The sun's dying light cast long blue shadows across the snowy yard even as the pink and orange hues in the sky promised a beautiful sunrise in the morning.

When she was a teenager, snow had always been either dingy gray or rust-red and burned any skin it touched. Snow back then had been feared—it heralded winter, the season of starvation. Winter's freezing cold sucked the life out of any who were unprepared, and during the Hard Times being prepared was as rare as having as clean snow.

She never had any regrets about being the leader of the Saviors, or what they'd accomplished, although some days she took more pride in her work than others. It was at times like these, as she watched the gentle, white, nourishing snow fall and was buoyed by the comfort of a full pantry and a working, well-stocked wood stove, that Nova delighted in sitting back and fully enjoying the fruits of her labor.

That is, she'd have been able to enjoy the peaceful scene if her husband and eldest daughter would stop fighting.

"I don't believe this! All my life you've told me that my abilities should be used to help others, and now that I actually want to do something, you're not letting me," Kaleo said.

Caleb, Nova's husband and Kaleo's father, shook his head. "This is a delicate situation, and you're asking us to allow you to go chasing after danger like a dog chasing its tail. You're not ready yet. Let the authorities do their job and handle it. You need to focus on deciding what you want to do after you graduate high school. Spring is just around the corner; your graduation will be here before you know it."

"What I want to do is to find out who's kidnapping those Abled kids and stop them. Why is that so hard to understand?"

"You're too young and immature to be trying to track down kidnappers. Leave it to the adults, Kaleo."

Nova grimaced and Kaleo recognized the opening and threw her hands in the air.

"Young? Immature? When Mom was my age, she was already working for the government and traveling to foreign countries, and when you were younger than I am now, you were living on your own to send money back to your family. I would have thought that, of all people, you two would understand. If the great Sifter and Architect, the leader of the Saviors, won't help me do this, then I'll do it on my own!" Kaleo shouted before storming out of the room.

Nova leaned back in her armchair and looked at her husband. They'd been married for twenty-two years, and sometimes she still couldn't believe how blessed she was that he'd fallen in love with her.

Right now, the love of her life was sitting with his arms crossed, staring into their lit fireplace, the flickering light from the fire casting shadows across his face. His curly dark hair had only the faintest touch of gray, and a few more wrinkles appeared every winter, but to Nova the passage of time only served to make him that much more handsome.

"She's right, you know. I wasn't that much older than she is now when I made my first trip to South America," Nova said.

"Yes, I do know, but thanks for the extra reminder. It just gives me more reason to say no."

"It wasn't a terrible trip; it's when I first met you."

"And also when you almost died."

"It was the Hard Times. Everyone almost died."

Caleb shook his head and turned to Nova, his brown eyes wet with tears. "She's my daughter. *Our* daughter. Our firstborn. How can I let her do what she wants and put herself at risk? Surely someone else, anyone else would be better."

"You're right; she's your daughter through and through. I recall more than once having to physically drag you out of dangerous situations to keep you from sacrificing yourself for the greater good. I hate to break it to you, honey, but if you think that our children will stand by while others are hurting, you're in for a rude awakening. Don't forget that

Katherine just started back at school last month after being suspended for fighting because one of her Abled classmates was bullying that poor non-Abled kid."

"This is a bit more involved than standing up to a bully. Were you even listening to her? She wants to go after whoever has been stealing those Abled children. What's an eighteen-year-old going to do that the police or government can't?"

"She has a point—the police are too unorganized and the government isn't making much progress because no one trusts them. The damage we did in that regard years ago is still being felt, unfortunately."

"But to go after them by herself? She's a teenage girl, not some masked vigilante. She should be worried about finding a date to her high school dance, not hunting down criminals."

"If she was your son, would you still feel the same way?"

Caleb at least had the good sense to look embarrassed. "Yes, of course I would," he said, but his tone wasn't convincing in the slightest.

"She's a teenage girl with a danger sense that activates some type of energy shield. She's not a helpless sheep caught out in the rain, Caleb. She's showing every sign of turning into a powerful, vibrant, strong young woman who can take care of herself. We need to nurture that, not stifle her."

"But she's my baby girl."

Nova moved over to sit next to Caleb on the couch and wrapped him in a hug. "She'll always be your baby girl, no matter what."

They sat in silence while Caleb processed things. Eventually, he patted Nova's hand and she released him.

"You three are my family. The only family I have left. I love Kaleo and Katherine so much"— he paused, eyes brimming with tears—"but this world is dangerous for them. Kaleo isn't that much older than the teenagers and children being kidnapped. What if whoever she goes hunting for instead turns the tables and takes her away too?"

"We can take precautions. Maybe not overtly as Sifter and Architect, but last time I talked to Mod and Wiper they seemed to be itching for something to do and might appreciate a change of pace. Sniffer said his nephew has been upset by the disappearances as well. Maybe we can form a team."

"Kaleo, Mod, Wiper, and Sniffer's nephew? Sounds like an odd makeup for a team, and I don't think I like the idea of Kaleo and Eye's son being the only young people on the team."

Nova raised an eyebrow. "You don't trust our daughter?"

Caleb snorted. "I don't trust any teenage boy around my daughter, especially when there isn't any competition. It's too easy for feelings to grow in a vacuum. Besides, how would we fund such an endeavor? Business is good, but not good enough to pay four people for who knows how long."

Nova paused to consider her next words carefully, mindful of years of history and ill will they might bring to the surface. "Last I heard, Troy Heinstein's kids keep getting into trouble. He may be willing to help us with funding if we allow his son and daughter to join the team."

"Absolutely not. Not after what he did to Kayleigh and Leo. I'm not trusting his spawn anywhere near my little girl; they'd probably be more likely to set her on fire and let her burn than do anything to actually help."

"His daughter is a couple of years older than Kaleo, and I think his son is a year younger. Apparently, Wiper has been following the son's career in the small-time Abled fighter rings and said the son is good, but Troy didn't know about his fighting until recently and doesn't approve."

"It's probably not prestigious enough for his perfect blue blood and too violent for his yellow belly."

"I don't have the exact details, but it sounds like Troy's son isn't afraid to stand up to him. If he's good enough to rise through the Abled fighter ranks, he should have at least some gumption and skill."

"I still don't like it."

"We have to do something. What if it was Kaleo or Katherine who were abducted? Others don't have the resources we do. For all we know, this could be the beginning of another cult like Manipulator's. These are our people, and our daughter wants to help them."

Caleb looked at the ceiling again and exhaled slowly. "You and I could go after them and leave Kaleo and Katherine out of it."

"And risk exposing that we're still alive and making both our daughters targets? Kaleo and her team can be the boots on the ground, gathering information and reporting back. If we're careful, we can keep them out of danger but still allow them to help. They can be our eyes and ears, and it will keep her from striking out on her own and potentially getting into trouble without any support."

"You think she'd do that?"

"You heard what she said, and you know she got a dose of stubborn from each of us. We'd be foolish not to take her seriously."

"We never should have let her start organizing the reports from our network. That was a mistake. She shouldn't be having to worry about this. She's so smart, Nova. Both girls are. She could go to school, to *college,* and do things we never got the chance to do because we chose the hard path."

"It's her path to follow, and if she chooses to walk in our footsteps, it's not like we can lock her up in a tower and keep her safe forever."

"It wouldn't be such a terrible idea. I can raise a tower, and we can keep her there until she starts thinking logically again."

"You know that wouldn't work. Let me talk to Mod and Wiper and see if I can get in contact with Troy. Maybe if we give her a reconnaissance job it will kill two birds with one stone—satisfying her and shedding light on the problem."

"Fine." Caleb sighed. "I'll go talk to her and smooth things over. I'm just so worried that she'll get hurt."

Nova leaned her head against his shoulder as she watched the soft snow fall outside. "She will get hurt, it's a part of life, but we've raised her to be strong. We've given her the tools to succeed, to not only survive but thrive when life gets difficult. Now all we can do is to trust that she'll use those tools when she needs them."

Part One

Chapter One

7 years later; 6 years Post-Betrayal

Kaleo floated on cool water in the darkness. At the edges of the water, where it sloshed against bare rock, a horde of strange animals prowled. Their skins were covered in rainbow flames and cast shadows against the towering walls surrounding her lake. Kaleo wasn't worried; she somehow knew that the monsters couldn't burn her in the water, and that she would be safe as long as she stayed within its comforting embrace.

The water began to sink.

The monsters were drinking greedily, and when the heat from their skin made contact with the water it hissed, evaporating into steam that soon created a hazy mist drifting over the lake. Through the water vapor, Kaleo watched the monsters change form as they drank, transforming slowly from terrible creatures of nightmare into bright and gentle fantasy beings that slept peacefully on the lake's shore.

The water continued to evaporate, turning the large lake into a pond. The cool water that had moved in laughing ripples and gentle waves was now warm and still. As she watched the monsters prowl ever closer, Kaleo tried a different tactic. They seemed to love the water, so she opened her arms wide, inviting them to bathe in the shallows.

It would have worked, but she'd gravely miscalculated how much water they required, and all too soon the pond turned into a puddle, and the water turned stagnant. As the pond shrank, the remaining monsters growled and snapped at Kaleo, and the heat from their skin burned her.

She knew she should try to escape, but the water that had once been her savior was now a suffocating mud keeping her imprisoned. She struggled as best she could, but she'd been fighting for so long and was so tired that it was no use. She was trapped.

Just as the heat became unbearable and the monsters crouched to pounce, their attention was diverted to a newcomer standing on the ridge of the lake that had become her grave. Kaleo tried to call out, to tell the intruder to run to safety, but it was no use. She felt a thump, the little water left in her puddle trembled, and a great rushing wind filled the space. All the monsters, the heat, and the pressure were sucked away, and Kaleo was suddenly left alone in the pitch black, gasping for air that wasn't there.

Kaleo heard a scraping sound somewhere above her head and looked up to see a crack of light followed by a light breeze whispering past her face. She inhaled deeply, savoring the sweetness of the fresh air. The bright light of day touched her face, and the gentle warmth of the sun was a welcome contrast to the burning heat she'd endured a few moments before. Kaleo opened her eyes to the light and saw the face of a handsome young man staring down at her.

She smiled. She knew his face, the face of the one she loved. The sight of him brought to mind memories of laughing, of comfort, and of a love that made her heart feel full even on her hardest days. His hair was sweaty and sticking to his forehead, his face was covered by a film of dirt and grime, and his eyes were creased in worry, but he was there, stroking her cheek with his finger and mouthing words to her that she couldn't understand.

She closed her eyes and relaxed. She was safe.

THUD.

Kaleo opened her eyes.

She was lying in a hospital bed in a well-lit room. Several flower arrangements and plants sat on the windowsill, and a stack of get-well cards stood on her bedside table. Kaleo reached out to pick up a card, only to be distracted by the sight of multiple tubes attached to her arm. She slowly turned her head to follow the various lines and tubes to an IV pole with several bags.

A rustling across the room drew her attention.

"Good morning, Kaleo. I'm so glad that you're finally awake," her mother said from a seat by the window with her own IV pole next to her.

"Where's Stefan?" Kaleo's voice was a croak as she tried to gain her bearings in the unfamiliar room. She shook her head to try and banish the disoriented sensation, feeling as though she'd just awakened from an intense dream.

"He stepped out for a bit. I'm pretty sure he's spent every spare minute here watching you. He didn't want to leave, but I told him that I'd keep an eye on you so he could work. I'm sorry if I woke you up; I'm still not quite used to toting this pole around with me wherever I go."

"Where am I?" Kaleo let her head fall back on the pillow as a wave of fatigue washed over her.

"You're at the National Abled Taskforce headquarters. We repurposed one of the overnight suites into a makeshift hospital room for you. How much do you remember?"

"I tried to stop the missile... and then I just had a lot of very strange dreams. What happened while I was out?"

"Director Stone got a call from Homeland notifying him of a terrible mistake—a nuclear bomb had been launched on American soil, and it had coincidentally hit where President Hamilton was staying overnight during his tour of the American West. Homeland wanted NAT to do as much cleanup and reconnaissance as possible before they sent in the specialists.

"Stefan, Wiper and I traveled to the nearest military base along with our resident explosives expert, Nicole, to get our bearings before going in. When he realized that you tried to stop the bomb on your own and were still missing, Stefan lost his mind and went after you. Nicole and I followed when we were able, and I cleaned up whatever radiation you hadn't already taken care of. Wiper stayed behind at the military base to do any damage control in case you revealed your identity." Nova held up her arm with several IV lines attached. "And now you and I are a matching set."

"This is some type of anti-radiation medication?" Kaleo asked as she looked down at the lines in her arm.

"Something like that. I'm sure Katherine could tell you more. We transferred you up here as soon as we could, and I followed yesterday. It's been two days since we rescued you, and another two since the bomb was launched."

"The President and the others—are they okay?"

"They're perfectly fine. I'm sure that as soon as they know that you're awake, they'll stop by for a visit."

"Did they tell you what really happened?"

Nova nodded, her face grim. "Johnson made another play for the presidency while Hamilton was trying to get back into contact with the outside world. I'm guessing Puppeteer and his camp were surprised to hear that Hamilton survived, and shocked that he didn't have so much as a scratch on him. I'm not sure what the plan is next, but it sounds like the sacrifice Phoenix made combined with the power demonstrated in stopping such a large bomb bought us some time while they plan their next move."

"If that's the case, I need to get back to normal fast."

Kaleo tried to sit up but was far too weak to do much more than tense her muscles. At that moment, Katherine and Lucy Hamilton, the First Lady, walked into the room.

"Kaleo!" Katherine cried out before embracing her older sister, despite the constraints of the hospital bed and IV pole.

"We thought we heard talking and wanted to check," Lucy said to Nova.

"Kat, I can't breathe," Kaleo gasped. Katherine gave her one more squeeze before backing away and assuming a more professional demeanor.

"I'm glad to see that you're awake. Now, let me do a quick exam," Katherine said. Kaleo nodded and glanced at Lucy, unsure of why the First Lady was in her hospital room dressed in scrubs.

"Lucy's your nurse, dear. We needed someone who could keep an eye on you, and she volunteered when she heard you were going to need care," Nova said.

"It would have been a lot of work to find someone trustworthy, or for Wiper to monitor their memories, and I thought that it was high time I repaid some of my debt to you," Lucy said.

"Debt? There is no debt."

"Hush, child. You rescued Adrian once and saved John's life at least three times now. That's worth far more than a couple of baths and making sure you're comfortable while you recover," Lucy said firmly.

"And speaking of your recovery, I think we need to have a little heart-to-heart." Katherine sat on the edge of Kaleo's bed and placed her hand on the blanket over Kaleo's leg.

"That bad, huh?"

Katherine nodded, her lips pressed in a thin line. "Stefan and Mom told me about what happened. I'm not quite sure how you managed to convert the radiation into light and sound, but whatever you did, you're going to be paying for it a while."

Kaleo tried to laugh but could only manage a pitiful chuckle. "Are you trying to tell me that I won't be going out into the field tomorrow?"

"I'm trying to tell you that you won't be field-ready for a very long time. For a normal patient who only wanted to go back to baseline, we'd be looking at several months' recovery at least, if ever. With my abilities, Mom's abilities, and your abilities all combined..." Katherine paused and frowned, eyebrows drawing together in thought. "Maybe a month if we're extremely lucky, probably much longer. You should be very dead right now, so this is completely uncharted territory."

Kaleo frowned. "What happened? I remember trying to stop the nuke, and then I was so tired and everything else feels like a fever dream."

"You almost gave me a heart attack, that's what happened," Stefan said as he walked through the door. "Thanks for the phone call, Nova."

"You're going to give yourself an actual heart attack if you don't take it easy, Stefan. You may not have been exposed to as much radiation thanks to your suit, but that doesn't mean you're anywhere close to one hundred percent, and I know you couldn't have gotten here from your office so quickly unless you used your abilities," Katherine said as she crossed her arms and glared at him.

"Give me a break, Doc. This was for a special occasion. It's not every day that Sleeping Beauty wakes up." He smiled and bent down to kiss Kaleo.

"Hey, beautiful," he whispered as he looked into her eyes.

"Hi," Kaleo whispered back.

"You two probably have a lot to talk about. Kaleo, I'll be back later to go over some things with you. C'mon, Mom, I think that it's about time to change your IV bags and let these two get caught up," Katherine said.

After her mother, sister, and Lucy left the room, Stefan dragged a chair over to sit next to Kaleo's bedside and reached for her hand. "I've been so worried about you. I can't believe you decided to wake up when I wasn't here," he said.

Kaleo smiled and squeezed his hand. "You can thank my mom. She knocked her IV against the cabinet and it woke me up."

"I can't believe I didn't think of that. If I'd known it was that simple, I'd have gotten a marching band in here yesterday." Stefan shook his head and caressed her cheek, his eyes filling with tears. "I was so afraid I'd lost you. Don't ever do that to me again."

"No promises."

"Promises... that's right. Speaking of promises..." Stefan fished a thin chain out of his shirt and pulled it over his head. He unclipped the ends and slid off Kaleo's engagement ring. "I believe this belongs to you, young lady. I wanted to put it on as soon as we got you transferred here, but Lucy overruled me for safety reasons."

Kaleo held out her left hand and he placed the ring on her finger. "There we go, much better," he said, kissing her hand.

"Did President Hamilton tell you what I told him?" she asked.

Stefan nodded. "January seventeenth sounds perfect to me, and since it's just over three months away we'll have plenty of time to plan, especially with you being on light duty for the foreseeable future."

"Light duty? You're going to really enjoy hovering for the next few months, aren't you?"

"You know I am." Stefan swallowed and frowned. "Before we talk about what happened, do you mind if I grab a drink of water?"

"By all means, go ahead. I'll do my best to not fall back asleep."

"If you do, I'll just find the nearest IV pole and start bashing it against the wall."

Kaleo smiled and closed her eyes when Stefan left the room, glad for the chance to rest. The brief conversations had drained her energy reserves alarmingly, and it felt like her eyes had hardly closed when she heard footsteps.

"I see you're still obsessed with playing the hero, although these dramatics are really beginning to wear thin," Audra said, and Kaleo's eyes sprang open.

Audra was standing at the foot of her bed, winding a lock of golden hair through her fingers.

"Go away, Audra. I'm not in the mood for this," Kaleo said, and turned her head to look out the window, blatantly ignoring the other woman.

"I can't believe Stefan put that sorry excuse for a ring back on your finger. Don't get used to it, there's no way he'll actually go through with marrying you."

"This was a custom ring he made using the gold from his mother's jewelry and the stone from my grandmother's engagement ring. He put a lot of thought into it," Kaleo said defensively, unwilling to let Audra insult her fiancé's taste.

"He didn't even buy it new and just used a bunch of old recycled materials? Pathetic."

Kaleo tried to raise a barrier to block out Audra's words but to her horror, while she could still sense the energy flow in the room, she couldn't manipulate it.

Audra smirked when she saw Kaleo's panicked look. "Do I sense that your abilities aren't working anymore? Let me get this straight: you don't have abilities, you can't get out of bed on your own, and you don't have any hair. Who would want to marry a trainwreck like you?"

Kaleo touched her head and felt a cloth cap. When she pushed her fingers underneath the edge of the cap and felt only smooth skin, her eyes filled with tears. Her hair, with its well-formed gentle waves, had always been her pride and joy, and she'd taken great care to ensure it was always shiny and healthy.

"You're crying? Really?" Audra scoffed. "Maybe Stefan had the right idea—a pathetic ring for a pathetic person."

"Kaleo is a hero," Stefan rumbled from the doorway. He stepped into the room, his eyes flashing. "The only pathetic person here is you, Audra. Kaleo was more than prepared to put her life on the line for this country, and she did it without complaint. You couldn't even risk a few bruises to save two innocent children and your teammate at the riots two months ago. You've never taken a risk in your life for the people you love, if you're even capable of loving someone who isn't yourself."

"She doesn't have abilities anymore. Did you know that? I know her family is strong, but do you really want to tie yourself to such a weakling?"

Stefan's nostrils flared, and his fists clenched and unclenched at his side. "I don't care about her abilities. I'd marry her if no one in her entire family had abilities. In fact, I'd marry her even if it meant giving up my abilities." He took a step closer to Audra. "Kaleo has more strength in her pinky toe than you do in your entire body. If I ever hear you harassing her again, I'll fire you so fast you'll be on the street before you can blink."

Audra's eyes narrowed for a moment before widening into an innocent expression. "I'm sorry, Stefan, I don't know what came over me."

"Get out," he growled. "And stay away."

He turned his back to Audra and sat next to Kaleo, rubbing her hand.

"You didn't have to say that," Kaleo told him after Audra slunk out of the room.

"Yes, I did. I should have said it a long time ago. From here on out, if she so much as looks at you wrong, let me know and I'll talk to Zeke and get it taken care of."

"I don't want to make things awkward for NAT, or make it look like you're playing favorites."

"Sweetheart, you single-handedly stopped a nuclear bomb and saved the life of the president, two governors, and a state-pact leader. If Audra had any sense, she'd be trying to make friends."

"She was right, Stefan, I can't use my abilities anymore. The last time this happened, it was five years before I could do anything."

"Don't worry about it. You're probably just so exhausted you don't have the energy to use your abilities."

"What if they abandoned me again?"

He smiled. "If that's the case, I'll be selfishly relieved because I won't have to worry about you risking your life on any more missions. I'm sure you'll still be able to keep working with Hamilton, and I see no reason why you couldn't still be the NAT liaison."

Kaleo frowned and touched her scalp. "Speaking of marriage, maybe we should postpone the wedding. You wouldn't want a bald, ugly bride."

"You couldn't look ugly if you tried, and I couldn't care less if my bride was bald, as long as she was you." He kissed her temple. "It's up to you, love, but I think that you're beautiful just as you are and don't see a need to push the date back. You'd be a trendsetter. If it helps you to feel better, we can always get you a wig."

"Trendsetter or not, let's talk about what's been happening the past several days, and then we can get started on the wedding plans," Kaleo said, leaning back on her bed.

Chapter Two

Katherine was correct in her initial assessment of Kaleo's weaknesses and deficits. Nova worked on separating radioactive particles from Kaleo's body, and Katherine on targeting her medications and helping her body heal—but even then it took Kaleo a day and a half to gather the strength to dress herself and sit on the edge of the bed. It was another day before she was able to stand for a few seconds, and two more days before she could take a step with the help of a walker.

Stefan was by her side through it all, encouraging her at every step and providing her a steady shoulder to lean on. Twice she pushed herself too far and fell, and twice he caught her.

"Darling, you shouldn't work yourself so hard. You know what Katherine said—it's going to take time for the medication to reach its full effect and for your body to heal," he chided her after catching her a third time.

"Don't worry, I'm only pushing myself because I know I have you there to catch me." She smiled up at him. "Besides, we don't have much time. I want to be on my feet and able to dance for our wedding, not having to use this walker to hobble around like an old woman in my wedding dress."

"Well, if that's all that you're worried about..." Stefan scooped her off her feet and swayed with her from side to side.

"Stefan, put me down. This is ridiculous," Kaleo squealed.

He laughed and kissed the top of her head. "I'm sorry, I could have sworn that you said that you wanted to dance, and the wish of my future wife is my command. Besides, I've got to use these muscles for something."

"Stefan, you better put your future wife down, or your future sister-in-law and mother-in-law are going to throw a fit," Kaleo's dad said from the doorway.

Stefan sighed and set Kaleo on the bed. "Good idea. I'd hate to start off on the wrong foot with my new family."

Caleb clapped Stefan on the back. "Good man. I'm glad to finally get some more testosterone in the family. I love my girls, but sometimes I feel a little outnumbered."

"Glad I could be of service." Stefan bent down and kissed Kaleo's forehead. "I have to head into work now, sweetheart. Rest up and maybe you can convince me to help you practice your walking later. I love you."

"I love you too, Stefan. Don't work too hard."

As the days passed, it seemed like almost the entire task force walked through the door of her makeshift hospital room at one time or another to pay their respects. Todd, Michael, and President Hamilton all stopped by at least once as well, although try as Kaleo might, she couldn't convince any of them to talk politics or tell her about what happened after they'd gotten away safely. Stefan had already told her what he knew, but that still left a gap of several days at the army base before the arrival of the task force.

"I've been explicitly banned from talking about work by your mother, and your sister, and my wife," President Hamilton said solemnly before a corner of his mouth twitched. "Although as president I do believe that it's within my rights to tell you that everyone made it to the base safely, and that while some of the other agencies made a big to-do about investigating the cause of the weapons malfunction, at my direction NAT has been making inquiries of their own and Director Stone and Stefan are nothing if not efficient and thorough."

"It was Puppeteer, or one of Johnson's supporters, wasn't it?" Kaleo asked.

Emmerson Johnson had been the original elected president, with John Hamilton his vice president. After Johnson suffered an ill-fated stroke at a party on the night of his inauguration, Hamilton had stepped into the vacated role. Johnson had made a miraculous recovery in the past several months, no doubt due to the influence of a man named David Rockhill, otherwise known as Puppeteer, the leader of an Abled supremacist group whose abilities allowed him to fully control those he touched like puppets on a string.

"I'm not allowed to tell you."

"You didn't deny it, so I'm guessing it's a yes. Do we have any proof?"

"My lips are sealed."

"Fine. Do people know that Phoenix is the one who stopped the attack?" Kaleo asked.

Hamilton shook his head. "We've done our best to keep it under wraps considering the delicate nature of your condition, but I'm afraid there were a few leaks which have led to rampant rumors. The good news is that thanks to Wiper we believe your identity is safe." He patted her hand and stood up. "That's all I can tell you. Any more, and I'd be risking the wrath of three very powerful women."

"I understand. When can I go back to work? Next week?" Kaleo frowned. "That is, if you even want me back. My abilities aren't working at the moment, and I can barely stand on my own, so I'd be a terrible bodyguard."

"Mod's been masquerading as you for the past several days at the White House, but the plan is for you to take the next month off due to your poor great-aunt whose health is rapidly declining. From what I understand, she's expected to pass away soon. If your doctors clear you in a month's time, we can talk about starting you back slowly."

Kaleo smiled. Her fictional great aunt's illness had served as the official excuse for her absences in then-Governor Hamilton's home office when her alter-ego, Phoenix, worked as his bodyguard on the campaign trail. "And what if my abilities aren't back by then?"

"We'll adjust your responsibilities; if the past week has been anything to go by, we need Kaleo's organizing and cat-herding skills on a daily basis just as much as we need Phoenix for special occasions."

Kaleo considered protesting but thought better of it. Long conversations still tired her greatly, and if she started back at the White House before she was ready, she'd only be a hindrance. "I understand, sir. Thank you for stopping by."

"You are very welcome. Thank you for everything you've done." Hamilton saluted Kaleo and left the room.

As the days passed, and despite her best efforts, Kaleo's abilities didn't return. She grew increasingly concerned, and when the Professor stopped by Kaleo's room she asked him if he could help her, but he'd only shaken his head.

"You need to rest and recover now. Whether or not you have abilities is of secondary importance at the moment, and I fear that if you rush yourself, your abilities may take longer to come back. When you are cleared by your medical team, if your abilities still are not back I will see what I can do," he said as he set another plant and a small stuffed animal on her windowsill.

By the end of her second week awake, Katherine's radiation medicine and Nova had worked their magic, and Kaleo was strong enough to go home. Her excitement at leaving her hospital room was tempered by Katherine's and Apathy's warnings that she still wasn't back to normal, and that her recovery would be a long one. However, even their stern warnings weren't enough to completely dampen Kaleo's spirits.

It had been a long time since she'd taken a vacation or a day off that didn't directly follow a NAT mission, and Kaleo had to admit, if only to herself, that it was nice to lie around, read novels, and take as many naps as she wanted without feeling like she was letting someone down.

Like clockwork, every day as soon as he got off work, Stefan made the drive to her house, where they spent the time planning their upcoming wedding and their life after marriage. Stefan's attentiveness was almost stifling, and he spent most of the evening jumping up to get her anything she asked for or looked like she might need—but when Kaleo teased him, he only shrugged and took her face in his hands.

"I almost lost you, and for a time all I had was hope that somehow, against all odds, you'd survived. Can you blame me for savoring every moment with you that I get?" He teared up, his face crumpling in an effort to hold back the tears. "Darling, I was terrified you'd died a horrible death, alone and in pain, and that there was nothing I could do. It felt like the gates of heaven had opened up for me when we got engaged, only to be slammed shut in my face when I realized what you'd done. You're a hero; you're *the* hero. Please let me take care of you. Give me this time to do my part."

Kaleo smiled and pulled Stefan into a hug. "Don't worry, I won't leave you again, and I'll let you hover all that you want... at least until I get better, that is."

"Thank you," he said, his words muffled in her cap.

She didn't tell him she was grateful for his hovering. Loath as she was to admit it, her body constantly ached all over and Kaleo could feel how close to the limit she'd pushed herself. If she truly had lost her abilities, she knew she would have to find a new purpose in the world again. Stefan, with all his hovering, and despite the pressures of his job, never once seemed to care if she'd ever be able to return to her role as Phoenix.

A week and a half after she'd been released home, Stefan had to lead a mission and was out of town for three days. While he was gone, Lin and Nicole, her two best friends, kept Kaleo company.

"So, Lin, how are you and Brant doing? Does he suspect anything about Phoenix?" Kaleo asked as they sat around her dining room table and played cards.

A pretty blush bloomed on Lin's face. "We're doing great. He told me last week that he loves me. And no, he doesn't suspect a thing. He keeps on asking when we're going to do another double date with you and Stefan, but I told him about your poor aunt and her failing health, and he accepted it hook, line, and sinker."

"Your aunt was a great cover story, by the way. I can't believe how much mileage you've gotten out of it," Nicole said.

"Yeah, I can't believe it either. Who would have thought when I was campaigning with Hamilton last year that dear Aunt Cindy would become so important." Kaleo laughed. "What about Ashley? How's she doing?"

"She's good. She wanted to come but was concerned about any lingering radiation and wanted to play it safe with Nicholas."

"I understand. I assume she's still in hiding?"

"Brant's still keeping her existence under wraps, and as far as we know, Puppeteer hasn't found out that she's alive."

Kaleo nodded. Many years before, Puppeteer had been part of a team with her, Lin, Ashley and her brother Brant, and Kaleo's first love, Reader. They hadn't realized that Puppeteer was a double agent for an Abled supremacist group called the Pure until it was too late and he betrayed them—leaving both Reader and Ashley dead and Kaleo missing for a year. Brant's quest for vengeance against Puppeteer had left him without his left hand, and he'd never quite forgiven Kaleo for not being able to stop Puppeteer and protect her team.

Things had changed when the summer before, Ashley was rescued. Unwillingly pregnant with Puppeteer's child, she had been a captive of the Pure since the betrayal. She'd readily forgiven Kaleo's unwilling role as a puppet in the betrayal, and chose to raise her baby boy, Nicholas, to be a good man despite his evil father.

While she been presumed dead, Ashley's brother Brant had inherited a successful transport and shipping company, giving him the means to shield his sister and nephew from any who would wish them ill.

"Good. Tell her I said hello when you see her next, and that I'm looking forward to seeing her and Nicholas whenever Katherine clears me for it."

"Will do. Now, what about you and Stefan? How's wedding planning going?"

Kaleo ate a piece of cheese from the snack tray. "It couldn't be going better. He's been wonderful, although we haven't made any concrete plans yet because I'm still considering postponing it."

Nicole set down her cards and took the chips in the middle of the table. "Postpone the wedding? Why?"

"I don't exactly look like how I imagined I would..." Kaleo trailed off as her fingers touched the side of her head.

"That's fixed easily enough with a wig. Or, if it helps, I'll shave my head and you can just tell everyone that you shaved yours because I have cancer and you're such a great friend you didn't want me to feel alone on your wedding day."

"Nicole, stop that," Lin said as she rolled her eyes.

"Why? It would be the perfect cover story. We can pick some easily treatable kind of cancer and a month after the wedding I can be cured."

Kaleo smiled. "Speaking of the wedding, Nicole, you've been one of my closest friends since we met at Broadman University, and Lin, you've been there for me ever since we reconnected after the Betrayal. You've both been so supportive throughout everything, and I couldn't have asked for better friends. Will you be my bridesmaids?"

"Of course," Nicole said enthusiastically.

"I would love to," Lin added.

"I assume Katherine is your maid of honor?" Nicole asked.

"That's right."

"Good. Then don't worry about the hair. I'm sure between the four of us we can get something figured out. I'm not going to let you walk down that aisle with any regrets," Nicole said firmly.

Lin nodded. "Same here. Hey, not to change the subject, but what's the plan for tomorrow? Are you still stopping by NAT?"

"Yes. Stefan gets back from his mission late tonight, so I'd like to surprise him at the office and say hello to everyone. Do either of you happen to know what his schedule looks like?" Kaleo asked.

"From what I remember, he's got mission planning in the morning, followed by a couple of interrogations. After lunch, Laura and I have some reports that he needs to review, but after that it's just paperwork," Lin said.

"So we can hang out over lunch, and then I can surprise him before he gets too into immersed in his paperwork. Does that work?"

"Works just fine with me."

"I'll have to take a raincheck for lunch. It's my turn to be a NAT ambassador to one of the local schools," Nicole said.

One corner of Lin's mouth twitched. "You? An ambassador?"

"What can I say? Kids love to see things explode. You should get on the list to sign up, Lin. It's actually really fun."

"I'll look into it, but lunch works for me tomorrow, Kaleo."

Kaleo smiled. "Great. I'll pick it up and meet you there."

Chapter Three

Stefan tapped his finger on the table before putting his head in his hands. He and Taylor had just finished interrogating one of the men they'd apprehended the day before when he'd led a NAT mission to take down a black-market smugglers ring, and while the interrogation had gone well and they'd obtained a confession, he had the sneaking suspicion there was something he was missing.

The door opened and Audra entered. She shut the door softly, and he watched her walk to the mirrored wall separating the interrogation room from the recording room before turning back to his notes.

"I'm sorry, I won't be but a few more minutes. I'm just wrapping a couple of things up," Stefan said as he continued to write down his thoughts.

He knew from experience that if he didn't get everything written out now, there was a good chance he'd forget something that might be of great importance later. He didn't worry about Audra trying anything; Laura was on the other side of the mirror, waiting for him to finish so that they could go over some of her reports, and he assumed Zeke would be down soon to keep an eye on Audra's interrogation and make the recording.

"No worries, you've still got plenty of time. Looks like you and Taylor got done early."

"Yeah, we did." He chuckled as he wrote out another few sentences. "She's gotten better at engendering trust and not seeming so closed off and suspicious, which makes things go much smoother and saves us time in the long run."

There was silence for a few minutes, and Stefan finished writing down his thoughts and completing the paperwork on the desk. He sighed and stretched over the back of his chair.

"I didn't know that I'd be so easy to replace," Audra said quietly from her seat next to him.

Something in her tone made Stefan freeze.

"I never said that; you're an important part of the team," he said lightly before turning to face the mirror. "Laura, please let Zeke know that I'm done here. Once you do that, we can go over the reports that you were asking about.

"Laura isn't in the control room," Audra said as she twirled a lock of blond hair through her fingers. "I saw her and Taylor upstairs just a few minutes ago."

"I see. Well, I better get going then so you have time to prepare," Stefan said as he gathered his things. He kept his face as neutral as possible, not wanting to let Audra know how uncomfortable he was being alone in the room with her. He still felt sick when he remembered how Audra had cornered him in his office and forcibly kissed him several months before.

Audra giggled. "You don't have to rush out you know, I promise I don't bite... unless you want me to, that is."

"I think it's best for everyone if we keep some distance between us. I don't want people to think the wrong thing." Stefan tried to stand up, but the sudden movement made his head spin and he sank back into the chair.

"Poor Stefan... you must be so tired of having to worry about what Kaleo thinks," Audra said as she sat on the table facing him.

"I really need to get going. I'm sure that Zeke wouldn't appreciate me micromanaging his interrogation." Stefan tried to stand again, but strangely his muscles still refused to cooperate.

"No need to worry about that. Zeke isn't going to be here for the interrogation. In fact, there isn't an interrogation. I was just hoping that I'd be able to spend some quality time with you." Audra uncrossed and recrossed her legs.

"This is inappropriate, Audra. I'm sorry if I've ever given you the wrong impression, but I have no interest in spending any type of quality time with you."

"Is that actually you speaking, or is it Kaleo?" Audra's lips curled in distaste when she said Kaleo's name, and Stefan wondered how he had ever found her even the slightest bit attractive.

"It's me. Leave my fiancée out of this."

She sighed and stood up, leaving room for him to move. "If you truly feel that way, then go ahead and leave."

Once again, Stefan tried to stand. The heaviness in his limbs had somehow gotten even worse and his head felt stuffy, like he'd suddenly developed a cold.

"You better leave soon, Stefan. Otherwise, I'll just have to assume that you don't really want to leave." Her smile was predatory, like a cat's as it watched a mouse caught in a trap.

"Audra, what have you done?"

Audra walked behind him and fastened handcuffs around his wrists, then connected them to his chair.

"You know my abilities, Stefan," she whispered into his ear. "With my breath, I can create a wide range of emotions and sensations in my targets. Luckily for us, this room is very well insulated, which means you get the full force of what I can do."

Stefan shook his head. Ever since Audra had kissed him, he'd known that she harbored feelings for him, but he'd done his best to make it clear he had no interest in her without blatantly stating it so as to not risk embarrassing her. Now, sitting in the isolated interrogation room, tied to a chair and unable to move, he was regretting not spelling everything out explicitly.

"No, don't shake your head at me. I know exactly what you need," Audra purred. She pushed a chair in between Stefan and the table and sat in it so their knees were touching, before placing her hands on his legs. "You're a very handsome man, Stefan, do you know that? You deserve the best, and only the best."

"Kaleo..." He was silenced by Audra's finger on his lips.

"I don't want to hear that imposter's name anymore. Right now, this is just about us. A strong man like you deserves a strong partner."

"Kaleo's the strongest woman I know."

Audra's eyes sharpened and she slapped him across the face. "I said none of that!"

"She's the love of my life and far better than you'll ever be," Stefan spat. Audra might have tied his hands behind his back and paralyzed him, but he wouldn't stand for her speaking ill of his fiancée, even if it became harder to form coherent sentences with every passing minute.

"Is that right?" With her hands, Audra traced his body from his knees to his chest and then his neck. At the same time, she straddled his lap, eyes hungry.

Stefan looked down to see the skirt that she'd been wearing had slid up around her hips and her shirt gaped so far in the front that he could see all the way down to her belly button. Then her hands were on either side of his head in a viselike grip, forcing him to look at her.

"She won't be the love of your life for much longer," Audra said as she breathed into his face.

Try as he might, Stefan couldn't break free from her grasp. Audra's sickly blue eyes became his world, and before he knew it, she was kissing him.

He wanted to throw up, to scream, to push her off him and run as far away as he possibly could, but his body still wouldn't move.

Audra pulled away from the kiss and looked into his eyes. "How did that feel?"

It took Stefan a moment to find his voice, and it took him a few seconds longer to think of the perfect thing to say: "If kissing Kaleo is heaven, that was more like kissing a dirty wet mop."

Even in his numbed state, Audra's slap made his other cheek sting. "A wet mop? I see that you require more convincing. Don't worry, dear Stefan. I've had plenty of practice. By the time I'm done with you, you'll be begging me for more." Her voice started out as a growl and ended in a kittenish purr.

"Please, Audra, don't do this." Even to his own ears, Stefan's voice sounded like a whine. His plea was cut off when Audra leaned forward to kiss him again, this time forcing her tongue into his mouth.

He wished he could control his movements so he could bite Audra's tongue in two.

"Now, who do you want the most right now?" she moaned as she licked his neck and her hand groped him over his pants.

"Kaleo. It will always be Kaleo."

He felt the sting of her nails digging into his neck. "Give in, Stefan, you know you want to. How does this feel?"

"Disgusting."

She shifted over him and grabbed the back of his head with her hands. For a moment they sat there, with her breathing into his face and him trying to inhale as little as possible. Unfortunately, holding his breath wasn't his strong suit, and several new lungfuls of Audra's breath made Stefan feel both lightheaded, and very turned on.

"I know that you're not immune to my breath. If you stop resisting me, I can make you feel pleasure unlike any you've felt before. Wouldn't you like that?"

He closed his eyes, not wanting to associate Audra's face with the feelings building in his body. Instead, he thought of how beautiful and happy Kaleo had looked when she'd agreed to marry him, how she'd begged him the night of their engagement to make love to her, and how much he wanted her.

"Yes, that's right, Stefan. Close your eyes and enjoy yourself. I'll make you feel wonderful, and in return you'll realize that you've been wasting your time with Kaleo and be with me instead." Her hands moved down his chest to his inner thighs.

"Never."

Her grip on him tightened painfully, and he couldn't stop the whimper that escaped his lips.

"What was that?"

Stefan opened his eyes and mustered every shred of defiance he still had. Audra's abilities had indeed worn down his defenses, and even though his mind felt as dirty as if he'd been rolling around in mud, his body craved some form of release.

"You'll never be enough. No matter what you do, you'll never be better than her."

"Take that back," Audra hissed.

"No!"

"Fine then. I see I'll have to play dirty. You better change your mind soon, or I'll be forced to break you. It's your choice." Her smile was ice cold as she breathed in his face again, and at the same time unlocked his handcuffs.

Audra took his hands and brought them up to her hips. Instinctively, Stefan grasped her tightly and she sighed into his face once more.

"You see? You want this too."

Stefan closed his eyes, gritted his teeth, and shook his head.

"Mmm... yes, Stefan, keep on grabbing me like that," she groaned as she moved her hands back to his thighs. "If you're a good boy, I'll give you a real present. Now, just answer one question for me: Who do you want to pleasure you right now?"

He whispered the name too quietly for Audra to hear.

"Oh? What was that?" she asked, leaning closer to him.

"Kaleo. It will always be Kaleo. I love Kaleo!" he shouted with all his strength, which admittedly wasn't much. Fighting against Audra's influence proved to be too difficult, and he felt as though his mind had torn free from his body and surveyed what was happening from far above.

He had only experiences this once before, when he'd been in horrible pain, trapped under a building, and unsure if he'd make it out of the situation alive. He knew it meant he had no more will to resist. Pushed past his limits, Stefan slid his hands under Audra's skirt and pulled her closer to him, even as tears trickled down his cheeks.

"What is going on here?" Kaleo's voice penetrated into the fog that had overtaken his brain.

Several things happened at once. Stefan felt a wave of fresh air hit his face, and it cleared the worst of the fog from his mind. He opened his eyes to see his fiancée standing in the doorway to the interrogation room, and for a brief moment Stefan wondered if he was having a real mental break and had started hallucinating. At the same time, Audra hissed, and her grip on him loosened. Stefan took the opportunity to shove Audra off his lap.

"Kaleo, it's not what you think. You have to trust me!" he tried to shout, but his words were awfully slurred and his voice far too quiet. He jumped to his feet, unsure whether he most wanted to rush to Kaleo's side or run far from Audra.

His legs almost collapsed, and Stefan lurched backward before falling down, unable to catch himself.

"I'm sorry," he whispered.

Kaleo turned to Audra with fire in her eyes. "What did you do to him?"

"Do to Stefan? Nothing that he didn't want." Audra flipped her hair with her hand. "I told you he'd would come to me when he got bored with you. I'm surprised you haven't figured out by now that we've been having quite the torrid affair. All those late nights and weekends that he spent working in the office? Those were with me. You never had a chance. He never loved you, he just loved your family connections."

"You're lying. It's pathetic." Kaleo scoffed as she twisted her engagement ring around her finger.

"I'm the pathetic one? You're the one who has no abilities and hasn't been able to get out of bed for the past week. I'm surprised you could even find the strength to hobble in here. Add all that on to the baldness, and I'd say the only pathetic person here is you." Audra cracked her knuckles. "Perhaps it's time that I teach you a lesson, and then you can watch me show Stefan just what he's been missing out on. It shouldn't be too hard to return to where we were."

"No, Kaleo," Stefan groaned, but the two women were so focused on each other they weren't paying any attention to him. He couldn't let Kaleo face off against Audra in her current state; she was far too weak.

Unfortunately, he wasn't telepathic— Audra had drugged him too much to think straight, let alone move.

Kaleo settled into a fighting stance. "I don't need my abilities or my hair to fight you. Hit me with your best shot."

Audra took a step towards Kaleo, and the room went dark. Stefan heard a thud and a muffled cry, and then the lights were back on.

Lin was standing between Kaleo and Audra, her fists clenched at her side. Audra had a hand over her nose, and Stefan could see blood seeping out between her fingers.

"You like preying on the weak and helpless?" Lin hissed. She stepped towards Audra and punched the other woman again. "You think beating up others makes you stronger? That taking of advantage of them makes you more powerful? You think that just because you've always gotten everything you ever wanted, it makes you better than everyone else?" Lin punctuated each question with a ferocious punch. Stefan had seen less intensity in prize fight boxing matches, and all Audra only appeared able to hunch forward and protect her face.

"Lin, stop," Kaleo said, reaching out to grab Lin's shoulder.

Lin stood over a crouching Audra and spat on the floor. "Now that you're on an even playing field, you aren't so brave, are you? You aren't anything special, just another bully. If you ever threaten Kaleo again, you answer to me for it, and next time I won't be nearly so nice."

"You'll pay for this," Audra growled, blood still streaming from her nose and several cuts on her face.

"Do your worst. I doubt it'll be anything worse than I've already had to deal with."

"I'll make you both pay for what you've done. Stefan loves me! He doesn't deserve trash like you, he deserves me!"

Lin kicked Audra and shrugged at Kaleo's sharp look. "She deserved that. If she'd actually spent time learning how to defend herself instead of manipulating others, maybe this wouldn't have been so easy."

From his vantage point on the floor, Stefan watched Kaleo cross her arms and take a step away from the door. "Get out, Audra, and leave. You're done."

"You don't have that authority. The only people who can fire me is Zeke, Director Stone, or Stefan himself, and judging by how Stefan was acting earlier, I wouldn't be surprised if he told Director Stone that it was all a misunderstanding and asked to keep me around. He definitely seemed to be enjoying himself when it was just he and I."

Stefan heard the crackle over the intercom from the interrogation control room.

"You'll never be enough. No matter what you do, you'll never be better than her."

"Take that back."

"No!... Kaleo! It will always be Kaleo! I love Kaleo!"

Stefan looked up to see the lights on in the control room and Laura on the other side of the mirror.

"It's over, Audra. You crossed a line today. Give up and withdraw," Laura said into the microphone.

Kaleo turned to face Audra. "It sounds to me like even when you were trying your best to drug Stefan and assault him, all he could think about was me. Now, go. You have fifteen minutes to clear your desk before I call security. If they won't remove you from the premises, I'll call the police."

"You're not going to get away with this. He'll be begging for me now that he's gotten a taste of a real woman." Audra sneered before walking out of the room with her head held high.

"Taste of a real woman? I should punch her again just for that." Lin squared her shoulders before glancing over at him. "Are you going to be okay? Need any help? He looks pretty out of it," she said with a nod towards Stefan.

Perhaps it was the open door and fresh air in the room, or maybe the fact that Audra had left, but Stefan's thoughts started to settle and his muscles began responding to his brain's commands. "Don't worry about it, I'm already feeling better," he said as he tried to sit up.

Kaleo crouched next to him and traced his cheek with her fingers, her gentle touch a welcome change from Audra's stinging slap. "Are you sure? Do I need to take you to the hospital?"

"No need for that, love. I think I just need some rest and a chance to cool off. Her abilities have me a little frazzled." Stefan could still feel the effects of Audra's abilities in his system, and he knew that she'd been trying to infuse him with so much lust that he'd lose control. Now that Kaleo was kneeling next to him, he had a difficult time reining in his boosted desires.

Kaleo peered into his eyes and seemed to come to a decision. "We'll be fine. Lin, go make sure Audra leaves and doesn't cause any more chaos on her way out."

"Will do," Lin said grimly.

"And Lin?"

"Yes?"

"Thank you. I'm not sure that I could have taken her on; I'm pretty worn out from sitting around upstairs and then running down here. One punch and I'd have definitely been on the floor."

"No worries, it's what friends are for." Lin smiled. "I'm just glad I could help."

"I'll talk to you later."

"Yeah, sounds good."

After Lin left, Kaleo looked up at the mirror. "Laura, you still there?"

"Yep."

"Go with Lin and make sure she doesn't attack Audra again. If you can, let Director Stone know what happened too. I'm going to take Stefan home and get him settled."

"Roger that. You babysit Stefan, and I'll babysit Lin."

"I don't need to be babysat. I'm not a child, I've just been drugged," Stefan grumbled. He hated how slurred his words sounded at the end of the longer sentence, and his movements were still much too sluggish for his liking.

Kaleo down next to him and leaned her head on his shoulder. "Hush now, my turn to hover."

"I swear to you that I didn't know she was going to do anything. I thought Laura was still in the control room when Audra came in, and by the time I realized what Audra was doing, it was too late."

"I know."

He turned to look at her. "You know? How?"

"I was going to surprise you after your interrogations today. Lin and I were eating lunch in the kitchen, waiting for you to get done when Laura ran into the main room. She said Audra had told her that Director Stone wanted her help, but she had to wait for him to finish up a meeting and by the time she had a chance to talk to him, he didn't seem to know what she was talking about. She was suspicious about what Audra was up to in here and listened in... and... well, once she told us what was happening, wild horses couldn't hold me back."

"You're the most beautiful horse trainer I've ever seen," Stefan murmured as he kissed the top of her head and kneaded her side with his free hand, letting it drift up to the line of her bra under her shirt.

"And you're acting more frisky than normal. Are you sure you're okay?"

"Like I said, she drugged me. It was hard enough resisting her, and I didn't even want her." Stefan leaned down to brush his lips over Kaleo's temple. "But you, darling, are a completely different story, and I want you *very* much."

Kaleo shook her head and snorted. "Calm down, lover boy. Remember that I don't have my shield anymore, and I'm too weak to physically push you away if you start taking things too far."

Through the haze, something in her words triggered an alarm in Stefan's mind. "Are you okay? Are you hurt?"

"No, nothing like that, although I may have overextended myself when I ran here. I need a little longer to rest before I help you up and drive you home."

"You don't need to do that. I'll be perfectly fine in a few minutes," he protested.

"You and I both know that's not true. Once Audra uses her ability on someone, they're under the influence for at least several hours. You've not only been drugged, you've been physically and sexually assaulted. If Laura hadn't thought to check what Audra was doing, it would have been much worse."

"I had it under control."

"Oh, you did?" Kaleo reached over to pick up the discarded handcuffs from the floor. "So these were just for show? Should I keep them for the honeymoon?"

"Men don't get raped by women. We're too strong," Stefan said lamely, afraid that if he admitted the truth, Kaleo would think he was weak. When he proposed to her, he'd promised to always protect and provide for her, but now it seemed that she had protected him. Even worse: without Lin, Audra would have hurt Kaleo, and he wouldn't have been able to stop it.

Kaleo brushed the hair back from his eyes. Stefan felt his heart swell as he looked at her, and he took the opportunity to steal a kiss.

"Stefan, what happened to you here, just a few minutes ago, was terrible and wrong, and there was nothing that you could have done to prevent it. It doesn't make you any less of a man."

He looked away from her.

Kaleo sighed and hugged him. "It'll be okay, sweetheart," she whispered as she held him close. "I still love you. Tomorrow, after you get her influence out of your system, we'll start looking into therapy for you, okay? You've been carrying so much on your shoulders lately... your job, all of the stress with my health, wedding planning, and now this. Don't worry; we'll be okay, and I don't love you any less. We'll get through this, but I want to make sure you have space and time to process everything."

They sat in silence for another minute or two before Kaleo rocked to her feet and held a hand out to Stefan. "Let's get you home, honey. You need to rest."

He took her proffered hand and let her help him to his feet. Once he was up, he swayed like a newborn fawn on unsteady legs.

Kaleo wrapped one of his arms around her shoulders and smiled up at him. "Lean on me if you need to. Don't worry, I can support both of us."

"You shouldn't have to."

"Get used to it, I hear that marriage is all about the give and take, and it's my turn to give."

They made their way to the parking garage where she helped him into her car and drove him back to his apartment. As they drove, and as he thought of how kind, and good, and beautiful Kaleo was, Stefan couldn't resist putting his hand on her thigh.

Kaleo glanced at him and grasped his hand. Emboldened by her lack of protest, he began to slide it further up.

"None of that; you don't want to distract me while I'm driving, do you?"

"Maybe I'm just trying to get you warmed up for later."

"Don't get yourself all hot and bothered now, I'd hate for you to be disappointed," she said as she moved his hand back to his own leg but didn't let go.

Chapter Four

At Stefan's apartment Kaleo helped him up the stairs and got him settled on the couch.

"Have you eaten lunch today?" she asked as she took stock of the contents of his fridge.

"No, I was going to get something to eat on my lunch break while I talked things over with Laura."

"I thought so. I left your lunch at NAT, but I think I can at least make you some eggs and ham or something."

It only took a few minutes for Kaleo to whip something up, and Stefan spent most of the time marveling at how effortlessly and efficiently she moved around the kitchen. Almost before he knew it, she was setting a plate of food in front of him and settling on the couch by his side. He made short work of the meal.

"You certainly ate that fast enough," Kaleo said after he'd cleaned his plate.

Stefan chuckled and leaned back against the arm of the couch to look at her. "It was delicious, as always. However, I think that I already know what I want for dessert."

Kaleo's eyes grew big as he wrapped his arms around her and kissed her passionately.

"Stefan..." she whispered several minutes later when his mouth shifted from her lips to her neck.

He recognized her tone of protest and drew back, suddenly understanding her earlier reluctance.

"I'm sorry," he mumbled as he sat up straight and looked down at his hands. "I'm sure you don't want me right now, not after what happened."

"No, Stefan, that's not what I meant." Kaleo scooted closer to him, seemed to reconsider, and sat on his lap, wrapping her arms around his neck. "I want you just as much as ever. Nothing that happened today has changed how much I desire you, or how much I want to marry you. I just want to make sure I'm not taking advantage of you while you're in a delicate state."

"You want me? Even though earlier Audra was..."

"Audra forced herself on you. Don't you dare forget that," Kaleo said fiercely. "You were the victim, Stefan, and I'll make sure she's punished for what she did. But no, my hesitation is because I don't want you to wake up tomorrow and feel regret about anything we do now."

"Please... Kaleo, love me. Show me how much you want me." Stefan felt himself tear up, and he hated how emotional he was. "I feel so dirty right now. I'm not worthy of you; if you hadn't walked in when you did, I wouldn't have been able to resist her any longer. She broke me."

"She did no such thing," Kaleo said before kissing him like he was the sun and she was a flower who needed him to survive. Kissing her and feeling her body move under his hands soothed Stefan and grounded him. Being so close to her felt as right as Audra's advances had felt wrong.

Sometime later, Kaleo pulled back. "Feeling better?" she asked as she pressed her forehead to his.

"A little. Some more kissing definitely wouldn't hurt."

Her laugh was like the patter of spring raindrops. "Sometimes I think you'd be perfectly fine spending all day kissing me."

He wrapped his arm around her shoulders and pulled her close, loving the way she snuggled up to him. "That's not true, I'd eventually want a little more than just regular kisses," he whispered into her ear.

She was quiet, and for a moment he worried he'd pushed her too far. His fear was banished when she looked up at him with melting brown eyes. "Just wait three more months and you can have all you want."

"I'll hold you to that." Stefan traced her cheek with his thumb. Doing so gave him an idea, and before he'd thought it completely through, he was moving into action.

Kaleo squealed as he jumped from the couch, pulled her up, and tossed her over his shoulder.

"Stefan, put me down. This isn't a good idea; you were so unsteady on your feet just a few minutes ago that I had to help you up the stairs. Don't you dare drop me!"

He laughed as he carried her out of his living room. "Don't worry, love, I'm feeling perfectly steady right now."

As he stepped into the hallway, he heard a thud.

"Ow, you shoved my foot into the wall." Kaleo pounded on his shoulder with her hands. "Put me down before you break something."

Stefan pivoted in a circle. "Put you down? Where? There's no room in this hallway. Maybe you should stop kicking my wall with your foot!"

"I'm not a koala. My feet need to be on solid ground." Now he could hear the laughter in her voice, and it made Stefan's heart swell.

"You're not? My mistake. Guess I should set you down somewhere after all then," he teased as he carried her into his room.

"Not the bed. Don't you dare. Stefan!" Kaleo shrieked as he dumped her on his bed and dived in after her.

"Now it's my turn to be the koala, you can be the solid ground," he said as he wrapped his arms and legs around her.

Kaleo giggled and hugged him back. "I'll be your solid ground anytime."

He kissed her hand and lay next to her on the bed. "So, what do you think?" he asked.

She looked around, clearly confused. "I've seen your room before, Stefan. I helped you move in, remember?"

"But you've not really seen it from this view. You always sleep in the guest room."

"True. I think that it could use a light feminine touch."

"Lots of ruffles and pink?"

"Exactly." She rolled on her side and looked at his dresser against the wall. "I was wondering where you put that."

Stefan followed her gaze to the black and gray glass wolf statue that she'd given him the week before as a late engagement present.

"I wanted to be able to see it when I woke up, at least until I can see your beautiful face instead."

"You remember what I told you about it?"

He nodded. "Something about if I'm ever in trouble, or in case of an emergency, I should break it? Is it actually a camera? Are you spying on me?"

Kaleo shook her head and settled back into the pillows. "It's not like that. Just trust me, okay?"

"Trust you? I suppose I can do that."

"You already tried to sweep it for bugs, didn't you?"

"Couldn't find a thing."

Kaleo yawned and Stefan rolled to his side and leaned on his elbow. "You tired?"

"Exhausted. I wasn't expecting today to be as mentally or emotionally taxing as it was."

He stroked her arm, reveling in the smoothness of her skin. "I'm pretty beat too. How about we take a nap?"

"Are you asking me to sleep with you?" Her mouth curled up into a half smile.

Stefan laughed and kissed her nose. "Of course, it's all part of my master plan."

"Fine, you win. You probably need to sleep off some of Audra's influence anyways. How long does it normally take for her abilities to wear off? Four hours or so?"

"For an interrogation dose, yeah. I think she gave me quite a bit more than that."

Kaleo frowned. "I hate to get my outside clothes in your bed."

"Don't worry about it, although if you want to take your shirt and pants off, I certainly won't complain."

"How about I just borrow some of your clothes?" Kaleo asked as she rolled out of the bed and opened his closet door.

He put his hands behind his head as he lay on the pillows, making sure to flex his arms just enough to give her a pleasing view. "That's fine. Any chance I can watch you get changed?"

A blush spread over Kaleo's cheeks as she laughed and picked out a shirt and pair of sweatpants. "No dice."

After she emerged from his bathroom dressed in her new outfit, Kaleo slid between his sheets. "These are comfy. You might not get them back until after the wedding."

"A missing shirt and pair of pants in exchange for my fiancée sleeping in my bed? I'll take that deal any day of the week," he said as he burrowed in after her.

Kaleo found him under the blankets. She stroked the scratch marks Audra had left on his cheek, and Stefan closed his eyes at the gentle caress.

"Are you sure you're okay?" she asked.

He opened his eyes to look at her. "I'll be fine, as long as I have you."

"Always."

Stefan held Kaleo close, reveling in the intimacy of her touch. She trusted him. She loved him. She was precious to him. He wasn't sure who fell asleep first, but her presence drove his demons away and helped him to relax.

Chapter Five

Audra frowned. After being forced to pack her things under the watchful eyes of Lin and Laura, she'd been escorted to her car. However, while they could force her off NAT property, no one could stop her from parking across the street. A few minutes later, Kaleo's car appeared, and Audra followed it to Stefan's apartment. She stopped in front of a café, from which she had a good view of the parking garage entrance.

It had been several hours since the incident at NAT, and every passing minute only increased Audra's ire. She knew what feelings her abilities would have engendered in Stefan, so she knew exactly what he and that harpy were doing in his apartment.

Audra dug her fingernails into the steering wheel. It should have been her. This entire time, she was the one who deserved to be at Stefan's side. He was by far the most powerful unattached man at NAT and, knowing his abilities, she was sure he could take down Architect in combat. Stefan deserved to have a woman who could help his career, and if he'd chosen her, between his connections and her abilities they could have been one of the most powerful couples in the country. She loosened her grip and told herself they still could be a power couple; despite what the little bald mouse might think, this was far from over. Everything was ready; all she needed was for her prey to move.

As she waited, Audra mused over the unfairness of it all.

Director Stone had recruited her for the task force fairly early on, and at first she and Stefan had bonded over being the only non-Saviors officially on the force. She'd helped him with several investigations as part of her day job back in Chicago, and he'd given every indication that he was working up the courage to ask her out. The wait had nearly driven Audra crazy with anticipation—she'd known she wanted Stefan within a week of meeting him. The man practically oozed strength, and his air of mystery made him much more desirable.

She and Stefan had taken coffee and lunch breaks together, and everything had been proceeding to plan, although more slowly than she'd have liked when Adrian Hamilton had gotten himself kidnapped. Hearing the news, Audra felt in her bones that it was time to act, and she decided to make her expectations clear to Stefan when he came back from the mission.

Disaster had struck in the form of the plain daughter of Sifter and Architect. Audra felt her eyebrows pull together at the memory and forced herself to relax—wrinkles weren't attractive, and her face was perfect as it was. Or, at least, it had been perfect until Lin punched her, and Audra made a mental note to go to an abilities healer; if she wanted to be Stefan's significant other, she needed to look the part—and bruises, scratches, or scars would have no place on her body.

To Audra, it was painfully obvious why Stefan would choose Kaleo over her. It couldn't have been beauty, or brains. Kaleo only beat her in one category: connections. Even though she knew why he did it, Audra still couldn't understand how Stefan was able to tolerate his relationship and fake being so happy. Sure, Kaleo was well-connected, but she was drab, boring, and didn't have the strength of personality that a man of Stefan's caliber deserved.

Audra certainly couldn't blame Stefan—if someone else came along who surpassed Stefan's potential, she would drop him in a heartbeat. When she'd first joined the task force, she'd briefly toyed with the idea of luring Architect away from Sifter but had eventually discarded the idea; Architect was too old and didn't have the fire that she was looking for, and Sifter didn't seem like the type of woman to take kindly to interference in her relationships.

It had been almost embarrassing to watch Stefan chase after Kaleo like he was a dog running after an old bone. Back in Chicago, Audra could tell if Kaleo was in the cafeteria by the way Stefan kept glancing in her direction. Once Kaleo joined the task force, it was even worse, and watching Stefan and the others fawn over the young woman whose only claim to fame was her pedigree and stopping a couple of bombs almost made Audra sick.

She was the best interrogator the task force had, and arguably one of the best in the nation. She received job offers from other agencies regularly, and her abilities had led to hundreds of confessions from the most seasoned and hardened criminals. But did she ever get recognition for all she did? No; everything always went to the plain young woman who'd somehow twisted Stefan around her finger.

Audra had been trying to do Stefan a favor, to break him out of his funk with Kaleo. He'd changed since he started dating her. The intense, driven, burning pillar of strength had softened. Now he smiled freely, took more breaks, and easily designated more high-profile tasks and missions to Zeke, giving the lesser mission leader the chance to take the glory and credit. Stefan's burning ambition was being smothered, and his potential squandered.

She'd always assumed Stefan would come to his senses eventually, but she'd recently begun to suspect that he was in far too deep.

The first clue had been over a month before, when she'd been on Stefan's team during the first task force games. Most of the active members of the task force had been split into two teams and pitted against each other in a modified game of Capture the Flag. Stefan was the last man standing in the arena, and instead of accepting the glory for himself, or sharing it with his deserving team, he had given the trophy flag to Kaleo in a sickening display of affection.

Audra could have overlooked his lapse of judgment at the time, and even ignored his temporary insanity in proposing to Kaleo—but she couldn't excuse how he'd talked to her in Kaleo's hospital room, daring to unequivocally take Kaleo's side and threatening to fire Audra for speaking the truth. The fact that he seemed incapable of recognizing just how ordinary Kaleo was and how much he was throwing away by continuing to be with her rang the warning bell that finally woke Audra to the desperate nature of the situation.

Kaleo was dangerously close to ruining him, which was something Audra couldn't allow.

Audra's original plan of seducing Stefan and waking him up from his string of bad decisions might have been foiled, but she would not be denied justice. Kaleo's car pulled out of the parking lot and Audra shifted hers into reverse. She followed Kaleo's car at enough distance to not cause suspicion, and when it pulled into an empty driveway in a residential neighborhood, she made note of the address and drove further down the road to a charging station with a phone.

After she'd made the necessary contact, Audra drove back to Kaleo's house, her fingers tapping impatiently on the steering wheel. She glanced at the clock while parking and smiled when she realized she'd have just enough time for a little fun before her plan was put into action.

Audra made sure to have sufficient trusting-breath ready to go before she knocked on Kaleo's door.

"Kaleo, I know you're there. Please let me in. I've been doing a lot of thinking and wanted to apologize," she called out as she knocked again. Only a fool would open the door to her after what she'd done earlier; Audra had no doubt that Kaleo would let her in to talk things out.

Sure enough, the porch light turned on, the door cracked open, and Kaleo peered out at Audra.

"You have two minutes," Kaleo said.

"I wanted you to know that I've been doing a lot of thinking since what happened earlier today, and I'm ashamed I took things so far. I guess you know by now that I've had a crush on Stefan for a long time, and I thought that maybe if I just showed him what he'd be missing, he'd decide that he wanted to be with me.

"It was foolish of me, I know, and I can't believe that I let him get between us. You've always seemed so cool, and I guess I just felt so threatened by you from the beginning that I never stopped to think that we didn't have to be enemies."

Audra forced crocodile tears to her eyes and was proud of herself for the show that she was putting on—it was truly worthy of an award. She gulped, looked down at her feet, and rubbed her arms for good measure. It was imperative that she get inside, where her abilities would be most effective.

Kaleo scowled, twisting her already ugly face into a hideous expression. "Why the sudden change in attitude?"

"I never meant to force myself on him... My abilities just make me so tired, and I've been using them so much that I never get any sleep and it makes me irrational and causes me to make bad decisions. Surely you can understand, can't you? I know when you use your abilities it makes you tired, but I'm the opposite; if I use my abilities I can't sleep much at all."

Kaleo was nodding as if she understood, and Audra wanted to laugh at how smoothly everything was going.

"I understand what you're saying, but it doesn't change things with NAT. What you did was inexcusable."

"I know." Audra shivered again and looked around. "Do you mind if I come in, just to warm up and better explain myself? My car's heater stopped working earlier today."

Kaleo sighed and opened the door for Audra. Her insufferable dog was lying in front of the fireplace, and when the animal saw the new visitor, she immediately stood up and started growling.

"Rosie, stop that. She's here to apologize," Kaleo said sharply, but the dog didn't stop, and even took several menacing steps towards Audra with her hackles raised.

"I'm sorry, she's usually not like this with visitors. Please, have a seat," Kaleo said to Audra, who had to fight to keep from rolling her eyes. Why Stefan had let the flea-bag into the task force, she would never know.

Audra took a seat on the old, worn-out couch and swallowed her distaste. There was no hint of luxury or style in Kaleo's small house—the main decorations seemed to be plants, books, and dog hair.

As soon as she sat down, the dog lunged towards Audra and snapped at her leg.

"Rosie, no. I am so sorry, Audra, I don't know what's gotten into her. Please, give me a second to let her outside so that she can calm down," Kaleo said as she grabbed Rosie's collar and pulled her towards the back door.

"Don't worry about it; she didn't get me," Audra said through gritted teeth. It had taken almost all her self-control to not kick the dog.

A line of glass birds on the mantle caught her eye, and Audra turned to get a better look at them.

"Stefan got those for me," Kaleo said after letting Rosie out. She sat on the couch opposite from Audra. "The blue and yellow one was from when we first started dating, the green and red one for our first Christmas, the light pink and blue one for our anniversary, and the red and white one was an engagement present."

"How... nice," Audra said. The nerve of Kaleo to show off her cheap trinkets from Stefan like they actually meant something was quite grating, and for a moment she ground her teeth together before forcing her jaw to relax.

"He's always been so sweet and thoughtful," Kaleo said with a smile, unaware of Audra's brief change in mood. She frowned and reached up to touch the beanie that covered her ugly bald head. "Now, what else did you want to talk about?"

"Well, I don't want to take up too much of your time"—Audra checked her watch; only fifteen minutes remained before playtime was over, so she needed to get started soon—"but I wanted to make sure you knew how sorry I am for trying to come in between you and Stefan. I always thought he just wanted to be with you because of your family, and I never thought about him actually loving you for you. I'm so embarrassed about what happened. I can't believe I lost control like that. Please forgive me."

Kaleo narrowed her eyes and stared at Audra, wasting precious time before she finally spoke. "I'm sorry, Audra, as much as I'd like to believe you and forgive you, I simply can't. What you did was really messed up. It's Stefan's decision to forgive you, or to press charges, and I'll support him in whatever he chooses. You can't just spend the last year and a half making my life hard and then expect me to drop everything and accept your apology when you realize you've made a mistake. I think it's time for you to leave."

Audra was rather surprised that the stupid girl had a backbone, but her surprise was swiftly replaced with annoyance at Kaleo for making things more difficult than she'd originally anticipated. She walked over to Kaleo before falling to her knees and grabbing Kaleo's hands in her own. Such a display of submission made her want to gag, but she needed to get closer to Kaleo for her abilities to take effect.

"Please, Kaleo, I'm sorry for all the pain I caused you. I'm sorry for all the horrible things I said. I've been so jealous—you have Stefan, a supportive family, and so many friends who love you. If I could do it all over again so that you and I were friends, I would," she said, infusing her breath with her abilities.

Kaleo sighed and shook her head. "I wish we could have been friends too, Audra. Maybe one day, many years down the road, we can get over this."

"Thank you, that means so much," Audra exclaimed as she threw her arms around Kaleo. After hugging her rival, she pulled back and placed her hands on Kaleo's shoulders. "You have no idea how much this means. I won't waste this chance you've given me."

"I didn't say anything about–"

"Really, Kaleo, I appreciate it. Now I'll be on my way. Thank you for your time."

"Here, let me show you out," Kaleo said. She halfway stood, before collapsing back on the couch.

"Oh, having some trouble, are you?" Audra snickered, twisting a lock of hair around her finger.

"Audra, what did you do?"

Audra didn't have to keep the sneer off her face anymore. "You honestly think I'd have a change of heart so soon? I know you're naive, but I would have thought that after what I did to Stefan earlier you'd be at least a little smarter." Audra punched Kaleo in the stomach to ensure she'd inhale a big breath full of abilities. "We don't have long, so let's have a little chat."

Audra stood and walked over the mantlepiece, surveying the glass birds Kaleo had been so proud of. "I always knew you were ugly and weak, but now I see you're childish too." She picked up the first bird, turned it over in her hand, and looked at Kaleo. "What kind of grown woman would be okay with paltry gifts like these, let alone proud of them?"

She let go of the bird. It shattered into pieces on the brick hearth.

"You really think Stefan loves you? I hope you know that the only reason he was even able to touch you this afternoon is because he was still thinking about me. If you hadn't interrupted us earlier, he would have been putty in my hands." She picked up the next bird.

"You're wrong. Are you really so self-absorbed that you don't see that Stefan truly loves me? You've thrown yourself at him what—twice now? And both times he's tried to fight you off and came running and apologizing back to me. You are nothing to him; actually, now you're less than nothing," Kaleo said.

Audra rolled her eyes. "Sure, he and I are in a bit of a rough spot at the moment, but I've had to deal with more resistant men. It's nothing a couple of hours won't fix."

"You're a monster."

The second bird shattered on the floor. "I am strong. Maybe someone like you, who's always had things handed to you on a silver platter and who rides the coattails of her parents wouldn't understand, but I had to fight and claw my way up from the back hollows of Alabama to be here now, and I'm not going to let a spoiled princess like you stand in the way of my goals."

"You think this is going to make Stefan like you more, let alone love you? Why can't you accept that he chose me, Audra? There are plenty of men out there; you could have your pick of any of them."

"I picked him. The only problem is he's suffering from a prolonged lapse of judgment. That will be remedied once I remove you from the equation." The third bird shattered and Audra smiled. She checked her watch and frowned. Only ten minutes left—not nearly enough time for everything she wanted to do.

"You're not just a monster, you're insane," Kaleo sputtered from the couch, weakened and paralyzed by Audra's abilities.

"You're the insane one, thinking that you could ever hold on to a man of Stefan's caliber with your weak grasp."

"I've stopped a rally bombing, survived a factory explosion, saved your friend from an angry mob, and contained a nuclear bomb. I am not weak."

Audra waved her hand in the air. "Say what you want to try and defend yourself, it still won't change anything. From my vantage point, you're lying there helpless and I have all the power."

"Only because you're a snake. You've always been jealous of me. What did I ever do to you? Are you really so threatened by me?"

Audra hissed and threw the last bird to the ground. She picked up a shard of glass and stalked over to Kaleo. "Jealous of someone like you? Don't be so offensive. Is a lioness jealous of a worm? Is a shark jealous of a minnow?"

She grabbed Kaleo's wrists in her left hand and placed her elbow on Kaleo's head to hold it steady against the side of the couch. Judging by Kaleo's lack of struggle, her abilities were in full effect, but Audra was taking a page from her future boyfriend's playbook and playing it safe. She took the shard of glass and cut a deep line from Kaleo's left forehead down to her jaw.

"I'd happily carve an 'A' into your face, but that might implicate me when they eventually find your dead body, so I'll settle for leaving my mark in a less obvious way," Audra giggled before leaning back to look at her handiwork as a thick stream of blood ran down the side of Kaleo's face.

"Hmmm... you're asymmetrical. Perhaps I should add another line to even it out; it's the least I can do," Audra mused, running the shard over the right side of Kaleo's face before shaking her head. "No, I think we'll leave it like this. Symmetry is beautiful, so it's not something that the likes of you should ever deserve."

There was a brusque knock at the door in a pattern that Audra recognized, and she smiled. "Ah, there's our other guest, and just in time to keep us from getting bored."

She opened the front door to reveal a tall, burly man with stringy hair standing on Kaleo's porch. "Hello there, Rodney, it's nice to see you again."

"Where's the mark?" he asked, shouldering past her into the house.

"On the couch. We were having some fun before you got here."

He glanced at Kaleo and shrugged. "Whatever. Now, what are you going to tie her up with?"

"Nothing. My abilities paralyzed her and will remain in effect for at least another few hours. That should be more than enough time for you to do your job."

"Both of you should be glad that my abilities aren't working, otherwise you'd be in big trouble," Kaleo said.

Rodney glanced at Audra. "You didn't say she had abilities."

"I didn't? I must have forgotten. It's not worth mentioning," Audra said flippantly.

Kaleo scoffed and craned her head to look at Rodney. "Not worth mentioning? I am Phoenix. Whoever you are, if you call the police right now and subdue Audra, I can make it worth your while, and many very powerful people will owe you a very large favor."

For a moment, Audra was unsure whether Rodney would listen to Kaleo, and her mind kicked into high gear as she tried to figure out a backup plan.

"Phoenix? Likely story. Even if it was true, I don't want any attention from the circles Phoenix runs in." Rodney unslung a large duffel bag hanging over his shoulder and set it on the ground before turning to Audra. "Where's the bathroom around here?"

Audra shrugged. "You think I know? Go look for one."

He ambled off, and Audra looked down at Kaleo, debating what to do now that she had a few extra minutes.

Inspiration struck, and she reached out to grab Kaleo's left hand. Kaleo did her best to ball her hand into a fist and resist, but she was as weak as a newborn. "No, no, don't be like that," Audra murmured as she breathed directly into Kaleo's face. Once the extra dose of breath took effect, it was the work of a moment to force Kaleo's hand open.

Audra slid the engagement ring off Kaleo's finger and examined it in the soft light.

"So small... he really must not have been trying," she said as she slid the ring on her finger and shook her head at how plain it was. "If he had proposed to me with this cheap thing, I'd have been offended that he thought so little of me. I guess that just highlights the difference between you and me; it's the difference between trash that takes whatever it can get, and class that knows what it deserves."

Audra stood and surveyed the ring for a moment more before she took it off and dropped it amongst the shards of glass from the shattered birds.

"Don't worry, you won't be needing it or anything else where you're going."

Kaleo opened and shut her mouth several times before screaming for help.

Rodney's arm snaked over the couch and held a cloth over Kaleo's mouth. Within fifteen seconds, she was out cold.

"Your abilities were enough to keep her under control, huh? I think you overestimated yourself," he said.

"Shut up and don't forget who you're working for, dirty old man," Audra snapped. "You should be grateful to me for not reporting you to the authorities immediately when I tracked your little crime ring down."

"Make all the threats you want, but don't you forget that now I have dirt on you too," he growled as he picked up Kaleo's limp body and stuffed it into the duffel bag. "Help me carry this bag out to the car."

"That wasn't part of the plan. I'm paying you; I shouldn't have to help you."

"It's either this or add another thousand on for being annoying," he grunted.

Audra scoffed but picked up the smaller end of the bag. They walked it out to her car and heaved it into the trunk. Once she was satisfied that Kaleo wouldn't be causing any more trouble, Audra went back, shut the door to her house, and turned off the porch light, hoping no one would realize that Kaleo was gone until it was far too late.

"Going to be hard to get that bag through security," Rodney said as they pulled up to the train station.

Audra shook her head and drove past the public entrance to the section of the train station marked for private trains and VIPs. "No need to worry, I've got it covered."

They pulled up to a line of luxury train cars with the words "Heinstein Transport" painted along the side.

"Does the owner of this train know what you're using it for?" Rodney asked as they drove on board.

"Does it matter? Wait here for a second."

Audra enjoyed the feeling of his eyes raking over her face and her body as she got out of the car to speak with the Heinstein representatives.

Brant hadn't known the real reason why Audra had needed his train car, but he'd at least had the good sense to buy her continued silence with a little free train ride, no questions asked. Audra smiled; it wasn't nearly enough to make up for the blows Lin had dealt her earlier, but there was some poetic justice in Lin's boyfriend aiding her plan.

She wondered if Brant had ever told Lin about their history. Judging by his hushed voice over the phone when she'd called, and how easily he'd agreed to lend his private train for an unspecified errand, she would bet he hadn't. Audra made a mental note to reorganize some files in a certain safe deposit box; if she ever got in trouble, her leverage over one of the richest men in America would prove invaluable.

"We'll be out of the city and in the country in about thirty minutes. You can pick whichever stop you want before we reach the Eastern Seaboard tomorrow morning to do the deed and dispose of the body—but whatever you do, don't make a mess here. Brant knows I used this car, so Kaleo's blood showing up will implicate me. If you want to be efficient about it, you could probably just throw that duffel bag off the train; I'd think that would be more than enough to kill her. Once I have proof that you've finished her off, I'll give you the rest of the money," Audra said disinterestedly as she sipped from a glass of wine and lounged on the couch.

"Yeah, about that... I think that I'm going to change the terms of our deal."

"Change the terms of the deal? I hired you to kill her." Audra frowned. It appeared that her little puppet was trying to break free of her control.

He shook his head and reached across her to take a swig from the wine bottle. Audra wrinkled her nose as she caught a whiff of mildew and body odor.

"If she has any abilities at all, she's worth more alive than dead to me. Don't worry though, doll, I'm a professional and I have a reputation to uphold. I'll smuggle her overseas where she'll never be found; I've heard there's good money in the gladiator market there. Either she'll make it as a gladiator, or she'll end up as one of the slaves working for the gladiators. It's a shame that you marked up her face like that though—means less profit for me."

"You can't do that. We had a deal," Audra complained.

He slapped Audra. The force from the blow knocked her back to the couch and the wine in her glass spilled on her blouse.

"I said that I'm changing the terms of the deal. Either you accept that and give me the money nicely, or I'll take it from you."

Internally, Audra screamed in rage. Externally, she plastered a fake smile on her face. "Fine, if you insist; as long as the trash is taken out I don't care how you do it. Now, to celebrate our new deal, why don't you pour me another glass of wine since you so carelessly spilled mine?"

When Rodney poured her second glass, Audra took care to breathe into his face as unobtrusively as she could. It might take longer than she'd like, but she would eventually wear him down until he was as docile as a lamb and took orders like the good little soldier he was.

By the time Audra was halfway done with her glass, the world began to spin. She blinked. She hadn't had enough to drink for a buzz, but the harder she tried to focus, the more out of sorts she felt.

"Looks like those pills are finally starting to take effect; I was worried I'd have to dose you again," Rodney said from the other side of the cabin as he poured himself a large glass of something the color of amber. Audra shook her head; she could have sworn she'd been sitting beside him.

"It's not so nice when you're the one drugged, is it, princess? You really must think I'm dumb to try that little breath-trick on me after you'd already used it on my buddy back at my hideout," Rodney said.

It took Audra a moment to remember how she'd used her abilities to convince one of the other thugs in Rodney's circle to take her to the smuggler's warehouse that doubled as their headquarters. Originally, Audra had planned to report the location of the smugglers to NAT but had thought better of it and reported their competitors instead, reasoning at the time that it never hurt to have unsavory contacts who owed her for their existence.

"What did you do to me?" she slurred.

"I don't have abilities, so I have to make do with more traditional methods. The drugs I slipped into your drink were calculated based on my guesstimate of how much you weigh, although now that I think about it, I didn't account for the alcohol, so you might be in for a pretty rough time. Once you've passed out, I'll search you and your car for the money or anything else that I find interesting. By the time you wake up, I'll be long gone with my prize."

Audra shook her head, feeling too fuzzy to be angry. "That's not fair. We had a deal."

"The deal is off; sweet dreams, princess."

Chapter Six

Stefan woke up with a splitting headache and a resolve to ensure Audra never had the chance to do to anyone else what she'd tried to do to him. When he turned his head to see the soft light and muted warm colors of the winter sunrise filtering through his window, he was surprised to find that he'd slept through to the morning of the next day. He briefly remembered waking up some time the day before to go to the bathroom and guzzle down a few cups of water before rejoining a sleeping Kaleo in bed.

He rolled over, ready to pull Kaleo close, only to find his arms were reaching out to an empty bed.

He smiled, not surprised that she'd left before he woke up.

Stefan tried to call Kaleo's house to say good morning. When she didn't pick up, he briefly considered driving over to check on her and make sure she was still feeling okay but decided against it. She was a grown woman who didn't like it when he stifled her, and she'd already had to put up with so much in the past day. He settled for getting dressed in his favorite suit and tie, and promised himself he'd stop by her house later.

When he walked into his office, he found Director Stone waiting for him.

"Hello, Director. To what do I owe this pleasure?" Stefan asked as he sat in his chair.

"I think you can guess. Laura and Lin filled me in on what happened yesterday."

"I see. My apologies for not contacting you directly. I was... indisposed."

"I bet you were."

An awkward silence fell between the two for a moment until Stefan cleared his throat. "What's on the docket for today?"

"Lots of meetings: you and I are going to have a good talk, and then we're going to head over to my boss's office, and we'll see where to go from there. I don't suppose that you happened to take a saliva sample and swab yesterday?"

Stefan shook his head.

"That's unfortunate. Zach could have used that to analyze if Audra was using her abilities."

"She was."

"I know you think so, and that's what Lin and Laura said—but with accusations like this, we need to have proof… especially considering your history with Audra. Without proof, it makes our case shaky, and if she decides to go scorched-earth she could accuse you of rape to muddy the waters."

"So what's going to happen?"

"I'm sure human resources will want to talk to you. They'll also probably need Kaleo to give a statement, and we'll need Audra to also give one, but you don't have to be here for that."

"Shouldn't we notify the police and file a charge against her or something?"

Director Stone frowned. "We could, but it will have huge consequences for NAT. Can you imagine what people will think if the media starts reporting on how one of our top investigators assaulted her boss? It will cast suspicion on all our investigations and any confession obtained by her."

"Legal told us that it was okay if either she or Taylor used their abilities, as long as they didn't force a confession. We have the recordings that it was all above-board."

"I know that, and you know that, but the general populace? They'd eat up the drama of such a salacious scandal, and that could do irreparable harm to our reputation."

"It just doesn't seem right."

"It's not, but it's for the good of the task force. Most likely, we'll conduct an internal investigation, Audra will be fired, and that will be that."

It was much less than Stefan was hoping for, but still better than nothing. He summarized what had happened to him the day before, from the moment Audra joined him in the interrogation room to whenever she left. Once he was done, Director Stone drove them over to another building where Stefan repeated his story to Stone's boss.

As Director Stone and his boss hashed out the best plan of action for NAT and Stefan moving forward, Stefan ate lunch in the next room over. He tried calling Kaleo's home phone but wasn't able to reach her again, which was strange yet not so out of the ordinary as to cause concern.

After they were done, and once Stefan was back in his office, Nicole knocked on his door and asked if he'd talked to Kaleo recently.

"Not today; I tried calling her earlier but she didn't pick up. Why?"

"I was just wondering. I tried to call her last night when I heard what happened to see how she was doing, but she didn't pick up. Same thing this morning, and Lin said that she just tried to call her a little bit ago and didn't get a response either."

"That is odd, but maybe she just wanted some time alone to think." Stefan checked his watch. "I'm going to take off early today, have a quick workout, and then I'll head over and see how she's doing."

"Sounds good to me." Nicole sat on the couch. "And how are you doing?"

"Never better. Can't you tell?"

"We've been co-workers for long enough that I can tell when you're feeling off."

"It's been a hard twenty-four hours."

"I bet. I always knew Audra was a snake."

He nodded. "I know. I know you tried to warn me that she wanted to be more than friends that one time, too. I shouldn't have blown you off."

Nicole shrugged. "Well, not much we can do about it now. Maybe next time you'll listen to me."

"I definitely will."

During his workout, Zach stopped by to take a sample for his lab.

"Do you think it will help?" Stefan asked after Zach swabbed his mouth and had him spit in a cup.

"Honestly? It's probably too far out for anything to show, but it doesn't hurt to try." Zach crouched next to the bench Stefan was sitting on. "Are you doing okay?"

"Yeah, I guess."

Zach fished a business card out of his pocket and handed it to Stefan. "I thought you might want this, just in case. It's a card to a therapist who specializes in these types of things. No pressure to go to him, of course, just thought you might want the option."

"Thanks, Zach. I'll look into it. I appreciate it."

"Anytime." Zach stood up and gestured to the barbell loaded with weights sitting on the rack behind Stefan. "Do you need a spot?"

Stefan shook his head. "I'm good. I'm not pushing it today and I've got the safety bars if something crazy happens. I think I'd rather just be alone for a bit."

"I'll let you get back to your workout, then. If you ever want to talk, you know where my lab is."

"I do. Thanks, Zach."

After his workout, Stefan dropped by his apartment to change, called the number on the card Zach had given him, and arranged his first therapy appointment for the end of the week. Once everything was settled, he picked up a bouquet of Kaleo's favorite flowers and drove to her house.

Stefan parked behind her car in the driveway and felt a sense of hope when he saw the lights on in her living room. When he knocked at the door, he was already imagining how it would feel for his beautiful fiancée to welcome him with open arms. When he didn't get a response, he got his key out, only to find the door already unlocked.

The open door was unusual, but he reasoned that perhaps Kaleo had gotten his voicemail and assumed he'd let himself in. When he walked through the door, something about the atmosphere sent shivers down his spine and made his hair stand on end.

"Kaleo?" he called out, only to be met with silence.

Every step further into the house only increased the uneasy feeling in his gut.

When he rounded the corner of the entryway, the scene that greeted Stefan was like something out of a nightmare.

There were dark stains on one of Kaleo's couches that looked suspiciously like dried blood, and he guessed the colorful piles of glass on the fireplace hearth were the birds that had once been so proudly displayed on the mantle. For a moment, Stefan froze, feeling like his world was crumbling around him.

"Are you here, sweetheart? Is everything okay? Please answer me." Stefan couldn't keep the panic out of his voice, but there was still no response.

He heard scratching and whining at the back door and rushed over, afraid Kaleo had fallen outside and hadn't been able to call for help. When he opened the door, there was only a very cold Rosie and no sign of her mistress.

"Where's your mama, Rosie? What happened here?" Stefan asked the dog, who clung to his side with her tail uncharacteristically between her legs.

His next action was to search the house, and still not finding his fiancée, he called her mother, hoping against hope that Kaleo was with her and that there was a perfectly logical explanation for everything.

Nova picked up on the second ring. "Hello, Stefan. How are you doing?"

"Please tell me Kaleo's with you, or that you know where she is," he said.

"She's not with me, and I haven't talked to her since yesterday morning. Why? What's going on?"

"I'm at her house. There's blood on the couch, and the glass birds are broken, and Rosie was outside by herself and is acting really weird. Nova, she's not here."

A long pause on the other end made Stefan think they'd gotten disconnected. "Nova? You still there?"

"We'll be over soon. Call the police, we'll call Director Stone," she said before hanging up.

That phone call set off a firestorm of events. Within three hours, the entire task force with the help of the police and some trusted White House security staff were scouring Lincoln for the missing Kaleo. Sniffer had been out of town on consulting work, but he hopped on the first flight back to Lincoln to assist in the search as soon as he heard the news.

Some suspected that Stefan had a hand in Kaleo's disappearance, and Stefan had to agree that the timing of Audra's assault on him created a very suspicious set of circumstances. However, thanks to the security cameras at his apartment building and the faintly positive results from the mouth swabs, he had an alibi.

When Sniffer was finally able to join the search the next day, he found an invaluable piece of evidence—a single long blond hair—and asserted he could smell Audra's scent on a piece of glass.

The days after Kaleo's disappearance felt heavy, like an ocean of water was pressing on Stefan and weighing him down. When he went to therapy for the first visit at the end of the week, it was with a heart that felt like it'd been ripped in half.

He'd told Brant about Kaleo's disappearance, along with a few details of what had happened before, and his friend rolled his eyes. "Look, I like Kaleo and all, but isn't this kind of her M.O.? She thought you were cheating on her, so she made sure you were doing okay, and then she left. She probably didn't have the heart to break up with you in person. I'm sure she'll be back in a few weeks or months or something."

If Brant had said it at any other time, Stefan would have punched him without a second thought. However, he'd been through too much to do more than shake his head. After he went home, Stefan decided not to waste any more of his time with Brant. He needed friends he could trust, who would support him and Kaleo—and if Brant still couldn't get over the betrayal, he didn't pass the test.

As the day progressed, he ironed out the logistics of Kaleo's disappearance with her family, who welcomed him into their fold with open arms. Stefan was all too willing to assume responsibility for Rosie and check up on Kaleo's house once a week, while her parents agreed to pay her rent until they found her.

It wasn't until the next week that a lab test performed by Zach on the hair Sniffer found confirmed Stefan's fears beyond a shadow of a doubt: Audra had been at Kaleo's house.

Armed with the new information, Stefan continued his search with increased vigor. It didn't make a difference. Kaleo was gone.

Chapter Seven

Kaleo woke up with a racing heart and a dry mouth. She couldn't see anything in the pitch black and fought back the urge to scream, instead choosing to channel her distress into action. She fumbled in the darkness, her movements restricted by some type of fabric, until she felt the backside of a zipper underneath her fingers. Kaleo had no idea what had happened to her while she was out, but she knew that with Audra's treachery it couldn't have been anything good. It took her a painfully long time to open the zipper, but then she was through.

Only to be confronted with what felt like an ocean of cloth.

There, in the darkness, Kaleo lost all sense of time. Her mind wandered, and when she began to hear growls and see bright flashes of light and ghost figures that disappeared when she tried to touch them, she worried that she was going insane. She started counting, using the numbers as a way to ground herself and mark the time. Some time after ten thousand, her stomach growled. At fifteen thousand, the hunger increased and was followed by a desperate thirst. Eventually, both sensations were joined by a need to go to the bathroom. Still, nothing changed.

As time passed, it was hard to know what was sleeping and what was a waking nightmare. She became so hungry her stomach felt like it was tying itself in knots. After a certain point, she could no longer stop her bladder from emptying itself. The hunger and thirst became overwhelming, and Kaleo feared she would die alone and afraid in the dark.

There was a rustling in the cloth, and she saw daylight. Kaleo tried to reach towards the light but couldn't lift her arm very far.

"Ugh, what is that smell? It's like something died in there."

"She probably almost did, Rodney. My bags keep things hidden, they don't stop time. She's been in there for almost three days with no food or water." A hand reached in and pulled her out into the light.

"Help me," Kaleo croaked, her voice raspy from disuse. Her eyes refused to focus in the brightness, and all she could see was several sets of colorful blobs.

"She's awake."

"Of course she's awake; did you not just hear anything I said?"

"Is the bathroom ready?" The gruff voice was vaguely familiar, but Kaleo couldn't quite place it.

"All cleared. She won't be able to hurt herself in there."

"Good."

Someone dragged Kaleo across the floor and deposited her in a room. As her vision slowly cleared, she found a toilet and sink in front of her.

"Get yourself cleaned up. You've got ten minutes, and don't even think of trying to lock the door or doing something stupid," the gruff voice said before leaving and closing the door.

Kaleo complied, still trying to figure out where she was and what was happening. The last thing she remembered was seeing Audra on her doorstep. After that, things became really fuzzy and painted in terrible shades of fear and helplessness. Her face was pale and drawn in the mirror, and with trembling fingers she touched the angry wound that ran from her left temple to her jaw. It hadn't been dressed, and patches of her skin were stained red and caked with dried blood.

Her soaking wet clothes smelled horrible, but loath as Kaleo was to wear them after wiping herself off, she had no other option. A knock at the door interrupted her before she could figure out how to better clean them.

"Come on out now, and no funny business."

Kaleo squared her shoulders and opened the door. She'd drunk some water from the sink and it had helped clear her mind and refresh her spirits. An older, burly man stood across the room. His long hair hung over his face in greasy strings, and he was dressed in baggy and unkempt clothing. She faintly recognized him as the man who'd helped Audra kidnap her. Next to him was a man dressed in a white button-up shirt and khaki pants, whose sandy hair was tied back in a bun.

She knew that she needed to get away; any friend or acquaintance of Audra's was no friend to her.

"Come over here. We've got some food and water for you," the greasy man said.

Kaleo took a step forward before bolting towards what she hoped was an exit door. She didn't make it very far; she was still far too weak from the nuclear blast and whatever Audra had done to her, and the men caught her before she'd even taken a few stumbling steps.

A blow knocked her off her feet, and she was picked up and unceremoniously dumped onto a chair. The older man held a knife to her throat while the younger man tied her wrists and legs to the chair, paying no more attention to her struggles than if she'd been a moody infant. Once she was secured, both men stepped back.

"Here, drink this. You must be terribly hungry and dehydrated," the younger man said as he held a cup up to Kaleo's lips. She briefly considered spitting it in his face but resisted the impulse—she was so thirsty, her throat felt like sand. She sipped at the liquid in the cup and made a face; it tasted like chalk.

"Drink up now. We can't have you getting sick on us," Greasy said.

She finished drinking and scowled. "Who are you? Where am I?"

"I'm Rodney, and he's Bags. Where you are doesn't matter. We're taking you to one of the gladiator training centers in Europe. If you have useful abilities for combat, you'll be put into the ring. If not, you'll work as one of the servants."

"Whatever Audra offered to pay you, I can pay ten times in ransom. Just let me make one phone call and you'll have all the money you've ever wanted."

"Likely story," Rodney scoffed.

"Please, you have to let me go. If you don't, it could have terrible consequences for the country."

"Too bad, sweetheart. Just be glad that I didn't follow the terms of the original deal; if I'd done that, your dead body would be lying alongside the railroad tracks somewhere."

Kaleo sat up and threw back her shoulders. "I am Kaleo Hughes, daughter of Sifter and Architect, aide to President Hamilton and liaison to the National Abled Task Force. You have to let me go."

Rodney raised his eyebrows. "Oh, really? You're all that *and* Phoenix? In that case, I really can't let you go. Those NAT dogs have been trying to take down my smuggling gang for a while now. Perhaps I should cut your tongue out. It'll be much harder for you to tell anyone who you think you are when you can't speak."

"Stop it, Rodney," Bags said. "We both know there's no way that this woman could be any of that; if she was truly the daughter of Sifter and Architect, let alone Phoenix, she'd have been more than powerful enough to avoid getting caught in the first place."

Kaleo felt her eyes begin to grow heavy against her will. She fought to stay awake, but it was a losing battle.

"I suppose you're right. I've adjusted the drugs anyhow. I don't think she'll give us too much trouble for the rest of the trip as long as we keep her quiet. When does the ship reach port?"

"A week and a half."

"Good, then it's time to relax. One of us can keep an eye on her during the day, and we'll bundle her away in your bags when it's time to sleep, or if she starts causing too much trouble. The drugs should keep her calm, but I don't want to risk anything because we weren't on our toes."

Their voices faded away, and Kaleo was left floating on a calm gray sea.

Once again, time melded into a seamless band of muted colors and half-awareness. Kaleo knew there was something important going on, that she needed to wake up and do something, but the fatigue in her limbs and the fogginess in her brain were far too great to shake off.

Every now and then, usually when she was woken to go to the bathroom and clean herself, Kaleo would get a jolt of clarity before her mind faded back to the mental equivalent of a gray cotton sky. Once, she was able to pull herself together and recognize that the liquid shakes were drugged—but when she refused to drink, Rodney pushed her head back and held her nose until she was forced to swallow every last drop.

Time passed in a kaleidoscope of colorful blurs and waking fever dreams until one day Kaleo found herself on the floor of an unfamiliar room. Even as she tried to process where she was and make sense of the world, someone kicked her in the side.

"Get up, you worthless girl," someone above her said harshly.

Kaleo was kicked again and dragged to her feet by an iron grasp on her shoulder. She clutched her pounding head with one hand and was rewarded with a slap across the face.

"I said get up! I told them I needed reliable servants, not druggies. We don't have any room for freeloaders around here; you'll earn your keep or I'll beat it out of you."

Kaleo looked up to see a gaunt woman with graying hair pulled back into a severe bun staring down at her.

"Well, I see that at least you're not so drugged out that you can't wake up," the older woman scoffed. She kept her iron grasp on Kaleo's shoulder and pulled her down the hallway.

"What's going on? Where am I?" Kaleo asked as she struggled to keep up with the older woman's pace.

Her questions were rewarded with an arm shake so vicious she was surprised it didn't dislocate her shoulder.

"Quiet. You better not be one of those talkers. I don't like girls who don't know their place. Behave yourself, or I'll send you to work with Cook. You're too old to be one of his favorites, so you might even last a month or two in the kitchens."

Kaleo kept her mouth shut and focused on her surroundings. They walked through an old wooden building; the damp air clung to Kaleo's skin like a shroud, and the heavy sky outside was like a wet wool blanket stretched overhead. For a moment, Kaleo wondered if she'd died and was being escorted to a dreary afterlife.

"You are fortunate enough to have a contract with the Atlantic Trading Company, which has paid off your debts to your creditors. If you keep your head down and work hard, you should eventually pay off your contract, at which point you will be free to leave. I have been informed that you tested positive for Saban-40. Should you have useful abilities, especially in the gladiator arena, you may be able to pay your contract off much faster."

The woman paused to open a closet door, grabbed a change of clothes and a faded red sash, and thrust them into Kaleo's hands.

"Here, put the clothes on and tie the sash around your waist. It will tell everyone else that you're Abled. Know that even if you were the most powerful Abled in the world, you're living in my house now and I won't coddle you. No matter your abilities, you will do the same amount of work as everyone else. If you want to try out for the gladiators, you'll do it on your own time, after the rest of your work for the day is done."

"Gladiators?" Kaleo echoed. She'd heard of the gladiators in Europe, and how they were much more ruthless than their American counterparts called the warriors, but she'd never cared enough to learn more about it than what she heard in passing.

"What do you mean, 'gladiators'?" The severe woman fixed Kaleo with a sharp glare. "Oh, that's right. You're American, aren't you?"

Kaleo nodded.

"You Americans... For a country that takes great pride in toughness and grit, your gladiators are laughably weak. We've had a couple of them travel over for the world championships in Rome, but none of them even got out of the first round or two. I think that only one person has ever even made it to the quarter finals, and that was a quick match that didn't end in his favor. If you're an American Abled, I wouldn't even dream of trying to be a gladiator to buy out your contract faster. You'll just end up dead."

Kaleo followed her into a hallway lit by several candles and torches hanging on the wall. Several other men and women of various ages were wiping down the walls and scrubbing the floor.

"Where's Portia?" The older woman's voice cracked like a whip.

"I'm here, Miss Fulbright. How can I help you?"

Portia stood up from her scrubbing, keeping her eyes downcast and her hands clasped demurely before her. Kaleo judged from a few wrinkles on the sides of her mouth and handful of gray strands in her hair that she was just on the younger side of middle age.

"I've got a new one here. Teach her the ropes and keep her out of my way. It's only a matter of weeks until the Highland Abled Tournament, and I've got my hands full managing all the gladiators and their various needs. I asked Mr. Dexter to get me more experienced servants, but all he's done is buy this inexperienced fool."

"I understand, Miss Fulbright."

Miss Fulbright's brows drew together. "One more thing—I was told this girl is addicted to pills. Watch her like a hawk, especially when you're cleaning the pharmacy, and don't think that you can get away with shirking your chores just because she's going through withdrawals."

"Thank you for the information, Miss Fulbright. I'll do my best to train her."

After Miss Fulbright left, Portia looked Kaleo over and frowned. "I don't know who you are or what kind of experience you have, but we work hard here. We're almost done cleaning this hallway, and then we'll move to the outer chambers." She handed Kaleo a scrubbing brush and a towel and they followed the others into another hallway lined with windows overlooking a dreary sea.

"The combination of damp weather and cold makes for fast mold growth and a lot of mud. The gladiators are training all this week on the other side of the island, so Miss Fulbright is having us do a deep cleaning of the entire training complex before they get back so they don't interfere with our work. We're a little short on manpower, so we're running behind. I don't care what kind of withdrawals you're going through, you're going to carry your own weight or I'm going to throw you through one of those windows and tell everyone that you couldn't handle the pressure and decided to end it all."

"I'm not addicted to drugs. I was only drugged because I was abducted from my home," Kaleo said as she followed the example of the others and started scrubbing the floors.

Portia glanced at her from the corner of her eye. "That sounds like an interesting story. Tell me more."

Relieved at finally being believed by someone, Kaleo told Portia as much as she dared. She left out her alternate identity as Phoenix and the identity of her parents, but she stressed that she wasn't where she belonged, and that anyone who helped her return to her home and loved ones would be well rewarded.

After she was done with her tale, Portia asked plenty of questions. Before Kaleo had the time to fully answer one, the hallway was declared clean and they moved to the next room. Their group continued their cleaning until a ringing bell signaled a quick break for lunch. That afternoon, Kaleo helped to oil and polish all the wooden window frames, doors, and stairs in the rooms that had been scrubbed clean earlier in the day. As they worked, Portia told Kaleo all about life working for 'the company' as she called it. It sounded like a life that matched their surroundings—hard, rough, and gray, with little warmth and less joy.

They finished just as the sun was setting. Kaleo paused to look out over the water and allowed herself a moment to hope that Stefan had already figured out where she had been taken and was already on his way.

"Has anyone tried to escape?" she asked, Miss Fulbright's words from earlier in the day echoing in her head.

"Escape? Like tried to leave the island without paying off their contract? Yeah, several have, but very few have been successful. We're on one of the northernmost Scottish isles. The nearest island over there, while it looks fairly close, is over half a mile away and the sea is rough. Even if you were a strong swimmer... well, even if you had a swimming ability, you'd die of cold. The only way off this island is one of the boats in the little town by the harbor on the southern shore. They guard those boats pretty carefully, and everyone knows that catching an escaping servant comes with a large reward."

"We work here but can't leave? Sounds like we're slaves."

"I believe the legal term is indentured servants. Someone tried to make a stink about it some time ago, but nothing came of it." Portia shrugged. "I don't mind it so much. It's a pretty nice deal for someone like me, with no other connections and no abilities. I get three square meals a day, a place to sleep, and clothes that keep me warm. It's hard, sure, but it's honest work."

Kaleo frowned as she looked out over the sea. "No offense, but I hope that I don't have to stay here long enough to know what you mean."

Chapter Eight

Her first week at the Atlantic Trading Company was brutal. Kaleo had always maintained an active lifestyle, but manual labor all day, every day meant a different kind of work. She might call it a miracle that she kept up with the others, considering she still hadn't fully recovered from the radiation poisoning and had been off bed rest for only a few days before being abducted. As the days passed, she occasionally heard whispers as she passed others in the hallway about how drugs could sap the strength of addicts.

The whispers didn't faze Kaleo; at least Portia seemed nice, and by the end of the week Kaleo had made a friend, albeit a temporary one. She fully believed there was a good chance of rescue every day, which kept her spirits up and helped her to push on even when it felt like her hands were scrubbed raw and her entire body ached fiercely.

The cleaning crew took their meals in the main hall at one of the lowest tables, below the security guards, the empty table where the Abled fighters sat, and the high table where the fort manager, Miss Fulbright, and any visiting administrators or important personages ate.

"Ugh. Soup and plain bread again? This is like the fourth day in a row. I'm getting sick of it," one of the other cleaners said on Kaleo's third day as they ate the evening meal.

"Are you surprised? With the gladiators gone and Mr. Dexter taking his meals in his office, cook is probably doing the bare minimum to keep Miss Fulbright satisfied," the woman sitting across from Kaleo said.

"Of course he is. I overheard him asking her to send him a new girl or two. She didn't seem to take too kindly to the idea, considering how quickly he goes through them, but you know she wouldn't dare make him too angry."

"Why not? Does he have a terrible temper?" Kaleo asked.

The women speaking frowned at her and wrinkled their noses as if they'd smelled something bad. After an awkward silence, they exchanged glances and one shrugged.

"It's never a good idea to make cook angry. He could easily poison someone's food just enough to cause them a bad night or two without too much suspicion."

"And no one has thought to try and get a new cook?"

"He has a talent for good food, even when it's soup for four days in a row. Now, stop butting in and asking all your questions or maybe I'll tell Miss Fulbright that you want to go work in the kitchens."

The other woman giggled. "Look at her face, she doesn't have any idea."

"You're right, she must be too dumb to put two and two together." The woman sitting directly across from Kaleo sneered. "Let's just say that cook prefers his helpers on the young and pliable side. You wouldn't fit in there at all."

They were interrupted by Portia directing them back to their work. Later that night, as Kaleo lay wrapped in a blanket on a borrowed pallet in the maids' quarters, she thought back to the discussion at the dinner table. After turning what the women said over in her head, she decided to remain skeptical, as she'd learned all too well how easy it was for rumors to get started at the Atlantic Trading Company.

At the end of the week the Abled gladiators returned, and everything changed.

Kaleo was helping Portia sweep the main entryway when the gladiators arrived on horses. From the little she'd gathered over the week, Kaleo understood the fighters had been intensively training for the upcoming Highland Abled tournament in Inverness. Kaleo paused in her work and watched them ride in, evaluating each new member. While she was currently a servant, if her abilities worked she would be looking at her peers. As the group approached, Portia yanked her hand down, forcing her to kneel.

It wasn't a large group; about ten Ableds followed a man wearing a blue scarf that denoted his non-Abled status. From what she'd overheard of the various conversations around the fort in the past week, Kaleo guessed that the old man was Sven, the training master for the company.

At his side, riding a fiery chestnut, was a woman with a pinched face with long black hair flowing around her shoulders. As Kaleo watched, the chestnut danced in place and tossed its head, mouth foaming and tinged with pink. The reason for the blood became apparent when the woman sawed viciously on the bit in its mouth to regain control.

Kaleo frowned. Learning to ride had been a necessity in the rural area where she'd grown up. Cars were still scarce in a post-Hard Times world. Once upon a time, she'd loved horseback riding, but after the betrayal, being so high off the ground had made her feel insecure and robbed her of her enjoyment.

Despite her recent lack of practice, she hadn't forgotten her skills, and Kaleo could tell that the woman was being needlessly vicious with her mount.

Her disapproval must have been evident, as the woman made eye contact with Kaleo and frowned.

"Why is this ugly thing looking at me, Portia?" the woman asked as she reined in her horse.

Portia raised her eyes from the ground and realized for the first time that Kaleo had been blatantly staring at the group. "I'm sorry, Miss Servina. She's new here and doesn't know any better yet. Miss Fulbright gave her into my care, although she's been rather slow to learn and we think that she's had her brain addled by a history of drugs."

As she spoke, Portia palmed the back of Kaleo's head and forced it down.

"Lower your head to your superiors," Portia hissed under her breath.

"Take care to teach her well. If I see Scarface looking at me again, I'll give her another scar to add to her collection," Servina taunted. "Now, finish up whatever you're doing and prepare my bath for me."

Portia only released her grasp on Kaleo's head after all the other Ableds had ridden past.

"Next time, you will not hesitate to kneel before them and bow your head. Servina must have been in a wonderful mood to tolerate your insolence."

"Insolence? I was simply looking at her." Kaleo protested.

Portia scoffed. "You listen to me, girl. I've done my best to train you this past week and prepare you for your new life, but your arrogance is off-putting. Whatever type of drug-induced things you think happened in your past, you're no better than any of us other servants, and you're certainly not in the same league as the Abled fighters. Learn your place and act with the appropriate subservience, or it'll be taught to you."

"Fine, whatever. I won't be here for that much longer anyway," Kaleo's voice shook, surprised as she was at Portia's sudden change in attitude.

"Is that really what you think? That your knight in shining armor will save you? That your family wants you?" Portia spat on the ground. "Grow up. You're an indentured servant, and you won't be leaving for a very long time. People like you are trash. If you weren't, you wouldn't be here."

"And what about you? We're not trash, we're people."

"Oh, no, I'm not a slave like you. I choose to live here, and my loyalty has been rewarded with the esteemed role of being Servina's maid. I find your insolence to her personally offensive." Portia leaned closer to Kaleo, all traces of her formerly sweet attitude gone. "Any slight against her or her honor is a slight against me, and even if she's gracious enough to let you live, I'll make your life a living hell if you don't learn the proper subservience."

"Ah, there you are, Portia." Miss Fulbright broke into their conversation. Both Kaleo and Portia looked up to see the gaunt woman stepping down from the entryway across the courtyard. "Servina is here. Go and tend to her."

As soon as she heard Miss Fulbright's voice, Portia's attitude transformed from vindictive into what Kaleo now recognized as sickly sweet and too submissive, with her hands clasped in front of her dress and her eyes downcast. "Yes ma'am."

"And I see that you've got the newcomer with you. How is she coming along?" Miss Fulbright fixed Kaleo with her hawklike eyes.

"She is... passable, ma'am. I've had to listen to her constant ravings about her home and how her family and lover will come and save her, but she can at least do the simple jobs satisfactorily. It's very distracting, but I've managed to keep us on track, although I worry that she may influence some of the more impressionable cleaners."

Kaleo bristled. Portia had encouraged her to talk about her life and asked questions to draw out her stories. Now she recognized it as a ploy to get to know her so she could better tear Kaleo down. The person she had thought might be her friend had turned in the blink of an eye into an enemy. Kaleo didn't know what game Portia was playing, but she resolved to not get lured into another round.

"I see." Miss. Fulbright frowned. "Well, at least she won't be a total waste then. I'll keep her with the cleaning staff for now."

"Are you sure? With someone this desperate, just coming down off her drugs, I'd hate for her to be tempted around all those chemicals. She also upset Servina as the gladiators were riding in by not showing proper deference. She might be better suited for the kitchen, where no one would see her. I'm sure cook will get her whipped into shape in no time. Plus, she'd be out of the way there and wouldn't cause any problems," Portia said sweetly.

"Portia, are you questioning me? I would think that someone of your status would know better," Miss. Fulbright snapped.

Portia shrank into herself even more. "I would never presume to question you, ma'am. I only seek to help this company run smoothly, and I know that you've been so busy attending to the Ableds and managing your other important responsibilities that you don't have time to bother with these trivial matters. I am sorry if I caused any offense."

Remembering the rumors about the cook and not wanting to risk a position change, Kaleo decided to go for broke. "Miss Fulbright, I'm not addicted to drugs. I have never taken drugs recreationally in my life. My state when I came here was because I was forcibly abducted and drugged against my will. If you will simply allow me to write a letter or make a phone call, I promise you that whatever amount there is in my contract, my family will pay twice that to have me returned safely. I –"

"You see?" Portia cut in. "She's clearly delusional. Just look at her, practically skin and bones, wasted away from her addiction. She's clearly unhealthy, and those drugs must have fried her brain. Keeping her around would only enable her to spread her lies to others who are more gullible and more likely to cause trouble."

Miss. Fulbright narrowed her eyes and surveyed the two women before nodding her head. "Portia, I do believe you're right. I'll move her into the kitchens."

"But, my family–" Kaleo was interrupted when Portia slapped her across the face. The sting of the blow on her healing cut was almost as bad as the sting of the insult.

"Quiet, disrespectful girl. The nerve of you to question Miss Fulbright. I'm starting to think that the kitchens are too good for you."

"That's enough, Portia. Her brazenness will soon be rectified. Now, girl, come with me."

Kaleo did her best to ignore the smug look on Portia's face as she followed Miss Fulbright.

When they entered the kitchen, for the first time all week Kaleo felt truly warm. It was a large room with windows lining one wall and several fires burning merrily against the other. Even as she took in the hubbub of the bustling room, the distinctive smell of freshly baked bread wafted past her nose.

"Chef Hugo, I need to speak with you," Miss Fulbright called out from her station just inside the door.

A large man dressed in a dingy brown cap and a stained apron that might have once been white waddled over to them. Two small black eyes peered out at Kaleo from under heavy brows in a red face, and with every step he took his double chin jiggled.

"How can I help you, Miss Fulbright?" he asked in a voice far too nasal and high-pitched for his large frame.

"This girl is new to the company and has been working with the cleaning crew for the past week, but I believe she'd be a better fit here. From what I understand, she came to us after a long drug binge, and she's got an attitude. I've been informed that she is fairly slow on the uptake, but that with the proper training she can learn to be proficient at simple tasks. Supposedly she's Abled but has yet to demonstrate any abilities. I leave it up to you to find a suitable place for her."

The cook leered at Kaleo. "I'll try my best. Never let it be said that I looked a gift horse in the mouth."

"Thank you, Hugo. I also wanted to inform you that the fighters came back today, and it sounds like they've been sharpening their appetites all week."

"I understand and have already made preparations. Dinner will be ready at the usual time."

Miss Fulbright turned on her heel and sailed out of the room, leaving Kaleo alone in front of the creepy cook. He smiled without blinking and stared at Kaleo long enough to make her uncomfortable.

"I do believe that I have time to show you around before the dinner rush begins in earnest," he said eventually, and offered her his arm. Kaleo folded her hands together in front of her dress and looked down, mimicking Portia's posture and hoping that he would leave her alone if she didn't encourage him.

"Ah, a shy one? Don't worry, I'll soon break you of that."

Compared to Miss Fulbright's long and purposeful strides, the pace of Hugo's waddle was easy to follow as he ambled around the kitchen. He explained what each table, station, and hearth was for, and Kaleo couldn't help but notice that compared to the cleaning servants who were a mix of men and women of all ages, and who always chattered while they worked, the kitchen staff were quiet, female, and with a few exceptions all either pre-teen or teenagers.

After her tour, Kaleo was assigned to one of the prep stations where she spent the rest of the afternoon chopping a mountain of potatoes, carrots, and other root vegetables. She was still exhausted and sore from the week spent cleaning and doing laundry, and by the time dinner rolled around, her hands and arms were so tired she could barely lift them.

When Hugo rang the dinner bell, half of the kitchen staff peeled off their aprons. Like a line of dancers, they each grabbed a tray filled with plates of food and exited to the dining hall, led by Hugo, who had replaced his stained apron with a clean one.

Once Hugo and the others left, everyone remaining behind started to clean and the conversation gradually grew louder, only to quiet again when Hugo and the others returned from the great hall. Kaleo followed the lead of her fellow servants and grabbed a bowl, spoon, and cup from a large pile before getting in line. At the front of the line stood Hugo, leering at each girl before spooning food into her bowl. Kaleo did her best to ignore him, and while most of the girls split up to eat in several small clusters, she sat off to the side, unsure whether she would be welcomed into any of the groups, and even less sure whether she wanted to try to make friends after what had happened with Portia.

The serving girls ate quickly and spoke in hushed whispers before cleaning their dishes. Then, instead of going to bed or doing more chores as Kaleo would have expected, the other girls simply sat in silence as the atmosphere grew tense.

Across the room, a young woman who seemed around her age kept glancing at Kaleo. Despite Kaleo's best efforts, they never made eye contact, although she had the eerie sense of being carefully watched.

She'd been so absorbed in trying to figure out what had caused the sudden shift in mood that Hugo's nasally voice at her elbow startled her. "Don't think that I've forgotten about you, girl. We need to get you a kitchen uniform and some bedding. Follow me."

Immediately after he'd uttered the words, the atmosphere in the room lightened and the hair on the back of Kaleo's neck rose. She followed him out of the room with her weight shifted to her toes, ready for anything.

"You'll be sleeping with the others there," Hugo said, gesturing down the hallway before turning in the opposite direction. He opened a plain wooden door to reveal a medium-sized room. A large bed had been pushed against a wall, facing two large chests. Thick wooden beams ran across the low ceiling.

As Kaleo was looking around, the door shut behind her.

"Here, have a seat. What did you say that your name was?" Hugo asked as he walked over to one of the chests and began rummaging around.

"Kaleo," she said without sitting down.

"Kaleo. It's pretty. A pretty name for a very pretty woman."

She tried not to laugh; without hair and with the scar, pretty wasn't a word she'd have used to describe herself. "You're too kind."

Hugo turned around with his hands full of clothes. "It has nothing to do with kindness. You see, Kaleo, my kitchen is my kingdom, and like any king I like to have things run a certain way. It is easiest to achieve this harmony if everyone understands each other. Surely you can see how good communication is key for everything to work smoothly."

"Yes, I do."

"Good, good. Then you'll understand that the best communication occurs when all the orders come from the top, the head of the kitchen—which would be me—and that to facilitate this communication total trust is key."

Kaleo watched him circle her. "That sounds like a tall order for all of your new members. I was taught that trust should be earned, not given freely."

"An admirable lesson. Misguided, but admirable." He held the clothes out to Kaleo, but when she reached out to take them, he stepped back.

"We have a rule in the kitchen: nothing is free. If you wish to receive a new uniform, you must first take off what you're wearing."

For a moment, Kaleo was struck dumb. Once his words sank in, she drew herself up. "In that case, I think the clothes I'm wearing are perfectly fine."

"Oh, you think so?" Hugo's laugh sounded remarkably like a squealing pig. "And what about your bedding? You'll have to earn it, and the price is a night here."

"I'd rather sleep on the cold floor," Kaleo snarled, all too certain now of the source of the strange atmosphere in the kitchens earlier.

"Come now, don't make an enemy out of me. Just as you have to trust me, I have to trust you, and what better way to learn more about each other than by enjoying an intimate evening together? I have clean sheets, and my mattress is made of down. I'm sure that you've had a terribly hard week working with the cleaners and maids. All it would take for you to enjoy the luxury of its softness is a few minutes with me."

"Forget the cold floor, I'd rather sleep outside in the rain."

"Never let it be said that I forced a girl. You're all the same anyways; soon enough you'll come crawling back to me. If you beg nicely, I might even reward you with a drug of your choice. It's easy enough to hide things amongst the kitchen produce shipped to us."

Kaleo clenched her jaw and stared Hugo down in the light of the brightly burning candle on the side table. "Is this what the rumors were about? The young girls are much easier to manipulate, aren't they? Some of them were young enough that they probably didn't even realize what you were doing."

"I will not have such vulgar accusations," Hugo hissed. He raised his hand as if to strike her.

"Don't even think about it," she said with as much steel in her tone as she could muster.

Something in her voice, or perhaps in her glare, stopped his hand from descending.

Without another word, Kaleo shouldered past him. She made her way down the hallway back to the room where the other kitchen servants slept and paused outside the door when she heard voices within.

"Do you think he'll let her stay the whole night?"

"I doubt it. She's so old, and did you see that huge scar on her face? She'll be lucky to get a couple of hours' rest, and that's only if he falls asleep after he's done."

Someone giggled. "Rest... as if anyone could sleep with his terrible snoring."

"It's still better than the floor."

Kaleo opened the door and walked into the room. In the light of the dying fire, everyone turned to look at the newcomer, and her heart ached when she saw all the girls who were sleeping on blankets set on top of mats of straw. She stood for a moment in the doorway, surveying the room. Unfortunately, all the spots around the fire had been taken, leaving the only available space on the outer edges.

She made her way to an empty place in the far corner that shared the same wall as the fireplace. She might not have been able to form a shield, but her abilities allowed her to sense a slight increase in temperature coming from the stones of the wall, and even a few degrees of warmth was better than the damp chill that hung around the outer edges of the room.

As she tossed and turned on the cold stone floor, Kaleo tried to remember how it felt to be cuddling with Stefan in his bed. She knew he was probably worried sick, and her resolve to hold on until he could find her was strengthened. She smiled in the darkness when she imagined what he would have done if he'd heard Hugo proposition her.

Her thoughts turned to what Stefan would have thought of Audra's betrayal, and she shook her head to clear it; there would be plenty of time to unpack that can of worms when she was safe. Now, thinking about the past and trying to process what Audra had done would only upset her, and she needed all her energy to survive.

The next morning, Kaleo woke up at the same time as the others—an easy thing to do when she'd barely slept. When she entered the kitchen, she was snidely directed by Hugo to turn the huge, heavy roasting spits in one of the hearths.

After a long night on the stone floor, the warmth of the fire was like a breath of life to Kaleo's cold body. The work was hard, but she appreciated the chance to use her muscles. Peeling the potatoes the day before had been a welcome change of pace, but she needed to stay as active as possible if she were to have any hope in continuing her recovery.

It was a bonus that as the spit turned she was able to practice reaching out with her abilities during the monotonous work. While she still couldn't create anything with the energy she sensed, feeling the various flows eddy around the room gave her a sense of comfort; she'd worked hard at that skill, and the last thing she wanted was to let it get rusty from disuse.

Her second evening in the kitchen, Kaleo reached the front of the dinner line and Hugo asked her to join him in his room. When she refused, he dumped her bowl of food into the trash.

The next day, Hugo forbade anyone from feeding her, and even went so far as to assign one of the younger girls to watch Kaleo and keep her from eating under penalty of losing her own food if Kaleo had so much as a bite to eat.

Kaleo held strong. She was able to siphon off some warmth from the fire, and while it wasn't nearly as satisfying as eating, and she could still feel her stomach grumble in complaint, the lack of food didn't weaken Kaleo. She was greatly encouraged by the thought that even if she could never create a shield again, she hadn't lost all of her abilities.

The next morning upon waking, Kaleo found a slice of bread and a hunk of cheese wrapped in a dirty cloth by her head. She looked around the room as the other women began to get up, and made eye contact with the young woman who'd watched her on her first day in the kitchen. The woman glanced down at Kaleo's hand, which held the wrapped food, looked into her eyes again and ever so slightly nodded. Kaleo was sure to scarf the food down before anyone could see what she held. Once she was done, Kaleo looked up to thank the other woman, but only saw a flash of blue as her benefactress walked out the door.

The day was much the same as before, with Kaleo assigned to the roasting spit and being denied all food. That evening, when Hugo asked her to join him, Kaleo denied him again. For her defiance, he ordered her to clean out the fireplaces and dump the ashes in the bin outside. It was a dirty task and a long walk to and from the bin, made harder by the cold night air. Kaleo gritted her teeth and controlled her form to lift correctly; if she was going to be assigned manual labor, it was important that she at least make the most of it. To add insult to injury, her minder followed her around to ensure that she didn't try and steal any food scraps to ease the grumbling in her belly but didn't otherwise lift a finger to help.

It was hard to not feel resentment towards the girl, but once Kaleo learned that by watching her, her minder was able to eat double rations, she wasn't as begrudging; the girl was so painfully thin that it looked like it would take an entire year's worth of double rations to get her up to a decent weight.

By the time Kaleo finished cleaning the hearths, it was well past midnight. She washed her face and hands, and made her way to the sleeping quarters for a few hours of rest before they all got up early the next morning to start breakfast.

Surprisingly, her cold sleeping spot had a new neighbor. While Kaleo was curious and feared that this might herald a new type of attack, her body was too exhausted from all the lifting and moving of the day to be kept from its rest, and she sank to the ground.

"If you want to hurt me, you can try it now, although I'll warn you that it won't go well for you," she said into the darkness.

"I think I'll pass," her neighbor whispered back.

"That's too bad; it would have been nice to work out some anger."

"Save that anger for later. I have no fight with you." There was a pause, and Kaleo felt a cloth bundle pressed into her hand. When she carefully unwrapped it, she smelled another slice of bread and piece of cheese. Immediately, she shoved the food into her mouth.

"Thank you. My name is Kaleo, what is yours?" she whispered after she'd eaten her small meal, suddenly overcome with tears by the kindness of the stranger.

"Reina, and don't mention it. There aren't many here that can stand up to Hugo. Well, honestly, none besides me so far. If he doesn't intimidate them into it, they fold on the first day of hard duty and little food."

Kaleo turned on her side to try and see more of the other woman's face. "What do you mean?"

"You know exactly what I mean. There's a reason he likes the young ones, and it's not because they're great conversationalists. They don't even have to be enthusiastic about what he wants, as long as they give him access."

"Why hasn't anyone done anything yet? Surely there's someone you could tell."

"No one cares. Just about everyone here is on a multi-year contract, and most of them were either sold by their families for food for their siblings or parents or brought here to learn a trade because the orphanages were too full." Reina snorted. "I'm not sure they're learning to cook, but a few are getting great training on how to prostitute themselves."

"How can you stand by and watch him? Unless you're a part of this too? Is this a trick?" Kaleo already regretted eating the food, suddenly afraid that Hugo had drugged it and given it to Reina.

A sharp elbow hit her side, and Kaleo gasped.

"That was for insulting me. Do it again and I'll slap you," Reina growled.

"Can you blame me? As far as I see, it looks to me like you've already joined the club. How many nights did those blankets and a good meal cost?"

Kaleo was ready for the blow, and when her abilities alerted her of something moving her way, she blocked Reina's leg with her own. She blocked the next kick with her arm.

"I guess that was a fair question," Reina said, and sighed. "I came here as a maid for an Abled fighter. My mistress was killed in the arena, and Portia doesn't like competition in any form, so I was sent here to work. I already had my own bedding and a certain level of respect from others, as I'm not a contract worker and can leave any time that I like. I made it clear to Hugo, as I suspect you've already done, that no part of me was for sale, and that I'd stay out of his way if he left me alone. Since then, I've stayed for my own reasons."

"And you've not helped any of the others? You've just sat back and let Hugo molest them?"

"Most of them were already here before I was. Look, I've got my own goals. I don't have the time or energy to help anyone else. Judging from the rumors I've heard in the dining hall, you've also got something to live for. Take a piece of advice from someone who's been doing this longer than you: it's best if you keep your head down and work. We're in the middle of nowhere, so you're on your own to survive until your time is up."

"I'm on my own? Why bring me the bread and cheese then?"

There was a long pause, and she began to wonder if Reina had fallen asleep.

"Most of the girls here are Abled, and even if they don't have any real abilities to speak of, after they submit to Hugo they fall under his sway no matter how much they hate him. Even the non-Abled ones are too young to stand firm against such an authority figure, especially when it goes against what's expected. You held out against him, even when the deck was stacked against you, and it reminded me of my old friend," Reina whispered.

Kaleo racked her mind for the most recent research theories when it came to Ableds. Despite graduating from school well over a year and a half before, she still liked to keep up on new discoveries and recent research in the field of Abled studies. "Hugo has abilities?" She hadn't seen him wear the red scarf or belt reserved for Ableds in the Atlantic Trading Company, but then again he almost always had an apron on.

"Yeah, something about knowing exactly when the meat is done to the perfect temperature. Pretty lame if you ask me."

Kaleo frowned. She'd briefly hoped that Hugo would eventually lose interest in her and turn his attention to someone who was more receptive, no matter how despicable that would be. However, his being Abled changed things. Due to the shifting nature of Abled group dynamics, he risked losing control if he let her live peacefully without submitting to him. She inhaled deeply and tried to sort her thoughts so as to figure out her best course of action as she processed the new development.

After a long time, she gave up. There was no denying it—she and Hugo were on a collision course, and she had no intention of letting him break her.

Chapter Nine

The confrontation with Hugo came about much sooner than Kaleo originally expected. The next morning, one of the girls who slept directly in front of the fireplace was found dead. Delia was her name, and it had been her turn to get up early and get the fires started and the water boiling for the day. Instead, she'd used the time to fashion a noose out of the casings used for sausages and hung herself from the rafters.

From various overheard conversations, Kaleo gathered that Delia had been one of Hugo's favorites, and she'd been so anxiety-ridden about his preoccupation with Kaleo she'd decided her life wasn't worth living anymore.

"It's a pity," Reina said as she and Kaleo washed dishes together. "Delia was one of the sweet ones, although not the brightest in the bunch by far. Oh, well, I hope she's in a better place now."

"How can you say that so flippantly? This is terrible," Kaleo said. "The poor girl killed herself after three days because her abuser wasn't giving her enough attention. She couldn't have been any older than twelve."

"She's not the first, and she won't be the last." Reina shrugged at the horrified look on Kaleo's face. "Why do you think we had the space in the kitchen for you? You've got to toughen your skin, or you won't make it here."

"It can't be cheap to run through that many contracts."

"You're assuming the 'contracts' are so long because of their expense. In reality, it's more because they value your labor so low. That's the whole reason Hugo works to save money wherever he can—so he can afford to hire new girls to replace those who can't take it anymore."

Kaleo pursed her lips but didn't say anything more, unsure how to respond.

That morning, Hugo was conspicuously absent after cutting down Delia. Kaleo understood why he'd been gone when he walked back in later that afternoon, leading a young girl by the hand who had a red belt tied around her waist.

"Ladies, this is Yvonne, the newest addition to our crew," he announced before directing Yvonne to help prepare the vegetables and peel the potatoes.

"That's how he always starts them out. If they hurt themselves, he can take them back to his room for 'medical care.' Those are the dullest knives in the kitchen, so they're easy to slip and get cut on," Kaleo's minder said from her seat as she watched Kaleo turn the roasting pig.

Kaleo glanced over at the young girl. "So you do talk."

The girl shrugged and Kaleo turned her gaze back to Yvonne. She'd never been particularly good at guessing other people's ages, but like many of the girls who worked in the kitchens Yvonne was on the younger side, probably in her early teens. When she was first introduced to everyone, she wore her sleek, long black hair loose around her shoulders; now it was tied back in a low ponytail. Her dark almond eyes stole glances around the kitchen, and a small frown creased her brow as she worked hard to skin the mountain of potatoes in front of her.

Yvonne's demeanor reminded Kaleo of a young Lin, and her heart twisted in her chest. She turned her attention back to the roasting meat, only to hear someone cry out a few minutes later. When she looked across the kitchen, she saw Yvonne clutching her hand.

"Oh no, my dear, did you cut yourself?" Hugo was already at Yvonne's side, and Kaleo felt her temper rise. "That looks very deep and uneven. Come with me and we'll get it taken care of. You won't even feel the cut by the time we're done," he said lightly, and took Yvonne by her uninjured hand.

Kaleo stepped forward. She knew she was being foolish, and that she should heed Reina's advice and keep her head down, but she'd hate herself if she didn't act now. The timing was truly unfortunate—her abilities and body grew stronger every day, but she was still nowhere near full strength. It didn't matter; she was out of time.

"No, you don't," she said.

Hugo turned around. "Excuse me?"

"I know what plans you have for her, and I can't allow it."

The only sound in the formerly noisy kitchen was that of the bubbling soups and the hiss of fat from the roasting meat hitting the fire.

"What do you mean you can't allow it?" Hugo threw his head back and laughed, and his smile turned cruel. "I see I was mistaken—you're a spirited one after all." He shoved Yvonne away and grabbed a large meat cleaver off a nearby countertop. "It's time to teach you a lesson, girl."

Kaleo narrowed her eyes. As gross and despicable as he was, Hugo still had a large physical advantage over her. She'd spent enough time in the gym to know that even a skinny teenage boy could best her in a test of strength, and Hugo was a fully grown man. Just the day before she'd seen him easily lift a pig onto a roasting rack that was difficult for four of the older girls to remove.

On the other hand, due to his large size, she guessed she could probably move quicker than he could, at least for short bursts. Endurance-wise, it was anyone's game; if she'd have been in top form she could have outlasted him, although thanks to the effects of the radiation she couldn't be certain.

The one thing Kaleo was sure of was that when it came to Saban-40 concentrations, she had the upper hand, which meant there was really only one course of action she could take.

Kaleo drew herself up and stared Hugo down. They were stationed on opposite sides of the kitchen, with the main walkway between them, and the fate of an innocent girl hanging in the balance.

Instilling as much authority as she could into her voice, and doing her best to maintain a confident demeanor, Kaleo stepped forward. "Drop the knife, Hugo. You know you can't win."

Hugo's laugh made her skin crawl. "So you want to do this here? Fine then, once I win this challenge, it's going to make forcing you to submit all that much easier."

"We'll see about that," Kaleo said.

Yvonne whimpered and clutched her hand to her chest. Hugo looked down at her, and then around the kitchen where everyone had stopped their work to watch. "Why don't you sit down? This won't take but a moment," he said to Yvonne before walking towards Kaleo.

She stood her ground. For all her outward bravado, Kaleo wasn't quite sure how exactly challenges worked, although she'd heard Dr. Saban talk about them briefly at a family dinner several months before. Her mother had always been the unquestioned Abled leader of NAT, and Kaleo had very little experience on what to do now that she'd initiated a challenge, or exactly how to win one.

What she did know was that no matter what, she couldn't back down, not just for her, but also for Yvonne and all the other young women Hugo had taken advantage of. She grabbed a rolling pin off of the table nearby and balanced her weight on the balls of her feet.

Hugo misread her posture. "Frozen in fear? Good, you should be."

Kaleo almost laughed when she saw the way he held his knife; it was a great grip for slicing bread, but completely ineffective for a fight.

For the time being, Hugo seemed content to stand still and try to intimidate her. His tactics gave Kaleo hope that he was bluffing; she'd practiced knife-fighting with Stefan enough to know that it required a certain level of mental fortitude—and either skill or brief insanity for a truly effective attack. She adjusted her grip on her rolling pin. Unless Hugo wanted to kill or severely injure her, this was all for show.

If he was bluffing, it was time to call his bluff.

Kaleo stepped forward. "Oh yeah, you think I'm afraid of you, big man? You think I'm cowering over here because you're scary? No, I'm simply trying to figure out the best way to carve you up." She grabbed a chef's knife off the table and twirled it around her fingers the way Stefan had taught her. It didn't do anything from a practical standpoint, but it looked really cool, and she sensed that half the battle would be won by looking like she knew what she was doing. She pointed the knife at Hugo and took another step forward. "You think that I have anything to lose here? Big mistake."

Hugo stepped back. "You wouldn't do anything to me. They'd kill you for it. You're just detoxing from the drugs."

"Drugs?" Even to her own ears, Kaleo's laugh sounded unhinged. "I've never done drugs in my life. But even if I had, you know what detoxing drug addicts do? They act irrationally, and right now I'd rather die than watch you touch any of these girls again, sicko. Drop the knife and kick it over to me before I gut you like a fish," she growled as she stalked towards him.

Hugo's face blanched, and he did as she said, even going so far as to hold his hands up in surrender.

Kaleo dropped the rolling pin and picked up the meat cleaver. With a swing of her arm, she brought it down on the nearest table, burying the blade an inch in the wood. Hugo flinched.

Kaleo lowered her voice as she stepped into his personal space. "Now, let's get some things straight: from here on out, you're going to pretend like everything is normal. As far as Miss Fulbright or anyone else is concerned, this didn't happen"—she brought her other knife up to his throat—"however, behind the scenes I'm the new boss here, and if you so much as even think about touching one of these girls, I will punish you in painful and unexpected ways. You won't die, but you'll wish that you did." She moved the tip of the knife to his groin. "Am I clear?"

Hugo swallowed. "Very much so... ma'am."

"Good." Kaleo stepped back. "Now tell everyone else so we're all on the same page."

"I'm the head of this kitchen in name only. You're the real boss," Hugo said quietly.

Kaleo shook her head. "Louder."

"You're the real boss," Hugo repeated.

"Good. And what happens if you touch any of these girls again?"

"I'll be harshly punished for it."

"That's right. If you harass them again, I'll remove your family jewels and make you wear them as a necklace," Kaleo said. She looked around to gauge the reactions of the other women. Many had eyes almost as wide as dinner plates, but none of them stepped forward in Hugo's defense. Reina had one eyebrow raised.

"Today we're removing all the supplies from Hugo's room. He gets to keep his bed and personal items, but everything else will go in our sleeping room. As such, there shouldn't be a reason for any of you to go to his room ever again, and if he tries to lure you there, I want you to immediately tell Reina or me, and we'll take care of it. Things are going to be very different from here on out. Any questions?" Kaleo asked.

When no one said anything, she nodded. "If anyone has any personal questions that they don't want to ask in public, come and find me. We need to finish getting dinner ready, or someone will get suspicious and wonder what's going on. After dinner, we'll move the supplies. Let's get back to work."

After everyone returned to their jobs, Kaleo turned to Hugo and handed him a long wooden spoon and a pair of tongs.

"What are these for?" he asked.

"When I said that I don't want you touching any of them, I meant it."

"What if I need to move someone out of the way?" he whined.

"Then you can ask them nicely to move or use your utensils to nudge them gently. I believe I've made myself clear as to the consequences of you touching any of them under any circumstances. It's your choice to make," Kaleo said with a pointed glance at his crotch.

Hugo harrumphed and moved away, presumably to check the doneness of one of the roasts.

"I thought that I told you to keep your head down," Reina said at her elbow.

She shrugged. "Someone had to do it, and I'll be glad to actually get a full meal tonight."

Kaleo walked to where Yvonne was sitting and knelt in front of her. "Hi there, I'm Kaleo. What was your name again?" she asked.

"Yvonne," the girl said timidly.

"It's nice to meet you, Yvonne. I heard that you cut your hand. Can I take a look at it?"

Yvonne held out her hand. It was a superficial wound, though one that bled profusely. "That's quite a cut. How does it feel?"

"It stings."

"I bet it does. The good news is that it looks like you just sliced the skin pretty good. I don't think you damaged the muscles underneath. How about we get it cleaned off and bandaged, and then you sit and watch everyone else work for now? After dinner we'll have time to take care of it properly. Does that sound okay?" Kaleo kept her voice as gentle and soothing as possible.

Yvonne nodded, and Kaleo led her to one of the sinks where she washed the cut with soap and water and wrapped Yvonne's hand in a clean towel. After she was done, she directed the young girl to a spot near the hearth close enough to be warm without being stifling, where she could keep an eye on the newest addition to the kitchen without being disturbed.

The rest of the preparations for dinner went off without a hitch. Immediately after Hugo and the servers returned, Kaleo ordered everyone to Hugo's room and supervised the removal of all the supplies he'd been holding hostage.

After successfully liberating their supplies, Kaleo and the others left Hugo alone in his room and retired to the kitchen. The mood was much lighter than it had been before, although Kaleo could still feel an undercurrent of tension and saw a number of darted glances at the door.

Once she was satisfied that the most pressing matters were taken care of, the second thing Kaleo did was to make sure Yvonne's hand was cared for properly. When they saw her gently bandaging the cut without asking for anything in return, several other girls stepped forward to tell her about their own injuries and illnesses. Most of them were rather benign cuts, although one girl had burned her forearm severely a few days before but hadn't told anyone about it to avoid drawing Hugo's attention. Kaleo took one look at the angry-red, weeping burn and sent the girl to the infirmary for treatment.

As the days passed, the mood in the kitchen continued to lighten. Hugo still wandered around and directed the cooking, but now he used his spoon or tongs in place of his hands, and Kaleo watched him like a hawk from her station at the roasting hearth. Despite not seeing any indication of rebellion, Kaleo stayed on her guard, not trusting Hugo to give up his position so easily.

Her caution was rewarded a week and a half into the new arrangement, when Kaleo picked up her soup bowl to eat dinner after a long day. Yvonne, who'd already started eating, gasped and slapped Kaleo's bowl out of her hands.

Kaleo flinched. In the past week, Yvonne had all but become her shadow. From the little she'd told Kaleo, the quiet girl had been sold to the company on a six-year contract in exchange for enough money for her parents to apprentice her older brother and then drink themselves into a stupor.

Judging from the round burn scars on her skin, Kaleo guessed that Yvonne's life hadn't been an easy one. The fact that she'd done the bare minimum to stand up for the girl and ensure her safety, combined with what the other girls had told Yvonne about Hugo, had apparently been enough to earn the young girl's undying loyalty, and she rarely left Kaleo's side when they weren't working.

"Everything okay?" Kaleo asked as everyone turned to look at what had caused the commotion.

"It's poisoned!" Yvonne cried, shoving her bowl as far away as she could.

A flurry of conversation broke out across the room.

"What do you mean, poisoned?" Reina asked from her seat across the table.

"I—I don't know, it just doesn't taste right," Yvonne sputtered.

"How do you know?"

"It's my abilities. They tell me when something is wrong with my food." Yvonne shrank into herself and looked down at the table. "I only got them a few months ago. My pa used them to know what was safe to eat from the trash bins behind the restaurants when he'd lose our food money gambling on the back-alley Abled fighters. That's why Miss Fulbright sent me here to the kitchen."

"And you think that there is something wrong with your soup?" Kaleo asked.

Yvonne nodded. "It doesn't taste rotten… just weird. Chemically."

Kaleo frowned and walked over to where Freya, the serving girl on duty, had been ladling the soup into bowls for everyone. She grabbed a clean spoon from the drawer, dipped it into the pot, and smelled it. She couldn't sense anything different, but when she handed it over to Yvonne, the girl tasted the soup and made a face. "Same thing. Something is really off."

Kaleo looked at Freya. "Do you know what the problem could be? Has anyone interfered with this since we served it to the main hall?"

Freya gulped and shook her head.

Kaleo raised her eyebrows. "Are you sure, Freya? You were in charge of the soup tonight. If you know something, you should tell me. I don't want anyone to get sick or have any problems. There won't be a punishment if you tell me, as long as you do it right now."

Under her intent gaze, Freya withered. "I'm sorry, miss, but he told me that if I didn't do this, or if I told anyone, then he'd punish me. Please don't hurt me, I didn't have any choice. I'm really, really, really sorry. I didn't want to do it."

The words came out in a rush, followed by a flood of hysterical tears.

"Hey! No one eat the soup," Reina called out as Kaleo tried to calm Freya down.

"Freya, listen, you have to tell me everything," Kaleo said.

"It was Hugo. Two nights ago I had to use the toilet after bedtime, and when I was done and walking back to the sleeping room, he cornered me in the hallway and gave me a small packet and said that if I didn't add it to the soup on my night to serve the meal, he'd make sure that I had a terrible accident in the kitchen and wouldn't be able to work anymore. I had to do what he said, Miss Kaleo. If I lose this contract and can't work, then my mama and little sister will have to give the money back and live on the streets again," Freya said.

"Thank you for telling me," Kaleo said. She turned back to Yvonne. "Did Hugo know about your abilities?"

Yvonne shook her head. "The broker who sold my contract to Miss Fulbright only told her that I was good with food."

Kaleo nodded and stood, turning to address the whole kitchen. "Has Hugo asked anyone else to do anything? Please, don't be afraid to speak up. You won't be punished."

One of the girls raised her hand. "He asked me to make sure that the door to the sleeping room was unlocked tonight."

Another girl piped up, "And he made me show him where you slept!"

"Did he touch any of you?" Kaleo asked. Everyone shook their heads no. "I see. Well, I'm sorry, girls, but no one should eat the soup. Looks like it's bread and water and whatever cheese or other leftovers we have available tonight."

"What's going to happen to us?" Freya asked.

"Like you should care, traitor," someone snarled from the back of the room.

Kaleo shook her head. "None of that, now. We can't afford to let him divide us. Freya and everyone else, I trust that if something like this happens again you'll come to me as soon as it happens?"

Freya and the others nodded.

"Thank you for owning up to it. It was an easy mistake to make, and I know how fear can be a powerful motivator. Thank goodness Yvonne caught it when she did. Now, no one worry. I'll take care of this," she said as she exchanged looks with Reina.

Chapter Ten

Later that night, after everyone had gone to sleep, the door creaked open. A large shadow entered and skirted around the room to Kaleo's sleeping pallet. The room was silent, save for the shadow's heavy breathing, and there was the flash of a knife and a flurry of movement in the dim light.

It took a minute for the shadow to be satisfied with its work, and it bent down to the pallet to check for a pulse. Apparently what it found was satisfying, as it bundled the limp form up in a blanket and glided from the room.

The shadow lumbered down the hallway to Hugo's room, where it shoved the bloody blanket and its contents through the open window. The room was against the outermost wall of the fort facing the sea, and the bundle fell almost twenty feet before lying still on the rocks wet with ocean spray. The shadow pumped its fists in the air in victory before pouring itself a glass of wine from the decanter on the desk.

"I'm sure you're feeling very proud of yourself right now, eliminating your competition like you just did." The flare of a match and subsequent lighting of a candle illuminated Reina's face.

Hugo's mouth opened in surprise, then his expression devolved into a sneer. "Your friend is gone; I disposed of her all too easily. You better watch your back because you'll be next."

"Not likely," Kaleo said as she stepped into the faint pool of light cast by Reina's candle and used the flame to light her own. "I knew that you had problems, but I'd hoped to spare you. Unnecessary bloodshed only breeds more bloodshed."

"Kaleo?" Hugo blinked, frowned, glanced out the window, and shook his head. "You're dead."

"Dead? You mean from you stabbing me and throwing my body out the window?" Kaleo snorted. "Thankfully, no. That was tomorrow's pig that we were going to roast for dinner. It's good that it's extra cold tonight; I think that we may still be able to recover it tomorrow morning to use for breakfast."

For someone who had just been told that instead of murdering his enemy he had instead stabbed an already dead pig, Hugo recovered from his surprise remarkably well. "It doesn't matter. You can't do anything. You need me, and I won't stop until you're out of my way," he said, his face twisted into a grimace of hatred.

"So you didn't challenge me like an Abled with honor would? That's too bad, although not entirely unexpected."

Hugo swayed on his feet and looked confused.

"Well, Reina, I guess I'll let you take it from here if you're still sure," Kaleo said.

Reina's smile was grim and her hazel eyes glinted in the light of the candle. "I'm positive."

"You think that you can take me? I'll throw you out the window too, blondie," Hugo slurred.

"I doubt that. It sounds like those sleeping pills that we crushed up and put in that pitcher are already taking effect. I guess what they say is true—you really shouldn't mix alcohol and medication," Reina said.

"You won't do anything to me, you're just a lady's maid without a lady."

Reina raised an eyebrow and her smile was almost a snarl. "You foolish, foolish man. You think I've stayed here in the kitchens because I had no better options?" She hefted a coil of rope in one hand, swinging the end back and forth like a cat stalking its prey. "I'll show you what this 'lady's maid' can do, because you won't live long enough to tell anyone else."

Kaleo left Reina to her own devices and headed back to the sleeping room. When they'd discussed what to do about Hugo, Reina had been adamant that she would handle him and had refused all offers of help.

"Everything is fine. You all can go to sleep now. He's not going to bother anyone ever again," Kaleo said softly, and heard a couple of muffled cheers in response.

Someone had thoughtfully replaced the fake pallet on which they'd put the pig with her own, and Kaleo sighed as she slid between the blankets, although she remained alert until Reina settled on the pallet next to hers.

"It's done," Reina whispered.

"Understood," Kaleo replied. She rolled over on her other side to face the cold wall and buried her head under her blankets, pulling them tightly around her. In the comfort and safety of the cocoon, Kaleo finally relaxed.

She wasn't sure how long Rodney had kept her drugged, but she guessed it had taken at least a week to travel to Europe by boat. That, plus the past two weeks she'd spent at the Atlantic Company meant that she'd been away from her home and family and friends for almost a month; possibly more. She missed them so much: her parents, Lin, Nicole, Rosie, and above all, Stefan. She'd done as he would have wanted and played it safe, trying her best to stay out of the drama, but she couldn't do so any longer. If it hadn't been for Yvonne's abilities, she'd be dead. Now that she'd survived, she had an entire kitchen looking to her for leadership.

Kaleo recognized that ever since she'd stopped the nuclear bomb, she'd been playing defense and only reacting to situations that arose. In fact, as she lay in the dark, she realized she'd been playing defense for much longer. She'd had that luxury before, supported by a strong team that enabled her to not have to push herself forward. She had no luxury now, and her complacency and belief in human decency had almost gotten her killed.

Tears rolled down Kaleo's face as her heart broke. She loved her old life and missed it terribly, but that Kaleo wouldn't be able to survive. She'd been lucky, but luck would only carry her so far. Reina had stepped up to deal with Hugo, but Kaleo couldn't always rely on others. For better or for worse, Kaleo was now the undisputed leader of the kitchen and that meant she would need to step forward for everyone's benefit.

She curled up in the safety of the darkness and quietly cried until she had no more tears. She'd had a supportive family, a good job, and the love of an amazing man, but now that life was as out of reach as the sun in this ever-gloomy place. When her eyes felt dry and scratchy and her chest hollow she took a deep breath and calmed herself. Stefan might be looking for her, but that didn't mean he would be able to protect her. She missed him so much, but she couldn't let her homesickness distract from her current reality.

She knew her focus had to be on getting stronger, so that when she was rescued she could help in the upcoming war in America. Until then, her job was to stay safe and play the game as well as she could so that none of the young women in the kitchen would be preyed upon so easily again.

Kaleo mentally steeled herself. She locked the vulnerable, easygoing part of her personality into a box, and tucked that box away in the darkest, most secret part of her heart. Just as her abilities had enabled her to grow a protective covering to shield herself from the worst of the radiation from the nuke, she would now need to grow a skin of steel to protect herself from anything her new life could throw at her.

She woke the next morning with a new attitude and outlook on life. This Kaleo wasn't horrified at the way Hugo's dead body hung from a rope tied around his neck to the beam in his room. This Kaleo had the presence of mind to coordinate with the others ahead of time so that when Miss Fulbright was notified, they already had a plan. This Kaleo recognized that Hugo was a broken man who would have only continued to hurt others if he hadn't been stopped.

The story told to Miss Fulbright was that Hugo had grown very sullen and withdrawn after Yvonne rejected his advances and had taken his own life. Bridgett, who was the oldest woman in the kitchen, volunteered to coordinate the kitchen duties until a better cook could be brought in.

Bridgett's abilities allowed her to warm the air by several degrees, making her a genius at baking bread and pastries. The younger girls respected her and had often gone to her for comfort, but she was far too mousy to challenge Hugo. She'd been most grateful when Hugo was dethroned by Kaleo.

The pig that had served as Kaleo's body double was recovered at first light and served at dinner in the main dining hall to great compliments. After almost a week of culinary successes, it was announced that the search for an official head cook would be postponed indefinitely due to Bridgett's skill.

The news came as a great relief to Kaleo. Bridgett had no problem letting Kaleo be the true Abled leader, and in return Kaleo led by example and worked hard. Every day, turning the roasting spits felt easier—and on her good days, if she concentrated very hard, she could begin to feel a tingling sensation in her hands that boded well for the eventual return of her abilities.

With the death of Hugo, the atmosphere in the kitchen permanently changed for the better. Now, instead of the girls being afraid to speak out or make loud noises to prevent drawing too much unwanted attention, the kitchen was filled with singing and chatter. Even if the trauma that many of the girls had suffered was too fresh to allow them to laugh, they could at least breathe freely.

Unfortunately, as Kaleo grew stronger and the Abled dynamics in the kitchen solidified, they drew notice from other corners of the company. Under Hugo's rule, the kitchen had been avoided by everyone due to his creepy nature and temper. Once the news of his death spread, they had quite the influx of curious visitors.

Many of the gladiators stopped by to challenge Bridgett and were surprised when she accepted their challenge and almost immediately caved to their influence. Every single one of the newcomers left the kitchen thinking they'd proven the strength of their abilities and walked out like strutting roosters.

Late one evening, after most of the girls had gone to bed, Kaleo, Reina, Bridgett, and a few older girls stayed up to enjoy a rare quiet evening chat.

"I always feel so bad about those poor gladiators wasting their time. I hate to think about how many fights it's probably caused back in their barracks when they find out I've submitted to everyone who walked through the kitchen doors," Bridgett said as she mended a kitchen towel.

"Don't worry about it. They're just trying to prove they've got enough Saban-40 to make someone submit and get a leg up on the competition. The head trainer wouldn't want to designate someone as a leader only to have them fold once they're confronted with a good team," Reina said.

"You're doing a wonderful job, Bridgett. No one suspects anything, and this means that we're averting any real challenges." Kaleo stopped sharpening her kitchen knife and looked around the circle. "My Saban-40 may have been strong enough on its own to win Hugo's challenge, but he was overconfident. Any of the real fighters will be ready for a physical fight. They didn't dare challenge Hugo because of the mental authority they'd already placed him in–"

"And probably because they were afraid he'd poison their food," one of the other girls said.

Kaleo smiled. "Probably because of that too. They don't care about maintaining a hold on their challenge here, they just want to prove that they're stronger than someone."

"The fools don't even know that they didn't win anything." Bridgett snorted.

"But one day they might figure it out. Do we have a plan for that?" Reina asked.

"The more time I have to recover, the better our chances are," Kaleo said. She looked around the circle; she'd already told them an abridged version of what had happened to her, so they understood where she was coming from, and as far as she knew these women either believed her or didn't care about her past.

"What happens if you get saved from this place like you think you will?"

"Yeah, what about that letter you wrote?"

Kaleo sighed and looked down. One of the first things she did when she took over the kitchen was to hide a small letter to her family in the produce order, and she continued to send a new letter out every week to either her family or Stefan, hoping against hope that one of the letters would find their way to America.

"We'll cross that bridge when it comes to it. Now, not to change the topic, but I saw several of the new maids here earlier. What's the latest gossip?" Kaleo said, not wanting to even entertain the hope that she would be found until it was a sure reality.

"Servina's in top form going into the tournament in two weeks' time. Sounds like she's got a solid chance of placing, which will increase her chances to get an offer in Rome."

"What's in Rome?"

"The top echelon of the gladiator leagues. Everyone who's anyone will eventually make their way to Rome, and it's a dream of many gladiators to get picked up by one of the top training centers."

"Oh, I see. Good for her." Kaleo glanced over at a teenager who'd snickered. "Or not? Not good?"

"She's driving everyone crazy with her demands. I've heard that even Portia has just about had it with her, and that woman is her loyal lap dog. Servina is strong, but the rumor is that if her head gets any bigger she won't be able to even fit in a man's helmet."

"Ugh. Serving her and the other gladiators is the worst, and Celtic, the one with the perfect brown hair is the worst of the worst. Two days ago he tried to grope me when I was serving him," Reina complained.

"Maybe that's because you keep on going to his room at night," Bridgett said. Reina glared at her, and Bridgett shook her head. "Don't give me that look, young lady. What you do on your own time is none of my business, but you can't play with fire and not expect to get burned. If I wasn't up at all hours of the night using the toilet, I wouldn't have known anything."

Kaleo frowned. "Do I need to adjust the assignments? I don't want trouble if he's getting too friendly during working hours."

"Better not. Miss Fulbright doesn't want an Abled serving them for fear of accidentally upsetting the dynamic, and I don't want any of the other non-Ableds to have to worry about it. Hugo was enough for them to deal with; they don't need any more trauma... and Servina is rather temperamental."

"If you're sure, then we'll keep it like this. Let me know if Bridgett needs to speak with Miss Fulbright."

"I'll be fine. We don't need any more scrutiny at the moment, and I know how to handle myself. I'll talk to Celtic. If nothing else, I'll just do my best impression of Kaleo when Miss Fulbright or one of those other Ableds is in the kitchen and no one will notice me," Reina teased.

The others laughed and Kaleo chuckled along with them. When anyone important was visiting she kept her head down and pretended to be busy. It was a strategy that seemed to work well; no one cared about a former drug addict with a scarred face who was lifting large bags of flour, moving wheels of cheese, or working around the hearth.

The next two weeks passed in a blur of routine. Kaleo grew used to ordering her team around in as unobtrusive of a way as possible, and her strength continued to grow. The day Servina won the Highland Abled Tournament was also the first day Kaleo managed to activate her abilities and create a thin layer of energy over one of her hands, which burned like a small flame.

The kitchen girls had grown quite close, bonded by their shared trauma and hard work, and when word spread that evening in the sleeping room that Kaleo had grown strong enough for her abilities to manifest, Bridgett insisted on breaking out a jar of candied nuts she'd been saving for a special occasion.

Kaleo had celebrated along with them while wondering at the dark red color of her abilities and trying to hide her sadness that Stefan wasn't there to celebrate with her.

Yvonne, who remained her ever-present shadow, seemed to sense her mood. "Don't worry about it, Kaleo. I'm sure that he'll be coming for you any day now. He has to," she said as she snuggled up to Kaleo after the celebrations.

Kaleo smiled. She'd told the girl all about her fiancé, and Yvonne had latched strongly onto the masculine ideal that he represented. As she brushed Yvonne's hair, Kaleo hoped that one day hearing the stories of Stefan would help the beautiful young girl hold any would-be suitors to the highest of standards and keep her from settling for far less than she deserved.

Servina and the other gladiators returned. Flush from her victory, Servina's arrogance, entitlement, and demands increased exponentially. She constantly complained that the food wasn't up to the standards of what she'd been served in Inverness, and Reina began to come back to the kitchen wearing any food that Servina had deemed sub-par.

Despite the bullying, Reina refused to be replaced, and Kaleo wondered what her end game was—and if Celtic, the Abled with whom Reina had a physical relationship, played a part in it. Encouraged by Servina's boldness, the other gladiators began harassing the servers both at the meals and outside the dining hall until Kaleo requested Bridgett take it up with Miss Fulbright.

Their concerns were shot down by Miss Fulbright, who insisted it was simply the Ableds giving in to their more brutal nature. Once Servina was transferred to Rome, she claimed, things would calm.

Two nights before Servina was due to leave, disaster struck.

The kitchen was already short-staffed due to a terrible cold that had sent several of the girls to the infirmary, forcing Kaleo to reorganize their duties. In the hubbub of the dinner rush, one of the girls who normally served the non-Abled guards and support staff was distracted when pulling a batch of rolls out of the oven, and badly burned herself on the hot baking sheet.

"Kaleo, look at her hands," Reina said as she held the hands of the crying girl under running water.

Kaleo took one look at the red and white welts forming on the girl's palms and nodded. "You're right. We'll have to send someone else. She can't serve like that."

"She has to. All the non-Ableds need to serve the fighters, and everyone else is either too busy or too young. We're stretched too thin."

"All right, then I'll go," Kaleo said as she pulled off her apron and made sure her red sash was tied appropriately around her waist.

"You don't have any training, and if you mess something up and someone from one of the higher tables notices you it's going to cause a problem," Reina protested.

"We don't have any choice. I waited tables for a semester or two in college, so I'm not totally out of my element here. Besides, it's an easy night. We're just serving bowls of salad and spaghetti and refilling some drinks, so it shouldn't be too bad," Kaleo said.

When she walked out of the kitchen, her hands piled high with food, Kaleo made sure to keep her head down. The first course, a salad, was served without issue, although Kaleo couldn't help but keep both an eye and an ear on the gladiator's table. Reina had been having to deal with more drama from Servina every day, and Kaleo wanted to see firsthand just how badly the situation had deteriorated.

Kaleo served the main course without incident. Her table, full of various cleaners and support staff, was engrossed in conversation, so she was one of the first to finish. She retreated to the wall, where the other servers stood until they saw someone who needed a drink refill.

It was the perfect spot from which to watch the commotion that broke out.

Celtic stuck out his foot and tripped Reina, who dumped the bowl of spaghetti she was serving onto Servina. The resulting shriek was loud enough to wake the dead, and everyone in the room turned to look at the gladiator's table.

"You clumsy fool. I've had enough of your bumbling. Why they let a non-Abled dog like you serve us food is beyond me," Servina spat as she stood from her chair.

Kaleo's body immediately tensed and the hair on her arms stood on end. She'd heard the others talk about Servina's abilities: long nails sharp as knives, and a penchant for using a whip embedded with shards of broken glass in the gladiator ring. Servina's temper was as deadly as her abilities—she'd earned her name by beheading her opponent when she'd tried out for the Atlantic Trading Company, and she lived up to her reputation. Portia might not have been Servina's first maid, but she was the only one so far who hadn't been gravely injured.

Servina slapped Reina across the face.

"Aye, give the poor lassie a break, Servina. It's not her fault she's clumsy," Celtic drawled in his thick Scottish accent.

"Are you afraid that I'll ruin the pretty face of your little infatuation, Celtic?" Servina replied. She grabbed Reina's face and scrutinized it. "I know you haven't had any luck with her lately. Maybe I should punish her for denying her betters."

"Go ahead and do whatever ye want to, I couldna care less." Celtic shrugged and sipped from his cup.

"Is that so? In that case, where should I make the first cut? Maybe on the side of her mouth so you could kiss it better? Or would you prefer that I slice a lovely little red necklace across her throat to make it look like one of those noodles that she spilled on me? She's working here as a servant, so it's not like anyone will miss her."

The blood in Kaleo's head began to pound. She'd seen enough friends become injured, traumatized, or die to last a lifetime. She stepped forward.

"That's enough. Leave her alone," she said, her voice ringing out clearly in the silent room.

Now everyone was staring at her.

"And who are you to be giving me orders?" Servina spat.

Suddenly remembering herself, Kaleo held up her hands and worked to keep her voice calm. "I'm just a humble serving girl and a friend of Reina's. Please don't hurt her, she didn't do anything wrong. Celtic tripped her. It's his fault. Punish him. Leave her alone."

Servina shoved Reina to the ground and stepped towards Kaleo. "I see by your clothes that you're one of those kitchen-rat Ableds. Are you daring to challenge me?"

The mocking and condescending tone that Servina used cracked something open in Kaleo, like a dam that had been holding far too much water and was at its breaking point.

"Only if you insist on it," Kaleo said as she drew herself up and stepped forward again. "Nobody likes a bully, so I guess it's high time someone taught you a lesson."

"Servina! This American isn't important. She was a drug-addicted Abled sold on contract here. She didn't cut it as part of the cleaning or maid crew, so she was sent to the kitchens. It seems that even the useless cook wasn't able to cure her of her attitude. She's not worth your time," Portia called out snidely from her seat at one of the lower tables.

"Shut up, Portia and know your place. A drug addict of no consequence dares tell me what to do?" Servina's tone rose into a shriek as she turned to Kaleo. "Back down now, and maybe I'll only give your friend here a scar on her face that matches yours."

Portia's voice and the reminder of what had been done to her were the straw that broke the camel's back. Kaleo's temper, which had simmered under the surface since Audra's betrayal, finally boiled over. Her abilities had returned slowly over the preceding weeks, like a daffodil breaking through topsoil in the snowy spring, but now they flared to life like a blooming sunflower feeling warm summer sun for the first time.

"Back down? To you? A two-bit bully whose ability consists purely of having sharp fingernails?" Kaleo scoffed. "Forget going to Rome; you need to go to the nearest manicurist."

Servina charged forward with an ear-splitting scream and Kaleo met her halfway across the room in a hastily cleared open space. Servina didn't seem keen on banter and lashed out at Kaleo, but her claw-like nails only met air.

As Kaleo dodged Servina's attacks, she realized she was falling back into her old patterns. No one could beat her on defense, not with her shield, but something told her this fight wasn't only about outlasting the other person. To declare victory, she needed a solid win that demonstrated both her strength and Servina's weakness. Anything less, anything that left even the smallest doubt, could mean trouble in the future. Hugo had been relatively harmless, but even so, if not for Yvonne, Kaleo's broken body would probably still be lying on the rocks by the sea. She was tired of running, of hiding, of being the nice girl and the responsible adult.

Servina thought that she could do whatever she wanted simply because she'd won a stupid tournament.

Kaleo had single-handedly stopped a nuclear bomb.

Portia and the others discounted her because she was American. They conveniently forgot that her country's heritage included the Saviors, a handful of Ableds who'd earned their name by saving the world. Kaleo decided it was time to educate everyone as to what American Ableds were capable of.

Servina's next punch was already slicing its way through the air. Kaleo caught it in her hand. The energy from her abilities, which crackled with a bright red light, prevented Servina's nails from slicing through her flesh.

Joy, fierce joy, untamable joy, raced through Kaleo's body while the red light raced up her opponent's arm.

Servina yelped. She backed away from Kaleo, but the damage had already been done and the skin of her arm was burned.

"You'll pay for that!" Servina shouted before charging Kaleo again.

This time, Kaleo didn't have enough time to prepare and simply held her arms in front of her head, protecting herself with a shield. When she felt Servina's hands make contact, Kaleo pushed forward with all her might. The force of Servina's blows lessened, and Kaleo stepped forward to take advantage of her opponent's momentary loss of balance. She grabbed Servina's throat and pinned her against one of the columns that dotted the main dining hall. The red light covered Servina's head and neck, and through narrowed eyes Kaleo watched Servina claw at her hands. Then Servina went limp in her grasp, the fog of anger lifted from Kaleo's eyes, and she let go.

Servina slumped to the floor and Kaleo realized far too late that her opponent had been trying to tap out and submit. Kaleo's energy field had completely covered Servina's head and upper torso, and the areas where the light had touched were now horribly burned and blistered. Miraculously, Servina was still breathing, although her eyes were closed. In the chaos that erupted around her, Kaleo couldn't ascertain anything else.

A gentle hand pulled her several feet back. "C'mon, we'll let them get this sorted. You don't need to be here right now," Reina said.

"I'm sorry, Reina. I didn't mean to kill her," Kaleo said numbly as she watched a hive of people surround Servina's crumpled form.

After a moment's pause, Reina guided her away. "If this is your ability and you don't want to be in the gladiator arena, I see why you've been hiding in the kitchen. Although I've got to say that it would have been useful last week when we were having difficulty getting a nice char on those roasts."

They walked through the kitchen doors. The news had already spread, and everyone crowded around them.

One of the louder girls piped up from the back. "Reina, did you really almost get cut up? And did Kaleo actually kill Servina?"

Kaleo sagged against a table, suddenly overcome with exhaustion.

"What are you all doing standing around? Stop talking and get her a chair!" Reina barked.

"Yes, get her a chair. It wouldn't do for our newest gladiator to faint dead away."

Kaleo looked up to see three people standing in the doorway. One man she recognized as the manager of the Atlantic Trading Company, Mr. Dexter, another as the Abled trainer, Sven, and the third person was Miss Fulbright, who had so many veins standing out on her forehead and neck that she seemed about to have a stroke.

"You insolent girl. How dare you! All that hard work, wasted," Miss Fulbright screamed and slapped Kaleo across the face.

The blow knocked Kaleo out of her numbed state of mind, and her anger flared to life again at the insult.

"I'd be careful if I was you, Eugenia. If you do that again, you may end up like Servina," Sven said.

"She's hardly a person, no better than an animal, and I will treat her as such. Look at her—out of control! She's dangerous, and she just ruined a large company investment," Miss Fulbright said.

Kaleo looked at her hands to see them glowing red and exuding a ragged, crackling energy. With a deep breath, she calmed herself and released her abilities.

"I'd say she has more control than you give her credit for. Servina was well-trained and battle-hardened, and this young woman took her down as easily as I'd take down one of our new recruits."

The manager frowned. "Get to the point, Sven."

Sven shrugged. "The way I see it, you didn't lose an investment. You still have someone to send to Rome, and in my professional opinion you may have just exchanged a bar of silver for one of gold, if you can convince the Boar's Head to take her."

Miss Fulbright scoffed. "Gold? This girl just got lucky. She wasn't even strong enough to sway the others to her side; you saw how they swarmed around Servina when she fell."

"I saw nothing of the sort. In fact, I believe it was your own non-Ableds who swarmed Servina, perhaps to ensure the wicked witch was actually dead. Now, girl, what is your name?" Sven asked.

"Kaleo. My name is Kaleo Hughes, and I was forcibly abducted from my home in America and sold here. If you contact my family, they'll be more than happy to pay whatever fee you require for my contract," Kaleo said as authoritatively as she could, hoping that now that she was talking to the boss of the company, perhaps someone would actually listen to her.

"You see? She's delusional. Her ex-boyfriend sold her to us under a contract, and she was too drugged out to even care," Miss Fulbright said.

"That's not true, and you would know that if you'd even taken a moment to listen to me. I was drugged, but it was against my will," Kaleo said as her fists clenched at her side and began to tingle. "I can give you the phone numbers and addresses of several people, any of whom will vouch for me and pay whatever price you deem fair. If you're still unsure, you can contact the American embassy and they can make the necessary arrangements."

"Is that so?" Mr. Dexter nodded. "Then it's settled. If you'll give those numbers to us, I'll personally make sure they're contacted."

Kaleo breathed a sigh of relief. Miss Fulbright looked like she had swallowed a lemon, but Kaleo didn't care; her nightmare was almost over.

She gave Mr. Dexter the phone numbers for her parents, Katherine, and Stefan. The next day he informed her he'd made contact with her parents, and they'd agreed to buy her out of her contract.

"They must be very wealthy to agree to that price without any hesitation, but it's their money. Say your goodbyes and gather your things; you ship out tomorrow," he said.

Kaleo was on cloud nine as she made her final preparations and said goodbye to everyone in the kitchens. It wasn't necessarily easy, but the sting of leaving the girls and women she had worked with for the past couple of months was eased by the promise of going home, and she had been reassured by Mr. Dexter that the kitchen workers would be cared for after she left.

Not everyone was as excited as she was, and Yvonne avoided her for much of the evening. When Kaleo finally cornered her in the kitchen pantry, the younger girl's eyes were red and watery, as if she'd just finished crying.

"Hey, what's the matter?" Kaleo asked as she sat on a wheel of cheese to get closer to Yvonne's eye level.

Yvonne sniffled. "You're the leader and you're leaving. What's going to happen to the rest of us?"

"You'll be fine. Reina and the others will be here, and they won't let anything bad happen to you," Kaleo said. "Don't worry, you'll be able to learn how to cook—and once you work your contract off, you'll have skills you can use to find a decent job. Plus, I'll write you letters, and if you have any more issues just let me know and I'll come over and beat everyone up, okay?"

Yvonne hugged her and pressed her head into Kaleo's side. "Can I come visit you in America and meet Stefan?"

Kaleo hugged her little friend back and grimaced, thinking of the troubles that America was about to descend into, if it hadn't already. News on the island from the outside world was lacking, and the little they got was usually European-focused. "America isn't a safe place for you right now, but one day you can, I promise. I'm sure that Stefan will be delighted to meet you."

After she'd said her final goodbyes, and just before Kaleo was about to leave the kitchen for the last time, Reina stopped her.

"Hey, good luck out there... and thank you," Reina said.

Kaleo nodded. "Thank you too. I couldn't have done it without you."

When she walked out into the main courtyard, several people were waiting for her. A middle-aged, balding man introduced himself to her as Joseph, the assistant manager for the Atlantic Trading Company and the man who would be escorting her home. They rode horses for two miles to the dock, where a boat was waiting to take them to the mainland.

After the boat, they traveled by train to an airport.

"Your parents wanted you home as soon as possible, and agreed to pay for a chartered private flight," Joseph said by way of explanation as they walked out to a medium-sized plane.

"Where are we flying to, and when do we touch down?"

"New York, and in about twelve hours. We'll get there early in the morning, local time."

It took Kaleo a while to fall asleep on the plane as she thought about everything that had happened to her in the past two months. Most noticeably, the scar Audra gave her had healed well, but it was still far too fresh to be fully covered by makeup. She wondered if Katherine would be able to help it heal in time for the wedding.

The wedding... It would probably have to be postponed at least another several months to give them time to get everything in order. She wondered if Stefan would still want to marry her, considering everything that had happened.

Kaleo's stomach churned as she looked out the window and remembered the terrible burns covering Servina's body. Guilt threatened to consume her. She hadn't meant to kill the other woman, only to stop her from hurting Reina. Her parents had always emphasized the importance of using her abilities for good; to protect people, not for violence. She didn't know how she'd tell them what she'd done.

After accepting a cup of warm milk from the flight attendant thirty minutes into the flight, Kaleo finally began to feel tired and leaned her chair back to rest. When they touched down it was still dark outside, and she woke up very groggy. As they'd disembarked, she was somewhat surprised to find no one waiting for her on the tarmac.

"Your family called me just before we touched down; they've been detained in their travels and have arranged to meet us at a nearby hotel later this morning," Joseph said.

Kaleo nodded and climbed into the waiting carriage, too dazed to question why they didn't have a car.

As they drove through the streets, she looked out of the small windows. "New York is much darker than I remember," she said.

"We're driving through the outskirts right now. The hotel we're traveling to is near the airport and outside the city limits. We arranged to meet them here to get away from other prying eyes," Joseph said as they stopped in front of a gate.

Kaleo nodded as the gates opened. The moon was partially obscured by clouds, and under its soft light they drove through what looked like a great expanse of lawn. She wondered what kind of hotel this was; large amounts of useless grass seemed quite wasteful and old-fashioned.

They pulled up to a beautiful building made of stone and wood at the end of the driveway. Joseph was the first to get out. He held the door open for Kaleo and guided her inside where a small group of people sat behind a reception desk and smiled as they walked in.

Though her thoughts were still a little fuzzy from her nap on the plane, the way the receptionists looked at her felt off. Kaleo shook her head in an attempt to clear it. She approached Joseph to hear what he was saying, but he'd already finished speaking by the time she reached the front desk.

One of the receptionists stepped forward. "This way, miss. I'll show you to your room," she said in thickly accented English

Kaleo hefted the small bag with her meager possessions over her shoulder and followed. They were almost out of the room when the woman turned her head to smile. "You'll like it here. We're the most prestigious training center in Rome. Gladiators from all over Europe fight for the chance to train here before the games."

Kaleo stopped.

"We're not in New York?" she asked. Joseph cursed behind her.

"No, of course not. We're in Rome." Her guide looked confused, glanced over Kaleo's shoulder, and then her eyes widened as she realized her mistake.

In an instant, Kaleo's world streamlined and narrowed. Her priorities reorganized themselves until she had only one thought above all others: escape.

She turned on her heel and sprinted for the door. She was three steps away when a hand grabbed her shoulder. Kaleo turned and lashed out with an arm wreathed in red. Her assailant yelped in pain and released her.

As she burst out of the building, Kaleo realized that what she had previously thought a grass lawn was instead a field of dirt—no doubt a training area for the gladiators who lived in the facility.

Kaleo ran across the open ground as if the devil himself chased her. Somewhere, bells tolled and guards materialized out of the shadows to surround her. Kaleo slowed down just enough to maintain her abilities but didn't stop. She barreled into the first guard and shoved him out of her way. Her red shield crackled across her hands and arms, burning anyone who tried to touch her.

She fought her way across the yard, knowing that if she crossed the front gates into the city proper, she had a chance. She'd spent enough time in the Atlantic Trading Company to know that behind closed doors anything could happen without fear of reprisal. If she made it to the freedom beyond, some passerby might take her to the American embassy. If she could fight her way free, she would finally wake up from the nightmare of the past several months.

When she was two thirds of the way across the open ground, Kaleo's limbs grew heavy. While she continued to fight, a strange throbbing sensation developed in her neck, weighing her down. The guards backed away but remained in a circle, keeping pace with her as she stumbled towards the front gate. Kaleo used the rare moment of reprieve to lift her hand to her neck, where it throbbed the worst, only to have her fingers brush over a wooden stick.

She plucked the object from her neck and surveyed it in the bleak light of the moon. It was a small dart, hardly longer than her finger, feathered with what looked like some type of cotton fluff on the end and a tip so dark red it was almost black. As she struggled to account for the new development, Kaleo sensed she was running out of time.

After another step towards the front gate, her legs collapsed. Kaleo refused to give up, dragging herself forward with her arms until even they stopped working. Her field of vision decreased until she could only see the front gates and the freedom they symbolized. She feared that if she didn't reach them, she would never see Stefan or her family again.

Her head fell to the ground, and she was barely able to muster the strength to turn it at the last moment so as not to break her nose. In the distance, a figure in white, illuminated by the moon, walked towards her with arms open wide.

Try as she might, Kaleo couldn't fight the inevitable, and her vision faded to black.

Chapter Eleven

With a grunt, Stefan finished his bench-press rep, racked the barbell, and sat up.

"Dude, you blasted through that last set. Good job," Trevor said as he slapped Stefan on the back.

"Thanks, you want to do another set?"

"No, I'm good. Want to grab something to eat?"

Stefan checked the time and nodded. "Yeah, but I can't take too long. Rosie's waiting for me at home and she's going to need a long walk this evening."

After grabbing their things, they drove to a local Mexican food restaurant.

As they sat down and placed their orders, they chatted about work and Trevor's family. The younger man was proud of one of his sisters, who'd recently discovered she had the ability to create a light breeze in a room.

"She's a little disappointed because it's not nearly as powerful as mine was at the beginning, but I told her to keep on practicing. My mom and dad think she'll always be weaker, but I guess we'll see," Trevor said.

"How's she been taking it? I know my brothers were jealous when they realized I had abilities and they didn't."

"She's been okay so far. It doesn't hurt that she's been making good use of it by keeping the house warm this winter." Trevor paused as their food was served, and glanced at Stefan. "Is there any news?"

A now familiar pang ached in Stefan's chest. "None."

"That's too bad. How long has it been?"

"Two months."

"Ouch. I'm sorry, man."

"Yeah, me too." Stefan took another bite of his food. "We're going to find her though. It's just a matter of time."

"That's right. If anyone could find her, it would be you. Have you talked to Brant lately?"

Stefan shook his head. "He thinks Kaleo just ran away on her own, and I haven't had the time or energy to hang out the past few months."

"I understand."

"Why? Is he doing okay?"

"Yeah. I don't talk to him much, but he seems happy."

"Good for him."

After they finished eating, Stefan said his goodbyes to Trevor, paid, and hopped on his motorcycle.

He hadn't had much of a chance to ride the bike recently, as he usually took Rosie with him to work at NAT. Today was only different because the night before Taylor had volunteered to stop by and let Rosie out in between her various errands and media events around town. Stefan loved Rosie, but she could be a little distracting at times, and he'd taken Taylor up on the offer.

It had been nice to have a day to himself in the office, but Stefan was ready to get home and relax with his dog. As he navigated traffic, he decided Rosie should come along to Kaleo's house; while he performed his usual the mid-weekly checkup, she would have a chance to run around in the fenced-in backyard and burn off some excess energy.

The ever-present hollow ache in his chest grew sharper when he thought of how his life should have been. The last time he'd seen Kaleo, she was nestled under his arm, with her head on top of his chest and her fingers tracing soothing circles on the back of his hand. It was one of his most cherished memories: knowing that though he'd have a lot to process, she'd be by his side, supporting him and helping him through it all. Not a day went by that Stefan didn't regret falling asleep and letting her go.

Two months was a long time. At first, he'd taken heart from the fact they had a suspect in Audra—but despite Stefan's best efforts, as time passed it was as if Audra had disappeared like smoke in the wind, and the investigation had stalled. He was even limited by whom he could interrogate and what he could say. The last thing anyone wanted was to draw attention to Kaleo's disappearance, and the story of her aunt could only hold up to so much scrutiny due to the public nature of her parent's lives. In certain circles, finding her had been made a top priority, but every lead had so far turned into a dead end.

Still, even as days turned into weeks and weeks turned into months, Stefan refused to give up. He'd promised Kaleo that if something ever happened to her, he'd find her, and Stefan refused to break that promise. The trail might have gone cold, but Stefan had no choice other than to believe one day he'd feel a nibble on the many lines that he had cast, and the fact that their wedding date was a month away only increased his resolve.

Kaleo's disappearance had done much more than just throw his life into disarray: the persona of Phoenix was too valuable as a deterrent to lose, and it was a matter of national security to create a suitable stand-in.

The solution had come in two parts: first, Nova stepped up and volunteered to wear the Phoenix helmet in place of her daughter. Fortunately, she was similar enough in height and build to Kaleo that she could pass the physical attribute test when she was fully geared up, although the sticky question of what to do about Kaleo's abilities remained.

Thanks to a combination of creative engineering by Jeffrey and Lin's light manipulation abilities, they were eventually able to come up with a complete solution: Sifter would act as the physical representation of Phoenix, and Lin would be stationed nearby to create the effect of the shield by using very small blue lights that had been added to Phoenix's uniform. The addition of a small fog machine created a blue shield that seemed capable of stopping any projectile. All it took was one carefully placed "angry" citizen to throw a water bottle that was rebuffed by a hidden Lift, and their illusion was complete.

It wasn't perfect, but Phoenix's reputation had grown fearsome enough to prevent anyone from testing their illusion any further.

Stefan had almost finished organizing a mental list of things that needed to be done by the end of the day when he opened the front door of his apartment.

The first thing he noticed was actually a lack of noise—normally he could hear Rosie's whines and barks of anticipation as soon as he inserted his key into the lock.

"I'm home, Rosie," he called out, but received no response. He walked over to her crate, only to find it empty and open.

"You silly girl. Did Taylor forget to lock your crate, or did you figure out how to open it?" he asked as he removed his motorcycle gear, hung it in the entryway, and set his helmet on the kitchen countertop. He still didn't hear anything from Rosie, but he knew where she might be. When he was at home, she'd taken to either napping on the couch or on his bed if she was very tired. A quick glance at the couch confirmed it was empty, so he made his way to his bedroom.

"Did you have a good day today, little girl?" he asked as he rounded the corner, before halting mid-step.

Audra sat on his bed, cradling Rosie in her arms. She looked up at Stefan as he entered the room, and his heart dropped.

"You know, I never understood why everyone loved the ankle biter so much. I was always worried she'd give me fleas or something," she said as she stroked Rosie's limp head.

"What are you doing here, Audra?" he asked, almost choking on his anger in his rush to get the words out.

"Surprised to see me?" Her smile chilled him to the bone.

"How'd you get in?"

"You're not the only one who knows how to pick a lock."

"Where's Kaleo? What did you do to her?"

Audra's smile devolved into a frown. "It's been two months and you're still hung up on her? I thought I gave you more than enough time to pretend to be worried and get over the break up."

"We didn't break up, you did something to her. Don't try and play games with me." Stefan stepped into the room and readied himself to activate his abilities. He didn't trust Audra holding Rosie in her arms, especially when the dog was so dear to him and Kaleo.

"Not another step closer, unless you want me to slit the furball's throat," Audra said, gesturing with a black knife.

Stefan froze and held up his hands. "There's no need for that. I'll talk to you, just put Rosie down. She's only a dog, and she's innocent in all this."

"Put Rosie down? When she's my main bargaining chip? Do you think I'm dumb?" Audra laughed. "Of course, you must be used to Kaleo, so perhaps you really thought that would work on me. You ought to be thanking me for releasing you from her shackles. A man like you deserves so much more."

Stefan didn't like the unhinged way Audra was talking, or how limp his dog looked, and tried to change tactics. "Why are you here and what did you do to Rosie?"

"It's rather poetic, actually, I did the same thing to Rosie that I did to her owner: Breathed in her face just enough to drug her. It was too easy with her being locked in her crate." Audra patted the top of Rosie's head. "You know, I've never liked dogs, but I'm grateful that this one at least gave me a second chance to talk some sense to you." Stefan tried to inch forward, and Audra shook her head and pressed the knife to Rosie's neck until he backed away again.

"Don't think for a second that I'm getting sentimental and you can take advantage of me. It would be even more poetic to kill Kaleo's dog using a shard from the silly glass statue that I assume she got you." As she spoke, Audra shaved a spot on the side of Rosie's neck.

Stefan's eyes slid to his bedside table, where the black wolf statue Kaleo had gotten him as an engagement present had sat. For the first time since entering the room, he realized the statue was no longer in its spot, and that shards of black glass were scattered over the floor.

"Fine, Audra. Let's talk. I'm all ears," he said, leaning against the door.

"Oh no, we're not going to talk any more. You're going to come over here, lie on the bed, and let me make love to you. Then, once you've realized what you're missing out on, you're going to take me back to NAT and explain to Director Stone that you've made a mistake, and you want him to let me rejoin."

"You're insane."

"And you're very brave to be saying such things to me when I have the life of your precious mutt in my hands."

"How do I know that she's even alive? She hasn't moved or whimpered at all. You could have very well already killed her." Stefan bluffed with a confidence he didn't feel.

Audra smiled. "You've always been so smart. It's one of the things I loved first about you." She pinched Rosie, and the dog whimpered. "See? She's fully awake, just paralyzed. Here, I'll even make you a deal: kiss me once, and I'll let go of Rosie."

"You'll use your abilities when I do?"

"But of course. A girl should always use all the tools at her disposal to seduce her lover."

"I'm not your lover."

"Not yet. Don't worry, I promise to make it enjoyable for you." Audra adjusted her grip on Rosie and pressed the glass shard to the dog's neck. "Now, hurry up and come here. I want to take my time enjoying you."

"Why do you even want me? Don't you understand I'm not attracted to you? That I don't want you? My heart belongs to Kaleo."

"Yes, but after today your body will belong to me." Audra smiled. "A long time ago, before she betrayed me, Laura heard you and Kaleo talking in your office and told me all about it. Why else do you think I seduced you the way I did? You poor man, having to go for so long without some kind of release. I look forward to seeing you actually enjoy yourself."

"I could never enjoy being with you."

Audra scoffed and rolled her eyes. "I'm tired of this conversation. Either you come here right now, or you stand there and I finish what I started with Rosie. Maybe I'll tell you what happened to Kaleo as a reward for good behavior."

For two months, Stefan had felt wildly out of control, as if Kaleo's disappearance had transported him onto the back of an angry, rabid rodeo bull, but as Audra's words sank in, everything solidified and clarified. Loath as he was to admit it, he'd hit a dead end in his search for her, and now here was Audra herself offering him a break in the case.

Granted, the break came at a high price, but he was desperate. He'd made a promise to the love of his life, and it was time to take back control and fulfill that promise. Kaleo might hate him when she found out what he'd done, but she'd be safe, and that's what mattered above all else.

"Fine. We have a deal," he said.

"Lovely. Now come here and kiss me. Once you do, I'll release Rosie and we can get started."

Stefan did as Audra said.

He sat on the bed, took a deep breath, and leaned over to kiss her. When she breathed into his mouth, he could taste the cloying sweetness of her abilities. He tried to pull away, but Audra's hands clasped behind his head and she refused to release him from the kiss. Stefan's mind numbed as his libido spiked.

One of Audra's hands let go of his head, and he heard a clink as she set the shard of glass on the nightstand, followed by a thud as she pushed Rosie off the bed.

When Rosie's body hit the floor, Stefan tried to break away to make sure she was okay, but Audra wrenched at his ear and forced his head still.

"I'm not done with you yet, and if you don't convince me that you actually want me, I'll never tell you anything about Kaleo."

"That wasn't part of the deal."

"It doesn't matter. You don't have any negotiating power now."

Stefan flinched, but he couldn't afford to go back; one mistake and he wouldn't get the information he desperately needed. He grabbed a handful of Audra's hair and pulled it hard, forcing her to look up at him. "A kiss. That's what you wanted. I've held up my end of the deal. Now you're going to tell me everything you know about Kaleo or I'm going to make you pay," he growled.

"Yes, just like that," she said as she leaned forward to kiss him again.

"Oh, you like that, do you? You like it when I take control?" Stefan asked. She breathed into his mouth again, his arms and legs began to strangely shake, and her lips curled into a smile beneath his.

Audra wrapped a leg around him. "The only thing better than a big, tough man like you controlling me is when the tables turn," she said, and in one smooth movement pushed him over so that she was on top of him.

Stefan twisted and rolled her onto her back. "You can't force me to do anything."

"So you want this after all?"

He thought of Kaleo and how she'd taken care of him and cooked him lunch the last time he'd seen her. He remembered her face the night they had gotten engaged and the joy and love shining through her eyes as they talked about their wedding plans. Every minute with her had felt so right, like he was exactly where he belonged. Kaleo was the love of his life, and he would do whatever it took to get her back, no matter the cost.

"Yes, I want this, Audra. You have no idea how much I need this," he said, thinking of Kaleo.

"I'm glad you've finally seen the light," she said as she kissed him again and climbed on top of him before locking his wrists to his bed frame with a handcuff.

"You don't have to do that," Stefan said as an icy sliver of fear crawled down his spine and the reality of the deal he'd made hit.

Audra smiled sweetly. "Oh, but I do. I know how fickle you men can be. This is just in case you change your mind before my abilities really take hold."

Without any other option, Stefan lay back and let Audra do her worst. "Do you like this?" Audra asked as she removed her shirt and leaned over him. Stefan chuckled at the absurdity of her words, and she took it as an agreement. "I bet Kaleo never did anything like this. That goody-two shoes would never know how to please a man. I hope Rodney taught her a lesson or two, and that he wasn't gentle."

Stefan bit his tongue as he nuzzled Audra's neck, careful to not say what he was truly thinking.

Suddenly he heard a male voice, and then Audra was jerked off the bed. To Stefan, it felt like his last shot at finding Kaleo was being pulled away from him, and he roared in desperation and kicked out.

"How dare you!" Audra screamed.

"Audra? Is that you?" Brant asked.

Stefan looked around to see Trevor standing next to the side of his bed, Nicole by the window, and Brant just within the door.

"What are you three doing here? Get out! I was so close! She was about to tell me what she did to Kaleo!" Stefan shouted and thrashed around.

Nicole pulled on Stefan's handcuffs. "All right, Audra, where's the key?"

"The key? I must have lost it." Audra said, batting her blue eyes.

"Trevor, see if you can find some paper clips in a desk somewhere."

As Trevor searched for the paper clips, Nicole, Brant, Audra, and Stefan stared at each other.

"So, do either of you want to explain what's going on? Is this your way of getting over the breakup, Stefan?" Brant asked.

"Obviously I'm not here right because I want to be," Stefan snapped. "Nicole, Rosie is on the floor by the bed. Can you check on her?"

"While she does that, I'll just be on my way," Audra said.

"Brant, don't you dare let her go," Stefan growled.

Nicole picked up Rosie as Trevor came back into the room with paper clips in hand and began working on the handcuffs. As he waited to be released, Stefan explained what had happened. When he was done, he paused and frowned. "Now, what are you three doing here?"

"A few months back, Kaleo gave me a pager and asked me to do her a favor. She told me that if it started going off, it meant that you were in desperate trouble and needed help and that I should go straight to your apartment. About thirty minutes ago it started squawking," Nicole said.

"Same thing for me," Trevor added.

"Lin was the one who gave me the pager. She said Stone had told her to ask me to do the same thing... but I guess that was a lie," Brant said.

Stefan checked Rosie over and patted her head. She still looked rather dazed, but he took it as a very good sign that her tail wagged furiously.

"Are you feeling okay, little girl? Did the nasty woman hurt you?" he crooned.

"Brant, tell them to let me go right now or you're going to regret it," Audra said.

Stefan looked up to see an embarrassed expression on Brant's face. "Brant? What's going on? How do you know Audra?"

"It's nothing; I'll tell you later," Brant said, refusing to meet Stefan's eyes.

Stefan shrugged and turned to Audra. "Tell me what you did to Kaleo, now."

Her eyes were wide and innocent looking. "I don't know anything about what happened to Kaleo."

"You're a liar. Who is Rodney and what role did he have?"

Audra's eyes narrowed, her expression morphing into hatred as if someone had flipped a switch. "I'm not telling you anything about Kaleo or Rodney, and you can't make me. I know all your little tricks and I won't crack. You lose, Stefan—and now you've betrayed me, I won't ever take you back."

"Are you really that self-absorbed? I've never wanted to be with you, and I wasn't the one who betrayed you." Stefan gestured at the black glass littering the floor. "You betrayed yourself. Kaleo told me to break this statue if I ever needed help. Honestly, I doubt I would have done it no matter how you threatened me, but you did me a favor and broke it for me. Your hatred of her led to you accidentally triggering those pagers."

Audra licked her lips. "You missed your chance, Stefan. Even if I did know something, I definitely wouldn't tell you now."

"Mod was at NAT when we left. If they're still there, they may be able to get in touch with Wiper," Trevor said.

Stefan frowned and rubbed his face. "Why didn't I think of that?"

"I think I can guess, if that sweet smell is anything to go by," Brant said as he sniffed the air.

"I won't consent to him using his abilities. He won't be able to do anything," Audra said.

Nicole snorted. "You can drop the act now, Audra. We know that you were involved in Kaleo's disappearance. Shut up while we figure out what to do with you."

"You three keep an eye on her, I've got to make a phone call," Stefan said. He carried Rosie into the living room and set her down by her water bowl before gathering as much saliva as he could in his mouth and spitting it into a cup to have Zach analyze later. Next, he took a kitchen cloth and wiped his mouth before placing it into a paper bag and setting it beside the spit glass. Finally, he grabbed his phone and dialed the number for the NAT receptionist desk.

"Thank you for calling the National Abled Task Force. How can I help you?"

"Mod, this is Stefan. Audra broke into my apartment and tried to use Rosie as leverage to assault me. It's a long story, but I'm positive she knows what happened to Kaleo and is refusing to say anything about it or cooperate. Do you think Wiper can help?"

"Hold on, he's actually here with me right now. Let me ask him."

Stefan petted Rosie as he waited during the long pause.

"You still there?"

"Yes."

"Wiper said he can get the information. Are you alone with her?"

"No. Brant, Nicole, and Trevor are here."

"Bring her in and let Director Stone know."

"Understood. We'll be there soon."

Stefan hung up and exhaled.

It was decided that Nicole and Trevor would drive Audra to NAT, and Brant would drive Stefan. Stefan insisted that he was okay to drive, and that it was imperative that he take Rosie to the vet just in case Audra's abilities had somehow hurt her, but he was overruled by Brant.

"Dude, she's drugged you up. I'm not letting you drive a car or make any big decisions when you're like this."

"I'm fine. I don't feel off at all."

Brant shook his head. "Maybe you don't feel off, but I'm telling you that her abilities can do weird things to your head."

Nicole and Trevor looked at Brant curiously, and Stefan frowned. "How do you know?"

"She and I used to have something going on. I'll tell you later about it, but just trust that I've done enough drugs in my lifetime to know when I'm high, and her abilities definitely qualify."

"Brant's right, Stefan. You did say earlier that you forgot about Wiper," Trevor said.

"Fine, Brant can drive me," Stefan said.

After Trevor and Brant escorted Audra to the garage, Stefan and Nicole were left alone while he gathered Rosie's things. Stefan glanced at Nicole. "It wasn't what it looked like, I promise."

"So you're saying you weren't drugged into making a reckless decision, tied down, and assaulted?"

"I chose to kiss her."

"I could smell her abilities before we even broke into your apartment—sorry about that, by the way—but that much of a concentration would cloud anyone's judgment."

"How can you be so sure I wasn't trying to cheat?"

Nicole scoffed. "You? Cheat? On Kaleo? Stefan, I've watched you run yourself ragged the past two months trying to find her. You don't have to explain yourself to me. I know how Audra's abilities work, and I know how much you love Kaleo. I didn't doubt you for a second."

He closed his eyes and leaned against the door. "Thanks, Nicole. I think I really needed to hear that."

Stefan and Nicole joined Brant, Trevor, and Audra in the parking garage where Audra had been forced into Trevor's backseat. Once Stefan made sure that Audra was appropriately secured with a mask on her face to limit her abilities, he reminded Nicole and Trevor to take Audra straight to NAT with no side stops or detours before climbing into Brant's car holding Rosie on his lap.

Chapter Twelve

After dropping Rosie off for a checkup and climbing back into Brant's car, Stefan turned to look at his friend. "We don't have long before we get to NAT. How do you know Audra?"

Brant sighed. "Last winter I saw her hanging around a few the restaurants and bars I frequented. We ended up hitting it off and she was hot so... well... you know."

Stefan groaned. "Last winter? Let me guess, sometime around December?"

"Yeah, how did you know?"

"Did you know she worked for NAT?"

"She works for NAT?" Brant shook his head. "I had no idea. She told me that she worked in public relations."

"She was one of the people assigned to your security team after Operation Cuckoo. Please tell me that she didn't approach you."

"I was the one who made the first move. Why?"

"Apparently she likes to use her abilities to seduce men."

"Yeah, and she's pretty good at it." They rode in silence for several minutes until Brant pulled into NAT. "Hey, do me a favor and don't tell Lin about this, okay?"

"She doesn't know?"

"No, she doesn't. I didn't realize Audra worked at NAT until you just told me, although in hindsight I think I understand more about the dynamics at play. I've heard plenty of stories from Lin about the 'car blonde'."

"Are you going to tell her eventually?"

"I think I have to." Brant sighed and ran his gloved hand over his face as he tapped his prosthetic arm against the steering wheel. "Audra and

I had... an arrangement. I was dealing with some residual feelings from seeing Lin again after Operation Cuckoo, so every now and then I'd call her up, and in exchange for some favors she'd use her abilities on me so that I could feel something close to what I used to feel with Lin."

"What kind of favors?"

"The sexual kind. We always met up at her house when I was in the mood, and it was all about the sex, with no other feelings involved. I didn't realize until a few months ago that she'd recorded every single one of our hookups."

"I wouldn't have ever thought you'd be embarrassed of a sex tape or two."

Brant parked his car. "It's more than just a couple of videos, and the last time I went to her house was the day you called me in to identify Ashley after she was rescued, and Lin and I had that fight. We weren't officially dating, but we'd already spent one night together, and that's enough of an overlap to make me worried that Lin won't take it well."

Stefan nodded and they made their way to the interrogation viewing room, where they found Trevor, Nicole, Wiper, and a middle-aged Arab woman wearing Mod's blue and red checkered scarf.

"Nicole and Trevor told us about what happened. How are you doing?" Mod asked Stefan.

"I'm okay, just a little shaken up."

"I hate to ask this of you, but would you mind asking her to talk again before I send Wiper in there? Maybe she'll be willing to talk now."

Stefan shrugged. "Sure, if you think it'll help."

As he entered interrogation room, his heart rate sped up and his palms began to sweat. Stefan knew people were watching on the other side of the two-way mirror, but it did nothing to stem the rising tide of anxiety he felt when he sat across from Audra, remembering what had happened the last time they were in the interrogation room together. He swallowed his anxiety and took a deep breath.

"There's no use in you putting your business face on, I'm not going to tell you anything," Audra said before he could even speak.

With that opening salvo, the interrogation didn't go well. Stefan knew that he was off his game but still did his best to convince Audra to talk until he heard a tap on the interrogation window.

"This is your last chance, Audra," he warned.

"Or what?" Audra laughed. "It's obvious that you're at the end of your rope. I've never seen you so discombobulated, Stefan, and honestly? It's really not attractive."

Stefan stood. "Don't say that I didn't warn you."

When he walked back into the viewing room, he sagged against the door. "Please tell me you can do something," he said to Wiper.

Wiper glanced at Mod, who nodded. "It's time. Do whatever you have to do."

Wiper hugged Mod for a long time. "Oh, don't worry. She'll tell me everything she knows… one way or another," Wiper said as he turned back to Stefan. His gray eyes were sharp and his smile predatory, a stark contrast to his usual easy-going manner. Stefan had seen his fair share of criminals, and as he looked at Wiper he wondered what crimes the older man had committed.

After Wiper stalked out, Mod sighed. "I'm sorry that you all have to see this side of him, but it had to be done."

Everyone turned to watch Wiper enter the interrogation room. As soon as he walked in, Audra rolled her eyes. "Obviously I don't consent to this; you're just wasting your time."

"I won't lie: a part of me was hoping you'd say that. It's been a long time since they let me out to play, so I'll be sure to make this as painful as possible," Wiper said. In one fluid motion, he grabbed Audra's head in his hands and almost immediately, she began to shake and cry.

"What's happening?" Brant asked.

"Wiper doesn't require consent to use his abilities. In fact, if he doesn't care about the pain he causes, he's more powerful. When he's being careful, most of the time the people he uses his abilities on only feel a dull pressure, like the beginning of a sinus infection or a headache." Mod paused when Audra started to scream. "When he's not being careful, the sensation is more like a hot knife digging around in your brain and stabbing you all over."

"And he was a Savior?" Trevor was aghast.

Mod shrugged. "More of a Savior-adjacent, like Brant's father. His abilities were useful in some circumstances, but he was mostly just along for the ride." They frowned. "Sifter and Architect aren't going to be happy when they find out about this."

"He's kind of scary right now," Nicole said.

"This side of him is terrifying and can be very dangerous. Long ago we discovered that he could leave this aspect of his personality with me, in my true form. It's been over twenty years since he last had to use it, and he'd hoped that he wouldn't ever have to do it again—but I guess we all know what's at stake."

They watched in silence and listened to Audra's cries of pain. When Wiper finally let go, she slumped forward and cradled her head in her hands.

Wiper entered the viewing room several minutes later and handed Stefan a recording device. "Everything I could find is on here. Find Kaleo," he rumbled before punching Brant square in the face.

"Dude, what was that for?" Brant asked as he rubbed his jaw.

"Nice punch," Nicole said.

Wiper ignored Brant and turned to Stefan. "If I were you, I'd let Heinstein stick around when you listen to the tapes so you don't have to track him down to take your revenge."

"Is anyone going to fill me in here?" Brant asked.

"How's Audra?" Trevor asked, nodding towards the interrogation room, where she was still slumped forward.

Wiper's eyes were like two chips of ice. "I might have broken her. I don't care. For all her plotting and planning and what she did, she was already broken."

Mod took Wiper's hand in their own. "Do you need anything else from us, Stefan?"

"No, you can go. Thank you for your help. I let Stone know about Audra, and he said he'd contact Homeland and coordinate taking her into custody. He just needs someone to stay here and keep an eye on her until he can get everything settled."

"Don't let her out of your sight. She still knows who Phoenix is, and I didn't want to wipe that part of her memory until we have everything we need for sure," Wiper said.

Stefan nodded. "We'll be careful."

Wiper glared at Brant. "You and I will talk later."

After Wiper and Mod left, Stefan turned to the others. "Nicole, Trevor, I take it that you want to stay and hear what Wiper saw?"

"Of course."

"Yeah, man."

"What about me?" Brant asked.

One of Stefan's eyebrows rose. "Wiper seemed to think it was important you stay. I'll defer to him."

"Sounds good."

Stefan plugged in the recorder. Mod had indeed been correct; when Wiper didn't care about digging deep, his abilities were much stronger. Normally Wiper's abilities had a two-week limit, but his recorded voice started narrating detailed events from several months before.

Some things Stefan could have predicted, such as Audra being upset at the news of his engagement to Kaleo. Other things he would have never guessed: how watching him place the NAT flag over Kaleo at the Capture the Flag event had started Audra's descent into madness, and how their scene in Kaleo's hospital room had finally made Audra snap.

Stefan listened with tears in his eyes to Wiper describing how Audra had followed Kaleo home, smashed all her birds, and cut her face. The tears turned into anger as he heard about Rodney and Audra smuggling Kaleo away from Lincoln.

He had to pause the tape to pull Nicole off Brant when Wiper mentioned Heinstein Transport.

"Traitor!" Nicole spat at Brant after Stefan dragged her a safe distance away. "I'm driving straight to Lin's apartment right after this and telling her what you did, and I hope she drops you like a rock. How could you do that to Kaleo? To all of us? She saved your life, and the lives of your friends and family, and you repay her by betraying her."

"Betraying her? I didn't know that Audra had a grudge against her. I didn't even know Audra worked for NAT until today. And as for the other stuff, I don't have any clue what you're talking about," Brant said, a red welt already visible on his cheek where Nicole had punched him.

"You idiot. I read the reports. Phoenix saved your life, and Ashley's life, and I know that Kaleo used her shield abilities to stop the bleeding when Lin was stabbed even if it wasn't an official thing. You owe her several times over, you worthless excuse for a piece of garbage."

"Nicole, that's enough. That wasn't your secret to tell," Stefan snapped.

Brant's face had gone pale. "Phoenix? Are you saying Kaleo is Phoenix?"

"Yeah, she is, and despite the terrible way you treated her, she still saved your sorry—"

Trevor interrupted. "She *was* Phoenix, until she went missing. We've had to kind of get creative lately."

"But Phoenix is still out there. I saw a news report of her and some other NAT members guarding the President recently. Wait... *get creative?*"

Stefan had thought that Brant's face couldn't get any whiter, but he was wrong.

Brant put a hand over his mouth. "Lin mentioned she'd been helping Director Stone at the office more, but she hates field work. Please tell me that you have multiple people working at NAT whose abilities involve the manipulation of light."

Stefan shook his head and Brant's shoulders slumped.

"I hadn't heard from Audra in months when she called me. She said she'd gotten in trouble and needed help to start over in a different town, so I let her use one of my private train cars, and I arranged to leave a little money in the car to help her get started in her new life. I never would have guessed that she'd used it for... that."

"How did you even know Audra? Did Lin tell you about her?" Trevor asked.

"No, Lin never said anything. Audra and I had a prior history, that's how I knew her. For what it's worth, I refused at first, but she blackmailed me and I didn't think it'd hurt to let her use the train once and give her a little money to keep her quiet." Brant turned to Stefan. "Look, you have to believe me."

"Why should I? You've made it quite clear how you felt about Kaleo." Stefan couldn't keep the chill out of his voice.

"Yeah, I guess I did. That's why you've been avoiding me for the past couple of months, isn't it? Because I thought she'd run away on her own and kept trying to help you move on?"

Stefan nodded.

"Look, I know I've been a jerk to Kaleo in the past, but I was working through some things, and I've been trying to be nicer. We were cool before she left. Plus"—Brant swallowed—"if Nicole is right, then I owe Phoenix my life, Ashley's life, little Nicholas's life, and it sounds like I owe both Phoenix and Kaleo for Lin's life. I guess she never did stop protecting us after all."

"You got that right." Trevor snorted. Brant shot a look at him, but Trevor only shrugged. "Look, do you know how hard it's been for me to listen to you complain and make fun of Kaleo and not say anything? You've been acting like a fool."

"Only because no one told me *anything*."

"That was Kaleo's decision. She thought that you got along with Phoenix, and she didn't want to take that away from you," Stefan said.

"Of course she did." Brant sighed. "Look, maybe I've been a fool and an idiot and whatever else you want to call me, but I promise you all right now that I'll do whatever it takes to help find her." The color returned to Brant's face as his resolve settled into his voice like a granite boulder settling into a creek bed. "I'm going to make it right and make it up to everyone, and especially to you, Stefan." Brant lowered his voice and squeezed Stefan's shoulder. "You're like the brother that I never had. I know what it's like to lose the love of your life, and I'm going to help you find yours."

Stefan took a deep breath and nodded. "I'll hold you to that."

"What's mine is yours. Now let's find Kaleo."

Nicole punched Brant again before taking a step back and nodding. "I agree: let's find Kaleo."

Chapter Thirteen

The next day, as Stefan organized and tracked down leads, he received a phone call from Nova.

"Hi, Nova, how can I help you?" he asked as he motioned for Lin to continue sifting through the bank accounts of the smuggler named Rodney. With information they'd received from Wiper, it had been fairly easy to track Rodney's identity and begin to parse out his activity over the past several months.

"Earlier today I got a letter in the mail from Kaleo. She's being held against her will at a gladiator training center called the Atlantic Trading Company in northern Scotland."

"We found her?"

"I think we did."

Stefan practically leapt out of his chair. "Just tell me where she is and I'll be on the next flight out." When Lin looked over at him, he pumped his fist in the air in victory and started pacing, and she smiled and sat back.

"Hold your horses, Stefan. I know you want to go to her, but we need to plan this out. Her letter was brief, but from what she wrote, I don't think they'll let her go willingly. It's dated almost a month and a half ago and looks like it's been through a blender and a storm. I'm as excited as you, but we should proceed with caution."

"Okay, so I'll fly out tomorrow. That should give me plenty of time tonight to get things settled with Director Stone and Zeke. I'll stop by your house to plan with you and Caleb?"

"Sounds good to me. We'll expect you for dinner tonight."

"We found her, Lin," Stefan said after he'd hung up.

"You found Kaleo?"

"Yes, we did." Even in his joy, Stefan paused as he realized that not only had his intended sacrifice the day before been rendered moot, but that he had essentially cheated on Kaleo with Audra.

"What's wrong?" Lin asked.

"I really messed up yesterday," he said, afraid to say more in case Brant hadn't told Lin what had happened.

Lin nodded. "Brant told me about it. Don't beat yourself up too much; I know you were only doing what you thought was right at the time, and I'm sure Kaleo will understand."

"Brant told you? What did he say?"

"Oh, you know, the basics: how they found Audra on top of you, and you handcuffed to the bed and under the influence of her abilities again, and how he found out about Phoenix, and how he just conveniently forgot to let me know he'd been sleeping with one of my coworkers before we got together, and how he thought he was helping out the aforementioned coworker when she had to move suddenly and accidentally enabled her to abduct Kaleo and smuggle her who-knows-where," Lin said in a tight voice.

"Are you okay? That's a lot to process."

"Not really, but I don't want to talk about it. I'm happy for you, Stefan, really, but you and Brant are friends, and I don't feel right talking to you about my relationship with him," she said firmly.

"I get that, sorry for prying."

"No, it's fine. I'm glad that you're Brant's friend, and I hope you don't blame him too much for the past two months."

"Hard not to when he's a big part of the reason why she's been so hard to track down. I knew we were missing something," Stefan grumbled.

"I know, and I know that sometimes he doesn't make the best decisions, but he's really missed you, and he's feeling terrible about what happened. You were one of his closest friends. If you cut him off, it's going to crush him."

Stefan sighed. "I'll think about it, Lin."

Lin smiled. "Besides, once you find Kaleo and bring her back, she and I can have lots of fun complaining all we want about our well-meaning but occasionally clueless significant others."

"I look forward to that," Stefan said before excusing himself. He walked directly to Director Stone's office and requested the next week off.

Stone sat back in his chair and surveyed Stefan. "Is there a reason for this sudden request?"

"Yes. Have you had a chance to listen to Wiper's recording of Audra's memories?"

"I have, and I'm guessing you just got off the phone with Nova and want to follow up on the Scotland lead?"

"That's right."

"Why a full week off?"

"Nova has a bad feeling about the situation, and I want to make sure I don't have to rush back here if there's a kink in the plan. I'm going to talk it over with her and Caleb tonight, and then I'd like to be on my way tomorrow morning."

"How are your other projects going?"

"Ready to be passed off to someone else after a final review. Zeke should be more than able to handle them."

Director Stone nodded. "All right then, go ahead. You've got the vacation time, and I'd rather you go now before things start to really heat up here."

"How long do we have on that front?"

"Could be days, could be months. All it takes is one unlucky projectile for our cover to be blown, and then the dominos start to fall. The faster you can find her, the better for everyone."

"Understood. Thank you, sir."

"And Stefan, one more thing," Director Stone slid an envelope across his desk. "I am well aware that in the world of the gladiators, all roads lead to Rome. If you find yourself needing a contact there, I know of someone."

"You really do have networks everywhere." Stefan took the proffered envelope and glanced over the file. "He's young."

"Not that much younger than you. He and his sister escaped from one of the Pure's towns when he was hardly sixteen. They were the last case I worked before transferring up to the Midwestern Pact offices."

"If you had a source from the Pure, why didn't you say anything until now?"

"He was too young to know anything important, although he did give me a written statement and information that might have been useful—if it hadn't been conveniently misplaced almost as soon as I filed it. Arranging for him and his sister to travel out of the country was as much for their protection as anything. He's not the most cooperative or trusting source, and for good reason."

"Is his contact information up to date?"

"Within the past year, yes. His sister sends me Christmas cards. Hopefully you find Kaleo easily and don't need to use this, but it's good to be prepared just in case."

Stefan nodded. "Thank you, Director Stone."

That evening Stefan hashed out a basic plan with Nova and Caleb: he would fly first thing in the morning to Edinburgh and contact the American embassy there before traveling up to the address he'd found for the Atlantic Trading Company in the Orkney Islands, where he would show his identification and pick Kaleo up if everything went according to plan.

After he'd left the Hughes' house, he joined Brant and Lin at Brant's mansion for dessert. Once they sat down to eat, Brant offered him the use of a private jet, but Stefan declined. Once he realized that there would be no persuading Stefan, Brant insisted on paying for his airfare and giving him a credit card.

"I have my own money. Just because I'm not filthy rich doesn't mean that I can't afford anything," Stefan protested.

Brant rolled his eyes. "Just take it; it's literally the least I can do. When you find Kaleo, reserve a luxury hotel suite, take her shopping for whatever she wants, and then take her out to the nicest restaurant in town, all my treat. If you find her on the first day, spend the rest of the week touring Europe on my dime for all I care. If you spend less than twenty thousand, I'll be very disappointed."

Stefan shook his head. "I really can't accept this..."

"Just take it, Stefan. When Brant feels bad, he starts throwing money around like a toddler playing in the snow," Lin said, twisting a diamond bracelet on her wrist. Her tone was even more bitter than it had been earlier in the day, but Stefan thought it wise to not say anything.

"Seriously, though, she's right, and I believe the forecast mentioned a blizzard for at least the next week," Brant said.

"Plus, he won't miss it any more than you or I would miss ten dollars," Lin interjected.

In the end, Stefan agreed to take the credit card, and to use it. He had to admit as he turned the card over in his hand that it had a nice, solid heft.

The next day, Stefan settled into a surprisingly comfortable seat in first class on a flight to Scotland.

The flight felt much shorter than he'd expected, perhaps partly because of his excitement at seeing Kaleo again.

After a full day and a half of traveling, Stefan finally set foot on the island belonging to the Atlantic Trading Company, accompanied by Alex, a State Department employee who worked at the American Embassy in Edinburgh. Alex was an older man who'd worked in international affairs since before the Hard Times. His hair was stark white and he stooped, but from the little he said, Stefan gathered there was a wealth of knowledge behind the bespectacled eyes, and his handshake was surprisingly strong. The two of them walked the couple of miles to the company training compound, and Stefan was pleasantly surprised to find his companion maintained a good walking speed despite having to use a cane.

"Don't look at me like I'm too frail for a nice little jaunt, Stefan. I promise you my morning hikes with the missus are more difficult than this little walk," Alex said gruffly when he caught Stefan watching him as they approached the old fort the company called home.

"How can I help you, gentlemen?" the man stationed at the front gate asked.

"I am Alexander Porchenko, from the American embassy in Edinburgh and this is my companion, Stefan Peters. We are here to investigate your illegal detention of an American citizen, a Miss Kaleo Hughes. If you would be so kind, please let us in speak to the manager of this facility."

"One moment please," the guard said before disappearing through the open gate.

"You think it's wise to play our hand so early?" Stefan asked.

"We're not playing our hand, we're letting them reveal theirs," Alex said.

The guard returned within a few minutes. "I'm sorry, we aren't accepting visitors at this time."

"How unfortunate." Alex shrugged and pulled out a cell phone. "Ah, well, I'll be sure to relay this development to my supervisor, the American ambassador. If I remember his schedule correctly, I believe he's having tea with your minster of foreign affairs right now. I'd hate to interrupt him, but he takes these matters extremely seriously and has a vested interest in returning the young lady to her home."

"Hold on, hold on. I think there was a misunderstanding, let me double check," the guard said, practically falling over himself in his rush to exit the guard booth.

Alex tapped his cane and looked at Stefan over his glasses. "For your sake, and the girl's sake, I hope this is the only bump in the road."

Stefan nodded and clasped his hands behind his back as they waited. He'd dressed for the occasion in one of his nicest suits, although he and Alex had already decided that it would be best if he pretended to be a representative sent by Kaleo's family to track her down. They'd reasoned that everyone would be more open to talking to an impartial and professional detective than a desperate fiancé.

Soon enough, the guard was back and waved them through the gate. "You may enter. Have a seat in the courtyard and someone will be with you shortly."

Stefan and Alex waited in a stone-cobbled courtyard that looked like it hadn't seen either the sun or a scrub brush since the Hard Times. After almost thirty minutes, a middle-aged woman in an austere dress walked across the courtyard to him. Her mouth had more frown lines than laugh lines, and her graying hair was pulled back into a severe bun.

"The manager will see you now. Follow me," she said in a voice that cracked like a whip before turning on her heel and striding away.

Stefan rose from his seat and let Alex take the lead, making sure to not seem rushed or overeager. His research had informed him that the gladiator market was cutthroat, abounding in shady business practices, which had been confirmed by the American ambassador. Rodney had known that Kaleo was Abled, at least genetically if not in practice, so they were working off the assumption that she'd been sold as a potential fighter.

They were led into a well-furnished room occupied by an older man dressed in a pinstripe suit.

"Welcome, Mr. Porchenko and Mr. Peters. I am Angus Dexter, the manager for the Atlantic Trading Company. Please have a seat." The man gestured to the chairs in front of his desk.

"It's nice to meet you, Mr. Dexter," Alex said as he sat down; Stefan followed suit.

"Yes, you as well. Tell me, what can I do for you?"

"I am from the American embassy in Edinburgh and am assisting Mr. Peters here in his quest searching for a woman known as Kaleo Hughes. Mr. Peters is a representative of the Hughes family, who recently received a letter from their daughter that detailed her imprisonment here. Miss. Hughes went missing over two months ago, and foul play was confirmed. He has been sent to locate Kaleo and bring her back home."

Mr. Dexter frowned. "Do you have proof? We take such accusations very seriously."

"Yes, we do, and I'm glad to hear that. Miss Hughes has powerful friends in America, and if it turned out that she was held against her will here, it would not go well for you or your government," Alex said as he pulled a copy of Kaleo's letter out of his bag and placed it on the desk. "Feel free to keep this, we have made several copies and the original is in our possession at the embassy."

"I see. But how can I know that you are who you say that you are? We receive agents from other training companies more often than I would like. How am I to know that you're not trying to poach our talent?" Mr. Dexter asked.

Stefan kept his face neutral as he made a mental note that Kaleo's abilities must have returned if the manager referred to her in such a way.

"Wonderful questions. As you can see here, we have her driver's license, passport, and several pictures of her. We can also show you our identification if it would soothe your mind," Alex said as he set the documents on the desk beside the letter.

Mr. Dexter gulped. "These could be forged."

"If you still don't believe me, feel free to give the American embassy in Edinburgh a call. My boss is very interested in why you've been keeping an American citizen here against her will—and I'm sure the Ambassador and his good friend, the Scottish Prime Minister, would love to hear your side of the story and have you come in for questioning. As it is, I believe my colleagues are already lodging an official complaint with your government."

"That won't be necessary," Mr. Dexter said. He loosened his tie slightly. "There is, however, a problem."

Alex frowned. "I don't see how. Simply release Miss Hughes into my custody, and we will be on our way. If you cooperate fully with us, we will show mercy and allow the doors of the Atlantic Trading Company to remain open, with more scrutiny after an extensive audit. If you refuse to work with us, I'm afraid I cannot guarantee anything."

Stefan tried his best to not let his hands twitch at the idea of holding Kaleo once more.

"Well, you see, that's the issue. Frankly, I'm not quite sure how to say this, Mr. Porchenko—but there has been a tragedy. Yesterday Kaleo Hughes tried to escape by jumping from the walls of the fort to the sea below. Unfortunately, a witness reported seeing her struggle to resurface after hitting the water, and we suspect she drowned."

Stefan felt like the air had suddenly been sucked out of the room. As his mind struggled to grasp the words his ears had heard, he went into autopilot.

"Her death is rather fortunate for you in that it ties up several loose ends. You will forgive me for not believing such a convenient story without proof," he said evenly.

Mr. Dexter shook his head. "I'm afraid that's not possible. She became unhinged after murdering our top female gladiator and had to be isolated. Unfortunately, she burned a hole through her door and escaped before anyone knew what was happening. It was pure luck that one of our maids saw her jump into the sea. The only proof we have is one of her shoes that washed up on the beach this morning."

"We will speak with the witness and take a look at the shoe."

"Certainly, if you will give me a few moments to gather everything."

Stefan's eyes followed Mr. Dexter out of the room. Once he and Alex were alone in the office, he allowed himself one deep breath to calm his nerves.

"Rather convenient. Too convenient, I think," Alex said under his breath.

"They could still be watching us," Stefan said.

"I'd be shocked if they weren't. Do you feel up to asking the witness some questions?"

Stefan nodded, knowing that it was important for him to keep his cool, no matter how much he wanted to rage and scream. The mere thought of Kaleo's death, after they had gone through so much and he had gotten so close to finding her, made him nauseous.

Several minutes later, Mr. Dexter reentered his office with a shoe in his hand and a middle-aged woman following him.

"This is Portia, one of Kaleo's closest confidants and the witness to her death," Mr. Dexter said. Portia stood with her hands clasped in front of her and eyes downcast. When she was introduced, she raised her eyes to Stefan and nodded meekly.

Stefan stood to offer Portia his chair. She glanced at Mr. Dexter for approval before taking a seat.

"How did you know Miss Hughes?" Stefan asked.

"Miss Fulbright assigned her to me to teach her the ropes. We grew quite close the past few months. When she told me about her family, I felt so bad for the poor thing."

"I see. If that's true, why did it take so long for us to receive her letter? Didn't you try to help her at all?"

Portia swallowed and darted a glance at Mr. Dexter. "Well, you see, us housemaids talk amongst ourselves, but we try not to cause trouble. Kaleo told Miss Fulbright about her family, but that horrible man who brought her here had already poisoned Miss Fulbright's mind and told her Kaleo was addicted to drugs, so she just thought it was the ravings of someone on a detox."

"It wasn't until a couple of weeks ago that Kaleo gained a high enough standing to have mail privileges," Mr. Dexter broke in.

Stefan was positive they were lying; Kaleo's letter had been stained, crumped, and dated almost two months before. He remained silent, giving Dexter plenty of rope with which to hang himself.

Dexter lost the silence contest and broke first. "The timing is truly terrible. I am sorry for your loss."

Stefan ignored him and turned to Portia. "What happened?"

"Kaleo attacked Servina, our top Abled fighter. She was jealous of how much attention Servina was getting and couldn't control herself," Portia said. "Either that, or she couldn't handle living anymore and thought Servina could help her end it all."

Stefan raised an eyebrow. "And what happened after that?"

"After she killed Servina, we locked her up. She was a mess, apologizing and screaming."

"Yes, so I gathered. And then?"

"I was on my way to her room when I saw her running down the hall. I tried to stop her, but she wasn't listening to me and moved too fast. She climbed over the wall of the fort and jumped before I could do anything."

Stefan picked up the shoe on Mr. Dexter's desk and examined it, but despite how hard he tried to focus, he couldn't; in his mind, he could only see Kaleo jumping to her death.

"I would love to get a tour of this facility, you know, to see where Kaleo has spent her time in the past several months so I can accurately include her working conditions in the report to my employers," Stefan said after a long pause, trying to shake off his feelings of dread.

"Unfortunately, that won't be possible. Most of the keep is under scheduled renovation, and we cannot allow an outsider into the construction zone for liability reasons."

The room started to spin and grew stifling. "I see. Thank you for your time, Mr. Dexter and Portia. We will be in touch to follow up with you soon," Stefan said as he slipped the shoe into his bag.

"I don't see why they would need to follow up; that's all the information we have," Mr. Dexter protested.

Stefan sighed and rebuttoned his suit jacket. "I understand your confusion, but my employers are very powerful in America and loved their daughter very much. If her death is true, heads are going to roll, and mine won't be one of them. Our lawyers will be in touch."

"You'll also be hearing from representatives from the American embassy. A bit of friendly advice: if I were you, I'd prepare myself for an intensive investigation with heavy consequences should we find any wrongdoing on your part," Alex said as he stood and tapped his cane on the ground.

With Alex following him, Stefan walked out of the office without a second glance and continued on his way out of the training center. The path eventually split around a rocky outcropping, one side going back to the village and the other winding to the right towards the ocean. Stefan sagged against the rocks, needing a moment to rest.

Alex sat next to him. "What do you think?"

"She can't be dead," Stefan whispered. "She can't." He looked down the path leading away from the village and shook his head. "I think I need a moment. Would you mind?"

"Go ahead, I don't mind waiting," Alex said as he rested his cane across his knees.

"I'll be back."

"Take your time. It'll be nice to rest these old bones a bit."

Stefan pushed off the rock and turned down the dirt path. He followed it around the hill to another rocky outcropping that sheltered a few stunted trees.

With his back against a tree, Stefan sat on a rock and looked at the gray ocean crashing below. There was no doubt in his mind that Dexter had been lying through his teeth, and he hoped he'd struck enough fear into the man's heart to pave the way for things moving forward. He planned to stay the night at the small inn in the village and call Nova and Caleb to talk through their next steps, including asking the Hamilton administration to coordinate with the embassy and lean heavily on the Scottish government for an expedited investigation.

He didn't know how long he'd been sitting and watching the waves crash against the rocky shore when the hairs on the back of his neck stood on end. There it was again—the faintest sound of a footstep, and then the rustle of a branch as the person who had been watching him moved forward.

A young woman and an even younger girl made their way down the narrow path to him. The woman was around his age and the girl approximately that of the Hamilton twins.

"Can I help you ladies?"

The young woman, whose blond hair was up in a bun, was the first to speak. "My name is Reina, and this is Yvonne. Is it true that you are Stefan, Kaleo's fiancé?"

He was taken aback by the directness of her question. "I am. How did you know?"

Reina smiled. "Kaleo told us all about you. She was positive you'd find her and rescue her from this place."

Stefan swallowed. "She said that? Where is she?"

"Not here, that's for sure. She was sent back to America the day before yesterday."

"That's not what they told me—they said she tried to escape and drowned."

Reina snorted. "I can promise you that didn't happen." She paused when Yvonne tugged at her tunic and gave her a look. Reina rolled her eyes. "Go ahead and speak up, Yvonne. I know you can talk."

Yvonne shook her head and looked at the ground, and Reina sighed. "You'll have to excuse my friend here; she misses Kaleo, and she's a little awestruck and shy to be in the presence of the great Stefan."

"There's no need for that; I'm just a normal guy. Here, Yvonne, how about you sit down and tell me all about what happened with Kaleo?" Stefan asked as he patted the rock next to him.

Yvonne blushed and looked down, but with an encouraging nudge from Reina, she sat next to him and smoothed the fabric of her beige tunic out across her legs.

"I like your red belt," he said, fishing for a way to break the ice.

"Thank you. It means that I'm Abled. Kaleo had one too, but Reina's is blue because she doesn't have abilities."

"What happened to Kaleo?" he asked gently.

"They told everyone one thing, but I was acting as the taste tester and server for Mr. Dexter yesterday when he was on the phone, and I heard him talking about someone they sent down to one of the big training centers in Rome. Everyone thinks I'm dumb because I'm so small and young and I don't talk a lot, but I listen really good and I know what I heard. After Kaleo challenged Servina, they didn't have anyone to send to Rome, so it had to be her."

"Servina? I've heard that name before. Portia told me that Kaleo attacked her, and that guilt over her death caused Kaleo to snap."

"A few days ago, Kaleo challenged Servina because she was about to kill me," Reina said. "She said something about Servina being a bully and picking on someone her own size. I wouldn't trust anything that Portia says; she was Servina's maid and hated Kaleo from the beginning. If it hadn't been for Portia, Kaleo would have stayed on the cleaning crew and had a much easier time of things for the past two months."

"I see. So, you think Kaleo was shipped to Rome? Did she want to go?"

Yvonne shook her head. "The only place Kaleo wanted to go was back home. They must have tricked her, otherwise she would have never left here. She told me you'd find her any day, and that she just needed to wait and be patient. When Mr. Dexter told her he believed her and would be sending her back, she was ecstatic. She was content in the kitchen while she waited for you; she had no reason to try and escape because she was confident that someday one of the letters she sent would reach you and she'd be rescued."

"She sent me a letter?"

"Every week she sent letters to you, her parents, and her sister."

Stefan nodded and looked out over the ocean again, lost in thought.

"You're going to find her, right?" Yvonne asked.

"Of course I'm going to find her." When he turned to look at Yvonne, her eyes were as big as dinner plates.

"We better be getting back to the kitchens before they miss us," Reina said finally.

"I understand. Just one more question: was she happy? Healthy? Okay?"

"She missed you and her old life terribly, and she didn't have an easy time of it here, but she was strong. She survived."

"She *is* strong. And very nice. And she promised me I could come visit her in America one day," Yvonne said before turning to Stefan.

Stefan smiled for what felt like the first time in a very long time. "If that's what she said, then I suppose you'll have to." He reached into his bag and pulled out a business card. On the back of it, he wrote his personal cell number before handing it to Yvonne. "Here, when you're ready to visit us in America, call that number and I'll make all the arrangements. Thank you for everything, Yvonne, you've given me hope."

"You're welcome," she said as she took the card from his hand, shy once again.

"Now, go on, Yvonne. I'll be right behind you," Reina said as she shooed Yvonne away.

She waited until the younger girl was out of earshot and turned to Stefan. "It's not going to be easy to track Kaleo down in Rome. Dexter isn't going to tell you anything if he can help it, and the fact that she was able to challenge Servina so easily will make her a valuable fighter. I wish you the best of luck."

"Thank you, I'm sure that I'll need it." He gave Reina a business card as well. "If you find out anything else, please call me."

"Will do."

Reina waved goodbye before following Yvonne up the path. Stefan sat on the rock for a few minutes more to collect his thoughts, and then made his way down the path to rejoin Alex.

As he walked, something in Stefan's brain clicked, and he paused to pull Kaleo's shoe out of his bag. One glance at the shoe confirmed his suspicions, and he picked up his pace until he reached the rocks where Alex was waiting.

"Feeling better?" Alex asked.

"Much. The shoe isn't Kaleo's, and I just had two young women who worked with Kaleo in the kitchens seek me out and tell me that she isn't dead; she was sent to Rome in Servina's place."

One of Alex's eyebrows rose. "Those are two very large developments. How do you know the shoe isn't hers?"

"I've been shoe shopping with Kaleo enough to know what the wear pattern on the bottom of her shoes looks like, and it's not this. Plus, Kaleo isn't that much shorter than me, so our feet are roughly the same size. This shoe is far too small."

Alex nodded and stood. "I see. I was hoping the Atlantic Trading Company wouldn't live up to the reputation of the gladiator games, but it appears that my fears were valid. We can discuss the next steps when we head back to the village. Perhaps someone there knows more and will be willing to talk."

When they had almost reached the outermost buildings, Stefan heard the thunder of hooves and turned around to see a group of riders coming towards them. He and Alex stepped to the side of the road, only to find themselves surrounded.

Most of the riders were carrying spears, which they leveled at him while keeping their distance.

"To what do we owe this visit?" Stefan asked carefully.

"You've overstayed your welcome on this island. Take the next boat off and leave this place. If you're smart, you won't come back," said a burly man who Stefan assumed was the leader of the group.

Alex tapped his cane. "And if we refuse?"

"You two will either be walking onto that boat on your own two feet, or you'll be carried onto it in a body bag. The choice is yours." As he spoke, the head rider shook his spear and jabbed at them.

Stefan frowned when he assessed the situation. He'd traveled light; no knives were allowed on planes, and while he had the use of a taser, he was woefully out-armed. Even moving at top speed, he doubted that he'd be able to outmaneuver his ten opponents and their spears on his own, especially while having to worry about his elderly companion.

"I understand. We'll be on our way then," he said through gritted teeth as he held his hands up.

"We'll go with you, to make sure that you don't get lost on the way and forget where the boat dock is."

Chapter Fourteen

As Stefan sat on the ferry back to Scotland's mainland, he cursed his luck. He'd made progress tracking Kaleo through Audra's intel and might have only needed a couple more days to find her on his own. If Audra had made her move on him one week sooner, he would have rescued Kaleo before the Atlantic Trading Company discovered how valuable she was.

He took a bus from the ferry to the train station, where he called Director Stone's contact.

A man answered the phone. "Allen residence, this is Paul."

"Paul? My name is Stefan Peters. I got your number from Jason Stone."

There was a long pause on the other end. "Jason Stone? What does he want?"

"A favor. Specifically, for you to help me find someone. I'm getting on a plane to Rome soon and will be there probably in the next ten hours. Can you meet me at the airport?"

"Dude, I don't know you. I don't even know how Jason got this number."

"Please hear me out. I have money and I'll make it worth your time. Stone said you owe him a favor and he's calling it in now."

Another pause on the other end of the line, the sound of muffled voices, and then Paul was back. "Fine. I'll meet you at the airport. Call me when you know what time for sure."

Stefan and Alex parted ways at the train station; Stefan was headed to the airport and Alex was returning to the embassy.

"I'm sorry we couldn't find your fiancée, Stefan. I can promise you that we'll keep on applying pressure to the Atlantic Trading Company from our end. Perhaps if we can get a look at their books we can figure out where they sent her, although it may take some time. The wheels of diplomacy move slowly, especially in this political climate."

"I understand. If you find out anything else, please let me know."

"Of course. When you touch down in Rome, call me and I can give you the contact information for our embassy there. Perhaps they can provide you with more help than I was able to—although it would be prudent to warn you that while my ambassador and his staff are loyal to President Hamilton, I've heard rumors that other branches of the State Department may not be so accommodating."

"Thank you, Alex. You've been a great help."

Alex peered at Stefan through his wire-rimmed spectacles and reached out to shake his hand. "I've not been that much help to you, but I will accept your gratitude. Take care of yourself and please let me know when you find your fiancée."

Around ten hours later, Stefan walked through the exit of the airport. He scanned the small crowd of taximen and drivers. A fair-haired man wearing a black leather jacket and sunglasses held a beaten cardboard sign with his name scratched on it.

"Paul?" Stefan asked.

"That's me." Paul tilted his head to look Stefan up and down, and his sour frown deepened. "You're Stefan, I take it?" he said. His surprisingly thick accent made him sound like he'd be more at home in the woods of the American South than on an Italian street.

"I am."

"Great. Let's get going then. Where are you staying?"

"I haven't made reservations anywhere yet. Where would you recommend?"

"There's an inn not too far from my place that seems pretty clean. That is, unless you need somewhere nice so you don't muss those fancy shoes of yours."

Stefan shrugged. "I'm sure the inn will be fine."

Paul turned on his heel and Stefan followed him onto one of the many buses waiting at the airport.

"My neighborhood is on the other side of the city," Paul said before leaning his head against the window.

Any attempt that Stefan made at conversation was cut short by Paul.

"Look, I work at night, so I'm up way past my bedtime," Paul said as he adjusted his sunglasses. "Just to be clear, the only reason I'm helping you right now is because my sister asked me to. Otherwise, I'd be sleeping."

"I appreciate it."

"Yeah, you said you'd make it up to me, so before I show you anything, tell me what you were thinking as far as payment."

"Whatever you currently make per day, doubled."

"Triple it."

"I'll quadruple it if we find the woman that I'm looking for. If not, it remains doubled."

"Fine."

Paul didn't say another word to Stefan for the rest of the ride. Eventually, he reached up to pull the bell to let the bus driver know that it was their stop, and Stefan followed him off the bus.

"The inn is about two blocks that way," Paul said with a nod down the street. "I'll meet you in the dining room there at four. We can start work then."

"It's eight o' clock in the morning. That would be wasting the entire day," Stefan protested.

Paul's hand played with the flap of a peculiarly shaped pocket that ran the length of his thigh. "I worked all night and need to sleep. If you want my help, you do it on my terms."

Stefan glanced down the road. "Fine, four o'clock sharp."

Once he had checked into a room at the inn, Stefan sat down for a cup of coffee and breakfast. He'd gotten more than enough sleep on the plane, and he didn't want to waste any more precious time. The rest of the day was spent in researching the area and talking to locals, as well as withdrawing cash from Brant's card to pay for his expenses. The language barrier wasn't as bad as Stefan had feared; between his native languages of Romanian and English and his broken French, he made do.

The reconnaissance went well, although the monumental task he'd set for himself became apparent after several hours. Hearing that the gladiator games were big business was completely different than being on the ground and seeing just how much of the local economy was centered around the games, and Stefan compiled a list of the biggest gladiator training centers to visit with Paul.

When four o'clock rolled around, Stefan sat by the window in a cafe next to the inn and watched the passersby as he waited for his guide. Paul was right on time; in contrast to that morning, he'd removed his sunglasses, and his blue eyes were as bright as the cloudless sky outside. Stefan took in his worn clothes and shoes before Paul sat across from him.

"Have you eaten yet?" he asked.

Paul shook his head and yawned. "Just woke up a bit ago."

"How long do we have?"

"I start work at ten tonight."

"Get whatever you want and fuel up. We've got a lot of ground to cover."

After they'd ordered, Paul sat back and appraised Stefan. "So, what are you doing here?"

Stefan told Paul a very abbreviated version of the situation with Kaleo, and Paul whistled under his breath. "That's going to be a tall order. How long do you have here?"

"Two, maybe three days."

Paul mumbled something under his breath, flagged down the waitress and ordered something in Italian. She was back in a few minutes with two cups of coffee.

"Espresso. Drink up, we're going to need all the help we can get."

Stefan took a sip of his drink and nodded in approval. He slid the papers with the list of training centers to visit over to Paul. "I was thinking we'd start with the smaller training and recruitment centers today and work our way up. With any luck, she'll be at one of the smaller ones and we'll get her out with no trouble."

"Looks like you did your research." Paul looked over the list. "Most of these centers aren't in good parts of town. You'd get eaten alive. It's a good thing that you're paying me so well for protection."

"And interpreting services, don't forget," Stefan said dryly.

"That part of my services you may not need as much," Paul said as he stirred his soup. He looked up, sensing Stefan's surprise. "Did no one tell you? The gladiator games started around thirty years ago when the Saviors challenged the mayor of the city to a duel for some reason or another; I forget, and sometimes the story changes. The important part is that the Saviors won, were able to save the city or whatever, and the gladiator games were born. As part of a nod to its first champions, English is the official language of the gladiator games."

"That will be helpful; I'll be able to talk to them myself without your aid then."

"Where did you learn English?"

Stefan frowned. "My parents, why?"

"Your accent isn't American."

"My mother is from Romania. I was born and grew up on an army base there. My father moved my family back to the United States when I was in junior high."

"That'd explain it. You definitely have the American walk, so I was wondering why your accent didn't match your attitude."

"The American walk?"

"It's a kind of swagger usually most often seen in Americans and people who are much too arrogant. Either way, I think it's best if we pretend that you are a private investigator hired by a wealthy family to look for their wayward daughter, and I am your guide. If you need to speak, make your accent as thick as possible because some here look down on Americans. Sound good to you?"

"Sounds great."

"Good." Paul turned to look out the window, apparently done with the conversation.

Once they finished their food, Stefan checked his watch. "Well, shall we get started?"

"Sure."

"Lead the way."

That first day, after spending a solid five hours combing through the streets and various dirty and decrepit training centers, Paul and Stefan reconvened at the inn.

"Tomorrow I'll spend some time on surveillance at the top training centers. Maybe we'll get lucky and catch a glimpse of Kaleo," Stefan said.

"Sounds good to me. I meet you here, same time, same place?"

Stefan nodded.

The next day started off as poorly as the first, albeit in slightly more polished buildings. Whereas the day before Paul had been flashing the Italian equivalent of twenties to talk to the managers, now the bribes were in the hundreds.

Influenced by the amount of bribe money and the allure of a bought contract, several of the more well-maintained centers brought out a lineup of apparently every single brunette they had of average or above average height. As the day wore on, Stefan's patience wore thin and the flame of hope burning in his chest had begun to wane.

"Are you sure she's even in Rome? There are a ton of other companies and camps across Europe. If they sent her somewhere, it may have been to another place to get warmed up before the big leagues. If she was truly untested, the companies here may not want to risk giving up a slot until she better proved her abilities. They could be trying to train some of the American out of her as well, to increase her value," Paul said as they walked to one of the last centers on their list.

"She's here. She has to be."

They walked up to the large gates and repeated their often rehearsed speaking parts. After handing over a bribe, they were let into the compound and guided across the large dirt training arena where several people sparred.

Stefan cast a practiced eye across the fighters. They were certainly better than the average untrained person, but still what he would call mediocre.

"Are these your Abled fighters?" Paul asked their guide.

"Yes, these are some of our new trainees."

"I see mostly men. Some of the other centers that we've visited had a pretty even gender split."

"Women tend to have more powerful abilities, but they also tend to be physically weaker and can cause Abled dynamics issues. Lesser centers without our resources will take on more women to use in the less prestigious individual matches where team dynamics don't come into play. We prefer to focus on gathering and cultivating the best female talent that we can find with the goal of strategically placing them into teams where the strength of their abilities and leadership potential can really shine and highlight the strength of our male fighters."

They entered the building through a pair of heavy wooden double doors that led into an elegant lobby. Behind a polished stone countertop stood two smiling and smartly dressed receptionists.

One of them greeted the newcomers in Italian, and Paul stepped forward to explain the situation.

From Stefan's vantage point, either Paul didn't explain it very well or the receptionists didn't want to listen, and Paul's voice rose in intensity as the vehemence of his hand gestures increased.

"Paul, what's going on?" Stefan asked casually.

Paul muttered darkly under his breath as he turned around to look at Stefan. "They say that they aren't allowed to give any outsiders information. I've tried to reason with them, but they're stonewalling me and we're not getting anywhere."

"It looks to me like you've frightened them a bit."

"They wouldn't have to be frightened if they'd just give me a plain answer, but they won't even deign to look at a picture of her, let alone tell me if they've had any new recruits in the past week." Paul lowered his voice. "And don't even get me started on the insult of them speaking to us in Italian, as if we're too dumb to know a second language."

Four burly guards walked into the room through a side door and took up station in front of the receptionists.

"Oh, c'mon. This is overkill," Paul said before yelling in Italian at the receptionists, who shouted back at him. He pushed past Stefan to stand between him and the guards, and his hand drifted to the pocket at his side. "Don't worry, I've got this. If you can distract the scrawny-looking one in the back, I should be able to take the other three."

Stefan couldn't help but smile. He'd learned in the past two days that the only way to gain respect in the world of the gladiators was by a show of strength and power, and while he still hadn't told Paul about his own abilities, it appeared high time for a demonstration.

He took a deep breath and calmed his mind, deciding to forgo the taser. The world around him slowed down.

One of the guards shifted his weight forward, while the two behind him each took a step to the side to flank Stefan and Paul.

Stefan never gave them the chance.

The guard in front was pulled forward and thrown off balance into the reception desk. The other two guards had their legs knocked out from under them, and then Stefan vaulted the tangle of arms and legs to deliver a square punch to the last guard's jaw.

When Stefan turned around to survey the scene, he saw Paul standing with what looked like a bolt of lightning in his hand and an incredulous expression on his face.

"You were taking too long," Stefan said.

The fourth guard was still on the ground, and Stefan bent down to search his prone body. Once he found what he was looking for, he removed a knife from the guard's belt and twirled it around his fingers.

"Now, where were we? Do you think that little show was enough to get us some information?" he asked.

"I would say that it most certainly did," an older gentleman said in English as he emerged from a screen behind the receptionist's desk. He winked at Stefan. "And as the owner of this training center, I'd say my opinion goes quite far."

The gentleman turned to the receptionists and spoke to them quietly. Out of the corner of his eye, Stefan watched as the lightning bolt in Paul's hand dimmed until he was only holding a normal metal rod. Paul caught Stefan's eye, shrugged, and returned the rod to the long pocket along his thigh.

"Come, you two. I gather we have things to discuss," the gentleman said as he beckoned them forward.

Behind the screen, a door led to a luxurious office. Stefan walked in and sat in a chair across from the gentleman without hesitation, Paul following his lead after a moment's pause.

"Please, sit. My name is Elwin Nilsen."

"Your name doesn't sound very Italian," Paul remarked.

"That's because my parents were Norwegian. Now, how can I help you?"

Stefan listened as Paul went through their spiel once more. Elwin nodded along like he believed them.

"I see, and you think that there is a chance that this Kaleo Hughes is here at this facility?"

"We believe she might be."

Elwin shuffled through several papers on his desk. "Unfortunately, the only Ableds we house are already under contract, and we take great care to do our research to make sure that those contracts are valid. However, the show that you put on in the lobby was rather entertaining, so I will give you a tour of the facility anyway. Do you have a picture of the girl in question?"

Stefan slid a picture of Kaleo across for Elwin to look at; it wasn't anything personal, just her official headshot for Hamilton's office.

"This is an old picture. Her hair is probably much shorter now, due to an accident that occurred before she was stolen, and she may have a new scar on her face."

Elwin studied the picture and frowned. "I don't think we have anyone who looks like this here, but I will doublecheck."

It was a beautiful facility, and Elwin showed it off with great pride. Each Abled fighter had a room, and they could enjoy a community armory, an indoor training ring, and well-equipped medical facilities. It was almost enough to tempt Stefan to move to Europe and try his hand at gladiator fighting.

Unfortunately, despite Elwin requesting that all the female fighters be brought out, there was no Kaleo to be found.

The tour ended in the lobby, and Elwin handed Stefan and Paul a business card. "I will admit to having ulterior motives in giving you this tour. The little display you both put on in the lobby was quite powerful. Have either of you thought about being an Abled gladiator?"

"I'm afraid I have some rather pressing matters at home that I can't ignore," Stefan said.

"And my sister would kill me if I joined up, although after this tour I will say that it's very tempting," Paul added.

"Such a pity. Still, hang on to those cards just in case. It can be hard for Americans to break into the European scene, but I'd be glad to help you try. Please don't hesitate to reach out if you change your mind," Elwin said.

With a heavy heart, Stefan turned towards the door to exit the lobby. He paused when he saw a large swath of burned wood in the door.

"Did you set an angry gorilla on fire and then let it loose?" Stefan asked.

Elwin chuckled. "No, no, nothing like that. We simply had an Abled who was unsatisfied with their contract terms lash out in anger. Don't worry, we are taking steps to remedy the situation as I speak."

Paul raised an eyebrow. "I'd be careful if I were you, that looks like a nasty burn."

"We have the situation fully under control," Elwin said as he guided them out the door.

Later, after they'd visited the last training center without gaining any inkling of Kaleo's location, Stefan and Paul reconvened at a small cafe.

"So, what's the next step?" Paul asked as he ate a slice of pizza.

Stefan shook his head, letting his shoulders cave. "I have no idea. I have to go back to America soon, but I don't see how I can do that when she could still be here."

"And you're positive she didn't die trying to escape?"

"Yes. She's out there somewhere, I'm sure of it." Stefan withdrew a wad of cash from a hidden pocket and set it on the table. "Here's your fee—four days' worth of wages for two days of work. I guess this is where we part ways."

Paul glanced around as he put the cash into his pocket. "You're not staying in Rome for another day?"

"No, I think I'm going to take the train and hit up a couple of centers in Paris and London as I make my way back to America. Maybe one of them will know something."

"You're going to leave just like that?"

"I have to. I have people who need me. I can't let them down."

Paul nodded. "I'll keep an eye out, and if I see anything or hear anything, I'll let you know."

Stefan finished his drink and handed Paul his business card. "Sounds good to me. Tell your sister I said hi, and that I'm sorry I wasn't able to meet her."

"Will do." Paul surveyed Stefan's face and his normally serious expression broke into a smile. "You know, when I first saw you, I thought you were going to be insufferably arrogant and pretentious, but you're not so bad after all."

Stefan made his best attempt at a smile. "And I thought that you were going to be some totally unhelpful punk kid. At least you picked some decent places to eat."

"Hey, I had your back that one time," Paul protested.

"That's true. What kind of abilities do you have anyway? Lightning bolts?"

"I can impart solar energy to a metal rod, so basically, yeah."

"I bet that comes in handy."

"It makes my job as a bouncer much easier."

Stefan frowned. "Don't bouncers work at night?"

"I make it work."

Stefan tossed several bills on the table and stood to leave. "Well, it was nice meeting you, Paul. Keep in touch."

"I'm sure my sister will send you a Christmas card."

Later, as he left Rome, Stefan felt like he was leaving part of himself behind. He had never dared to think about what might happen if he didn't find Kaleo, and now he was having to face his worst nightmare: despite Reina's and Yvonne's assurances, there was a possibility that Kaleo was dead.

Stefan's mind swirled with dark thoughts as he looked out the window of the train to the night beyond. He was returning to America because his deeply engrained sense of duty refused to let him shirk his work. However, though his head told him it was the right thing to do, he couldn't shake the feeling that he was leaving his heart behind, somewhere in Rome.

Chapter Fifteen

Kaleo was freezing.

She opened her eyes to see a dimly lit, spartan room whose only light came in the form of a small window set too high up on the wall for her to see anything outside. Kaleo raised a hand to her neck, where her fingers brushed over a small welt, and she remembered the feeling of the dart against her fingertips.

She was so tired, but the room was too chilly for her to lie still for long, so she got up and paced.

And paced.

And paced some more.

The room was a large jail cell made of stone, with a bed, table, and a toilet and sink in the corner. The monotony of waiting was mind numbing, and the solid metal door seemed to muffle all vibrations, leaving her deaf to whatever was happening outside.

She tried practicing her abilities, and while she was encouraged by the crackling energy field she created, the meager sources surrounding her and the persistent cold that made her shiver deep in her bones forced her to limit the energy drain.

The small patch of sunlight moved several feet across the floor before someone unlocked the door.

A willowy woman in a flowy dress entered the room. She was almost as tall as Kaleo, and her long black hair hung around her face in loose strands and flowed with her languid movements.

"Have you cooled off yet?" the woman asked as she sat gingerly in one of the chairs at the small table.

Kaleo crossed her arms. "Let me go. I don't belong here. You have no right to keep me."

"We have a signed contract, which is enough of a right."

"The contract isn't valid. I should be free."

"Freedom is just a state of mind. You could be free here. You could be the freest you've ever been."

Kaleo frowned and said nothing more.

They sat in silence as the sun patch continued its march across the stone flooring. After a good amount of time, the woman stood.

"It seems that you still need to think your situation over. I'll be back tomorrow."

After the woman left, Kaleo tried everything to escape. The bed was bolted to the floor, so she couldn't use it to examine the bars at the window to pry her way out. The metal door was smooth from the inside and had no hinges she could dismantle, and nothing that she could pry loose. Her new abilities that burned things weren't strong enough to melt through any of the solid metal and drained her terribly in the cold room.

She did her best to remain calm and think of alternative ways she could escape or convince her captors to let her go, but nothing came to mind. As the light began to fade outside, a small window slid open within the larger metal door, and a tray of food was pushed through.

It was plain fare: bread, water, boiled vegetables, and beans, but Kaleo hadn't had anything to eat all day and the bland food tasted surprisingly good.

When darkness fell outside, the temperature in the room dropped further and Kaleo wrapped herself in the thin blanket on the bed and tried her best to fall asleep.

She didn't sleep well that night, and when breakfast came the next morning Kaleo forced herself to eat the oatmeal gruel and dried fruit. She spent most of the morning huddled in the blanket on the cold floor, trying to gather as much energy as she could from the weak sunlight that shone through the small window.

Sometime after breakfast, the door opened and the woman from the day before walked in again. Kaleo turned to face the intruder, but remained in the sun.

"Have you thought about things enough now?"

"What was I supposed to be thinking about? I don't know where I am, or what you want with me."

The woman sat down and pulled a piece of paper out of the folds of her dress. "You are a potential fighter in the service of the Boar's Head training company. I need you to sign this official contract before we can begin the recruitment process."

"You said that you already had a contract; just use that for whatever kind of slave labor you need me for."

"We do have a contract, but it's still linked to your former company. If you wish to continue here, you must sign the new contract."

"I don't want to be a recruit, or employed, or anything else. I just want to go home."

"Once you win enough money to reimburse us, you will be released from your contract."

"Call my parents right now and they'll pay to have me released."

"Unfortunately for you, that's not how this works."

Kaleo stood and walked to the table. She glanced over the contract just long enough to see how heavily weighted it was in favor of the training company, and without another word she ripped the paper in two pieces.

With a sigh, the woman stood up. "You're a fiery one, I'll give you that, but we've tamed dozens more spirited than you. Take a piece of advice from someone who's been in the game a long time: give in now, before we break you completely."

Kaleo stepped forward, body tense and ready to attack, sure that if she could just knock over the woman she'd hold her hostage and at the very least escape from the small cell where she'd spent the past two days.

She had no such luck. Before she was halfway across the room, the woman flicked her wrist and Kaleo felt a sting on her leg. She looked down to see a dart sticking out of her thigh. Just as she registered that she'd been hit, her entire leg went numb and she fell on her side, helpless, as the woman walked out the door without a backward glance.

Kaleo spent the rest of the afternoon crawling after the sunlight, her leg useless. By the time dinner rolled around, the effects of the dart had worn off enough for her to stand on both legs and walk over to the window, only to be disappointed by the slice of bread and cup of water provided.

The next morning, Kaleo awoke to find the sunlight almost gone. During the night, someone had covered the window with black cloth, leaving barely enough light to see in the already dim room.

Breakfast was another slice of bread and a small cup of water. Kaleo didn't bother getting up, instead lying in the cold darkness and chasing phantom lights with her eyes until the door slid open once more. The woman entered, carrying a small lamp and a bag slung around her shoulder.

"Are you willing to listen to me now?" the woman asked as she set the lamp on the table.

Begrudgingly, Kaleo sat in the opposite chair.

The woman smiled and pulled a piece of paper, a pen, and a small cup out of her bag. "Here's the contract. Once you sign this, you will officially be a potential recruit. If you live up to your reputation, you may very well become a Boar's Head gladiator, with all the privileges that come with it."

"And if I don't sign?"

The woman looked around. "All things considered, you still have a rather nice room here. It may be a little cold, sure, but it has a bed, a working sink and toilet, and even an open window that provides some fresh air. If you continue to be difficult, it can be arranged for all of that to be taken away like this." She snapped her fingers, and when Kaleo said nothing, she sighed. "It seems you need more time to think. I'll be back tomorrow, or maybe the day after. My patience is beginning to wear thin. Perhaps you will be more amenable next week."

She reached for the contract, but Kaleo was faster and slammed her hand down to prevent the paper from being taken away as she considered her options.

They sat in silence for a moment. Kaleo's head was bowed, but when she looked up, she shivered as the faintest hint of a predatory smile passed across the woman's face.

"You should know that in order for me to allow you to sign, you must also drink this." The woman poured a vial of liquid into a small cup on the table.

Kaleo picked up the cup. It felt strangely warm in her hand, and gave off a peculiarly spicy odor. "What is this?"

"A special type of medication. You'll forget almost everything in your long-term memory."

"Permanently?"

"Unless you drink the antidote, which contains many expensive ingredients and is difficult to make properly."

"Just so I'm clear: if I don't sign right now, you'll gradually take more and more meager comforts away from me until I either do sign or I'm dead?"

"Correct."

Kaleo sat back in her chair. "I don't have a choice, do I?"

"No, only the illusion of one. Your fate was sealed as soon as you drove through the Boar's Head gates."

There was a knock at the door, and the woman got up to answer it.

As she listened to the sound of hushed conversation, Kaleo sank into the depths of despair. Long ago, she'd promised Stefan that if something ever happened to her, she would hang tight and wait for him.

Well, she had waited. And waited. And waited some more. If she hadn't stepped up, Hugo would still be in charge of the kitchens, and who knew how many more girls he would have molested. If she hadn't stepped forward, Servina would have killed Reina. If she didn't step out now, she feared she would either die alone in the cold room or go insane.

"I'm sorry, Stefan, but this is a promise that I can't keep anymore," she whispered as she swallowed the liquid in the cup and picked up the pen.

The woman returned to the table, done with her conversation, and smiled when she saw the empty cup and signed contract. She gathered up the cup and the contract but left the pen on the table.

"It's customary for you to keep the pen you signed with. If you have good luck in the gladiator arena, you may be able to use it to sign the receipt for the antidote in a few years' time. I will leave you now; enjoy the last few minutes you have with your memories before they're locked away. Don't bother trying to cheat the system and make yourself throw up either. Most of the active ingredients have already been absorbed by the mucous membranes in your mouth, and vomiting will only complicate things," the woman said.

After the woman left, Kaleo sat alone in the shallow pool of the lamp's light, paralyzed by the magnitude of what she had done, her mind racing for any kind of solution.

She turned the pen over in her hand and had an idea. It was a ludicrous thought that probably wouldn't work, but it at least gave her hope. She might have been forced to sign the contract, but she wouldn't go down without a fight.

Kaleo quickly dug the pen into her thigh and scratched out several words. If something happened while she was inebriated that washed off the ink, with any luck she had dug hard enough to create a welt or a bruise that would still be readable after the drug took effect.

Just as she finished the last word, the room spun and a wave of exhaustion crashed over Kaleo. She stumbled to her cot and lay down. The movement caused an overwhelming wave of nausea, and she leaned over the side of her bed and vomited.

Even in the cold room, her body felt like it was on fire and Kaleo thrashed around, throwing herself on the floor in a desperate attempt to cool off. A soothing hand placed a cool washcloth on her forehead, and she opened her swollen eyes to see the woman in the flowing dress leaning over her.

"Don't worry, you will be fine. This is a necessary change—your metamorphosis from caterpillar to beautiful butterfly. We are your family now, and we will take care of you," the woman whispered, and Kaleo's world went dark.

Part Two

Chapter Sixteen

Recruit One woke to the harsh sound of a blaring horn. With a groan, she swung her legs out of bed and changed into her uniform. Her muscles protested fiercely at the movement, but she paid them no mind, having grown used to their near perpetual soreness. She ruffled her fingers through her short hair in an attempt to keep the unruly curls from getting matted before pulling on her socks and shoes.

The only benefit to living in such a small room was that everything was easy to find. Overall, the room was nice as long as she avoided thinking about how much it felt like a coffin.

Her fingers brushed against the words scratched on the wall at the foot of her bed, and as she passed through the door her spine straightened and her face settled into an impassive expression. No matter what happened, no matter what she saw, she would survive, and she would make it back to her room in one piece.

A group of women milled in the hallway. Recruit One ignored their daggered glances and leaned against the wall, careful to keep her back protected. Every woman in the hallway had been tested in some way or another and found worthy enough to be sent to the Tiber Recruitment Center, one of the best facilities in all of Europe when it came to matching new fighters with prestigious training companies and rich sponsors.

At least that's what she'd been told. None of the other women had memories, but they had the benefit of experience after fighting their way up for months or even years. She had none.

Recruit One shook her head to clear it of any distracting thoughts about her past—those were best kept for when she was safe inside her room. Now she needed to focus on sizing up her opponents and thinking one step ahead.

Once, at the start of the trials several days before, things had been different. She hadn't been the most outgoing in the group, but she had at least tried to be friendly. That had all ended when their first trial started. The trainers who ran the center had informed them that the group of thirty needed to be pared down into a group of fifteen, who would then move on to the next training round.

Their first trial had been a free-for-all on the sands of the training arena. Thankfully, along with her grooming routine and fighting skills, she hadn't forgotten how to use her abilities. Recruit One had emerged not only practically unscathed but at the top of the class.

Some of the others hadn't been so lucky. For them, the coffin-nature of their rooms had been an omen instead of a warning.

It wasn't a trial day, so the time passed in a highly regimented blur of sparring, strategy lessons, classes that discussed the basic biology of Ableds and their abilities, and workouts. At the end of the day, it was with a grateful sigh that Recruit One shut the door to her room and heard it lock behind her. The only source of light came from the small candle on the wall sconce outside her room and was barely enough for her to see a hand in front of her face. She didn't mind; she didn't need a candle to see.

She activated her abilities and encased her left hand in a red light, feeding its strength until she could see every aspect of her room. There wasn't much—she had a bed barely large enough for her to lie comfortably, a small trunk that housed her two changes of clothes and her pen, a water pitcher, and a cup. The walls were rough-hewn wood and covered in scratched words and symbols from all the recruits who had come before her.

Recruit One changed into her sleeping clothes and sat on the edge of her bed. For what felt like the hundredth time, she placed her hand on the wall, where she'd added her own words to tell her story.

Bird. Ring. Win. Family.

She thought as hard as she could, searching her nonexistent memories for any clue as to what made those particular words so important that she'd carved them into her leg with her initiation pen. The first two words were a mystery, but she understood the third all too well. On her first day with the other women, the workers in charge of them had taken all the recruits into a large room, sat them down, and explained their role: they were being assessed for the gladiator arena. The most powerful would go on to earn the title of "queen" and lead teams in Abled fights in the arena. Women Ableds usually had much higher Saban-40 concentrations than their male counterparts, and strong women were needed to prevent any interference from group dynamics that could throw a match before it started.

The days at the recruitment center melded together, although she was sure to mark each on her wall with a broken shard of pottery that she'd found hidden under her bed on her first day. There were more trials that took various forms: group fights, duels, fitness tests, intelligence tests, and survival challenges. She excelled at them all. She didn't remember who she had been before her time at the Tiber, but she knew if she ever wanted to find out, she'd need to win at everything.

As the group's numbers were whittled down and the competition grew fiercer, several women paired off. Recruit One didn't bother; their trainers had already said that those who made it through all the trials would be placed on separate teams. She saw no reason to befriend others who might one day be her enemies. Instead, she kept her eyes and ears open to gain knowledge of her future opponents' strengths and weaknesses and make up for her inexperience in the ring.

One morning, instead of being taken to the cafeteria for breakfast or to the training grounds for another test, the remaining women were finally escorted to a different area of the training compound.

Recruit One and two other women, Recruits Two and Three, were ushered into a room and told to sit. One of their trainers—Recruit One had never bothered to learn his name—spoke as another handed each of them a wrapped package.

"From here on out, you will no longer be identified by your number ranking. Instead, you'll be referred to by the color of the clothes that we have provided you. Please, open your packages."

Recruit One tore open the wrapping paper. The package contained several red shirts, black pants, and red socks. She looked over to see Recruit Two holding up a green shirt. Recruit Three had blue clothes.

"Red, Green, and Blue will be your new names. You should feel proud: you've made it to the final selection round."

The three women were led to a circular table in another room. After they'd taken a seat, a side door opened and nine men walked through.

"You twelve will be living with each other for the next few weeks as part of the selection process. We know you're all hungry, and have arranged for breakfast. Please, eat and get to know each other," the trainer said.

The newcomer men filled the open seats, and once everyone was situated, several servants walked out, their arms piled high with food.

Red was polite, but not chatty—a sharp contrast to her two female companions, who were positively bubbly.

The food they'd been fed in the days before had been nutritious, but not particularly tasty. This brunch spread was delicious, and she ate and drank her fill. After everyone had eaten their fill and only the scattered remnants of food were left on the table, the trainers who had been sitting against the wall stood up.

"Has everyone eaten enough?" a male trainer asked. When they all nodded, he smiled. "Good. The food you just ate, and the food you will be eating for the next week, has been laced with a medication to suppress your abilities. This will prevent you from using them until we taper you off the medication or provide an antidote."

"You did what?" one of the men said. He shoved his chair back and stood up, his small eyes and thick black beard making his face look like a thundercloud, especially when combined with skin mottled red in anger. "Are you stupid? I'm an Abled fighter. How am I supposed to fight if I don't have my abilities?"

"You are an Abled fighter, but abilities aren't everything; mental fortitude and strength are also required. In the past, some of our tests had false positives due to contestants finding some abilities more attractive or 'stronger' than others. The medication we gave you only limits the manifestation of your abilities, not the expression of Saban-40. This helps us to get a clear picture of how group dynamics will play without abilities muddying the waters."

"But what if my abilities never come back?" another man complained.

"There haven't been any cases of permanent side effects after the antidote has been administered. That's all the time we have for questions. Let me show you to your suite."

The group was led down a series of hallways and shown into a living space. It was explained that there were four rooms, with the three women sharing one and the men splitting the other three. The living space had a sink and cabinet with snacks along one wall, and off the main room was a shared bathroom with a handful of shower stalls and toilets. They were given an hour to unpack their meager possessions and acquaint themselves with the space. Red didn't have anything of her own beyond her signing pen, which now sat on the table by her bed, but she would have liked to run her fingers over the comforting words next to her bedside one last time.

No one needed fifteen minutes, let alone the full hour, and then it was back to training.

The first night, once everyone had returned to the suite after a packed day of training and classes, there was a knock on the door and a new trainer entered.

"Most evenings from here on out, you all will have two hours to relax wherever you wish within your suite, and then I will be back to lock you into your rooms."

"Locking us in? Are we children? Why don't you give us a warm glass of milk and tuck us in at bedtime while you're at it." The dark-haired man from breakfast scoffed.

The trainer shrugged, looked pointedly at the clock, and left.

Red felt a hand on her arm and turned to see Green standing at her side.

"Can I help you?" she asked.

"I really need a shower," Green murmured with a worried glance at the largest group of men across the room.

Red knew what she meant—several of the men had already made suggestive comments to her. From what she gathered, the trials process for men was much longer and more grueling than for women, and it sounded like they hadn't had feminine company in a while.

"Do you want me to keep lookout?" Red asked.

Green nodded her head vigorously. "I can return the favor if you want."

"I think I'll take you up on that, thanks."

They waited until no one else was using the communal bathrooms and showered without incident. Once they were done, it was almost time to be locked into their rooms, so Red and Green excused themselves from the predatory eyes of the men in the main room and retreated to the relative safety of their bedroom.

The next day, they repeated the same routine, and Red dared to hope things wouldn't be as bad as she'd originally thought. However, the night of the third day a wrench was thrown into the new routine when no one stopped by to lock their door.

Blue waited thirty minutes past their previous curfew and then stood from where she'd been lounging on her bed. "Well, I think our introduction time is up. I'm going to go back out to the main room and entertain any man who wants to join me."

"Introductory time? What are you talking about?" Green asked.

"Oh, that's right, I forgot that this is your first time at this stage, Green. Red, this is your first time in the trials at all, right?"

"That's right," Red said.

Blue checked her hair in the mirror and put her hands on her hips. "Well, then let me give both of you newbies a piece of advice. This is my third time in the trials and my second time at this stage, and take it from me: the only way you get past this point is to make as many alliances as possible with those guys out there. Pure and simple, it's a popularity contest. We've had the first two days for everyone to get to know each other, and now it's a free-for-all."

"You've heard what they've been saying about us. If you go out there, they'll know the door has stayed unlocked for sure, and who knows what they'll do," Green said.

Blue shrugged. "I don't care. It's been too long since I slept with a man, so I'll be more than willing to take care of whatever needs they may have. Maybe you should think about doing the same—it might be better for your gladiator chances.

Green frowned. "What do you mean?"

"They obviously put us here to see what kind of team we can command. Three women and nine men—they're seeing what groups form. Men are dumb, and I have every intention of doing whatever I can to get them to bond with me and follow me. I don't know about you two, but I personally don't enjoy this process and want to be done, no matter what it takes."

Green looked over at Red after Blue left, "Are you going too?"

Red shook her head and shifted her weight on the bed so that she could better lean back against the wall. "Saban-40 and group dynamics or no, I have no interest in any of the guys out there. I'll focus on staying professional and keeping hormones out of it."

Green swallowed and looked at the door as a chorus of hoots and whistles echoed from the living room. "The door is unlocked. What if they decide to come in here?"

Inspired by the clay shard that had been left in her previous room, Red reached over to the glass water pitcher on the side table, wrapped it in a spare blanket, and threw it on the ground. She took the largest shard of glass and set it on her bed.

"A woman with a weapon is safer than one with none," she said as she handed the second-largest shard to Green.

Despite her outer bravado, Red didn't sleep that night, choosing to keep vigil on her bed. The walls were thin, and she tried not to listen to the sounds that Blue or her male companions were making, and instead focused her attention inwards to ponder her four words.

It was much later when Blue entered with her clothes in her hands.

"Still up?" Blue asked.

"Can't sleep."

"Hope I wasn't too loud. You know, there were plenty of guys. You could have joined and had your own fun."

"I'll pass."

Blue nodded to where Green slept. "For someone who'd been so worried, she's sleeping well."

"I know," Red said, unable to completely stifle her tone of disapproval.

"Well, I've satisfied all the appetites that I could for today and believe that I've earned my rest," Blue said as she changed into her sleeping clothes, lay on her bed, and blew out her candle, plunging the room into darkness.

"Goodnight," Red said, still sitting upright on her bed.

She waited several minutes before deciding she wouldn't be able to sleep well with the door unlocked. Now that all three of them were in the room, she got up from the bed and listened by the door. When she was sure it was silent in the room beyond, she opened the door as quietly as she could and padded in her bare feet to the living area, where she paused, alert and on edge. The only light came from the moon shining through the window, and the room appeared empty. Red tiptoed to one of the wooden chairs placed haphazardly around the table and grabbed it before walking back to her room.

She was halfway across the space when she heard the scuff of a footstep down the opposite hallway. Red froze, afraid that any movement would give her away.

A man stepped into the main room. His short blond hair stood in tufts, and he carried a water pitcher in his hand—she guessed to refill it from the large water receptacle by the front door. Most of the men already had their own gladiator names, and while Red was still rather fuzzy as to who was named what, she believed his was Helios.

Despite her best efforts to remain invisible, Helios filled his water pitcher and turned around to look straight at her.

Red mustered a self-assured and dignified expression, even as her heart seemed to beat out of her chest. They stared at each other for a moment, and then Helios nodded, raised the pitcher of water in greeting, and returned to his hallway.

Once she was back in the room and had wedged the wooden chair under the doorknob, Red breathed a sigh of relief and climbed into bed.

Despite the added security of the chair, her sleep that night was disturbed. At one point, she heard Blue get out of bed and walk across the room. Red thought that Blue was probably just having a midnight bathroom break, but it didn't stop her from tensing her muscles, ready to leap up at a moment's notice if Blue tried to attack her.

Unfortunately, Blue's motives appeared much more insidious, and Red listened as Blue found the chair, moved it away, cracked the door open, and returned to bed. Red's first panicked inclination was to get up and replace the chair before reason took over and she decided to wait and see what happened, if anything. It was a calculated risk, but no one else knew about her glass shard, and Red was confident in her ability to defend herself with it.

Thankfully, nothing happened, and early the next morning Blue got up and replaced the chair.

"Do that again and I'll lock you out of the room next time," Red said once Blue had gotten back in bed.

"Try it, and I'll break down the door. In fact, I'm only a weak woman. I may have to bring the two biggest, most aggressive guys that I can find to help me get back in, and I don't think you want to be the one to give them the payment they'll demand."

"Is that why you took the chair away and opened the door? For a payment advance?"

"And what if it was? What are you going to do about it? You don't have your abilities, so I'd be very careful if I was you." Blue stood from her bed and tossed her hair over her shoulder. "Anyways, I'm going to shower. After the fun I had last night, I was too tired to do much, and no one likes a dirty girl."

The days passed in a blur of activity and sleepless nights, although Red and Green managed to work out an uneasy agreement to take watches during showers and at night. A full week later, the trainers came to escort everyone to their scheduled classes and training, separating the group into genders. Red and the two other women were led to a different room and told to sit in three wooden chairs before Green was taken to the next room. After another fifteen minutes, denoted by the ticking of a clock in the corner, the door opened and Blue was summoned.

The bells in the center of the compound tolled at the half hour mark. The door opened once more and one of the Tiber aides told Red to enter.

The room was plain, with only a wooden table and two chairs for furnishings. A small window overlooked the back corner of the training center, although it was placed in such a way that the bright Italian sun did not filter through. On the opposite side of the table from Red sat a tall, lanky man with dark brown hair and a thin face.

"Sit down and look into the evaluator's eyes as long as you can. Do not speak," the aide said before stepping out.

She did as she was told and sat in the wooden chair on her side of the table. When Red looked into the brown eyes of the evaluator, she noticed first the bags underneath them, and then the worn expression on his face.

Looking so intimately into his eyes made her uncomfortable, but Red resolved to not avert her gaze. She knew Green and Blue had each lasted fifteen minutes, and she refused to break sooner. After what felt like an eternity, the man ran his fingers through his hair, pulled gently, and left.

It was well past the hour mark when the aide escorted Red out of the room.

"Who was that?" she asked as the aide led her back to the suite.

"Viewer."

"Why was he there? What did he do?"

"He's an Abled who can see everything about you just by looking into your eyes. All your past thoughts, emotions, the events that happened to you... everything. Since he first appeared five years ago, he's been very helpful in identifying the best matches for teams, and also who has the best chance of making the cut."

"I see."

When she walked into the suite she shared with the others, the atmosphere was tense, and Red was immediately on guard. Everyone was sitting around the room, but Green and two of the men were missing.

"Where's Green?" Red asked.

Blue shrugged. "She washed out and was taken away,"

"And two of the men?"

"Same thing with them, I guess. When I got back, they were gone and the trainers aren't saying anything."

Lunch was the usual chicken and barley soup with bread and cheese, and that afternoon they had their normal regimen of weapons training, Abled classes, and conditioning. The classes were designed to give them all a basic education about Ableds, abilities, and how individual and group dynamics worked. Every now and then, something that was said in one of the Abled classes would make the back of Red's head tingle, as if an idea were trying to fight its way free—but it was always a fleeting feeling that she was never able to fully grasp.

After a full day of classes and training, Red was exhausted, and despite her best efforts to not think about it, she missed Green's company. The other woman's bubbly personality had been irritating at times, but Red much preferred it to the constant attention-seeking behavior of Blue.

That night she hardly slept. She hadn't forgotten how Blue had taken the chair away from the door, and she didn't trust the other woman to play fairly. Before she went to bed, she took an extremely quick shower and missed Green again. She hadn't realized how soothing it was to have a lookout until she was on her own and neither the bathroom nor shower doors locked.

The next day, during one of their classes, Red found herself nodding off. Thankfully, the teacher hadn't noticed, but she recognized that she couldn't focus due to lack of sleep. She'd been getting only the bare minimum of sleep with Green's help, and the night before had pushed her over the edge.

At lunch, Helios, the blond man with the spiky hair, sat next to her and struck up a conversation. It wasn't totally out of the ordinary; Red had made small talk with everyone in the group at one time or another. However, after a few minutes, he leaned closer to her.

"You're not sleeping well, I take it?"

Red frowned. "What would give you that idea?"

"I saw you nodding off in class."

"I didn't think I was that obvious."

"You weren't, but I've been watching you."

She raised an eyebrow at him, and he grinned. "I've been watching everyone, but particularly you women. Blue's made no secret of the fact that it's not her first time in the trials process and that you're the newcomer. Even if she hadn't said anything, it'd be obvious—usually you look like you're soaking up everything you can."

"Isn't that normal?"

"Not really. Most of us spent a good amount of time fighting for other, lesser recruitment centers before coming here. In fact, I took the memory drug two years ago. That's quite a bit of time to relearn a lot. You must have been pretty fresh from taking it when you came here."

Red nodded. "My first memories are waking up in the barracks for the trials. I don't remember anything before that."

"I knew it. You've done well for someone so fresh. That brings me back to my question—why are you having trouble sleeping? Is the stress wearing you down?"

"Not stress from the training. More that I can't trust Blue not to stab me in the back."

"What do you mean?"

Red paused to look around and consider what she should tell Helios. He'd been one of the quiet ones and hadn't joined in the ribald remarks of the small group led by Thunder, the dark-haired angry man who was a permanent fixture in Blue's orbit.

"How do I know that I can trust you?" she finally asked.

Helios chuckled. "You can't. At least, not long term. However, right now you can trust my motives. I'm here to win, to be deemed the strongest of the men, if not the strongest overall. To accomplish that, I have to side with the strongest female."

"And if you don't?"

"This wasn't a good day for you to be dozing off; we just covered this in class. The tests that accurately quantify the concentrations of the Saban-40 pheromone are expensive and hard to get, and even if you can get them, they're not very precise. What's the difference between a dark red and a very dark red? Not much. However, that small distinction could be the difference between a champion and someone who never makes it out of the unsanctioned matches. Fighters are expensive. That's why places like the Tiber are in such demand: to filter out the chaff. At this stage of the trials, they've sorted men and women into groups of relative strength, and now they're pitting us against each other to see who comes out on top. In the case of you women, that means they're looking at how many followers you can pull compared to your competition. In my case, and the case of anyone else with a Y chromosome, they're testing to see if we can recognize who has the strongest Saban-40 concentrations."

"Isn't that easy for you then? Just choose the woman everyone else is going with. How would they know any better?"

"Oh, trust me, they've got their ways. Plus, they're also testing our loyalty. Saban-40 is a big part, but it's not everything and it wouldn't be very smart to put wishy-washy Ableds into the ring of the small leagues, let alone the arena of the big tournaments. Yes, they need their queen bees, but what is a queen if her workers don't recognize her?

"Ableds of similar power also tend to flock together. In that case, all the mediocre Ableds would join together, and if I were to join them, it would make me seem mediocre as well."

"Sounds like a lot of guessing and leaving things up to chance."

"Welcome to the gladiator games. It's definitely an art, not a science."

"So why tell me all this?"

"Like I said, I've been watching you and I see things that you don't."

"Things like what?"

"Like the fact that for the past several nights, when you and Green went back to your room to sleep, so did several men. Others take their pleasure from Blue, if she's offering it, and then retire as well. Very few stayed with Blue beyond satisfying their own needs."

"I see."

"No, you don't, because last night when you retired, the pattern wasn't broken. Up until then, I wasn't sure if it was you or Green or a combination of the two, but now I think I've picked my candidate."

"For someone who just said that he didn't want to follow the mediocre crowd, it sounds like you're all about the popularity contest."

"Like I said, it's an artform, and this isn't my first time in the trials."

"You're staking a lot on bedtime."

"Perhaps, but that just means that I need you to follow through." He paused to eat another chunk of bread and cheese and chewed thoughtfully before speaking again. "Tell me, why aren't you sleeping well? I need you to be in top form, so help me to help you."

Red sighed and told Helios about Blue removing the makeshift chair lock the week before and cracking the door open, and what she'd said the next morning. He nodded along, his lips pursed in thought.

"Now that it's just she and I alone, I don't trust her not to pull something. Without my abilities, I'm too vulnerable on my own."

"You could always bring someone else into your bed. That would provide more protection," he said.

Red narrowed her eyes at him and leaned away. "And you're volunteering for such a post? Was everything that you just said a lead-up to such a proposition?"

"Of course not."

"How can I know for sure?"

"Many reasons. First and foremost, I don't find women attractive, so I have no interest in your body or anything physical, though I take it by your response that you wouldn't entertain that option even if I did."

She unclenched her jaw, but still shook her head.

"In that case, I suppose the other option would be for you to have a guard outside the door. It won't protect you from Blue if she tries to slit your throat, but we can keep any of her followers from trying something nefarious."

"We?"

A smile played at the corner of Helios' mouth. "I'm only the spokesperson. The others have decided not to reveal themselves yet for various reasons, but this trial has been rather unusual. With Green gone,

I think the end isn't too far away. Battlelines will be drawn soon enough, and I need you to be in top form for a challenge."

"A challenge?" Red echoed.

"Yes, a challenge. You really weren't paying any attention at all today, were you? When two Ableds of different strengths come in contact, somewhere deep in their lizards brains they compare their different concentrations of Saban-40 and establish a pecking order. Outside of the gladiator games it's not a big deal because other factors, such as personality, wealth, and age play larger roles in social determination.

"A challenge happens when Ableds don't like where they are in the pecking order, of if two Ableds of similar strengths come into contact and have to establish an order. There are different types of challenges, but the main thing to know is that once one is initiated, the person who backs down or submits is the loser."

"I think I remember hearing about that during the last phase of the trials." Red frowned. "They were talking about the difference between men and women or something, but didn't elaborate on the challenges then."

"Women generally have higher Saban-40 concentrations and thus have more powerful abilities despite being physically weaker."

"That's something I never quite understood—why not just have a team made up of women? Couldn't they just win over everyone else?"

"It's not quite so simple, but that's exactly why strong gladiators who are dependable and loyal are in high demand. A team of men loyal to their queen could steamroll a team made up of only women before the women could influence them enough to make a difference."

Red nodded. "So a strong queen is important."

"It's vital. A good queen can hold her own in the arena, has a strong enough influence to fight off the effects of other queens, and is charismatic enough to keep her followers loyal to her. That's also why you won't often see a direct challenge between two queens in a fight; if one loses the challenge, odds are her team will turn on her and recognize their new leader. In real life, it comes across as people preferring one friend over another. In the arena, it means a lost match, and possible death for the queen. Of course, like I said, multiple factors can come into play with Abled team dynamics. Sometimes a queen can lose a challenge and still retain her followers, but it's rare. Any other questions?"

Red shook her head. "That's a lot to process."

"There's a lot of nuance to these things that the classes won't teach you—and even the best of queens can't do everything on her own. That's why a good second-in-command is so important. Any good second will watch his queen's back and help rally the troops."

"A second in command? Is that what you're aiming for here?"

Helios smiled. "Usually, the second-in-command is the most powerful male on a team. If I'm your second, and you're the strongest, it makes me look promising. Without giving too much away, my abilities, while strong, aren't the most suitable for the arena, so it's vital I make up for their disadvantages by other means. If a queen is an investment on a house, a second-in-command is an investment in the house's security system."

"So you want to prove that you're a strong protector and can keep your queen secure." Red frowned. "Won't guarding me at night impact your sleep, and thus your performance?"

"Don't worry about that side of things, I've got it covered. What do you say?"

For the first time in the conversation, Red glanced over at Blue. The other woman was laughing with Thunder and letting him feed her a bite of his bread before she turned to the man sitting at her other side, brushing her fingers along his arm while asking him a question.

"I think I'll take you up on the offer," Red said.

"Great, leave everything else to me."

"You're asking me to trust you about an awful lot when I hardly know you."

"Like I said, don't trust me, trust my motives. I want you to win. I need you to win because it's my ticket to the next phase of my gladiator career."

"Unless you're a double agent for Blue."

Helios sipped at his drink. "I'm not, and being so disloyal would be unheard of and practically disqualify me from the trials outright, but you're quite suspicious. Good. That will serve you well."

At the end of the busy day, when they got back to the room, a trainer was waiting for them in the living space of the suite.

"Hello, everyone. We have decided to change the room assignments. From here on out, Blue and Red will each have a room to themselves.

Don't worry, your things have already been moved. You remaining men can figure out your sleeping arrangements however you wish. I suggest that you all rest up. Tomorrow will be a trial day, and you'll need everything you've got."

"A trial day when we don't even have our abilities yet?" Blue complained.

"Probably the same reason that they took our abilities away in the first place—they want to test our strength and skills without them," Red said.

"You think that you know everything, don't you, newbie?" Blue scoffed.

Red shrugged and sat by the window overlooking a small, shaded courtyard. "You're the one who asked the question. Don't ask if you don't want an answer."

"Watch yourself, Red. There's only two of us. It'd be a shame if something happened to you that prevented you from continuing."

"Take your empty threats somewhere else." Red had seen Blue's fighting skills and abilities during their recruit trials, and while the other woman wasn't chopped liver, Green had definitely been stronger, and Red knew she was stronger than Green by far.

"Now, now, let's not say anything like that, Blue," Helios said.

Red noticed several glances pass among the men.

"Oh? Have you made your choice then, Helios?" Blue asked.

"I'd just appreciate that you don't disqualify yourself so I actually have a choice to make."

Apparently Blue accepted his answer, as she turned away to talk to the small group of men in her orbit. With Helios' new insight fresh in her mind, Red looked around. It was true that a majority of the men were seated around Blue, but Red noticed for the first time that not all of them were actually paying attention to what the other woman was saying, and that Blue had chosen a seat in the center of the room, naturally placing herself in the middle of everyone.

Emboldened by Helios's words, and wanting to know exactly where she stood in the group, Red moved from her lone seat by the window to the table by the sink, on the opposite side of the room from Blue. On her way, she grabbed a small stack of papers from a desk sitting against one wall, and started folding paper airplanes to keep herself entertained. She set the stack of papers in the center of the table as an open invitation to the others.

After a few minutes, several of the men either had moved closer or joined her at the table.

"Paper airplanes? What are you? Twelve?" Blue said haughtily.

Red shrugged. "I don't think so, but my memory was wiped, so who knows?"

Blue scoffed again but didn't say anything else. After a few minutes, she stretched lazily and looked around the room. "Well, I'm planning on taking advantage of my new bedroom. Anyone who wants a tour is more than welcome to join," she said as she stood and walked to her room.

"I call dibs, lads. You'll have to wait until after I'm done to have your fill," Thunder said with a wink at the others before following Blue.

Red raised an eyebrow but didn't say anything until Thunder had shut Blue's door. Then, in an effort to drown out the noises issuing from Blue's room, she turned to her nearest companion, a large man called Hog and started up a conversation.

As she talked, Red took note of the style of paper airplanes that her companions made. Helios's were complex, and he took time to decorate each and cut the wings into intricate designs. Hog, on the other hand, seemed content to make the most basic airplane and then throw it as hard as he could. It was hard to tell with the other men; most lounged about but didn't move from their seats to either go to Blue's room or to join Red at the table.

After they'd worked through the stack of papers, Red glanced at the clock and decided to call it a night.

Red showered quickly before wishing everyone goodnight and returning to her new room to finish her routine. After her evening reflections, and just as she was preparing to get settled into bed, she realized that now she had a room all to herself and could ensure her door was wedged shut. All that she lacked was a suitable wedge.

She crept over to the door and listened for any noises outside. When she didn't hear so much as a whisper of conversation, she opened the door softly. She hadn't forgotten what Helios had said earlier, but she still felt vulnerable in the thin sleeping clothes she wore.

As she stepped out from the doorway, she almost tripped over something in the darkness. A large hand encircled her ankle, holding her fast, and Red's heart skipped a beat in fear.

"Red, is that you?" Hog asked.

"Yes," she squeaked.

"Ah, sorry about that. I wasn't expecting you to leave. Helios said you wouldn't."

"I was just getting a chair to lock my door with," she said.

There was a pause before Hog spoke again. "That's not a bad idea. Let me get that for you."

"Are you one of the men Helios was talking about?" Red asked when he'd brought a chair from the living room for her.

"Yeah, he told me not to be obvious about it because he didn't want Blue to challenge you out of fear, or to force the trainer's hand yet. Something about proving what we can do first. I don't know what he's got in mind, but he's been through enough trials to know the game."

"If he's been in so many trials, why hasn't he passed them yet? What makes you think he's giving good advice?"

"The fact he's even qualified multiple times for the Tiber trials says tons. A lot of people wash out after the first one or can't stay ranked high enough to come back. I know you're new, so you probably don't realize it, but being able to get this far in the trials is an honor that can make any mediocre fighter's career. It's not uncommon for those who have been in their fourth or fifth trial to go on and become a champion somewhere else. The training here is top-notch, as are the classes, and even if we wash out, it gives us the edge in the lesser leagues."

"I see. Well, thank you for the chair, but you really don't have to stay here all night. I'm sure I'll be fine now."

"I appreciate the thought, but Helios was right: you're our ticket out of here, and I'm not going to be the one to let the golden goose get slaughtered on my watch."

"If you're sure, then I won't stop you."

"Thank you, ma'am."

Chapter Seventeen

Red got a full night's sleep for the first time in several days and woke up feeling refreshed and ready to face the world. After a light breakfast, the group piled into two carriages and was taken into the forest for their first real trial.

Once they arrived, the trainer waited for everyone to gather in a circle and gestured at a path approximately twenty feet wide that led up a tall hill to an old stone fort. "In this trial, you'll attack that rocky outcropping which is being guarded by soldiers. To win, you must gain control of the fort."

One of the training aides unrolled a blanket, revealing a wide range of weapons.

"Here are the weapons at your disposal. Take your pick," the trainer said.

Red surveyed the weapons, unsure of which one to wield. There was a plethora of knives, swords, and ranged weapons, but they all felt weird in her hand. No one else seemed to have difficulty choosing a weapon, and she was soon left alone while the others discussed strategy several feet away.

Her hand hovered over a pair of swords before she withdrew it; she had a hard enough time keeping track of her form with one sword, and it would be foolish to think she could handle two. Her concentration was broken by a shout from Hog, who'd taken a few steps down the path. Judging from the handful of arrows and rocks littering the path and the rueful way Hog was rubbing one of his shins, Red assumed the soldiers guarding the hill hadn't taken too kindly to his curiosity.

She shook her head and grabbed one of the maces. It was on the lighter side and still felt odd in her hand, but as she tested it with a couple of swings she decided it would do for the moment.

"Nice of you to join us; we were just finalizing the plans," Blue said snidely when Red walked over and stood next to Helios.

"What kind of plans?"

"Those three are going to charge forward to distract the guards while the rest of us circle around the back and flank them," Blue said with a gesture at Helios, Hog, and another man.

"Obviously I'm not a fan of this plan and would prefer to not get turned into a pin cushion today," Hog said.

Red shook her head. "We don't know how many men our opponents have, and splitting the team up will greatly weaken us."

"What are you talking about? This is a great plan. They definitely won't be expecting a flank attack," Blue said.

"I'm not going to let you sacrifice Helios and Hog, Blue. Don't think I don't see what you're doing—they supported me yesterday, and now you're trying to get them injured and removed from the competition," Red said.

"Stop your whining, Red. While you were trying to pick your favorite toy, I gave them the orders. We already have a plan in place, now they just have to execute it," Blue said.

"I disagree. It sounds to me like you're only sending them off to be the distraction on the front while you and the others sneak around and take the glory for yourselves. We're in this as a team, and we should either all win or all lose as a team," Red said.

"You've got to be kidding me. This is a trial; it's every man for themselves here. Blue obviously recognizes who the strongest is, kid, so let her do her thing," Thunder interjected.

Red looked at the group of three Blue had ordered to take the front and shook her head. "I'm not going to condone those orders. Blue, if you feel so strongly about a sneak attack, you can take that route, but anyone who disagrees is welcome to follow me."

"Suit yourself. It's your funeral, and when we win this trial, it'll be your lost opportunity," Blue said. She waved Thunder and the remaining three men to the side, and they faded into the forest.

Red breathed a sigh of relief and turned back to the group, consisting of Helios, Hog, and a gladiator whose name she now remembered was Spike. "Okay, does anyone have a better plan than 'charge straight up the hill and wave your swords'?"

Hog shrugged. "Strategy isn't really my strong suit." Spike nodded in agreement.

"What does our leader think?" Helios asked.

Red frowned, but as she thought through the situation, she felt a glimmer of inspiration, and a hazy plan formed. Perhaps Blue hadn't been all that crazy to think that a frontal attack might be the way to go.

"They're not really aiming for us, are they?" she asked Helios.

"How should I know?"

"Because you've done these trials more than any of us."

"That doesn't mean I know the minds of the trial-makers. These trials are dangerous, you know that."

"Yes, so I've heard," Red muttered. She looked down at her armor and the weapon in her hand. "Hog, you were the one that got attacked. Can you do me a favor and walk back into the clearing that leads up to the fort?"

Hog shook his head. "No way. I'm not about to get killed for no reason."

"I understand. Well, I suppose good leaders shouldn't ask their subordinates to do something they're not willing to do themselves," Red said before hoisting the mace over her shoulder and trotting out to the path.

"Are you crazy?" Hog yelled behind her; Helios followed swiftly with a "Red, stop, come back!"

She ignored them, and before they could stop her she was at the point of the path where Hog had been attacked. As soon as she passed some kind of imaginary line, several stones were launched her way. Red held the mace in front of her face as a makeshift shield and the projectiles bounced off the shoulder of her leather armor with little more than a scratch. She took a couple more steps forward and was rewarded with an arrow skating off the armor on her thigh.

It was then that she was jerked backwards and found herself on the ground looking up at the sky.

Helios entered her field of vision, his mouth twisted in a snarl and his green eyes narrowed. "What do you think you're doing? You're going to get yourself killed."

"Am I?"

"Uh, yes, you are," Hog said.

Red hoisted herself to her feet and gestured up the hill to the stone fort. "I don't think I am. In fact, I don't think they want to kill us or hurt us at all." She turned to Hog. "You said last night that anyone who qualifies for these trials is automatically considered more powerful—and the further they make it, the more prestige they get, right?"

"Right."

"Which means that their contracts automatically increase in value?"

He nodded.

"So the contract of anyone who makes it to this stage would probably get a pretty good boost?"

"What are you trying to get at? We're wasting time," Spike said.

"This is the end game, right? The final stop before the serious gladiator stuff starts? Why would the trainers risk killing someone now, when they could still have potential or even become a champion after another couple of trials? It doesn't make any sense, and I don't think they actually want to kill us. We're assets right now, assets I'm betting they don't want to lose."

"Then now you're saying we should just charge straight up there? Are you insane? That's just what Blue wants."

Red shook her head. "Even if they're not really trying to kill us, it wouldn't hurt to be cautious. I'd bet they saw Blue and her group split off, so they're probably expecting us to be the diversion, not a full and serious attack. It'd be absolutely crazy to run straight up that fairway and think the four of us could take the fort, especially without abilities."

"You're telling me," Hog grumbled.

"But what if we stuck to the side of the path and used the trees as some protection? If my guess turns out to be true, they won't be trying to aim for the vital parts. It may give us the edge we need to push through and get up there."

"Or it'll get us killed," Helios said.

"No guts, no glory. Do any of you have a better idea? Every minute we wait here is another minute for Blue to figure out a better plan."

Hog and Spike looked at Helios for confirmation. He sucked on his teeth for a moment and shrugged, his mouth set into a grim expression. "It's a crazy plan, and I don't like it, but we really don't have many other available options, so maybe it's crazy enough to work."

Strangely, after they'd braved their way through what felt like a storm of stones and arrows and reached the fort at the top of the hill, they met no resistance.

Red walked forward, drawn through the old ruins to the center of the fort where a stone chair sat against a wall on top of a crumbling dais. The fort guards had withdrawn to line the wall of the plaza and were silent even as the sound of bowstring twangs and shouts could be heard from the other end of the fort, where Red assumed Blue and her team were making their assault. Something in her mind clicked into place, and with the support of her team at her back, even amongst their former enemies, Red boldly strode forward and sat on the throne.

At once, the guards stamped their feet and fell silent.

An armored man stepped forward, removed his helmet to reveal himself as one of their trainers, and stretched his arms out wide. "This concludes the end of the trial. Guards, go round up the others. Red and Red's teammates: your performance has been noted. You may all go back to the carriage and leave for the training center. There is no need to wait for the others in your trial group."

On the way back, as Hog and the others chattered about the trial, Red looked out the window. She felt a hand on her arm and turned to find Helios watching her.

"How did you know?" he asked.

She shrugged. "I just had a feeling."

When they got back to the training center, Helios declared he was going to take a nap, Hog and Spike said they planned on heading to the weapons room before getting a snack, and Red decided to take a shower while the suite was mostly empty. She still didn't necessarily trust Helios, but he'd so far given her no reason to distrust him, and she didn't want to wait until everyone was back and vying for a shower spot.

After a long shower that felt almost luxurious, Red toweled off, changed into clean clothes, and surveyed her face in the mirror. She was excited to see her hair had grown a fraction of an inch and covered her scalp in fuzzy dark curls. She traced the white scar on the left side of her face that ran from her temple down to her chin and wondered once more how she'd gotten it. Behind her, the door opened.

"Sorry, I'm almost done and then you can have the bathroom all to yourself," she said, stepping to the side of the sink with her back to the nearest stall.

"Don't worry about it. You can even join me, if you'd like," Thunder said.

"No, thanks; I'm just finishing up now." She bent forward to towel her head dry and decided to finish her evening routine later, when she wouldn't be disturbed by Blue's man.

Heavy hands grabbed her hips and pulled her roughly back and to the side. Red's first reaction was to freeze; her next was to stand upright and take a step forward and away from Thunder.

He was too strong, and his grip on her hips tightened. He shoved her forward against the sink and pinned her hips with his before forcing a washcloth into her mouth and pushing her face against the mirror.

"Almost done? I don't think so. We're just getting started," he said.

Everything was happening so fast Red didn't have time to think; she only knew that she was in danger. She tried to scream, but the washcloth muffled the sound to a loud hum.

Thunder kept his hand on her neck, and she heard the distinctive sound of a zipper. "You're not the prettiest broad I've ever been with, but I think if I don't look at you too much I can make it work," he grunted as his free hand pawed at her pants.

Red lashed out with her hands but only reached air, and Thunder tightened his grip on her neck. In a last-ditch effort, she angled a kick back, felt her foot hit flesh, and he released his grasp on her briefly. The momentary opening was all she needed, and before Thunder had time to recover, she pulled the washcloth out of her mouth.

"You're going to pay for that. I was going to take it easy on you, but now I'll be sure to make it hurt–" The rest of what he said was cut off when Red screamed at the top of her lungs.

The sudden noise threw Thunder off guard and he shifted his weight just enough to allow Red to shove her hips backwards and hit his groin. He grunted in pain and stepped back. She stomped on his foot and landed a punch directly to his nose as he doubled forward.

Red darted past Thunder to the door. Just as she stepped out, his hand closed on the hem of her shirt—but with a twist of her body she was free and running out into the living space, where everyone was gathered.

Helios stumbled out of his room just as Red ran into the living room. He rubbed his eyes, took one look at her face, and then looked past her at Thunder, who was emerging from the bathroom.

"What's going on?" Hog asked.

"Miss Princess over there doesn't know a good thing when it's sitting right in front of her, or rather, behind her. You'd think that someone who looks like her would have been grateful for the extra attention," Thunder said.

Red took several extra steps away from Thunder and tried to control her breathing and shaking hands, wanting to get as far away from him as possible without giving in to the fear coursing through her veins.

The expression on Helios' face darkened, and Red followed his gaze to Thunder's pants, which were still unzipped. "How dare you," Helios growled.

"No need to be jealous of the girl, Helios. I know these trials are hard for a man of your tastes, but you can't fault us normal people for our needs. Besides, you know how it is: when the lady says jump, you jump," Thunder paused, and a wicked expression crossed his face. "Although maybe that's not the case for you,"

"So did your lady say 'jump' then?" Hog asked.

"And what if she did? You all know that Blue's the strongest."

"Red was the one who won the trial," Hog said.

"Like that means anything," Blue snapped. "I would have won if she hadn't decided to go against my orders. I'm stronger than her, just like I was stronger than Green."

"That's not what I see," Red said.

Blue turned towards her in a fury. "You think you're strong?"

"I know that I am. Well, stronger than you at least."

"You're nothing. If that idiot over there hadn't fumbled in the bathroom, you'd be finished just like Green—another washed-up-trial candidate who couldn't take the heat."

"Didn't Green leave on her own?"

Blue's laugh was cruel. "Leave on her own? Sure, just like you would have 'left on your own' if Thunder had done his job."

"That's what happened to Green? What about the men who left?" Red swallowed down a wave of nausea.

"One of them tried to stop Thunder, so Thunder broke his shoulder and blamed it on the other guy. Told the trainers that the two candidates had gotten into a fight when one of them forced himself on Green, so they were disqualified and Green wasn't in any state to continue."

"The trainers believed him?"

"I can be very persuasive when I choose to be," Thunder said.

"You're despicable. You both are. Despicable and weak."

Blue's expression devolved into a snarl. "Say that again, I dare you."

Red stepped forward until she was an arm's length from Blue. "I said that you're despicable. You're also sad, pathetic, and a sorry excuse for a human being. Weakness and insecurity practically ooze from your skin."

Thunder and another man joined Blue, but Red refused to be intimidated. The way her heart was pounding, she had two options: channel the adrenaline into anger or faint—and she wouldn't give Blue the satisfaction of victory. Out of the corner of her eye, she saw Hog move to stand behind her, joined by Spike, Helios and two of the men who had been on Blue's team and didn't look keen to back her now.

"So what happens next?" one of the men standing behind Red asked.

"Any minute now, the trainers will come to take Blue and Thunder away. I know they don't like to interfere, but these are very serious accusations, and they probably want to protect their investments," Helios said.

"How? They don't know what's been going on."

"I suspect they've got at least one camera in this living space, to see how the group dynamics play out. You suspected so too, didn't you, Blue? That's why you had sex out here in the open, to entice whoever was watching to give you an advantage and overlook certain things. The problem is that now you've overplayed your hand and admitted to engineering what happened to Green."

Blue shrugged. "There isn't a rule against it. This is my last chance in the trials before I wash out due to age, and I'm not afraid to fight dirty to get what I want."

"Well, this is one fight that you aren't going to win. You're done, Blue," Red said.

Blue lashed out and slapped Red across the face. Red responded with a punch to Blue's nose, knocking the other woman to the floor. She heard a scuffle and looked up to see Helios and the other men holding Thunder back.

"Get them out, now. Both of them," she ordered the others.

"Where?" Hog asked.

"Put them outside the front door and lock it behind them. We don't want them or need them here, and we can't trust that Blue won't try to hurt Red if we let her stay," Helios said.

"No, you can't do this. I was supposed to win. You two over there—help me! We had an agreement," Blue said as she was manhandled towards the door, blood streaming down her face from her broken nose.

"You gambled when playing the game, and you lost, Blue. Good luck with the rest of your fighting career; you'll need it," Helios said as he shoved Blue and Thunder out and shut the door behind them.

The remaining group members sat in the living room and looked at each other. The only sound at first was that of Blue sobbing, and then Thunder yelling at her, and finally the two exiled fighters screaming terrible things at each other.

Then, whether the trainers came and removed the two troublemakers or they'd finally screamed themselves hoarse, there was merciful silence.

Red touched her cheek where it still stung from Blue's slap. "So, what happens next?"

Helios shrugged, apparently having used all his words for the day, and another man whose name she didn't remember spoke up. "This isn't my first time either, although it's certainly the most unusual one. In the other trials, the trainers and powers-that-be watched the pairings of men and women. After a couple more mock battles to determine who was the strongest in the groups, they'd make their decision. Now that we've only got you, and there are six of us, I don't know what happens next."

Later, when it was time to eat, the trainer who normally took them to the dining hall instead had everyone sit down.

"Due to unforeseen events, some adjustments to procedure will be made. Thus, there will be two more trials, and then we will announce your final placements."

"What does that mean? Will we have our abilities back?" Hog asked.

The trainer shook his head. "I can't tell you anything more; just know that for better or worse, your trials will soon come to an end."

Chapter Eighteen

Two days later, it was time for the second-to-last trial. The location was once again in a forest somewhere outside Rome. It took most of the day to reach the forest by carriage, leaving Red plenty of time to meditate and reflect.

Once they finally reached the location, the trainer held up her arms and gestured at the entire forest. "Your trial today will be similar to a game you played as children. Red, you have the belt I gave you?"

Red touched the red belt around her waist and nodded.

"Perfect. This game will be a combination of a chase and a race. Red, you'll be in front and given a five-minute head start. Whichever man crosses the finish line with the belt you're currently wearing around your waist will be considered the winner, and the rest of your ranks will be adjusted accordingly. The only rule for this trial is that you men can't attack each other unless your opponent has possession of the belt. This isn't a fight, it's a race."

"How do I win?" Red asked.

The trainer ignored her question. "Everyone, take your places. The racecourse has been marked by the yellow flags. You don't have to stay on course, but take care, it can be easy to get lost in the forest and we won't be sending anyone in after you."

Red took off at a dead sprint when the trainer rang the starting bell, wanting to put as much distance between herself and the men as she could. Once she was in the trees, she slowed down from her sprint to a run, and just as she was starting to get short of breath, she heard the second bell, signaling the start time for the men. The reality of being chased injected a new flood of adrenaline into her veins.

She was the slowest one in the group by far and harbored no doubts about her chances in a head-to-head race. Fortunately, she had a secret advantage: prior to their lineup, the trainer had pulled her aside and handed her a sack containing five small syringes and a roll of paper.

"These are fast-acting sedatives. Each one is enough to knock a man out for the duration of this trial, and this map is a rough description of the course. Use both of them as you see fit."

"But there are six men," Red said.

"I suggest you make your choice carefully as to who deserves to win."

Red jumped over a small log that stretched across the path and shook her head. She had no intention of crowning a man as victor.

She had five syringes and six men chasing her. That meant she'd need to take one man out of the running the old-fashioned way. Helios and Hog had been her two biggest supporters; she would do them the honor of incapacitating them with the syringes so they wouldn't be injured and would still have a chance to compete moving forward.

She had no clue how long the race was, but the rough map told her it would be no quick jaunt, giving her plenty of time and room to work. If she wanted to have the best shot at victory, she'd need to let the pack weed itself out a little.

At the nearest straightaway, Red veered off the path into the underbrush, crouched behind a bush, and stayed still. She calmed her breathing; if she was found at this critical juncture, all her best laid plans would fall to pieces.

The men's race had already spread out, with Helios and one of Blue's former supporters in front and the rest behind them. Hog was in the last group, running almost a full minute behind the leaders, and Red guessed his larger mass made it difficult to maintain speed.

After she'd seen all six men pass, Red stole out from her spot and went hunting.

The back three weren't much difficulty; due to Hog's huffing and puffing, Red was able to sneak up behind him and his nearest companion and stab each of them with a syringe before they knew what was happening. A blow to the side of the head with a thick tree branch easily took out the third man.

That left three others: Helios and two men who'd supported Blue until her ousting. To rid herself of man number four, Red used her map to cut through a wide curve and get ahead of him. She then leaped from the brush as he ran past, hurling a rock to his leg that produced a sickening crunch. He'd be out of the running for sure, and Red still had two syringes.

It took Red longer than she'd expected to catch up to the fourth man on the course, which meant she was nearing the end. She slowed down to check her map and calculated that the finish line was half a mile away.

"Have you gotten lost? Mind if I help you?" Helios asked as he stepped out from behind a tree.

"No, thanks; I think I've got it figured out, although I appreciate the thought," she said. Red was glad she'd already sequestered her special belt in the bag with the syringes so it wouldn't be easily stolen or torn away.

"Look, Red, I feel like we've grown a real connection, and I'd love to continue our partnership. You see, with you as the top female in our group, whoever you give the belt to will probably be considered the top male. Depending on what the sponsors want, that could mean we wouldn't be separated. You're a very special woman, and I don't want to lose you. In fact, what I actually want is to pursue this connection and see what kind of relationship comes from it," Helios said.

Red frowned. "You told me that you weren't attracted to women."

"I didn't think I was, but you changed that."

"Really? What's your favorite part of me?"

"Your beautiful hair. It looks so soft, and I've wanted to run my fingers through it for days."

Red stepped closer to him, putting herself within arm's reach. "You've been such a big help to me during this trial," she whispered.

"I've just wanted you to succeed. I knew you were different from the beginning, and I did the best I could to support you."

"Are you sure?"

"I couldn't be any surer. Please, Red, tell me you feel the same way."

She smiled. "Here, I propose a trade. A kiss for a belt. One physical object for another."

"I can do that." Helios put his hands around her waist. As he leaned forward and closed his eyes, Red plunged a syringe into the meatiest part of his shoulder.

Helios jerked in surprise, and Red took the opportunity to step out of his grasp.

"Why?" he asked.

Red raised one of her eyebrows. "Just a tip for next time: when a woman asks you what you like most about her, you might want to go with something that's a bit less masculine than a buzzcut."

Helios grinned and swayed on his feet, the sedative already taking effect. "I thought it was worth betting you'd forgotten."

"It was a commendable effort. Where's your buddy?"

"Up ahead. He's planning on waiting at the finish line to ambush whoever you gave the belt to." Helios said before crumpling to the ground.

"I see." Red grabbed her last syringe and slung the bag containing the belt around her shoulder before stepping around his body. "Have a nice nap, Helios. It looks like it's time for me to go win a race."

Chapter Nineteen

Red and the others walked into the sand-filled training arena. There were four men left; two had been cut after the race trial the week before due to poor performance and injuries. Now it was only her, Helios, Hog, Spike, and one of Blue's supporters who had somehow made the cut.

They were led to the center of the Tiber arena by a new trainer and stood in a line. Across the arena in the stands was the head trainer, Silver, who'd introduced herself to Red after the race trial. Silver was in deep conversation with the man sitting next to her and hardly spared a glance for the recruits.

At the end of the arena, several men dressed in suits were milling around the box seats. One of them whistled and catcalled the fighters. Red ignored him.

"Abled fighters, this is your final trial. Are you ready?" the trainer asked.

Red and the men all answered in the affirmative.

"This trial will be a battle royale between Red and the rest of you, to gauge your fighting skills, abilities, and assess your overall potential. If I were you, I'd do the best I could, because the men in the box seats are either owners of the top training centers in Rome or potential sponsors."

Red activated her abilities. After the race trials, the antidote to the ability-blocking medication was added to their food, and everyone's abilities had slowly returned over the course of the week. She'd missed the added dimension of sensation that her energy sense gave her, and Red reveled in the tingling that covered her hands as they were enveloped by red light.

"Red, please step away from the others."

She did as she was asked and turned to face her opponents, mentally categorizing their abilities and prioritizing them as threats. Helios could make any part of his body shine like the sun, Hog was extremely strong, Spike could touch someone and send their blood sugar levels out of control, and the last man, Candor, had an uncanny ability to know what his opponents were most insecure about, and to use his knowledge to break their concentration and will to fight.

Of the four, Helios was the best fighter and Hog the most obvious threat—but Red had been on the receiving end of Spike's ability in a training match, and she'd seen the way Candor's abilities had affected Hog when they'd last sparred.

She took a deep breath and nodded at the trainer. She was ready.

The trainer walked to the edge of the arena and lifted his hand before blaring the air horn to signal the start of the trial.

Immediately, Hog rushed Red. She created a shield, and he charged headfirst into it and promptly knocked himself out cold.

Helios, Spike, and Candor all glanced at each other and spread out around her. Judging by their cooperation, Red guessed they were content to work together until she was removed from the equation and they could battle it out alone.

She turned in a circle, careful to keep her senses open and her feet moving, knowing it was only a matter of time before someone broke the standoff.

"Well, get on with it!" One of the sponsors called from his box seat. "Take care of the girl and let the real show begin!"

Red growled. For a sport that placed such importance on the strength of its women and their influence on Abled dynamics, no one seemed to understand she was more than just a beautiful dog collar to keep the men in line, or a pretty weathervane to provide insight into the strength of her male counterparts.

She would show those pretentious men in their fancy suits what she was capable of. Helios had told her the night before that the trials occurred once, maybe twice a year, and that even making it to the final stage didn't mean anything if a sponsor didn't agree to foot part of the bill.

Bird. Ring. Win. Family. If she wanted the chance to be a full-fledged gladiator and regain her memories, she needed to impress a sponsor.

Red fed energy into her hands and launched herself towards Candor. He was the easiest of the three remaining men, and if she could incapacitate him before he used his abilities, it would decrease the chance of him distracting her at a critical moment.

Candor wasn't ready for her, and with a swing of her arm Red's mace made contact. It was a lucky hit that dislocated his shoulder and knocked him off his feet before he had a chance to say anything.

She could feel Spike and Helios close in behind her and raised a shield to separate them as she turned to face the closest attacker.

While Helios was forced to wait outside the shield, Red and Spike circled each other. His spear kept her from rushing in unprepared, and she knew better than to try and jump in the air; if she did, she could maintain a weak shield around her body, but not the larger bubble that separated them from Helios. Spike jabbed at her wildly, and when he overextended himself Red took the opportunity to duck under his spear, rush forward, and crack his knee with her mace.

Spike dropped his spear and fell to the ground; judging by the sound his knee made when her mace hit it, Red guessed he wouldn't be walking any time soon. She stepped away from him, dropped her shield, and readied herself to face Helios.

Helios' body grew brighter, no doubt in an attempt to blind her. Red closed her eyes and relied on her energy sense to let her know where he was. Fortunately for her, the energy from the bright light helped her to pinpoint his exact position even when her eyes were closed.

It wasn't a perfect fight, and Helios managed to land several glancing blows, but eventually Red saw an opening. She charged, swept his feet from under him, and followed him to the ground where her burning hand hovered just above his throat.

Red looked to the trainer who'd been running the trial for further direction.

"Okay, that's enough. Everyone into formation, on the double," the trainer said.

Red promptly returned to her feet. Helios lined up next to her, while the other two were still groaning on the ground.

As she waited, Hog lumbered to his feet behind her. She guessed he hadn't heard the trainer and thought the trial was still on. Red stopped herself from turning to face him, recognizing that she might be able to use his lack of knowledge to display her skills.

"Hog is sneaking up behind us. Trust me and act normal," she said to Helios under her breath.

She saw Helios nod in acknowledgement from the corner of her eye. The trainer was checking over Candor and Spike and wasn't aware of the new development; music playing over the speakers in the arena masked the sound of Hog's approach.

Hog made his move when he was within arm's reach of Red. He yelled and lashed out at her head with a fist the size of a roasted chicken. Red could feel the speed and power with which his fist swung towards her, and knew if she let it make contact she'd have a severe concussion.

With perfect timing, Red turned at the last second and caught his fist in her hand, letting her shield absorb the force before returning it to him in a flash of red light.

Hog yelped and clutched his hand, jerking it out of her grasp.

"The trainer said we were done. I won, Hog; it's over," Red said.

"Hog, I said that's enough! No more attacking. You either, Red!" the trainer called out, having been alerted to the situation by Hog's yell. Red ignored the useless trainer and let the red light dissipate as she stepped closer to Hog.

"Mind if I take a look? I'm sorry if I hurt you," she said.

Hog released his hand and held it out to her. She took it and examined it. "Did it burn you?"

"Not too bad, just like how a cup of hot coffee would burn if you try to pick it up before it's cooled enough."

"I'm glad," she said as she finished her cursory examination. While his hand was quite red, no blisters appeared to be forming and the skin looked otherwise good. Red released Hog's hand, turned to Helios, and shook her head to let him know that Hog was okay and wouldn't need any further medical attention.

Later, Red, Helios, and Hog relaxed in the living room of their suite while they waited for results. There was a knock at the door, but before Red could get her hopes up, the door opened to reveal a bandaged Spike and Candor.

"Don't look so glum, Helios. I'm sure whoever's in charge of sponsorships is only waiting for the ink to dry on your new shiny contract before they give it to you," Spike said as he hobbled into the room on crutches.

"What did the doctor say?" Hog asked.

"Something's messed up in my knee for sure, although we won't know for a few days if it's just some bruising and swelling, or if it's serious enough to take me out of the game."

"What about you, Candor?"

Candor scowled. "Mind your business," he said before walking to his room and slamming the door shut.

"I take it the news wasn't good," Hog said.

"Probably not. I'm not sure about him, but from what I heard, my chances for a major company were pretty much torpedoed by me lying on the ground and cradling my knee like it was a baby. Apparently, the correct response would have been to stand up and keep on fighting on one leg."

"I'm sorry," Red said.

Spike waved her off. "Don't worry about it, although apology accepted if it helps you feel any better. I've been doing a lot of thinking in the past couple of hours, and this is probably for the best."

"You're giving up on being a gladiator?"

"Yeah, if I don't get a sponsorship now, I think I am, at least at this level. I was good in the mid-leagues, even made a bit of a name for myself, but this is an entirely different kind of competition that I doubt I'll ever be ready for."

"What are you talking about? You did pretty well, all things considered," Red said.

Spike shook his head. "I just followed Helios' and Hog's lead."

There was another knock at the door, and as Helios went to open it, Candor slunk out of his room and took a seat at the table in the kitchen.

Helios spoke to the person at the door and came back with five envelopes.

"Five envelopes? That must mean that we each got a sponsor," Hog said.

"Not necessarily. Everyone gets an envelope."

"Are we going to all open it together?" Red asked.

Helios shook his head. "Let's not make a big deal out of it. Just open it up and tell us, if you want to."

Red took the envelope from Helios and examined it. The paper was dark green with a gold Tiber wax seal.

"Looks like I was right. No sponsor for me, just a reassignment to another training center somewhere in the south of France. It sounds halfway decent, and the weather should at least be nice," Spike said.

Red didn't hear what the others said; she was too engrossed in opening her own envelope.

Her heart dropped when she saw the page in front of her.

"You look like you saw a ghost there, Red. Not get enough sponsorship money to suit you?" Hog teased.

She shook her head and swallowed back tears. "I didn't get any sponsorship money. It's blank."

"Blank? It can't be blank." Helios snatched the paper from her hands. "I don't believe it. You were definitely the best choice, and you smoked all of us in those last two trials." He stared down at the page and shook his head. "It doesn't make any sense. That would mean..." He opened his own envelope, scanned the paper, and shook his head again. "I didn't get anything official today, but it says that several of the training centers in town are interested in having me try out for their sponsors who weren't invited today. That doesn't make any sense, though. How could I get something when you don't? There must have been a mistake. I'd have never thought..." He trailed off.

Candor's cutting laugh broke the silence. "She fooled us all. I should have stuck to my gut and backed Blue. Can't you three see it? Somehow Red tricked us. She's weak, and we're all weak for following her."

"I'm not weak–"

Candor interrupted her. "Weak. Useless. A fool who will never find her way back to the people who cared so little about her they let her sign up as a gladiator. That is, if you even have people who care about you. Maybe you were so alone in the world that you signed up to take the memory wipe and forget about your sad, desperate, miserable little life."

"That's enough, Candor," Helios said.

"No, it's not," Candor turned back to Red. "You tricked us all, Red, but don't trick yourself. You may have won a couple of rounds and ousted Blue, but you still didn't make the cut. Those sponsors know what they're doing, and they decided you weren't worth it. Obviously, since you, the weakling you are, defeated all of us, it means that none of us were as strong as we thought. You were supposed to show our strength, but you couldn't even draw a sponsor for yourself. You're all but useless, and you'll never be strong enough to know who you were before you threw everything away and joined the meat grinder of the gladiator games."

Red knew he was using his abilities to prey on her insecurities, but it didn't make his words sting any less. She stood up. "Helios, Hog, Spike, I'm sorry. I guess I wasn't your ticket out of here like you thought. I'll leave you alone," she said before retiring to her room with her head held high, refusing to let Candor see how wounded she was.

Later, long after she'd finished crying into a pillow, she heard a knock at her door.

"Come in," she said, sitting up with her back against the wall.

The door opened and Helios walked in. She shifted over on the bed to give him space to sit down.

"Delivery," he said as he lifted what looked like a half-empty bottle of a dark liquid and two glasses.

"What's that?"

"Something to drown our sorrows in, otherwise known as whiskey." He sloshed some of the whiskey into a glass before handing it to her.

"I thought things like this were reserved for victories."

"Victories... or crushing defeats."

She swirled the alcohol and sniffed at it. "It smells like wet, rotten bread."

"That means it's good quality, or, at least I think it does. The guards I convinced to give me this bottle sure charged me like it was good quality. Try it."

Red lifted the glass to her lips and took a cautious sip. It burned like fire as it slid down her throat, and she had a coughing fit.

"See? Told you it was good," Helios said as he downed his drink, poured himself another, and topped hers off.

"You probably hate me right now."

"Hate you? For what? Because I didn't get any sponsorship money? Despite what Candor would want you to think, those types of deals are rare. If anything, I'm happy I got the offer to move to one of the mid-range training centers around here."

"Mid-range? Did Spike get the better deal in France?"

"Not at all. Don't you remember, or did all those tears addle your brain? Rome is the center for everything gladiator. A mediocre center here is still a step above a good center anywhere else, which means more money and prestige."

Red wiped her face. "I'm glad that at least you're moving up. What happens now?"

"We'll go our separate ways."

"Will we ever see each other again?"

"I don't know. Probably not unless we end up on the same gladiator circuit. I hope we don't because, to be honest, I really don't want to face you in the arena."

"If I even make it to an arena."

"You will. I'm sure there was a typo or something. There's no way they're going to let you slip by. And when you do make it to the arena, I'll be rooting for you."

"Thanks, Helios. You're not so bad."

He lifted his empty glass to her. "You aren't either. Just so you know, Hog and Candor both got offers. I think Candor will be working the rest of his contract off at a desk in some government office or something, and Hog got a pretty nice placement at one of the centers here. Between you and me, I'm surprised he got it because he's not the sharpest tool in the shed, and strength abilities are common at the moment, but I guess his strength and willingness to follow orders even when you'd already knocked him down gave him an edge."

Red downed the whiskey in her glass and handed it back to Helios. "I appreciate you letting me know. It's hard to believe it's all over."

"It is, isn't it?" Helios stood and tottered to the door. "No matter what anyone says, I still believe you were the right choice. It was good to know you."

"You too, Helios. Thanks for all your help."

Chapter Twenty

Sharps never had the luxury of being a simple man. He'd done too many things and seen too much heartache not to understand that the world was a cruel, unforgiving place. As the weapons master for the Boar's Head training center, he'd taught countless gladiators how to fight, and then watched too many of them walk out onto the sands of the arena and spill their life's blood for nothing.

Granted, he'd also watched many of his students spill the blood of their opponents and go on to win their matches, tournaments, and championships. The Boar's Head was the top training center in Rome, and it was his duty to prepare their fighters for the reality of the arena. His coworkers contributed in their own way: Airmed for the injuries, and Enzo to coordinate everything else, but Sharps knew that if it weren't for his training, their gladiators wouldn't stand a chance in the arena.

He'd worked at the Boar's Head for over seven years, five of those as their weapons master, and had been in the world of the gladiators for nineteen. As a former gladiator who'd won several championships, he'd paid his dues and his contract long ago. Now he spent his time beating good form, quick thinking, and calculated aggression into his charges.

Sharps was a busy man, and he took his job seriously. He had enough experience to know when someone had potential and when they wouldn't make the cut, and due to his discernment and stellar track record, he was allowed to make recruiting recommendations to the Boar's Head owner, Elwin.

Attending the Tiber Recruitment Center training showcase had been a welcome distraction in an otherwise normal day. It was a good way to get outside the walls of the Boar's Head, eat catered food, and see what the newest crop of recruits had to offer. Even if Sharps didn't see someone he liked—and he rarely did—it enabled him to study the up-and-coming competition.

Sharps had been invited by Silver, a former gladiator of his who'd retired from fighting to work as the head trainer at the center. He'd been looking forward to catching up with his former student and hearing the inside scoop on her newest bunch of recruits. While Silver had never been a particularly strong gladiator, she'd been dependable and had a knack for making others work hard. After she'd paid off her contract and left for greener employment pastures, she'd stayed in contact with Sharps; he'd reciprocated by recommending her center to his boss as one to watch. It was a win/win situation: the Boar's Head was often allowed to be first in line to preview top talent, and their wealthy sponsors weren't afraid to pay top dollar for good fighters—which only led to increased prestige and connections for the Tiber Recruitment Center when their recruits won under Sharp's tutelage.

"Any insights?" he asked as he looked out across the sand before the start of the final trial.

"Yeah, the woman is the most promising recruit I've seen in a long time."

"High praise."

"Have you heard anything about her?"

Sharps shook his head.

"That's surprising. She was sent here by the Boar's Head for us to test out. From what I understand, she entered in the pre-trials straight from the memory wipe, got top placement, and hasn't settled for less since."

"How are her skills?"

"Good. She definitely had quality training before she got her contract. I'd say she's almost ring-ready, and with some polishing she'll be arena-ready in no time."

"Are you sure you're not lowering your standards after so long down here?" Sharps asked. Usually, it took a gladiator several years, if ever, to work up from the first memory wipe to the level of competition of Rome's unsanctioned rings. Once successful in the unsanctioned matches, it could take another year, if not more, to get a fighter ready for their debut in the arena.

"You'll see."

Sharps had seen, and Silver hadn't been wrong. There was something about the way Red moved and fought that tickled the back of his mind, and after leaving the recruitment center he went immediately to Elwin Nilsen, the owner of the Boar's Head, to give his report.

From what Elwin told him the next day, Sharps hadn't been the only one impressed by Red's show, and the recruitment center had made the decision to hold off placing her until all potential sponsors and training companies had more time for observation and evaluation.

Because Red's contract was still held by the Boar's Head, Sharps had priority to assess her. Depending on what he found, the Boar's Head would either pick her up with a sponsor, or they would let the Tiber auction off her contract to anyone who was interested.

The day before, Sharps could have sworn he'd seen something familiar in the way Red moved, something that reminded him of his pre-gladiator days. As he sat in the Tiber's training room and waited for the trainers to collect Red and bring her in for her evaluation, Sharps tried to convince himself that he was getting too old and seeing things.

Soon enough, Red was led in and told to stand in the center of the sand-filled ring. The trainer in charge of her sat at the edge of the room, presumably to ensure she wasn't injured; judging from the rumors flying around, she'd garnered a lot of interest.

In one well-practiced movement, Sharps drew one of his knives and sent it spinning towards Red. Instead of stepping to the side, ducking, or otherwise trying to avoid the weapon, Red instead continued her steady march forward and let the knife bounce harmlessly off a newly erected shield.

Sharps waited until she reached the center of the room and stretched his hand out. "I'm Sharps, weapons master for the Boar's Head training center. I'll be evaluating you today for my company."

"It's nice to meet you, Sharps. They call me Red," she said as she placed her hand in his and shook it firmly.

Sharps wasted no time with extraneous words, and immediately knocked her off her feet.

Despite his surprise attack, she adapted well, rolled with the punches, and was back on her feet in no time.

He had decided not to assess her with weapons, as he was more concerned with her basic skills, reflexes, and fighting intelligence.

Proficiency with different weapons could be taught with enough practice, as long as the foundation skills were there.

Fortunately, Red's foundation was rock solid. Sharps had at least forty pounds of muscle on her and judging by her youthful appearance, at least twice the years of fighting experience, but her reflexes were sharp and she used her shield fluidly to avoid direct hits.

They started out sparring slowly, and he gradually increased the speed of his attacks. All too often, he'd seen new fighters straight out of recruit camp demonstrate good form when they had time to think about their attacks and defenses, only to devolve into a mess of flailing limbs when the fight sped up. Red had no such issue. If anything, as he pressed his advantage, her fighting style morphed into something much more dangerous.

It was subtle at first, and so unexpected that it took Sharps several seconds to believe his eyes. As he forced Red to rely on muscle memory and instinct, she'd transitioned from the standard fighting forms of a new recruit into moves he hadn't seen in years.

Once he was sure of what he saw, Sharps stopped sparring, told Red to get a drink and rest for a few minutes, and retreated to his bench to think.

Long before his gladiator days, Sharps was in a Canadian special forces unit called the Ghosts. Decades had passed, but as he watched Red move, he remembered the missions his team had shared with their American counterparts, the Rangers. At the time, a Ranger called Apex had been developing a specialized style of fighting.

Sharps' ability to see the future in limited increments of time had helped Apex put the finishing touches on his fighting system. By the time their joint training exercise had ended, Apex had declared the new Ranger style all but complete. He'd then sworn Sharps and the other Ghosts to secrecy, forbidding them from teaching the new style to anyone save those they loved most, as the fewer people who knew of its existence, the less chance there was of someone figuring out its weaknesses.

Now that he finally recognized what had been bothering him the day before, Sharps resumed his sparring with Red. There was no doubt about it: Red was definitely fighting in the Ranger way, although he noted a few differences. As they circled each other, it became obvious that whoever taught Red had tailored several of the more difficult moves to her body type and gender; as a woman, she didn't have the brute strength that some of the moves required.

He could draw one of two conclusions: either she'd been a part of the Rangers, or a Ranger had loved her enough to not only teach her the style but also modify it for her. Rangers weren't weak, and if one had loved her, the chances were good she could command a gladiator team.

The Ranger fighting style and the fluidity with which she used her abilities made the decision easy: Sharps knew talent when he saw it, and Red had talent in spades. As he watched her walk out of the ring after the evaluation, Sharps noted the dignity and strength that characterized her movements. If the average Boar's Head gladiator had the "look of eagles," Red had the look of an entire flock.

After his evaluation, Sharps went directly to Elwin Nilsen and only had to wait thirty minutes before a receptionist waved him through. Sharps paused at the threshold and knocked on the open door to Elwin's office.

Enzo, the training master, was already seated against one of the walls. Sharps nodded at Enzo but didn't pay attention to him otherwise. While Enzo was technically his boss and in charge of coordinating the full spectrum of care for his fighters, he and Sharps had never gotten along.

"Sharps, yes, come in. I assume you just evaluated our new female prospect?" Elwin asked.

"I have," Sharps said, and walked forward until he stood in front of Elwin's desk.

"And what did you think?"

"If you don't buy her contract, she'll make a fool out of all our gladiators in the arena."

"I see. I'll contact our sponsors and see if any of them are interested in her. Thank you, Sharps."

"Sir, with all due respect, I'm not done yet."

Elwin raised an eyebrow. Sharps understood; he usually kept his thoughts to himself, but sponsorships could be risky. Most of the time, the sponsor was a wealthy individual or family who bought gladiator contracts like others bought a stable of horses to watch them race. Just like racehorse owners, if a sponsor didn't like how their gladiator was fighting, they could pay a fee and stop allowing them to compete.

"I would be neglecting my duty if I didn't give you my full recommendation: the Boar's Head should foot her entire bill and not seek out a sponsorship for the woman called Red."

Enzo scoffed. "That's preposterous. We already have more than enough potential queens ready to take the mantle of team leader, all of them with more years of experience. Now you want to bring this newcomer on without a sponsor? Do you have any idea how much it costs to keep one gladiator in fighting condition? That's not even factoring in how much work it takes to get recruits to the point where they can even step in the ring for a trial match."

"This is the same young woman who injured five guards and five upper-ring gladiators, correct? The one who nearly burned a hole in the main lobby door because she didn't like her contract? I'm telling you, she's one of the best I've ever seen. She'll need some time to get into top fighting shape, true, but she's got the skills and abilities to take her all the way."

"We can't afford such a lavish expenditure, especially with our current roster of women," Enzo said.

Sharps swallowed his frustration and played his trump card. "I'll be her mentor and take on her training personally."

The statement almost knocked Enzo out of his chair, and Elwin pursed his lips. Sharps could guess what the owner was thinking: in his seven years at the Boar's Head, he'd not once taken on a student.

His reluctance to be a mentor was uncommon. Even his under-trainers—experienced gladiators who helped him train new blood while finishing out their contracts—would occasionally take on a mentee. Being a mentor was a lot of work, involving extra practice, strategizing, and providing support for the mentee.

Sharps didn't have the time to train every gladiator and recruit to the highest level, so a mentor was responsible for organizing extra training and working to give their mentee the best chance. It was a lucrative option for those willing to do the extra work, as it was customary for a gladiator to pay their mentor a cut of the winnings. It was also a risk; if a gladiator failed in the arena, the mentor took part of the blame and could even be charged extra fees by the training center for ruining a potential prospect. Until now, Sharps had not been inclined to give up any precious free time to a mentee. After watching the American woman who fought like Apex's student and had abilities strong enough to crush four men in the ring, he decided it was time to break his neutral streak.

"You? Her mentor? If she's as good as you say, she should be given a more experienced mentor," Enzo said as he adjusted his tie.

Sharps ignored him; Enzo was notorious for picking the most beautiful of their recruits for "mentoring." In Sharps' opinion, the only thing Enzo could do reliably was ruin his charges' potential. While they'd had some limited success in the middle rings of Rome, Enzo's gladiators never failed to turn into prima donnas who complained more than they won—and once he tired of them, Enzo was infamous for dropping them by the wayside.

"You wouldn't want her, Enzo. She's got a scar a mile long, and her hair is shorter than yours. Not exactly a pretty face to add to your stable."

"Enzo does have a point. While you've done an admirable job as weapons master, you have no experience as a mentor, Sharps. Why should I allow you to be her mentor?" Elwin asked.

"Enzo assumes that because I've never been a formal mentor, I have no experience with it. He fails to recognize that a large part of my job is to mentor all our fighters. I make them stronger, train them to use that strength, and then train them to win. I've worked at the Boar's Head seven years, five of which have been as your weapons master. Unlike Enzo, I have personal experience in the arena, and have seen what it takes to win as both a gladiator and as a gladiator coach. Any mentee of mine will have the distinction of being trained by one of the few gladiators who has won both an individual, and a team championship cup. I know what it takes to win, and my record speaks for itself."

"And what happens when your mentee needs extra work? You'll shirk your duties to your other gladiators so you can train her?" Enzo asked.

"Are you saying that you prioritize your mentees over your work?" When Enzo sputtered a denial, Sharps smiled. "I'm more than capable of balancing the two. Despite what Enzo seems to think, or how he trains his mentees, I'm intimately acquainted with both the science of pushing my fighters to their limits without overworking them and the art of how to let them rest without babying them. If you want to know how I'd handle a mentee, look at how well my fighters have done over the years."

Watching Elwin's face, Sharps knew he didn't have to say more. Since he'd taken on the job of weapons master, the Boar's Head had risen from one of the many training centers in Rome to one of the most prestigious in the world.

"She speaks with an American accent. If we allow an American into the center, let alone pay for her, we'll be the laughingstock of the city," Enzo said.

"It's true that she's an American, but don't let that fool you. If anything, it means you may get her at a discount."

"Americans are useless in the ring, everyone knows that. No American has ever won anything in Europe or done well in Rome."

"Except for the Saviors, right?" Sharps muttered. For the first time since he'd walked into Elwin's office, Sharps turned to face Enzo. "I am Canadian myself and have met more Abled Americans than you could ever dream. The crux of the matter, and the reason why so many Americans who come here struggle, is that unlike the Europeans, the Americans recognize the full benefits of their Ableds. Strong Ableds are snapped up into good, stable, well-paying jobs before they even have to think about competing in their equivalent to our gladiator games."

"If they're so strong, then why don't they come over here and fight us? Are they scared?"

"The American warrior games pay much better and don't have the same barriers to entry that we do. Plus, like I just said, their strongest Ableds don't have to compete. That means weaker Ableds are able to make much more money without having to go up against the cream of the crop."

"If that's true, why are you so dead set on the American woman? Isn't she just more of the same?"

"That's enough, Enzo, I've made my decision," Elwin said. "Sharps, you've been a loyal employee and a hard worker. Your fighters have done well in the ring, and your judgment so far has been nearly impeccable. Thanks to our placement in the team tournament last year, and what would have been our win if we hadn't been robbed in the individual tournament, our coffers are full. You haven't asked for much, if anything, while you've faithfully worked here, and I will reward you by granting your wish. I'll put in a bid for the girl, and if the Tiber accepts it, she'll be your mentee. You can return to your training and I'll have my assistant notify you when the girl is ready."

"Thank you, sir," Sharps said. He turned around without acknowledging Enzo and left the office.

It wasn't until he was back in his small office that Sharps allowed himself to smile and clench his fist in victory. It might have been years, but he would guard Apex's secret, and he would honor his friend by making sure the intriguing American wasn't drowned in the tumultuous waters of the gladiator games.

Chapter Twenty-One

Red was woken up by a knock at her door. She had no idea how long she'd slept, only that the night before she'd been so exhausted from a full day of evaluations and assessments, she'd had no dreams after her head hit the pillow. She opened her bedroom door to find the Tiber head trainer, Silver, waiting for her.

"Rise and shine, Sleeping Beauty, time for you to move out."

"Move out?" Red echoed, her brain still foggy.

"That's right, move out. My manager received several offers for your contract last night and accepted one. Congratulations, you've been bought by the Boar's Head and are now their newest gladiator, and shall be known as 'Blade' henceforth. All you need to do is to sign your contract and make it official."

"Why Blade? I haven't used any knives."

"I don't know; maybe when you get there you can ask them. Come on. Get ready and get your things together. We don't have time to waste."

It felt weird for Red to leave her name when it had served her so well, but as she stepped out of the recruitment center for the last time, Blade let her old name drop like old clothes that had gone out of style and didn't fit. She was no longer a recruit at the mercy of finding someone to take her contract; she was now a gladiator.

"Did a sponsor buy my contract after all?" she asked Silver as they walked to the waiting carriage. The Boar's Head didn't seem to do anything halfway—the matched pair of bays looked completely identical, down to the strip of white just above their front left hoof

"Officially, I don't know."

"And unofficially?"

Silver smiled. "Unofficially, don't worry about it. Just know that your talents have been noticed."

Blade climbed into the closed carriage and sat across from two guards. The ride was uneventful and quiet, neither of the guards being the talkative type.

Finally, the carriage rolled to a stop and one of the guards opened the door and stepped out. When Blade followed, she blinked for a moment to let her eyes adjust to the light and tried not to gasp at the facility in front of her.

The Boar's Head was breathtaking. Compared to the recruitment center, which had an overall air of frugality, the white three-story stone building was accented with dark wood and had flowering trees at the end of the drive. It presided over the perfectly smooth dirt training field. A quiet serving girl gave Blade the chance to take in the view before leading her to a side entrance and then up a flight of stairs to her room in the women's wing.

"This is your room," the girl said as she led Blade down a plain hallway and opened a door. "Unlike what may be the norm at other centers, you won't have to share your room here. The women's bathroom is just down the hall; you'll find the toilets, sinks, and showers there."

"Do all the Boar's Head women live on this hall?" Blade asked.

The girl shook her head. "Only the unproven ones. Your room and board will be deducted from your winnings, and the leftovers will go towards paying off your contract. The more you win, the more privileges you earn. The top gladiators have their own suite of rooms or other special privileges. The system provides a great incentive to encourage our gladiators to do their best."

The serving girl left Blade in her room to get settled and brought a filling brunch consisting of a large plate of bread, fruit, meat and cheese several minutes later.

"I will be back in a little bit to take you to your mentor for your first training session. Please, make yourself comfortable," the girl said with a curtsy before stepping out.

Blade looked around the room as she ate. It was small, but clean and tidy. The door didn't lock from the inside, but a deep window in the far wall at least allowed her to look out at the training yard. She sat on her bed and watched the fighters practice, enjoying the peace and quiet.

Just after the sun reached its zenith, another servant led Blade to the training building of the weapons master, set to the left of the main hall. Compared to the bright outdoors, the room was dark and cast in shadow.

"Mr. Sharps, sir, I've brought Blade," the servant called out in a tremulous voice.

The man Blade had met the day before emerged from a door at the back of the building, wiping his hands with a cloth. "I see. Thank you, you can leave her here and be back in an hour."

The servant left, and it was only Blade and Sharps. Now that her eyes had fully adjusted to the relative darkness, she saw the room consisted of a large sunken pit in the center and racks of weapons along the far wall.

"Blade, huh? That's the name they gave you?" Sharps asked.

Blade nodded and turned back to him. "What about it?"

"Normally, they're not so obvious. Of course, normally the gladiators we pick up already have their own names."

Blade waited for Sharps to continue. Instead, he beckoned her to a wooden bench where a series of knives and daggers were set out. "I've got to get these sharpened and maintained before my afternoon sessions. Here, sit and we'll talk."

She took a seat on the floor next to the bench and accepted the knife he handed her. Sharps spent several minutes demonstrating how to sharpen a knife, and when he was satisfied she had the hang of it, he sat on the other end of the bench.

"As you might remember, my name is Sharps and I was the man in charge of evaluating your fitness to fight under the Boar's Head banner. My evaluation was convincing enough for my bosses, Enzo the training master and Elwin the owner of this center, to see your value and buy your contract."

"I thought sponsors were the ones who bought contracts?"

"Usually they are. Contracts are expensive, and very few centers have the money to buy their fighters. Even fewer centers want to risk an outright purchase when they can get some silly rich person to foot the bill and feed off the prestige."

"Oh. So I don't have a sponsor after all?"

"No, the Boar's Head is the sole owner of your contract." Sharps paused when Blade frowned and chuckled darkly. "It's a great honor for you to be bought by the center, and I'm sure it's already feeding into the speculation surrounding you. Between you and me, it's for the best. Sponsors would require you to go to their parties and show you off like a prized animal in their menagerie. Sometimes they demand certain outfits in the arena, or that their fighters use specific weapons or act a certain way. You won't have to worry about much of that; you are solely here to train and to win, not to be a prancing pony for them."

"Instead of parties I get to train all the time? Are you sure this is the better deal?" Blade's smile faded when Sharps frowned at her, and she focused again on sharpening her knife.

"Do you want to win?"

"More than anything. I have to."

"Why?"

Blade looked up to see Sharps staring at her; his dark eyebrows were drawn over his brown eyes like a thunder cloud over a hazy day.

"Doesn't everyone want to win?"

"Everyone has their own motivations."

"How do I know I can trust you? Isn't the unofficial motto for the gladiator games 'your friend today will kill you tomorrow'?"

He turned his attention back to the knife he was sharpening and switched out his whetstone. "If you can't trust me, you can't trust anyone. As weapons master, it is my duty to make sure each of my fighters is appropriately prepared for whatever can be thrown at them in the arena. Beyond that, I am your mentor, which means I have a vested interest in you winning."

"Oh." Blade looked down at the knife in her hand. "This is a beautiful weapon. Where did you get it?"

"I made it."

"That's cool. Did you make all of these?" she asked, gesturing at the racks of knives and swords.

"No, just my personal ones."

"If I'm your mentee, will you make me one too?"

A semblance of a smile tipped up a corner of his mouth and was promptly replaced by a frown. "Win enough matches and we'll see. You definitely won't get anything until I know you can take care of it—and judging by the way you're dulling the edge of that knife, we've got a lot of work to do."

The rest of their time was spent in silence, until a servant came to get Blade.

"Rest while you can; I'll see you in a few hours for a thorough evaluation to determine the best schedule for you," Sharps said.

Instead of taking her back to the room, the servant took Blade to a different building in the Boar's Head compound, located behind the main office and dorm and across a garden full of plants growing in neat rows.

Blade stepped into a long room with beds on either side of a center aisle and privacy screens pushed against the wall. Between beds, open windows allowed light and fresh air to circulate through the room. At the end of the room, behind a counter, men and women worked to process various types of plants. Whereas the weapons room had been dark, dingy, and smelled of sweat and blood, this new building was light and airy, with the sharp smell of antiseptic hanging in the air.

"I see our newest gladiator has arrived," a tall woman dressed in a white, flowy dress said as she walked up to Blade and her minder.

"Airmed, this is Blade. I've been instructed to bring her here for her initial health check-up."

"I am aware. I take it you've already introduced her to Sharps?"

The servant nodded.

"Good. You can leave her with me and return to your duties. I'll have one of my aides return her to her room when we're done." Airmed turned to Blade. "Hello there, I'm Airmed, the healer for the Boar's Head. I'm in charge of all aspects of the health of our fighters, from simple bruises up to life-threatening wounds. My abilities allow me to weave tissues together to reduce the severity of injuries. I can also transfer injuries from one person to another, although that's only used in exceptional circumstances due to the great cost incurred. Let's take a look at you."

Airmed led Blade to one of the beds and gestured for her to sit. She ran Blade through a series of tests, dictating her measurements to an assistant who wrote them down. When she was done, she leaned back on her stool and frowned as she played with the end of her long, black braid.

"Overall, you're in good health, but I'm finding a few concerning things. Your strength, in particular, isn't where it needs to be to send you into the arena. No, don't be alarmed. This is common with new fighters, especially women. I'll get you started on an accelerated medication and supplement program, and we'll get you into fighting shape in no time."

"How long before I'll be ready?"

"From a health standpoint?" Airmed licked her lips. "Three months before any serious arena fighting, maybe more, maybe less, although you can start competing in the lower rings when Sharps clears you. Everyone is different, and you're a new gladiator who just finished the trials, so it's hard to tell. Any other questions?"

Blade shook her head.

"Well, it was nice to meet you, Blade. Welcome to your new family."

After Airmed's assistant dropped her off in her room, Blade waited until someone else came to take her back to the training room. She was early and sat on one of the benches at the side of the ring while Sharps trained a small group of men until a clock chimed in the corner.

Sharps called the men into a circle and spoke for a few minutes before dismissing them. As they walked out of the sand pit at the center of the room, several of the men took notice of Blade and nudged each other, but she ignored them, and they all left without saying anything to her.

Her first real practice was enlightening in several ways. The testing was extensive, starting out with her endurance and strength, followed by a skills test with various weapons, and ending with an abilities demonstration that involved transforming her shield into various shapes. By the time they were done, Blade was dripping in sweat and felt like she'd run a marathon.

Sharps' face was impassive as he stood in the center of the sand ring, watching her. The frown on his face and the way his eyes narrowed made Blade worry she'd fallen short of his expectations.

"Well, you're not the worst new gladiator I've ever had," he said after a pause, and she breathed a sigh of relief.

He tilted his head. "Does that surprise you?"

She shrugged, and his frown deepened.

"Okay, kid. First lesson is your ABC: always be confident. If you ever show the smallest hint of insecurity, more experienced fighters will eat you alive. Every time you walk into the arena, you need to exude confidence. You have to believe you've already won and that the fight is just a formality before you can collect your prize. Anything less is a weakness. Any weakness makes you weak, and the weak die. You don't want that, do you?"

Blade shook her head.

"Good." He twirled one of his knives. "Let's see how good you are at dodging."

The objective was for Blade to stand on the opposite side of the room and do her best to dodge Sharps' attacks. At first, she used her shield to cover the entire room, and none of the knives Sharps threw made it past the shield, bouncing off harmlessly.

"Okay, now dodge without raising a shield," he instructed.

Blade nodded, and when Sharps threw the next round of knives she stayed stock still. The knives stopped in midair, their blades burning red.

"Nice trick, but that's not quite what I had in mind. Either way, it brings me to my next lesson for today: Don't give away all your secrets at once. If I thought all you could do was create a shield, I could be lulled into a false sense of security when I didn't see a shield. No one will expect you to stop projectiles in mid-air, which means it's best for us if you only use that particular skill when you really need it. If you can get good enough at dodging, you won't ever need to use it and we can keep it as a trump card."

"Okay."

The timer rang, and Sharps stepped out of the ring. "That's enough for today."

"That's all?"

"You're quite eager, aren't you? Don't worry, we'll put you to work soon enough. The first day is always easiest; we don't want to overwhelm our new fighters."

Blade was taken back to her room once again, where she waited until it was time for the evening meal. Dinner was a subdued affair in the great hall, a grand room with ceilings stretching over three stories and white marble floors shining softly under the light of chandeliers. The seating arrangements consisted of a raised table at the front, several smaller tables set for six, and two long tables further back with plates every few feet. Blade noticed that most of the conversation came from the top table, where Sharps, Airmed, and several men dressed in expensive clothes were sitting, and two of the front tables, which held one woman and five men each.

She was one of the last people to enter, and the servant led her to an empty seat at the long table where the other women sat.

As she walked forward, one of the men at the front table tapped his glass with a spoon and the room fell silent.

"Everyone, we have a new face today. I would like you all to welcome our newest gladiator, Blade. She is fresh out of a recruitment trial and is Sharps' new mentee. Welcome, Blade. I expect to see great things from you."

She kept her head high and acknowledged the polite claps with a nod before taking her seat.

"Is it true? Sharps is your mentor?" a woman sitting diagonally to her right asked.

Blade nodded.

"Interesting."

"Is it?"

The other woman glanced over her shoulder and leaned forward, partially out of her seat. "He's never taken a mentee while I've been here." Her eyebrows rose as she looked Blade up and down, and she frowned. "I can't imagine what he sees in you, though. My mentor is Enzo. He's been very good to me and makes sure I have the best clothes and opportunities to make the best connections. He told me that I may even have a chance at qualifying for the individual tournament next year."

"Qualifying for what?"

"Quiet, you two! No talking," one of the passing servers said.

Blade turned her attention back to her food. Later, after they'd eaten, she tried to catch up to the other woman to make conversation as they were escorted back to the women's wing but was rebuffed.

"Look, it sounds like you're new to this, so I'll make it very clear to you: individual women gladiators aren't allowed to do much beyond train and fight until we get a team. If your mentor had more mentees, you might be able to talk to them, but you're out of luck on that front as well," the woman said before walking into her room and shutting the door behind her.

That night, as the clocktower tolled, there was a knock on her door and Blade opened it to find a servant holding a tray with several glasses of white liquid.

"Nightly glass of milk. All the gladiators get it. Drink up, it will help you sleep," the servant said.

Blade nodded, took the milk, and drank it under the servant's watchful eye.

"What's your name?" she asked.

The servant, an old woman with gray hair, shook her head. "It doesn't matter. Goodnight, Blade."

Over the next two weeks, Blade spent most of her time training or fighting. At the Boar's Head, there was a hierarchy: the more someone won, the more they were rewarded with clothes, objects, or freedom. As the newest gladiator, Blade had no personal items beyond her signing pen, and her personal freedom was almost nonexistent.

With Sharps as her mentor, she was at least allowed to spend most of her days in the building that housed the armory and training area. While she wasn't allowed to interact with any of the fighters, she took up station on one of the wooden benches against the edge of the room and spent her time sharpening knives and watching whoever was currently fighting or practicing. In his spare time, Sharps allowed her to practice in the ring for extra training.

After one particularly hard session, Sharps stepped back from their sparring and appraised her.

"Why do you hesitate to go on the offensive?" he asked as he poured a cup of water and handed it to her.

Blade shrugged. "It feels different. Not as comfortable—like I know that I can do it, but that maybe I shouldn't."

"Do you know why?"

"No, but isn't that kind of normal? The memory potion locked away my long-term memory, so figuring out my hang ups is part of the process, right?"

"Sometimes, yes. But, sometimes small memories will slip through, and those things can help you to learn more about yourself. Have you had any of those?"

"Not really." Blade shook her head before she remembered the four words scratched into her leg. She frowned and looked at Sharps, evaluating if she should tell him about her words. He held her gaze calmly as she narrowed her eyes.

"I've only known you for two weeks. Can I trust you?" she finally asked.

"What do you mean by that?"

"You're supposed to be my mentor, and I'm your student. What exactly does that mean? Like, are you going to be there for me through everything, or should I be concerned that you'll eventually stab me in the back? I'm not allowed to talk to anyone else, but I'd prefer to stay quiet if talking to you means losing one day."

"I'm your mentor, which means I'm giving up my valuable free time to give you extra training and guide you through the gladiator world. It's true—the most important lesson for you is to trust no one. This is a tough world, but it's a world that you're part of until you can pay off your debt." He paused to sip his water. "With that being said: I'm no longer an active gladiator. I paid my dues, won my championships, and have no desire or inclination to return to the arena, so beyond having my name on a plaque or two somewhere and two championship cups gathering dust in my office, my true legacy consists of what my trainees do. Since you're my only mentee, you are part of that legacy, meaning if you do well, it reflects well on me. If you do poorly, then I will be remembered as the mentor who took a young gladiator full of promise and ruined her." He glared at her to make his point, but she refused to shrink under his gaze. "Because of that, I can promise you right here and now that if you win in the arena, you will always have me in your corner, and your secrets will be safe with me."

"And if I don't win?"

"It won't be worth my time to talk about you."

She looked down into her cup. "After I drank the potion, I used the pen to scratch four words on my leg. I don't know what they mean, but they must be important."

Sharps looked intrigued. "What were the words?"

"Bird, ring, win, and family."

"I can't offer any insight into the others, but if you give your training your all, I'll teach you everything I know—and from what I've seen, I'm confident you'll win," Sharps said.

She nodded, accepting his offer, and the corners of her mouth turned up into a small smile. "Sounds good to me."

Chapter Twenty-Two

After he watched Blade leave, Sharps retreated to his office. It was a little hole in the wall barely large enough to fit a small desk, but he rarely spent time there anyway, much preferring the open gym or his forge.

Sharps sat in his chair and absentmindedly dusted off his desk. Most of the fighters under his care signed up for glory or gold. European social mobility had only gotten worse after the Hard Times, and unlike their North American counterparts, Ableds in Europe had never been able to break free of the sense of "other" and use their abilities to increase their wealth or standing as a group. They were the entertainers and the workhorses of society; good enough to be an athlete, a bodyguard, or a mistress, but rarely a business owner or an aristocrat.

His own station at the Boar's Head was rather unconventional. Most fighters who won a championship retired, content to advertise whatever brands their sponsor arranged for them and live off the spoils for the rest of their lives. A life of leisure hadn't appealed to Sharps, and instead of retiring he'd worked as a weapons master for several smaller training centers before the Boar's Head had picked him up. Usually, the men and women in charge of running the centers wanted non-Ableds in positions of power to prevent any Abled-dynamics interaction from affecting the company's bottom line.

Sharps was a gladiator before the current system—with its sky-high expenses, myriad fees, and need for sponsors to subsidize the cost—came into place. He was the last gladiator to win a championship without a memory wipe and had seen the effect the wipe had on the subsequent fighters, and how aggressive and prone to risks it made them.

That was one reason why Blade was so unusual—as a fighter, she was careful. He didn't doubt her desire to win, but she didn't push the envelope. Sharps would have originally stereotyped her as one to rush into something headfirst. Instead, she was almost surgical, as if she were always thinking three steps ahead, even with her current bad habit of preferring defense moves over harnessing her full offensive capabilities.

He'd tried to throw her off during their sparring; despite his name and his proclivity for knives, Sharps' abilities had nothing to do with sharp objects. He was able to view the future in short bursts, no more than a few seconds at a time, at various increments—although while looking into the future, he was completely blind to what was going on around him. When he had the chance to use it appropriately in a fight, he knew how to throw his knives or place his weapons for greatest effect.

He wasn't any less accurate when throwing the knives at his mentee, but as soon as the weapons left his hand Blade seemed to extrapolate exactly where it was going and dodge.

Sharps rolled his eyes when he thought of her name. Supposedly, it was a great honor to have such a promising gladiator given a name that mirrored his own, but he suspected Enzo was trying to needle him. The training master hadn't tried to disguise his belief that Blade would wash out, or that Sharps had overestimated her strength, and linking their names would serve to heap embarrassment on Sharps if she failed.

Blade. Despite the politics behind the name, it fit her. When she was focused, her gaze was just as sharp as any knife that he could make, and her mind was like a razor.

Sharps had spent a good amount of time in the past two weeks talking to Blade, and judging from how little she remembered and her reliance on muscle memory, he'd bet a year's salary that she'd received a much larger dosage than the average fighter. In fact, beyond the knowledge she'd gained in classes that all recruits had to go through, Blade had almost no knowledge of the outside world. Airmed was one of the few in the city qualified to administer such a drink, and as she had once explained to him, it was tricky to balance locking enough memories away to remove any biases with not locking so much that the gladiator had to relearn everything.

Being strong enough to take the memory drug was considered a great honor, as it meant a gladiator had true potential. However, from what Blade had said in regard to the four words she'd scratched on her thigh, something about the entire situation felt rather suspicious to Sharps.

As he continued to think about his mentee, the sound of footsteps echoed through the training room outside. Airmed appeared in his office doorway, her long, loose black hair swaying freely.

"Hello, Airmed; to what do I owe this pleasure?"

"I'm taking Ox off training for the next several days. He pulled a groin muscle yesterday during one of his matches and it needs to rest."

"You can't repair it?"

"For something that little? Three days is all he needs before he's as good as new."

"I'll make a note of it."

Airmed wiped off his desk with the edge of her white dress, drawing Sharps' attention to her creamy skin. When she sat on his desk and crossed her legs, his eyes traced her delicate white feet in their brown leather sandals, traveling up her smooth legs to her plump thighs.

"It's been a while since we spent some quality time together. I won't be doing anything later this evening, if you'd like to stop by my room for a night cap," Airmed said.

"I can probably find time in my schedule."

"If you can't, I suppose we could always take care of business right now. I don't have any pressing matters at the clinic, and it looks like we're all alone," Airmed said as she uncrossed her legs and pulled the edge of her dress even higher up her thighs.

Sharps stroked her lightly just above her knee, sliding his hand over the exposed skin. "That works too. Give me a minute to lock the doors."

She licked her lips. "You have thirty seconds."

Chapter Twenty-Three

The harsh screech of his alarm woke Stefan. He rolled over, snuggled up to the sassy little redhead who'd been sharing his bed so often lately, and buried his face in her hair. Her body was delightfully warm in the cool morning, and she smelled like a mixture of lavender and honey; probably due to the shampoo he'd used on her long hair the night before when they'd showered together. He put his arm over her side and she turned to look back at him, soft and inquisitive dark eyes already knowing the mood he was in without words.

Stefan rolled back onto his back to stare at the ceiling, suddenly feeling lonely. It had been a long six months since Kaleo had been taken, and no matter what he did, the empty feelings refused to go away. Sensing his change in mood, his bed partner crawled over until she was lying on top of him and nuzzled his face.

The nuzzling he could stand; the licking he couldn't.

"No, Rosie, no licks. You know better." He groaned. Rosie wagged her tail, glad to get a reaction out of him, and did her best to wash his face with her tongue despite his protests.

He pushed her head away to emphasize his point before hugging her and sitting up. "Maybe today's the day, eh, Rosie? Think we'll make a breakthrough and find your mom?" As usual, Rosie didn't reply, but Stefan chose to take it as a good sign that her tail never stopped wagging.

While Rosie did her business and caught up on all the new smells in the backyard, Stefan got ready for work. First he turned the water boiler on to make himself a cup of coffee and then moved to the closet in the guest bedroom where all of his clothes were and picked out a suit. He laid his outfit for the day on the bed but knew better than to put it on before Rosie was crated. It had only taken once for a very muddy puppy to leave paw prints on his slacks and teach him a lesson about the timing of his routine.

As he walked out the door, he imparted one last glance at the now-empty fireplace mantel. He'd never forgive Audra for what she'd done. In one night she had shattered his life into pieces as sharp and brittle as the fragments from the glass birds scattered on the floor.

He shivered and climbed on his bike as the winter air nipped at his cheeks. As he backed out of the driveway, he reflected on the changes that the past months had wrought. For starters, Rosie was now officially his dog. When he'd accepted that finding Kaleo would be a marathon and not a sprint, it became obvious he should care for Rosie. Since his high-rise apartment wasn't suited for a pet, he had taken over Kaleo's lease.

He'd put all his clothes in the closet of her guest bedroom. It hadn't felt right to reorganize her closet or touch her things, and he had plenty of space in the guest room. However, he'd refused to sleep in the guest bed—his place was at Kaleo's side, but he'd settle for sleeping in her bed until he could find her.

Months might have passed since he'd last held her in his arms, but the loss still felt as sharp as when he first learned she'd gone missing. Stefan could tell his friends and family were worried about him from their sympathetic glances and kind words, but he didn't see why; he'd done his best to not give them any reason to question if he was okay.

Kaleo was still missing, but it was only a matter of time before he found her. In the weeks after his fruitless trip to Europe, it seemed at times like everyone had conspired to constantly check up on him and expected him to be depressed, but nothing could have been further from the truth—Stefan didn't have time to dwell on negative thoughts. His fiancée, the love of his life, the woman to whom he had given his entire heart, had been taken from him. Any time he wasted on self-pity or self-doubt was simply a distraction from the mission and more time they spent apart.

Thoughts of Kaleo never left his mind, but Stefan refused to let himself become a hermit obsessing constantly over her—part of taking care of himself was to make sure that he didn't get burnt out. Burnout was dangerous. Burnout could lead to making mistakes, or worse, to giving up. So Stefan made a point to continue with the social aspect of his life as he had before. Once a week he went out for a trivia night with Brant and Adrian, and he had a standing invitation to the Hughes' family dinners. He played the part he was expected to, even if it felt like he was the lead in a musical that had lost its sound.

The day passed as had all the others before, in a blur of routine, and that evening was trivia night.

Adrian, Brant, and Stefan met at their favorite bar twenty minutes before the game was scheduled to start and grabbed their usual spot, a booth along one of the far walls. The venue was packed, and the trio crushed their competition as usual and extended their winning streak for at least one more week. It was Stefan's night to buy, and after their victory he went to the bar to order a round of drinks.

While he was leaning against the lacquered wooden bar, a young woman took the seat next to him. "Is it always this busy?" she asked.

Stefan glanced over. Her long brown hair was styled in beach waves that nicely framed a face with bright hazel eyes and pink lips. "Yeah, trivia night draws quite the crowd. Otherwise, it's usually pretty chill," he said before turning his attention away from her, feigning to listen to the radio playing behind the bar. He tapped his left hand on the table in time with the music, making sure the silver ring he was wearing on his left hand was clearly visible.

He'd taken to wearing the ring to stave off any unwanted attention when he went out, announcing to everyone that he was there to catch up with Brant and Adrian, not to talk to women cruising for a man. Once he'd started wearing the ring regularly, there hadn't been a good reason to take it off, especially as his wedding day came and went without any indication of where his missing bride could be. The band was his constant reminder, a visible symbol to the world that matched the hidden one hanging on a chain around his neck and against his heart. Absentmindedly, Stefan brushed his fingertips over the outline of Kaleo's ring and made yet another promise to himself that he'd return it to its rightful owner. He looked forward to the day when he could take his silver ring off and let her slide a gold one in its place.

He was jolted out of his thoughts by a hand on his arm. Stefan flinched and noticed the woman he'd been ignoring was now leaning disconcertingly close to him. "I said, what's your name, and do you come here often?" she asked loudly.

"Yeah, we like to come here for a guy's night out every now and then, but it's not really a frequent thing," Stefan lied. The bartenders were busy mixing drinks for a large group of women a few feet down the bar, so he judged he'd have to wait a few more minutes before he could get his drinks and escape to the safety of his table. Instead, he settled for a pointed look at his ring, hoping she'd get the hint and leave him alone.

The woman placed her hand over his, trapping it against the table. "You know, I'd be more than happy to make one of your rare nights out extra memorable. I don't live that far from here; why don't you tell your friends that you're heading home early and meet me outside?"

"I–I don't even know you," Stefan sputtered.

She smiled. "That's okay. You're very handsome, and you look like you've got a lot on your mind. I'd love to help you forget some of it, even if just for a little bit."

"Forget? You think I need to forget?" Somewhere in the back of his mind, Stefan registered his volume was rapidly increasing, but he had no desire to stop it. "If I need to forget something, it's you and your grabby claws."

The woman looked around at the suddenly quiet bar and her cheeks flushed red. "Fine, I know when I'm not wanted. Maybe you should go home to your *husband*," she said, tone dripping in ice.

Stefan would have laughed if his blood weren't boiling. He stood from his chair and towered over her, purposefully making his voice loud enough everyone could hear him and slamming his fist on the counter for extra emphasis. "At least I'm not so desperate to approach a man with a wedding ring and try to convince him to cheat on his wife. You're pathetic, you know that? Absolutely pathetic. As if I could ever bring myself to stoop to your level and—" He was cut off by a hand clapping over his mouth.

"That's enough, Stef, let's not cause a scene," Adrian said into his ear.

Brant stepped between Stefan and the woman. "I think it's time you leave. Now," he said.

She huffed and turned on her heel, exiting the bar without another word. The large group of women followed her, shooting dirty looks at Stefan as they left.

Adrian removed his hand from Stefan's mouth but kept his arm around his shoulder and guided him back to their table.

Brant brought their drinks a few minutes later and shook his head as he sat down. "Can we all agree to try and not get kicked out? I don't want to lose our trivia winning streak on the technicality of being banned."

"They don't want women like that here anyways," Stefan muttered. He looked up from his drink just in time to see the grimace on Brant's face and the look he shared with Adrian. "How much did it cost you to smooth the bartenders' ruffled feathers and keep us in their good graces? A group that size was probably worth a pretty penny. I'll pay you back."

"Dude, don't worry about it. I'm more worried about you. For someone who's usually cool as a cucumber, you looked like you were about to tear her to shreds, and not in the sexy way."

"I'm fine, already forgotten about it," Stefan said. He tried not to think about how his raw heart felt like it was being stabbed with serrated daggers. He forced a smile to his face and did his best to lighten his tone. "Anyway, Adrian, how's little Josie? She's what? Two months old now? How are you liking being a dad? How's Kiana doing?"

"Josie and Kiana are both doing great, Stefan. You just saw them just a few days ago, remember? Are you sure you're okay? I know it's been a long time since you've seen Kaleo, and I haven't said anything until now, but the ring you're wearing–"

"Looks like a wedding band, yes, I know. Really, I'm doing fine. I just get a little frustrated sometimes."

"I'd say," Brant muttered into his drink.

"Like you have any room to talk, Brant. It's been what? A month since you and Lin broke up? I'm surprised—instead of finding someone to help you take the edge off, you're just moping around like she died."

Brant frowned. "I'd have thought that of all people, you'd understand."

"Understand what? The dangers of cheating on my girlfriend? Were you jealous that girl decided to hit on me tonight instead of you? I thought a little overlap was kind of your thing."

Brant drained the last of his glass and slammed it on the table, eyes spitting fire. "I've been trying to give you a pass lately because you've been through a lot, and most of it has been my fault since I always screw things up, but that was too far. You're not the only one hurting, and I'm not going to let you use me as your punching bag tonight. Goodnight."

"Brant..." Adrian said.

"Don't worry about me, I'm not going to do anything stupid. I'll talk to you later, Adrian."

Stefan focused on the bottom of his glass, refusing to watch Brant walk away. After enough time had passed, he looked up to find Adrian staring at him. "What?"

"What do you mean, what? That was a horrible thing to say to Brant. You know how much the breakup tore him apart and almost caused him to fall off the wagon again. Tonight was the first time I've seen him smile in weeks. What's gotten into you?"

"I told you, I'm fine. Just tired or something. Sorry for ruining your night. I'll go home now," Stefan muttered, unable to maintain eye contact with his best friend as he stood from the booth.

Stefan didn't go home; he was feeling too conflicted and off-kilter to go back to Kaleo's empty house and be surrounded by memories of her. He drove down the street a few blocks and parked his bike in an empty alleyway before pulling out his phone.

"Hey, Ashley."

"Stefan, is everything okay? I thought you and Brant and Adrian were at trivia night. Did something happen?"

"Yeah, something did—but don't worry. Brant's fine. I know it's late, and this is last-minute, but I was hoping I could come over and talk." He heard her sigh and regretted asking so much. "It's okay if you say no; I'll be fine. Don't feel pressured or anything."

"You can come over if you promise to babysit Nicholas for an evening for me."

"I can do that."

"Then sure. Nicholas is down for the night. I'll put on a pot of coffee and the door will be unlocked. You can let yourself in."

Within twenty minutes, Stefan was sitting at Ashley's kitchen table, cup of hot coffee steaming in front of him. "I'm sorry for disturbing your evening. I know usually when we do this, I give you a bit more of a heads up."

"What happened?" Ashley asked.

Stefan summarized the evening and stared into his half-empty cup. Ashley sighed and topped up their cups. "Okay, I'm ready when you are," she said after leaning back in her chair and closing her eyes.

He'd already thought up a list of statements on his way. Stefan chose his words with great care; hearing too many lies gave Ashley headaches that could turn into migraines if she wasn't careful, and he didn't want to cause her any extra pain.

"I hurt Brant's feelings."

"Correct."

"I should apologize."

"Correct."

"The woman wanted me to cheat on Kaleo with her and didn't care one bit that I was wearing a wedding ring."

"Correct."

"I love Kaleo."

"Correct."

Now for the tricky ones, the statements that Stefan wasn't sure about. He hesitated for a moment before plunging forward.

"When she asked me to go back to her place, I wasn't tempted at all."

"Correct."

"I've never cheated on Kaleo."

"You've already asked that before, but correct."

"Are you sure?"

"Yes, Stefan, we've talked about this. Audra forcing herself on you doesn't count, and you were under a lot of stress and affected by her abilities when she literally *broke into your apartment* and tried to kill your dog."

"I've wanted to cheat on Kaleo in the past."

"Ouch," she said, rubbing her forehead.

"Sorry, I had to make sure."

"I'll give you that one, just don't do it again."

"I'm going to find her."

"You know that's not how my abilities work. I can't predict the future, and if you honestly believe you're going to find her, then it'll read as truth, whether or not you actually do."

"I know. I'm going to find her."

Ashley shook her head and looked at him with pity in her blue eyes. "Correct."

He drained his cup and got up to wash and dry it before putting it back in the cabinet. "Thanks, Ashley, I really appreciate this. You've been a lifesaver."

"Yeah, yeah, yeah, save it until after you watch Nicholas," she said, waving off his thanks with a small grin.

"Fine with me. Do you have a day in mind?"

"No, but I'll let you know."

Stefan nodded. "Sounds like a plan."

As he was leaving, Stefan paused at the door and turned around to look at Ashley. "I'm fine."

"I think we both know the real answer to that."

"I'm going to be okay."

"Correct."

After he left Ashley's townhouse, Stefan went home, showered, and fell into bed, holding Rosie in his arms and pretending that Kaleo was just working late at the office and would be home any minute. Despite his tossing and turning, sometime during the night he fell asleep.

Chapter Twenty-Four

The next morning, Stefan stopped by Heinstein Industries.

"Hey, Enrique, do you know what time Brant will be in today?" he asked Brant's secretary.

"Hi, Stefan. Actually he's—"

Brant's voice echoed from his office's open door. "I'm in here, come on in."

Stefan entered Brant's office and found his friend sitting in a dark leather chair, facing the large expanse of windows with his back to the room.

"You're in early today," Stefan said.

"Ashley wants us to hang out later, so I thought I'd get everything done this morning." Brant swiveled around to face him, and they stared at each other in silence.

"I wanted to apologize for last night. You didn't deserve any of it," Stefan said.

"You're right, I didn't. But lucky for you, I'm getting better at forgiving people. Here, have a seat. What's up with you lately? I was trying to help you, and you jumped all over me."

Stefan sat and ran a hand over his face. "Honestly? It's been six months. Every day that goes by without news puts me that much closer to the edge, and the woman last night almost pushed me over."

"How's the search going from this end?" Brant asked. After Kaleo's abduction and Stefan's fruitless trip to Europe, Brant's guilt had been so intense he'd created a small detective agency for the sole purpose of finding her and offered Stefan a job as the leader.

"It's a bunch of dead ends. I'm sorry to say there's been very little return on your investment so far."

"Do you need more funding? How much?" Brant pulled a checkbook out of his desk and waited, pen at the ready.

Stefan shook his head. The team had a generous budget which he'd used to hire a couple of freelance detectives who spent most of their time out in the field sniffing out any clues. In fact, sometimes it felt like the hardest part of Stefan's duties was to judge what their little group actually needed, and to stop Heinstein from spending all his money on new toys. "I don't need more money, I just need a lucky break."

"A break," Brant said. "Is Stone working you too hard? I'm serious when I say if you want to leave NAT, I'll pay you a full time salary with benefits at a competitive rate."

"You're already paying me a salary, and it's way above market rate, last I checked."

"Yeah, well it needs to be considering your experience and particular abilities. The last thing I'd want is for someone else to poach you away."

"Like you're trying to do with me and the task force?"

"If it makes you feel better, I can make you head of my personal security or something official."

"I can't leave the task force, especially not now."

"Things are that unstable, huh?"

"Classified information. I'm already walking a fine line working here part-time."

"I know you're pushing full-time here, don't lie to me. At least tell me you're not working overtime for Stone on top of everything else."

Again, Stefan shook his head. After he'd checked with Stone to make sure that Brant's offer didn't violate his government contract, Stefan had taken on the extra work. With Zeke now fully onboarded, Stefan was working a steady forty hours for the task force, and a few extra hours in the morning or evening at Heinstein Industries was more than worth the pay increase and the extra manpower to search for Kaleo.

"At least that's something. What are you even doing with all the extra money?"

"Saving it up for when Kaleo gets back. I'm sure she's been through the wringer, and I want her to be able to live the rest of her life in peace and quiet and never have to work again, if that's what she wants."

Stefan stopped talking, his eyes feeling strangely moist. He lived simply, even more simply than before he'd met Kaleo, and squirreled away whatever he could. He had big plans for the money: a house in the country so she could have a garden as large as she wanted, with plenty of room for Rosie to run, and maybe a comfortable early retirement for them to enjoy their lives and raise an entire brood of children without having to worry about anything other than who would pick up the kids from school and baking cookies for class fundraisers.

If nothing else, once he found Kaleo and after the war was over he was going to take her on a no-expense-spared vacation for as long as she wanted. He had already started making plans as a way to fill his lonely evenings, and every week she remained missing was another week he had to ensure everything would be perfect when she got back.

And she would be back; it was only a matter of when, not if. He was going to make sure of it.

"Anyway," he said, shoving down his emotions yet again, "I'm sorry about last night. You're a good friend, and I appreciate everything you've done for me. I'm sorry that you and Lin didn't work out. Have you met anyone else?"

After Audra had been taken into custody, Brant had to explain to Lin how he knew Audra, and from what Stefan gathered later, Lin didn't take his role in Kaleo's disappearance well. The two had eventually made up—until, several weeks before, something terrible had happened and they'd broken up for good. Stefan wasn't quite sure what was going on, as Brant was uncharacteristically silent on the subject, and Lin had already informed Stefan that she was uncomfortable talking about her personal life with him due to his proximity to Brant.

Brant shook his head. "No, I'm just taking time to sort myself out a bit more before thinking about getting into another relationship. Lin had to put up with a lot, especially with the Audra drama, and I don't want to lose another good woman because I'm not up to snuff."

Stefan checked his watch. "Well, I better be getting to my main job. We good?"

"Yeah, we're good. Seriously, if you need anything else, let me know."

Chapter Twenty-Five

Blade stepped out into the afternoon sun and stretched, smiling as the warmth and brightness filled her energy levels and made her fingertips tingle. "Are you sure that you don't want to ditch the horse and run with me?" she asked Sharps.

He swung into the saddle. "I don't need the conditioning, and my old knees wouldn't appreciate the unnecessary work."

"Suit yourself. Once I get one of those snazzy championship cups, can we maybe dial it back on all the running?"

"If you win a championship, we can talk about it, although I think you'd drive yourself and everyone else crazy without the exercise."

"You're right." Blade frowned as a dull pressure started at the back of her head.

"Everything okay?" Sharps asked, and she had to suppress a smile. Despite his gruff attitude, he'd taken his job as her mentor seriously, and had gotten her into top condition over the past several months. She'd heard some of the other gladiators complain about their mentors and the lack of respect or quality training they had, and Blade counted herself lucky that hers was so attentive.

"I'm fine; my head just feels a little weird, is all," she said, and bent down to make sure her running shoes were laced securely.

"Okay then, let's go. It's a long run today. Twenty kilos out, then twenty back at a comfortable pace. If you're out of breath, you're going too fast."

Blade nodded and they walked across the training grounds of the Boar's Head compound. When they passed through the gates, she picked up a steady jog. Today would be the longest run she'd completed so far, and even though she wasn't feeling as good as usual, she was glad to be outside of the training center with all its rules and stifling schedule.

As she ran, the dull headache increased, but she ignored it. More time passed, and the headache was accompanied by a new dizzy feeling that made it hard to keep her balance. Blade slowed to a walk, afraid that if she kept running she'd lose her balance and fall.

"C'mon now, pick up the pace. We're almost to the halfway point," Sharps said.

Her vision swam. "Sharps, I think something is wrong."

The world went black, and Blade lurched forward.

She fell in the darkness for a long time. Her hands reached out to grab something, anything, but there was nothing to stop her fall. Just as she began to worry she'd gone blind, Blade saw a light ahead and realized that instead of falling she was now standing. The change in position was disorienting, not helped by the ground rolling under her feet, but the longer she stayed still, the harder it was to breathe. She took one step forward, and, finding it easier breathe, took another, moving faster with each stride until she was sprinting towards the light.

As she got closer, Blade recognized a figure within the light. It was undoubtedly male, with broad shoulders and short hair. Something was achingly familiar about him, and she sensed that if she could just reach out and touch him, she'd be able to leave her terrible nightmare.

He wasn't making it easy on her, and it seemed to Blade like the closer she got to him, the faster he ran away.

"Stop, please," she gasped between heavy breaths, but he didn't so much as pause.

With one last desperate burst of speed, Blade launched herself towards him. Just as her fingers stretched out to grasp his shoulder, she felt herself being jerked back by unseen hands.

"No, wait, let me go!" she cried out, but it was no use. No matter how much she scrabbled at the ground, she couldn't stop herself from sliding away from the mysterious figure and back into the darkness.

She woke up in an infirmary bed. A healing assistant was sitting by her bed, and when she saw Kaleo was awake, she called out for Airmed. Almost immediately, the healer joined her assistant at Blade's bedside.

"You gave us quite the scare there," Airmed said as she leaned over Blade to check her vitals. Her white dress made her look like an angel of mercy.

"What happened?" Blade asked.

"Sharps said that you passed out in the middle of your run and started having a seizure. We think someone messed up your supplements last night and accidentally triggered an underlying issue."

"I had a terrible nightmare."

"You did? Tell me what you remember."

Blade shrugged. "I can't really remember what happened. There was just so much fear, confusion, and anger."

"Are you sure you don't remember anything? It would help us if you could."

"I'm sorry, but no. All I remember is how dark and cold it was, and that I was running towards something. A light, maybe? I'm not sure," Blade said. It was the truth. The nightmare, which had felt so awful and real at the time, was now rapidly fading away.

"That's okay. While you were out, we gave you something to remedy the medication mix-up, and we'll keep a closer eye on it in the future. It wouldn't do for one of our top contenders for the individual tournament to have a seizure in the middle of the arena," Airmed said as she patted Blade's hand.

"Yeah, let's not do that." Blade looked at Airmed. "Is this going to impact my entry?"

"It shouldn't be a problem. It was just a simple medication error that won't happen again. Now I want you to rest for another hour and take it easy for the rest of the day."

"Taking it easy now? The tournament isn't that far away. Sharps is going to kill me for messing up his training plan."

"Don't worry about Sharps. I can handle him, and if he starts getting too huffy with me, I'll stick him with one of my sedative darts," Airmed said with a smile. She glanced at the clock, patted Blade's hand, and stood up. "I've got to be getting on. Remember: one hour's rest, take it easy for the rest of the day, and tomorrow you'll be as good as new."

Chapter Twenty-Six

Sharps tapped his foot as he sat in a chair outside Airmed's medical clinic.

Anthisma, the Boar's Head gardener, looked up from Airmed's herbal plants. "Worried about your mentee?"

Sharps didn't immediately respond. He and Anthisma had a working acquaintanceship that could almost be called a friendship on good days—Sharps gave Anthisma tips about the gladiator games, and Anthisma kept his eyes and ears out and repaid Sharps with a wealth of information tidbits. Despite their arrangement, Sharps still liked to make Anthisma work for his tips, and he suspected the gardener enjoyed their verbal dances almost as much as he enjoyed his winning bets.

Anthisma nodded. "I saw them carry her in, and heard them say something about how she fainted and you had to haul her back. What happened?"

The sting of the fresh incident still smarted, and for a moment, Sharps considered telling Anthisma to mind his own business, but decided against it.

"About halfway through her run, she collapsed. I'm not positive, but she was almost running late, and I don't think she had a chance to eat her full breakfast this morning. It was probably just a severe blood-sugar drop or something," Sharps said, toeing a thin line between giving the man just enough information to keep him satisfied without hurting his mentee's reputation.

In reality, within the span of ten steps Blade had gone from running like she didn't have a care in the world to collapsing in the middle of the road and convulsing. "Let me go... Stefan... Wait...Help me," she'd groaned through gritted teeth, and thrashed her limbs before going limp.

Sharps had tried to wake her, but she only continued to talk, begging to be released and allowed to go back to her family with frequent mentions of the name "Stefan." Once he ascertained she wouldn't be waking up and that something was very wrong, Sharps had immediately bundled her up and thrown her into the saddle, sitting her in front of him, where he could be sure she wouldn't fall, and stuffing her mouth with a roll of gauze to keep her from talking.

"That's too bad. Did you hear about what happened to Nightshade?"

"Unfortunately, yes, I was there when it happened," Sharps said.

"I heard her team was sparring with Lady Vestibulous's team earlier today when one of Nightshade's men hesitated to protect her, and it gave Vestibulous's team an opening they used to slice her up."

"It wasn't that bad, but she did get hurt."

"It's bad news for the Boar's Head that a junior queen and a star newcomer are both injured or sick. You think they're having to separate them inside?"

"They shouldn't have to, any more than they would for anyone else."

"But Blade is strong, and Nightshade is having enough difficulty as it is keeping control of her team. Surely the last thing anyone wants is to have Nightshade's men get drawn to Blade. If I was Airmed, I'd put Nightshade right up against the door and keep Blade as far away as possible to minimize any interference."

"You think Blade is that strong?"

"She's your mentee, isn't she? She's won me quite a nice sum of money, too. I've seen her in the ring and in the arena, and I wouldn't be surprised if she was called up for her own junior team next year."

"It would be her second year at the training center. Most women need to wait until year three or four before they're strong enough and have been around enough to control a team and get promoted to queen."

"Yeah, and most women take a year and a half or two years before you even consider letting them try to qualify for the individual tournament." Anthisma wagged his finger at Sharps. "You can't fool me; I know you're a wily old fox. You've got a very talented mentee, and enough ambition to push her as high as she'll go. At this point, it certainly looks like she's got more potential than Nightshade."

Sharps raised an eyebrow. Privately, he'd always thought that Nightshade might not have what it took to be a successful queen. Her ability to give others hallucinations and waking nightmares was powerful enough, but she'd always had an off-putting air about her. He'd voiced his reservations the fall, before there was discussion about making a new Boar's Head junior team, but had been shot down by Enzo. Despite his best efforts in the intervening months, Nightshade had struggled to bond with her team, and deep cracks were starting to show. They were around two months out from the team tournament, and if her team hadn't bonded to her already, the odds weren't looking good for Nightshade.

"I'm sure you've already thought about all of that, though, haven't you? I'm old enough to remember what happened when you were competing in your team tournament almost what—twelve? Thirteen years ago? You had the choice to either save your queen or win the finals match, and you chose to win. That was with a powerful queen, too. I may be just a gardener, but I know what it looks like when a queen doesn't make the cut." Anthisma rambled on, but his words struck home.

Sharps stood and walked into the building. Anthisma was right—Nightshade was lying near the entryway, the knife wounds she'd taken earlier on her leg and shoulder already bandaged. Against the opposite wall, far from anyone who came to visit Nightshade, lay Blade, who was looking out the window. Sharps turned away before she could see him and walked back outside.

Anthisma was still muttering to himself and tending the plants, and Sharps frowned as his mind went into overdrive. It was true—the performance of Nightshade's team did not inspire confidence in either their future as a team or her abilities as a leader. Even now, almost ten months after the team had been formed, it was a bad sign they were still hesitating to protect her and letting her get hurt.

He remembered how Blade had tossed and turned on the ground, her brow furrowed as she called out for help and begged to be rescued. Sharps had long suspected that not everything at the Boar's Head was above board but had tried to keep his nose out of where it didn't belong. Now, though, his mentee, a woman who had been loved by a Ranger and whose demeanor and spirit reminded him faintly of a girl he had loved years before, was calling out for his help.

Sharps squared his shoulders and walked to his training room. He couldn't change whatever circumstances had led to her being contracted by the Boar's Head, but he could do his best to make sure she survived the gladiator arena and won enough to escape.

Within the hour, Sharps was summoned to the conference room next to Elwin's office. He entered and took his seat, choosing to ignore Enzo and Airmed and stare down at the dark lacquered wood of the table as he waited for Elwin to arrive and the meeting to begin.

"You look shaken, Sharps," Enzo said.

He snorted at the dig. "I am perturbed by the events of the day. I don't get shaken."

"Anyone would be worried if their student had such an unfortunate reaction only a few months before the biggest event of the year. Especially when their student is so prized and has so much pressure on her shoulders."

"I know you don't speak from experience, as none of your students have ever been as successful, no matter how much time they've had. One would wonder how you were able to rise to the rank you have with no practical experience in coaching gladiators."

"Now, now, don't you two start," Airmed said from her place across the table.

"Start? Have they ever stopped?" Elwin said as he stepped into the room.

"Hello, sir." Sharps greeted his boss with a dip of his head.

Elwin sat at the head of the table. "Hello there. Now, let's get started, shall we? What is this I hear about an issue with Blade?"

"She was out jogging with me when she suddenly collapsed. Earlier, before we started, she complained of a headache, but I didn't think anything of it. By the time I dismounted, she'd started thrashing on the ground and I stuffed a roll of bandages in her mouth because I was afraid that she'd bite her own tongue off with all the gnashing of teeth she was doing—"

"--which we need to talk about, because you should never do that. She very well could have choked to death," Airmed interrupted.

"Peace, Airmed. Let the man finish his story," Elwin said.

Sharps nodded. "Anyway, I knew she needed medical attention, so I got her in the saddle in front of me and did my best to get her back here as soon as possible."

"Did you hear her say anything?" Airmed asked.

"I got that bandage in her mouth pretty fast, so no, I didn't," Sharps lied.

"Airmed, do you have anything to add?" Elwin asked.

Airmed flipped her long hair over her shoulder. "I have a new assistant who mixed up several medications last night. As a result, Blade received a supplement that I believe triggered an underlying condition and led to the appearance of new side effects. I suspect she's had this issue since we recruited her, but it's been managed so well without a triggering episode that it's been undetected until now. Never fear, sir, I have properly punished the assistant who made the mistake and have rectified the situation. Blade is resting now, and will be on relative rest for the rest of the day to give the medication time to work. By tomorrow she should be fine for a return to her normal training schedule."

"I don't like it. I know we've already discussed this, but I still think she hasn't had enough time as a gladiator to be pushed for the individual tournament so soon. With this delay, perhaps we should rethink her entry," Enzo said.

"That's ridiculous. She's currently undefeated in both ring and arena, and qualified for the tournament without any pushing from me," Sharps said.

Elwin pursed his lips. "I'm inclined to agree with Enzo. We don't want her entered if she's not completely ready. She's much too valuable an investment."

"She'll be more than ready. Sir, you've already seen her performance in her qualifying matches, and she's only getting better."

The training master scoffed. "Of course he'd say that; she's his student. He's just pushing her harder to get more glory for himself and not thinking about how it would affect the rest of us if she gets killed or irrevocably injured in the arena."

"That's not true. If anything, keeping her in the individual tournament will be much better for her in the long run."

"How so?" Elwin asked.

Sharps chose his words carefully. "She doesn't have the temperament required for a long-term gladiator. The way of life here will eventually drain her."

"You don't think that she's mentally tough enough?"

"No, it's not that. Right now she's surviving because she has set herself a personal goal of winning everything, but if you take that away from her, if you tell her this one mistake out of her control is enough to take her out of the running and that she won't have any truly meaningful matches for another year, I fear she'll lose her motivation. She doesn't have the natural brutality and need for a regimented life that makes for a successful long-lasting gladiator. She's like a shooting star, not an ever-present moon."

"How far along do you estimate she is in her training?"

Sharps frowned, calculating in his head. "Right now? She could make it into the quarterfinals easily, and would be a top contender in the semis. I'm not sure who else the other centers or free agents are in the tournament yet, or I'd be surer about her final chances."

Enzo snorted. "A top contender in the semis? Someone's confident."

Sharps shrugged. "Elwin asked for my opinion. I've trained our gladiators for the past seven years, and she's easily one of the best. She came in with a good amount of innate knowledge of her abilities and skill, so I've just had to put the finishing touches on her and get her strength up."

Elwin surveyed the room, and Sharps was careful not to look away from his eye contact.

"Sharps, do you really think she'll be ready?"

"Yes sir. I'd even be willing to foot the bill to bring Viewer in here if he says differently."

"You will? Then we'll do that."

"But sir, think of the girl's health. I don't want to endanger your investment if she's not ready," Enzo protested.

"If she's not, Viewer will tell us. For obvious reasons, Blade has great potential to be a powerful tool, but like any finely crafted weapon, she must be handled with great care when not in use. Airmed, if this happens again, it will be your assistants' heads and your own that roll. Am I clear?"

"Crystal, sir."

"Good. Meeting adjourned."

"Actually, Elwin, may I speak once more? I have another recommendation. It may sound unorthodox, but if everything Airmed has said is true, I have full confidence that Blade can pull it off," Sharps asked.

Elwin leaned back in his chair and gestured for Sharps to continue.

Sharps swallowed. "Let Blade also enter the team competition. She proved she can lead a team in her recruitment trials, and it will only increase her prestige if she wins. Right now we're counting on Lady Vestibulous's team to be our main entry, with Nightshade's team to fill the bonus entry slot we were given as a consolation prize after last year's individual tournament finals fiasco. Nightshade's team is still having a hard time bonding—as I'm sure you're aware, she was injured today in a team sparring match. Instead of rushing Nightshade's team and risk devaluing her prospects by being in Lady Vestibulous's shadow, why not give Blade a team? A wild-card team for our wild-card slot."

"The team tournament? Your ambition truly knows no bounds, Sharps. That five percent bonus you get from the winnings of your mentee must have gone to your head. The nerve of it, suggesting such a thing when she's still in the infirmary bed," Enzo said.

"If I know Blade, she's only in the bed because Airmed told her to stay there. She's more than capable, and having a rookie gladiator win both the individual and team tournaments, and an American at that, will be a huge prestige boost to our training center, and to her value. We'd have every sponsor in Rome flocking to us."

"Just a moment ago you were expressing doubts that she'd be able to compete in the finals of the individual tournament, now you're saying she's going to win both? Which is it, Sharps?" Enzo asked, a mocking smile plastered across his face.

Sharps ignored the pointed jabs from Enzo and made eye contact with Elwin. "I was being conservative in my estimates earlier because I don't want to mislead you. If I am being totally honest and not trying to hedge any bets, she's a top contender for both tournaments, dependent on her team. I hesitate to make any guarantees, but I fully believe that with just a little more time and fine-tuning, she could beat anyone, including our veterans and those who only fight in the underground rings and Black Arena."

"You're blinded because she's your mentee," Enzo said.

"I'm not. You've seen her fight in the arena, so you should know just how much potential she has."

"If you give her a team and throw them into the arena before they're fully bonded, she'll die. Two months is an unheard-of time for bonding," Airmed said.

"She's strong. I have no doubt that she'll be ready."

"We have protocols for this, and she's already too far ahead of them. At minimum, one year for training, one for getting prepared for the individual tournament, and then another for the team tournament if they pass the tests of the prior years. Blade has completed none of those steps. You say two months is enough to bond? Nightshade has had more than four times that and is still having difficulty controlling her team," Enzo said.

"Nightshade is not Blade."

"You're right, she has four more years of experience!"

"And despite all that supposed experience, a worse record. If you think the reason Nightshade's having issues controlling her team is because they haven't had enough time together, instead of her simply being weaker and less charismatic than we originally thought, you've been letting her use her hallucinations on you."

"Airmed, what is Blade's physical condition?" Elwin asked, his quiet voice cutting through the argument like a hot knife through butter.

"Once she recovers, she'll be as healthy as a horse, sir. For what it's worth, now that this option is on the table, I must agree with Sharps, albeit for different reasons."

"Explain, please."

"She's healthy as of now, but as we all saw today that can change rapidly. I've had to adjust her medications due to this new complication, and she's currently receiving a dose that is extremely close to the maximum safe dosage for her condition. We're treading a fine line at the moment because there is evidence of some people building up a tolerance for this type of medication. If her condition deteriorates any more, she may not be suitable for the arena next year."

"I see. I have much to think about. Sharps, I know you're a busy man; you may leave us. I will inform you later what we decide," Elwin said.

Sharps nodded, stood, and bowed before exiting the room. He knew he'd done the best that he could to advance Blade; now it was time to get back to work training.

Chapter Twenty-Seven

Blade looked around the meeting room. Just over a week had passed since her seizure, and she was feeling brand new. Her updated medication regimen was doing wonders at keeping her head clear, and she focused so much better that she wondered if her condition had been lurking just under the surface and impacting her more than she realized the entire time.

Sharps had told her he had a surprise for her in the Boar's Head conference room but hadn't said anything more. Knowing Sharps, that could mean anything from an extra workout to a new set of weapons for her to try. Blade had seen him forging his own steel knives and asked him several times to make some for her, but so far she'd been out of luck.

There were two other gladiators in the room whom she'd recognized from around the training center. For the most part, the rookie gladiators were kept separate from the others, and the no-fraternizing rules got strictly enforced, but the two sitting across from Blade were good enough to be alternates for one of the Boar's Head teams preparing for the upcoming team tournament.

One of the gladiators, Suerte, a short, compact woman with striking black hair and eyes set in an olive face, had an ability that enabled her to estimate the relative probability in any situation and use it to her advantage. The gladiator sitting across from her was Ox, a beast-like man who towered over everyone else at almost seven feet tall, and whose broad shoulders and facial features resembled those of a cow too much to be coincidence. Blade had heard the darker rumors surrounding each; supposedly Suerte was on the run from a South American gang she'd stolen from—and Ox's family had gotten a little too close to their dairy cattle during the Hard Times, getting infected with a different strain of the virus that manifested itself in his distinctively bovine features.

With the memory wipes, one could never be sure about such rumors; the rumors surrounding Blade included her being a former American assassin who was using the gladiator games as a retirement plan, and while she couldn't be certain of her past, a life as an assassin didn't quite feel right.

After Blade sat in one of the empty chairs, another man entered the room. He was tall and had long blond hair falling to his shoulders in loose waves. She recognized him as Neptune, the Abled who had made it to the quarter finals in the individual tournament the year before.

Neptune grabbed a cup of water, stuck his hand in it, and as he sat down twirled strands of the water between his fingers like someone else might do to a pencil. "Suerte, Ox," he said with a curt nod before turning his dark blue eyes to Blade. "And who are you?"

"My name is Blade."

"Blade? Not the rookie who's entered the individual tournament this year?"

"Yes, that would be me."

"Hmm. Interesting."

Not long after Neptune's entrance, Sharps and Enzo, the training master, also walked into the room. Enzo looked around and rolled his eyes. "We're missing one."

"Blade is here, so I did my job. You were the one in charge of getting everyone else in the same room," Sharps said.

Just as Enzo opened his mouth to reply, the door creaked open and a chill ran down Blade's spine.

A tall, thin man sauntered into the room. The top of his bald head shone under the lights, and despite the warm day outside he wore a rich red cloak over black trousers embroidered with gold and silver thread. His light brown eyes glinted with malice and greed, and his thin mouth was pressed into a line. From the descriptions she'd heard from others, and from her own glimpses of him around the Boar's Head, Blade supposed that the man was the Abled named Eagle.

While she'd heard rumors of Suerte's past, Ox's heritage, and Neptune's predilection for beautiful women, the rumors that swirled around Eagle were stories of injury, maliciousness, and death. If Neptune was the golden boy, Eagle was the boogieman.

"Thank you for finally showing up, Eagle. Please, take a seat," Enzo said.

Eagle shifted on his feet and Blade caught a glimpse of the black wings that gave him his name. "No, thank you, I will remain standing," he said in a raspy voice bordering on a quiet screech.

"Suit yourself; it makes no difference to me," Enzo said.

Blade watched Eagle saunter across the room to the opposite back corner. She didn't like him watching her. It made her uncomfortable, as if she were trying to ignore a hungry wolf waiting for the opportune moment to pounce. Her attention was drawn back to the front of the room as Enzo cleared his throat.

"Now that everyone is here, we can finally begin the meeting. Due to the tragedy of last year's individual tournament, the game organizers have granted us a bonus slot in this year's team tournament. You've all been gathered in this room because we are forming a second gladiator team for the upcoming team tournament. You each have been hand-picked for this team, and if you look around the room, you will see your fellow teammates."

"This can't be right. What about Nightshade? I thought her team was the next one up," Neptune said.

"That is none of your concern."

"Of course it is, if it's affecting the creation of a new team I'm expected to join."

"It has been decided that Nightshade's team will be given an extra year to prepare for the team tournament."

"So the rumors were true; she wasn't ready," Suerte muttered across the table.

"We have two women on the team. Everyone knows serious teams only have one queen, and the rest men. Was there a mistake?" Neptune asked.

"No mistake. There are two women to ensure there is a strong backup in case the fitness of your queen changes, as it is much easier to add a man to a team than to shift loyalties to a completely new woman."

"Who's doubting my fitness? I am more than capable of leading a team and have already proven myself. I don't need a backup, let alone a rookie," Suerte said, leaning back casually in her seat.

"I am sorry for not being clear: you're the backup, Suerte."

Blade suddenly found herself the center of attention. She held her head high and was careful to not shrink under the combined weight of their eyes on her. Enzo wasn't as successful at not wilting under Sharps' glare at his blunt announcement.

"We'll see about that," Suerte said. She stood from the table and stalked around its edge to stand in front of Blade, invading her personal space.

"Submit to me," Suerte said.

Blade almost laughed at the absurdity of Suerte thinking she could be so easily cowed. "No, I don't think I will."

Suerte narrowed her eyes. "I am Suerte, third-year gladiator at the Boar's Head. I have won thirty-two sanctioned matches and lost six. Who are you, rookie?"

Blade sighed and stood, stepping close to Suerte and drawing herself up so the shorter woman could feel every inch of their height difference. "My name is Blade, and I am your queen."

She was expecting the blow, and without giving her abilities away, she slowed Suerte's fist enough to catch it in her left hand and stop it six inches from her jaw.

"What do your abilities say about your chance of injury if I return that punch?" Blade asked quietly as she held up her right hand, now glowing red.

Suerte broke eye contact to look at Blade's hand. For a moment, there was a pregnant silence, and then she nodded and stepped back.

"That's it? You're just going to back down?" Neptune said.

"My abilities have gotten me this far, so it'd be foolish for me to question them. It's not my fault the people in charge want to play games with their money, and at least I have a spot in the team tournament now," Suerte said. She glanced at Blade and frowned before muttering, *"Esa chica es tan débil que no carga ni con sus libros, mucho menos con su equipo."*

"Soy más fuerte de lo que parezco, y tal vez el resto del equipo prefiera una mujer en vez de una enana," Blade replied without thinking.

Suerte's eyebrow rose. *"Ah? Hablas español?"*

Blade pursed her lips and scrunched her nose. *"Sí."*

Neptune cut in. "Anyway, how is this even going to work? Blade's training for the individual tournament—how's she going to be able to train with us as well?"

"Blade is my mentee and on an accelerated training schedule. If I were you, I would concentrate on working on your training instead of questioning her readiness," Sharps said.

"Didn't she just take the memory drink a few months ago? As a rookie, does she even know about the importance of the team tournaments? This is insane. Enzo, you can't be serious about signing off on this."

"Don't you want to be on a team? As I recall, you threw quite the hissy fit when you weren't considered for Nightshade's," Suerte said.

Enzo swallowed and looked at Sharps. "It has already been decided. Neptune, you should be grateful you've been placed on this team despite your previous outbursts and history."

"I won't let you down," Blade said.

Neptune ignored her. "Ox? Thoughts?"

Ox shrugged. "Suerte tested her. I fight when and where I'm needed, and if I am asked to fight on this team, I am content."

"Eagle?"

"Leave me out of this. I wouldn't be here if I had a choice."

"Are you satisfied now, Neptune?" Sharps asked.

Neptune glared at Blade and folded his arms across his chest. "I want to see her in the ring."

"She has an arena fight scheduled at the beginning of next week. You can see her in action then."

"No, I don't want to wait that long." Neptune stood and thrust his finger at Blade. "You and me, in the ring. Now."

"Neptune! This is highly irregular. Sit back down and accept your placement!" Enzo screeched.

"If she's going to lead this team, she's going to have to accept more intense challenges than this. I'm only one member of a team, not several members all working together. Might as well see if she has what it takes. I want a full match, weapons, armor, and everything. Let's see if this rookie is even half as good as you seem to think."

"I can't allow this. Sharps, you're her mentor; tell him this isn't acceptable!"

Sharps leaned back in his chair and nodded at Blade. "She can handle herself and it'll be good practice for her. Be careful, Neptune, and try not to get hurt too badly."

While Neptune opened and closed his mouth like a gaping fish, Blade walked out of the room. As she walked, she embraced her anger at the dismissive way in which the others had treated her. She'd worked hard the past four months, harder than anyone else in the complex. She'd gained pounds of muscle, strengthened her abilities, and honed her reflexes to a razor's edge.

And yet, despite how much blood, sweat, and tears she'd invested into her training, the others still refused to accept her. The unproven fighters were jealous of her success, and to the veteran fighters she was no more than an up-start rookie who hadn't yet earned her place in the gladiator world. Wherever she went in the training center, she heard whispers of how she'd only received her spot in the individual tournament due to favoritism; that as her mentor, Sharps had somehow thrown the matches that had allowed her to qualify.

No one believed she was deserving. Some of them had seen her performance in the arena and the way she'd stomped her opponents into the ground and still doubted her. Others could be excused; they hadn't heard the crowds scream her name as she raised her fist in victory.

She would show them.

Blade strode into the gym and made a beeline for the armory with its racks of weapons placed against the wall. While she had become familiar with everything the Boar's Head had to offer, Blade hadn't yet found one weapon or style of weapon that truly appealed to her. She eyed the racks with their organized variety of swords, maces, and bows, along with more exotic weapons like katanas, madus, and shotels.

She was drawn to a medium-length spear with a head almost long enough to be considered a short sword in its own right. She hefted the spear and, satisfied with its weight, set it aside as hers for the fight.

It was a simple matter to buckle on leather armor, and she was done by the time Neptune entered the space to get his own weapons.

With a derisive snort, Blade shouldered past Neptune, with spear in hand and a large hunting knife tucked into her belt.

As she waited for Neptune to finish suiting up, Blade let the bright Italian sun shine on her skin and warm her from the outside in. Even as a few droplets of sweat trickled down the small of her back, she basked. The energy from the sun filled her to the brim like a celebratory cup of wine after winning a big fight, and as the energy began to overflow, Blade incorporated it into her body to give herself a boost.

She was careful not to imbibe too much—the more she processed and used, the more fatigue she would feel later, and she assumed Sharps wouldn't take pity on her and give her a pass from training that day simply because of Neptune's distrust.

There were eddies in the energy patterns at the entrance of the training room, and Blade opened her eyes to find Neptune striding confidently across the field of dirt. His medium-length blond hair was held back by a helmet, and the sunlight glinted off his gold and silver chest plate. His right hand held a triton and his left a net. As he approached, he turned around slowly in a circle to wave at the crowd of onlookers that had already begun to form. A large water skin was slung across his back.

Blade took a deep breath and stepped forward to meet him in the center of the hastily drawn ring. They faced off against each other, separated by ten feet of space. At the side of the ring stood Sharps and Enzo.

"Neptune is challenging Blade for her spot as leader of our second team. As such, this fight will be under gladiator rules, but to submission, not death," Enzo said as he raised his hands in the air.

Blade tightened her grip on her spear; gladiator rules effectively meant there were no rules. The only honor in the ring was that which was bought through blood. As Enzo's hand began to descend, she reviewed all she knew about Neptune.

He was strong, fast, and a good enough gladiator to make it to the quarter-finals of the individual tournament the year before. Rumor had it that he would have been a shoo-in for the Boar's Head junior team if he had been less of a womanizer; the flightiness of his relationships called his loyalty and judgment into question, and he'd been passed over despite his obvious talent in the arena.

Neptune's usual modus operandi was to capture his opponents in his net and then deal a deadly blow with his triton. His ability enabled him to manipulate the form of the water in the bag slung across his back, changing it from sticky to slick in an instant and giving him an edge wherever his water could reach.

Enzo's hand dropped, and the challenge began.

Blade darted forward and jabbed at Neptune with her spear. He knocked the blade to the side, but she twirled it in her hands and whipped the butt around for a follow-up attack.

Neptune dodged, then threw one end of his net towards her legs, presumably to entangle her feet and make her fall. Blade jumped over the net, landed on one foot, and used her spear as counterbalance for another attack.

This time, Neptune was ready for her. He stepped to the side, lifted his weapon, and brought it crashing down on the midpoint of Blade's spear. The sudden force shoved her spear into the ground and splintered the shaft. Blade immediately let go of the spear and rolled to the side, the triton sweeping over her head with a whistle.

Despite Sharps' best efforts to break her bad habits, something about being on the defensive felt comfortable. Blade sensed the danger in the siren song of comfort; playing defense was only good if she was prepared to push the offensive when she had the chance.

"Stop playing around, Blade, and end this!" Sharps barked.

Blade knew better than to break her focus and acknowledge she'd heard his advice—she'd only made that mistake once and paid for it in pushups to fatigue the next day. He was right, she needed to win, and she couldn't do that if she was running away from Neptune.

Blade completed the roll and sprang to her feet, shield at the ready. Neptune far outclassed her in strength, and probably in speed, but she knew that when it came to abilities she had the upper hand.

Neptune had given her the perfect chance to show the entire training center what she was made of, and she wouldn't let such an opportunity go to waste.

It was time to attack.

Blade pivoted, picked up her broken spear, snapped it in two, and held both parts in front of her. Neptune was somewhat predictable in his attacks: sweep with the net, then jab with the triton. This time, when he jabbed, Blade caught the triton on the blunt end of the spear and twisted within his arms to jab him in the nose with her elbow. Before he could react, she was back out of his reach.

"That's it, I've been trying to take it easy on you. Time to finish this," Neptune growled as blood streamed from his nose.

"Oh? So you actually have more? That's good, I was beginning to get bored. Here, I'll even give you a moment to wash your face," Blade said with a faux yawn as she leaned on her broken spear. She heard a couple of snickers from the crowd and smiled—she wanted to ensure Neptune's body wasn't the only thing that took a beating.

The taunt worked, and a cord of water wrapped around Neptune's torso and cascaded down his arm. With a roar, he swung his net high at Blade's head.

It was Neptune's signature move: the net, heavy with water and weights, would stick to whatever it touched, and once he'd entrapped his prey within its confines, Neptune would manipulate the surface tension of the different strings of water until they entangled his opponent, at which point he would have all the time he needed to torture out a submission.

Blade activated her shield and reached up to mold it into an umbrella over her head. The net settled neatly across the top, and Neptune let out a shout of victory that was cut short when he saw Blade's feral grin.

She took the energy swirling around her, directed it into her outstretched hand, and pushed it into her shield in a surge of heat and vibration. Instantly, the water on Neptune's net evaporated and the fibers emitted a high-pitched whine from the energy flowing through them.

As the red tendrils of energy spread from her hand and traveled up the net, Neptune reached out to pull it out of her grasp, but to no avail. When the tendrils reached his hand, he yelped and dropped the net.

"You'll pay for that!"

"Give up, Neptune. You're outmatched here and you know it, even if you don't want to admit it," she said as she allowed the smoking net to drop to the ground at her side.

He rushed her.

With a shortened spear in one hand and its broken half in the other, Blade met him in the middle of the impromptu ring. They traded a flurry of blows, and thanks to her shield placement, Blade didn't draw so much as a scratch.

She sensed Neptune getting desperate, and she pushed her advantage. He swung wildly at her neck with his triton. She dropped to the ground, swept his legs out from under him, jumped to her feet, drew her hunting knife, and knelt on his stomach with her knife pointed at his throat and the head of her spear aimed at his chest.

Neptune raised his head from the ground and evaluated her calmly, even as his chest heaved for breath.

For a moment they were frozen in silence, and then Neptune nodded and held his hands up. "I submit. Blade won."

Blade kept her weapons where they were. "And as for my place on the team?"

"I accept your leadership and will train with you."

"Neptune has submitted; the challenge is over. Blade has won!" Enzo shouted.

Blade dropped her weapons and offered a hand to help Neptune up.

"I'll see you around," Neptune said as he shook her hand, before trotting off to join the other veteran fighters.

Blade watched him go and briefly envied him for the ribbing he took from his companions.

"You'll get there one day," Sharps said at her side.

"Will I?"

"If you want to."

"Okay." She turned to Sharps. "What's on the training docket for today? I assume you're not going to let me rest?"

"After that little match? If that got your heart rate up, I need to start doubling your conditioning," Sharps scoffed.

"Neptune was a quarter-finalist last year, wasn't he? Shouldn't that count for something?"

"Sure, it counts as a good warm up. Now, c'mon. We need to work on your footwork and aggression when attacking. You need more practice breaking out of your bad habits. And you won't be able to hear me yell at you in the arena if it happens again."

Blade nodded and picked up her weapons. As her hands closed around the two halves of the spear, it felt like she was holding an old friend.

"Hey, Sharps, do we have anything else like these? I really like how it feels in my hand."

"I'm sure we can find something."

"If we can't, will you make me one?"

Sharps huffed as he walked away, and Blade followed him with a smile.

Chapter Twenty-Eight

Stefan showed up to Ashley's townhouse at the promised time with Rosie in tow.

"Thanks for doing this, Stefan," Ashley said as she handed him a crying Nicholas. "You already know where everything is, but he's not feeling well today. I think it's just some colic, and the doctor said it's not contagious, but he's been extra fussy. I'm sorry; you've probably had a long day, but I really need to get out of the house..."

"Ashley, it's fine. Go have fun with Brant. Nicholas and I will be okay. Won't we, little guy?" Stefan said as he bounced the baby in his arms and did his best to pretend the cries weren't bothering him. It was almost two months since his first time babysitting Nicholas, and he was well versed in the nightly routine.

Ashley stood from her wheelchair to slip on a long coat and smiled at him, placing a hand on his arm. "I really do appreciate this, Stefan. Thank you so much."

"It's no problem. Anything to help a friend out."

Ashley kissed Nicholas's head, hesitated, and then kissed Stefan on the cheek before sitting back in her wheelchair and wheeling herself out the front door.

Stefan spent most of the time rocking the colicky baby in the nursery. He could easily see why Ashley needed a break—Nicholas might be small, but the normally quiet baby had inherited a robust pair of lungs. It was a much shorter evening than he expected when Ashely returned just after nine o' clock, explaining that she just didn't feel right about leaving her sick child for too long.

The next morning, after he spent a few hours in his small office at Heinstein Industries as was his norm, Stefan dropped by Kaleo's house, loaded Rosie onto the back seat of his car, and went to work at the task force. He'd completely given up riding his bike; he couldn't take Rosie with him, and he felt terrible about leaving her home alone all day. There was also a second reason for putting his bike in storage: he had no intention of getting into a wreck and risk postponing Kaleo's rescue even further.

Stefan walked into the task force building with Rosie at his side, fixed himself a cup of coffee in his second-favorite mug, waved at Laura who was working down the hall, and unlocked his office door.

He'd been sitting at his desk for a few minutes when Nicole dropped by with the day's mail.

"How are you doing this morning? Getting enough sleep?" she asked brightly.

"Doing just fine, how about you?" he said, purposefully ignoring her second question.

"I'm doing well. You know, your ability is super speed, not super sleep. You look terrible."

He sighed and lifted his coffee mug. "This is only my second cup this morning. Give me an hour or two and I'll be downright chipper."

"You know that's not what I mean."

"I'm doing the best I can, Nicole. That's all that anyone can ask of me."

"Maybe you should tell yourself that. You can only push yourself so far before you run off a cliff."

"Or make a breakthrough."

Nicole rolled her eyes and he smiled; a laugh would have felt too forced. "Don't worry, Nicole. Rosie's keeping an eye on me. She's gotten really good at telling me when I need to take breaks."

"You know, we're just worried about you because we care."

"I know, Nicole, and I appreciate it, but I'm fine. Once I bring Kaleo home, I'll be even better."

Nicole looked doubtful, and Stefan guessed she wasn't ready to leave yet. "Anyway, if I promise that I won't say anything to Brant, can you tell me how Lin's doing? I see she took today off," he said.

"She's doing fine, I guess. She said she was going out with Ashley Heinstein last night. Something about a much-needed girls' night out."

"Is that so? Brant mentioned something to me yesterday at the gym about going out with Ashley for some sibling bonding time, and I babysat Nicholas last night."

"He said that? Do you think...?" Nicole trailed off.

Stefan shrugged. "I have no clue."

"Well, I guess I better get back to work. If you need me, I'll be down the hall."

"See you around."

Stefan sipped his coffee as he worked his way through the mail delivery. Nicole was always kind enough to order it in the way he liked: domestic reports first with recognized sources as top priority, miscellaneous domestic mail, international reports from sources, and then unknown international mail.

He had worked his way through most of the stack when he paused at the sight of a medium-sized, beaten envelope that looked like it had traveled a very long way. Stefan noted the postmark from Rome, and the return address of "Paul Allen," and reached for the knife he'd been using as a letter opener.

A piece of paper fell out of the envelope, but Stefan paid it no mind as he opened the letter.

Stefan,
Is this her? Let me know if you want to come back for another visit.
Paul

With trembling fingers, Stefan picked up the smaller paper that had fallen face down on his desk.

At first glance, it looked like a baseball trading card but for gladiators. A warrior goddess stared up at him from the picture in the center. Her dark brown hair was styled in loose curls hanging just below her muscular shoulders and was held back by a thin silver headband, her arms were crossed across her chest in an intimidating pose, and the scar running from her left temple down to her chin imparted her a ferocious air.

Kaleo's eyes glared up at him from the paper, daring him to find her.

His second-favorite coffee cup dropped to the floor and shattered.

Stefan's mind raced a thousand miles a minute as he drank in her image. Then he inhaled, his mind snapped back to the task at hand, and the steps he needed to take crystallized.

"We found your mom, Rosie," he whispered. The words shot as much energy into his body as if he'd been struck by lightning, and he jumped out of his chair and scooped up the dog. "We found your mom, Rosie!" he repeated before setting her on the ground, grabbing the letter and picture, and running out the door.

"Everything okay, Stefan?" Nicole asked from her desk.

"We found Kaleo. Call the Hughes! Call everyone!"

After eight long months of dashed hopes, dead ends, and sleepless nights, the picture he clutched in his hand might as well have been a life preserver keeping him from sinking under the waves of despair.

Stefan could hardly believe it as he ran up to Director Stone's office and past his boss's secretary, bursting into the room without so much as a knock.

Director Stone looked up, nonplussed at the sudden interruption. "How can I help you, Stefan?"

Stefan threw the picture and letter down on Stone's desk and began pacing the room, the energy in his body too great for him to sit still. "We found her. Your source, Paul, the Abled guy in Rome, turned out to be valuable after all."

There was a long pause as Stone looked at the picture. "Well, good. What are you going to do now?"

Something in the director's tone made Stefan pause and turn to his boss. "I have to go to her, that should be without saying. We can't just leave her there."

"But we really can't spare the manpower either. You know as well as I do that with the way the midterm elections are heating up, the war could start any day. It probably would have started already if you and Zeke hadn't been working so hard—or did you forget all the missions you've been on?"

"Even more reason to go after her. The sooner we get Kaleo safe, the sooner Phoenix can help us."

"What if she doesn't want to help us?"

Stefan frowned. "What do you mean?"

"What if she's been hiding from us all this time? She certainly looks well cared for, and we can't afford to send a team out to get her. We're stretched thin enough as it is."

"Director Stone, this is Kaleo Hughes, our Kaleo. Nova and Caleb's Kaleo. She'd never leave us, and if anything, the reports from her friends at the Atlantic Trading company said she was excited and more than happy to be coming home. She never gave up hope that I'd find her."

"That was then. It's been six months since you went to Europe searching for her, Stefan. Eight months since she went missing. Something could have happened that changed her mind. Perhaps it was a new boyfriend, or she could have decided that this was all too much pressure for her."

"Why are you saying these things?" Stefan asked, narrowing his eyes. His boss always had a play; the hardest part was always figuring out what his endgame was.

Stone waved away his question. "It doesn't matter, I can't approve a rescue mission at this moment."

"I'll take time off. I've still got some vacation time built up."

"You don't have enough vacation time for such an endeavor; you already burnt through most of your accrued time when you went to Europe searching for her, and it won't be renewed for another few months."

"Then don't pay me while I'm gone. Call it a leave of absence or something."

"I simply can't do that."

"Why not, Stone? Why can't you do this? I've worked hard and done everything you ever asked for. Why can't you give me this? I have to go after her and find her. Now that I know where she is, I can't wait even one minute more," Stefan said as the blood rushed to his face and his hands clenched into fists at his side.

Director Stone slid Kaleo's picture across his desk towards Stefan and tented his fingers. Rosie whined by the door, sensing the tension in the room.

"I'm sorry, Stefan, but rules are rules. I can't condone you jetting off to Europe on task-force money to find your fiancée," Stone said.

"Of course you can. It won't even be task-force money. I'll pay for it."

"I'm sorry."

Stefan breathed in through his nose, out his mouth, and squashed down his anger. "Fine then, you leave me no other option. I quit, effective immediately. I'll leave my resignation letter on my office desk, and you can mail my things to Kaleo's house."

"You'd burn this bridge?"

"I'm not the one who's forcing the choice. But, yes, if it's either find Kaleo or burn a bridge, I'll burn down the entire city."

"I see. I'm sorry that it had to end this way."

"Yeah, me too, Stone. Good luck finding someone else willing to work like a dog for you as much as I have," Stefan said. He'd been so sure Director Stone would be overjoyed at the news that it hadn't even crossed his mind what he'd do if the director didn't sign off on the rescue mission. He picked Rosie up in his arms and walked to the door.

Just as his hand touched the doorknob, Stone spoke again.

"Stefan, take one last piece of advice from an old man. If she really means that much to you, don't waste any time. If you're going to throw away your career for this woman, then go to her as soon as you can."

"That was the plan. But, Stone?"

"Yeah?"

Stefan turned around and looked at his former boss and mentor one last time. He took in the salt-and-pepper hair that had begun to lean more towards salt than pepper, the wrinkles around the eyes and mouth, and the sharp eyes that hadn't lost any of their vigor despite the recent pressures they'd been under.

"She's not just any woman, she's the love of my life. She's the only woman for me. I told her that I'd find her, and I plan to keep that promise."

Glossary

Abilities: The new common term for superpowers. Pregnant women infected by the Virus of the Hard Times and then exposed to radiation from the solar flares gave birth to children who developed "special abilities" after hitting puberty. Abilities are believed to be an inherited trait.

Abled: A person with abilities.

Hard Times: A period of time in which a rapid succession of world-wide disasters almost led to the end of the world and the extinction of the human race. The Hard Times started with a pandemic that killed hundreds of millions of people and continued with solar flares that knocked out all electronics and a severely unstable climate that led to global famine, killing millions more. Thanks to the Saviors, the worst effects of the Hard Times were reversed, although there have been long-term consequences such as gas-powered engines being replaced by batteries powered on renewable energy sources, electronics such as phones, computers, and televisions being exorbitantly expensive, and most travel and shipping done by train or boat instead of plane.

Lincoln: Formerly known as Kansas City. During the Hard Times, Washington D.C. became unlivable and the American capital was moved to the newly-named Lincoln.

National Abled Task Force (NAT): A government agency made up of mostly Ableds to work on difficult or specialized cases. Headquartered in Lincoln.

Saban-40: A type of pheromone secreted by Ableds. Generally, the stronger the concentrations of secreted Saban-40, the stronger the abilities.

Saviors: A small group of Ableds with powerful abilities who reversed the multiple feedback loops causing extreme climate change and saved the world.

Author's Note

Thank you for reading *Rook*. Self-published books live and die by word of mouth, so if you have time, (and especially if you liked the story), I would greatly appreciate it if you would leave a review on Amazon with a sentence or two of what you enjoyed about the story.

Rook is the fourth book in a planned series of six: *Pawn, Knight, Bishop, Rook, Queen,* and *King*.

Queen has already been written, and *King* is currently being written. My current publication schedule is to release *Queen* in May, and *King* in late summer of 2023.

If you are interested in publication updates, I would highly encourage you to sign up for my newsletter at www.rghurleybooks.com. Doing so will not only give you access to a FREE bonus chapter from *Pawn*, but will also add you to a list of dedicated readers who get extra perks such as early-access for new books before they are officially published. If you don't see an email from me within an hour of signing up, check your promotions folder or search "Hurley Books" and make sure to click the confirmation button to opt in.

I am also on Facebook (RG Hurley), Instagram (@rghurleybooks), and TikTok (@rghurleybooks).

Have extra questions? Comments? Reactions? You can contact me directly at rghurleybooks@gmail.com

Made in the USA
Middletown, DE
07 May 2023

29717823R00158